Avenger

Sovereign Stars Book 1

Blair C. Howard

ISBN: 979-8-9862563-0-6

Dedication

For Jo, as always

From the Author:

The World of The Sovereign Stars!

In the year 2052, physicist Mark Holder discovered the Slipstream drive—a traversable wormhole drive—and mankind reached for the stars and began to colonize the galaxy. For centuries, mankind continued to colonize system after system without coming into contact with intelligent alien life. But man is a natural predator, warlike and greedy. After many generations of minor warfare, humanity faced a near-extinction-level event remembered now only as The Purge.

The vast majority of humanity did not survive The Purge. Those that did owe their survival to a few hundred Heroes—starship captains and generals—who brought an end to The Purge and began to restore order in the galaxy.

These Heroes are thought to have had a range of powers, including telepathy (commonly called Psy), telekinesis (commonly called TK), and even a form of second sight that allowed them to see events in the future and thus predict probable enemy movements (these are the Seers).

Over the centuries that followed the end of The Purge, these Heroes of old passed their powers down to their children. And so, the Heroic Families were formed, bloodlines that can be traced to the present day.

After The Purge, humanity embraced a form of monarchy. Each star system with a habitable planet (which serves as the Capital for the system) became a Kingdom in its own right. In almost all cases, the royal families can prove their bloodlines come from Heroic blood. Although, over time, the bloodlines became clouded, despite efforts to keep them pure.

Present Day, Year 3278

Mankind, now in a kind of golden age, has achieved a level of stability not seen since long before The Purge. People live for an average of 175 years. Kingdoms are actively colonizing once again, exploring out through the network of Slipstreams. Outposts and settlements become colonies, and colonies eventually become kingdoms in their own right.

Science rules the day, and even those of heroic bloodline do not have TK or Psy abilities. Most of humanity believes the stories of the Heroes are only legends and fairy tales.

The military is now partially unified and partially fragmented. No substantial war has been fought between kingdoms for more than two hundred years, so there is now a single United Sovereign Fleet (USF), but the Carrier Groups within this fleet pledge loyalty to a specific king and kingdom. Individual kingdoms also have a royal militia, a kind of security force.

Overseeing all of these kingdoms, the United Sovereign Fleet acts as royal peacekeepers and protectors. But what do you suppose would be the outcome if they had to face a threat from a superior alien race?

Hello, my name is Krista. I'm the *Avenger*'s artificial intelligence, her AI, and I'm going to tell you the story, the whole story.

Prologue

Falling Stars

New Hope
      Planet Typhon
      Persei Star System

Kyne Minnah had a headache. Several lines of code just wouldn't resolve themselves. He'd spent hours working through a dozen different options and nothing seemed to work. The glitch stared back at him, stubborn and embarrassing.

Elio and Tobin are going to wonder what I've been doing all week, he thought. *This bug is going to set the whole project back a week or more.*

Then, just when Kyne felt as if he was at the end of his rope, a network error hovered above his holographic display.

"What the vac?" Kyne muttered, keying in a query to the network center. The answer that came back was puzzling.

Kyne leaned back. *No connection?* The Slipstream network was offline? *What the vac's going on?*

The signal cleared the network center downtown, and the X-ray transmitters all seemed to check out, but the Slipstream network station wasn't responding. *Well,* he thought, *there's nothing I can do about that. I wonder...* He tapped the data pad on his arm and tried to contact the network center, but there was no answer. He stared at the lines of code, shook his head, leaned back in his chair and stared at the ceiling. *Damn it!*

He decided to go for a walk. The network going down was annoying, but at least it bought him some time to stretch his legs. *What time is it, anyway?* he wondered. He glanced again at his data pad. It was past midnight. *Stars, no wonder I'm seeing double,* he thought.

"Hey, Telsa," Kyne said as he rose from his seat. The AI chimed to let him know it was listening. "Put my gear to sleep. And unlock the front door."

Another chime and the holo faded as his computers powered down.

Kyne grabbed his hat. A notification chimed on his data pad as he stepped out of his front door. He ignored it.

The night sky was beautiful, a deep black ablaze with twinkling white stars.

The streets of New Hope were quiet and the air was cool.

When Kyne had first heard of the open invitation to move to the Persei System, one of the most distant star systems in Known Space, he'd ignored it. He wasn't the pioneer type. Why join a primitive, colonial settlement halfway across the galaxy? Then again, he did enjoy the quiet life. And his home planet, Odin, was a busy, over-crowded boisterous world. So Kyne went ahead and signed up.

Now, he traded a few hours a week of IT work for a small house at the outskirts of New Hope where he could dedicate most of his time to his real passion: developing games and apps with his buddies.

Of course, if the network was down he wouldn't be able to do much coding. Sure, Elio would be angry, but what was he to do? It was out of his control.

His data pad chimed again. Kyne pulled up the display and the face of Mole Barrion appeared, a recorded message. The older man didn't look happy; he sounded angry.

"Minnah, you promised you'd have the gravcars programmed before morning," Barrion grumbled. "I see that this still is not done. Please do not disappoint me, Minnah. I want the celebration tomorrow to be spectacu-lar. I need those gravcars. Do not... let me down." The image faded, the message complete.

Kyne sucked in cool air. *Damn it,* he thought. *I'd completely forgotten.*

Well, he decided, *no time like the present. With the Slipstream network down, there's no point in going back to the house, anyway.*

He changed direction, made a right at the next block. The garage where the gravcars were stored was no more than a twenty-minute walk.

The celebration, the first annual Founders Day for New Hope, was supposed to be a big deal. At least that's what Barrion was hoping. And Kyne had promised to take care of programming the gravcar parade to trace a route through New Hope's streets, firing pyrotechnics into the air and displaying holographic dancers. It would be quite a show, but Kyne still had to program the cars to follow the route the city committee had mapped out. The project was an easy thirty-minute job. He'd just been putting it off.

He was beginning to feel sleepy, so he picked up the pace. He decided he'd finish up programming the route for the gravcars and then walk home and go to bed. Then, while everyone else was enjoying the show and drinking enough synthol to fry their brains, maybe he'd be able to figure out why the Slipstream network was down. Was it system-wide or just on planet Typhon itself? His mind started to race as he considered the possibilities. There was nothing like a new puzzle to work through to get the blood pumping.

People were starting to wander from their homes, he noticed. *Late-night holodrama watchers, probably,* he thought. *Upset over the network outage, too.*

Kyne waved at several of his neighbors as they stumbled around their front yards in the dark. A few blocks farther on, a gravcar hummed by, flying half a meter above the street.

He didn't take any notice at first, but, at some point along the way, he saw people were standing in their front yards staring up at the night sky. He smiled to himself. *What do they think they'll actually see, the network satellites with their bare eyes?*

But, the closer he got to the town center, the more

people there were on the street, all looking upward, some calling out to each other and pointing. Kyne reflexively glanced up at the sky himself. And that's when he saw them.

Stars.

At least they looked like stars... at first.

But, unlike most stars in the night sky, these were not white, and they didn't twinkle. These stars burned bright blue.

More and more blue lights appeared in the sky above New Hope. They grew brighter and brighter until they were by far the brightest stars in the sky.

"What the vac?" Kyne said as he stopped walking and stared like everyone else.

Suddenly, sirens began to sound downtown. *An emergency alert? What's happening? Could it be pirates? They never attack anything on the surface.*

Then it began. A needle-like beam of blue light from one of the bright blue stars struck a building just a few blocks from where Kyne was standing.

There was an almighty thunderclap, and the building exploded into a million pieces.

Screams followed the destruction. The emergency alarm was joined by another, and then another until the air itself vibrated from the noise.

The blue stars were descending on New Hope, their blue beams raining death and destruction on the city.

Kyne ran, his heart racing. But there was nowhere to go.

Chapter One

Prince of Orso

The Orso Royal Palace
Planet Caerus
Orso System

Elio Lorne, Prince of Orso, stepped into his bedroom suite, his hair still wet from the steam shower. A robot servant stood at attention in the corner, its eyes glowing the dim blue of sleep mode. He finished drying his shoulder-length blond hair and threw the towel on his bed and slipped into a robe before plopping down on the cushioned chair in the middle of the suite.

He glanced sideways at the small stand beside the chair where he'd left his halo, a circlet of corinium and circuitry. He grabbed it and slid it onto his head. The halo had been adjusted to fit snugly just above his ears.

Elio loved moments like this—his first time accessing his halo with his new forearm data screen. He held up his forearm, the form-fitted polydyethylene data screen flexing with the movement of his skin. He'd had the latest version installed earlier that day. The vitals sensors of this new model no longer required the old-style wrist plugs. It had nano probes that inserted themselves through the skin into the nervous system. The Xion V15 would not available to the general public for another three days, but through his royal connections, Elio had received his a few days early. He smiled at the thought of the citizens lined up for blocks, waiting for the new version.

He tapped the touch screen on his forearm to take him to the main menu and selected "gaming." His data screen synced with the halo. He touched the sensor to activate the halo and felt the familiar tingling sensation of the nerve-jack. Then, less than a second later, he was no longer sitting in his chair in his suite. Instead, his avatar, a Middle Eastern boy, stood in a bare white room, holographic displays hovering in front of him, welcoming him.

With a thought, he accessed the control panel for Old Earth Assassin. He and his friends had been developing the game for months. Elio was in charge of the coding, Tobin handled research, and Kyne Minnah took care of graphics. They had advanced far enough to be able to play the beta version for the first two levels.

As the game loaded, Elio opened a second window and went over the code for the holographic connections. There had been some bugs in it last time they'd played, but those should have been corrected with the latest update.

The game began, and Elio was surrounded by the holographic realism of the game's universe. He was standing in a town square, surrounded by stone buildings with thatched roofs. The streets were crowded with people. Merchants in the marketplace hocked fruits, vegetables and other wares.

The setting was Old Earth, before the systems settlements, before the Slipstream, before The Purge and before humans developed the gifts of TK and Psy, *if they even existed at all*, he thought. The Earth of this historical time period was primitive: stone streets, horses and carriages, no computers or combustion engines. It was an ideal time to be alive on the first human planet.

Elio enjoyed the quiet, slow pace of this world. Since there were not many records of life before The Purge, he didn't know if the details were correct. But from Tobin's research, it was as close as they could get it, at least for now. They'd continue the historical research later.

He walked his avatar down the street. When he'd jacked into the game, it should have triggered notifications to Tobin and Kyne that he was there.

Where are they? he wondered. *They should be here.* He sent them a message. It didn't go through. *Bad connection? That's odd. The inter-system network hasn't experienced an outage for decades.*

Elio had heard about them, but the new servers on the Slipstream Control Stations had multiple levels of backup.

He continued down the street and was about to approach the spice seller when, suddenly, a loud beeping interrupted the game and everything froze.

"What the vac?" he said to himself.

"Your father wishes to speak to you, sir," a pleasant AI voice sounded in his halo.

"Not now, Dinka," Elio said. "I'm busy."

"The summons is urgent, my prince. The king wishes to speak to you. You must comply," Dinka insisted.

Elio swore under his breath, then said, "Fine. Exit to home and enter virtual briefing."

The world of the game faded away, and Elio felt his bones and muscles tingle as his avatar shifted from the small Middle Eastern boy to his normal, thirty-year-old, six-feet-six-inch self.

He was back in the stark white room for only a moment before his surroundings shifted again to a hologram of his father's Royal office.

Elio's father, Orson Lorne, King of the Orso System, was seated at a large, ornate desk.

The king was in his sixties and a little on the heavy side. He, too, was tall, as were all the decedents of the Heroic line and, like Elio, he had a mane of thick blond hair. Unlike Elio, he wore a constant scowl that contorted his bearded face.

The large room, the massive desk, the ornate, militaristic decor were all designed to strike fear in the hearts of visitors, but they had no effect on Elio.

"Father?" he yelled. "I was in the middle of something."

The king arched an eyebrow. "Another child's game, was it?" he asked.

"It's what I do," Elio replied. "I'm a gamer. It's important to me."

"It's a waste of time," the king said angrily, "and it

isn't fitting for the crown prince of a Sovereign System to waste so much valuable time in a world of virtual nonsense."

Elio looked around, waving his hands at the virtual replica of his father's office, then said, "Really? You're saying that while you're jacked into... this?"

His father's face turned a deep red. "I'm contacting you this way because I don't have time to waste waiting for you to cross the palace," he said. "This is a busy day. We have network outages throughout the Galactic Arm, and I have back-to-back meetings all afternoon."

"Right," Elio said and rolled his eyes. *Network outages?* he thought. That must be why he couldn't link up with his friends. One of them, Kyne Minnah, was way out in Persei System.

"Son," the king said, "we've gone over this before. You're a Royal. You need to act like one."

"By doing what?" Elio asked.

"By not spending your time playing these games for one." The king sighed. "This is not how our ancestors lived. It is not what they intended for us. They discovered these systems, colonized this planet and lived well. They had the Gifts. Our forefathers who founded this system had the strongest TK and Psy powers ever recorded."

Elio crossed his arms and said, "Ever recorded? That's the point, father; there are no records. None of us have those powers anymore. We don't even know if they ever really existed."

The king was taken aback. His cheeks shook as he jerked his head back in surprise. "How dare you?" he

said. "You will not speak of such things in my presence."
He pointed a scolding finger at him. "Their powers still
remain in our royal blood, even if we are unable to access
them."

"Really, father?" Elio asked. "Are you serious?"

"Of course, I am," he replied.

"You've been listening to the old priests too much,"
Elio said. "No such... *gifts* exist. Show me a recording of
one of them using the magical telekinesis or telepathy,
then I'll believe it."

The king stood and puffed out his chest. "It would
surprise me, my son, if you showed any potential to have
such powers."

"Why? Do you have them?" Elio said and held up his
hands sarcastically.

"The TK and Psy were a gift," the king replied. "It
allowed the royal class to break away, to be who they
were supposed to be. And you would not be sitting there
enjoying the fruits of their labors without those Gifts.
You may not believe in them, and I cannot make you.
However, I do ask and expect you to at least conduct
yourself like an honorable man. And you will not mock
the Gifts or our ancestors in my presence."

"Well, when the day comes that I develop telepathy,"
Elio said, "you will be the first to know. And then maybe
you'll treat me like an adult."

The king gritted his teeth and was about to say something when another form materialized beside Elio. "Ha!"
He scoffed when Duke Rodor Steren's plump form
appeared.

"Your Majesty," Steren said, bowing deeply. He glanced in Elio's direction and mumbled, "My prince."

Of all his father's dukes, Steren was the one Elio disliked most. The two-faced little man spent all his time at the palace kissing up to the king. Elio had no idea what the duke actually did to deserve his title.

"Good. Now that you're both here," the king said, "I'll make this quick. I want both of you to travel to Tor in the Pricus System first thing tomorrow morning."

Elio's mouth dropped open, but it was Steren who protested first.

"Certainly, your majesty, but Prince Elio isn't needed, sir. I'm sure I can handle things."

The king raised a hand to hush the duke. "I know you can handle the diplomatic proceedings, Rod. But I want my son to get some experience, to learn from you."

"Experience with what?" Elio blurted. "Eating with the correct fork? I don't want to live my life shaking hands with stuffy colonists, Father!"

"I'm not asking what you want, Elio," the king said. "I'm telling you. The Pricus System is requesting permission to set up mining outposts. The colony of Pricus City on Tor is under my jurisdiction. The governor has also requested our input as to how the operations are to be run."

Mining operations? Elio thought. *What a bore.*

Elio noticed the duke was steaming. Elio grinned. "You're not scared I'll cramp your style, are you, Rod?" he asked.

Steren self-consciously patted his long black hair.

"It's Duke Steren to you, you little shit," he muttered under his breath.

Elio grinned at him but didn't reply.

"I have spoken," the king said. "Everything has already been arranged. This is a simple mission. Shake a few hands. Kiss a few babies. Give the governor what he wants. That's it. Rod, I want my boy to get some experience."

The duke wasn't happy, but he gave another unnecessary bow and said, "As you wish, Your Grace."

"Well, I still don't want to go," Elio said, crossing his arms.

"You will go, even if I have to order a marshal and a dozen of my personal guards to drag you from your bed and throw you into the shuttle," the king growled.

Elio let out a long breath. He knew his father had to be obeyed. He'd be going.

"Fine!" Elio snapped.

"Good, that will be all," the king said.

Elio's father waved his hand dismissively, bringing up his personal display and, with another wave, the room dissolved, and Elio was back in white space.

He hit the escape command and returned to the reality of his room, sitting in his chair. He lifted the halo from his head and threw it on the table.

"Dinka," Elio said, pointing at the still, apparently sleeping robot.

"My prince," the robot responded.

"Find me some clothes," Elio said. "I have an errand to run. Oh, and I want some breakfast. The usual."

"As you wish," Dinka said.

Elio went to his bathroom to brush his hair. A few minutes later, another servant robot entered the suite bearing a tray of food.

He'd eat, get dressed and put on a smile, *but*, he thought, *if I have to go on this stupid mission, I'll do it my way.*

And that meant he had a little light hacking to do.

Chapter Two

The Queen's Pleasure

The Orso Royal Palace
Planet Caerus
Orso System

A quick walk through the palace and across the courtyard brought Elio and Dinka to the military compound.

Elio turned to his robot and said, "Dinka, find a terminal that can access the control tower, flight plans and royal orders."

"Yes, sir." The bipedal robot lumbered to the closest terminal. Elio liked this V6000 series of service robots. It was something about their humanoid form. Sure, Dinka was constructed from dura metal and carbon fiber composites with some very sophisticated custom updates designed by Elio himself, but Elio liked talking to a bot that had two arms and two legs. For some reason, he didn't like the old standard palace bots that made it feel like he was talking to a trashcan. Elio had also had Dinka custom-painted with a silver and black scheme to ensure the bot didn't look like an ordinary service bot.

Dinka beamed his access code into the terminal's scanner and began typing on the screen. The bot's ocular system could scan through lines of code far faster than even Elio could.

"Terminal 7H in the communications bay will work, sir. And it is currently open." The bot's oval-shaped head turned to look at his master.

Elio nodded. Dinka tapped in several commands, then signed off and exited the system.

"Thank you, Dinka," Elio said and set off through the military offices with an air of confidence, as if he was supposed to be there. The few soldiers and pilots who were around were used to seeing Elio in and around the compound, not that any of them had enough rank to question him anyway.

He checked the nearest tracking screen on the wall to see if Lieutenant Dravo, his Marine buddy, was in the building. Dravo could get him into the communications bay no problem. The marine was always willing to risk doing little favors for Elio as long as he got access to the Royal's social credit coding. They were great friends anyway, had been for as long as he could remember and, with Dravo's help, Elio had learned how to fly and handle DEW weapons, while Dravo was able to visit the high-class clubs and party with the rich and elite. It was a match made in heaven. Unfortunately, Dravo seemed to be absent.

Elio sucked his lower lip, thought for a moment, then

made up his mind and walked confidently into the communications bay. He found Terminal 7H and began tapping, typing, on the screen. The screen asked for his military identification number, and he typed in a generic maintenance code he'd found previously. That let him into the system. The maintenance department didn't have their passwords updated nearly as often as they should.

He opened the control panel and ACCESS DENIED filled the screen. A default settings code bypassed that, and he was into the system. He inputted a cross-site scripting code into the search field and the system began searching for possible password matches.

He minimized that window and searched for an open port in a new window. Port HH9Z would work. He opened that, and when it asked for a sixteen-character password, he went back to the password matches the system had found for him. There was only one match that had sixteen characters. After inputting that into the port, he was now in the control tower system. *Too easy.*

Elio grinned to himself. He really should bring up the flaws in this system to his father at some point. But then he wouldn't be able to have his fun.

Not only did his mind work more like a hacker than a politician, but Elio felt alive when he was solving a coding puzzle. Nothing made him feel more dead than sitting in a boring political meeting. It was the thrill of problem-solving, of using his intuition and knowledge of hacking that he loved. But if he got caught again... Well, his father had warned him there would be consequences.

Hacking was not a suitable occupation for a prince, which was one of the reasons he enjoyed it.

Elio found the royal orders for the Pricus envoy that had been entered into the system only that morning. If he was forced to travel, there was no way he was getting stuck in some spartan USF ship with that back-stabbing little bastard Duke Steren.

That being so, to the one USF Diplomatic vessel and battle cruiser escort ship assigned to the trip, he added *The Queen's Pleasure*, his personal yacht, to the clearance manifest.

The Queen's Pleasure was a gift from his long-departed mother. She passed just two weeks after his twenty-first birthday. *The Queen's Pleasure* was... special, sleek and fast, and Elio had tricked it out to suit his needs and personality.

Elio looked around. No one seemed to notice him. He saved the changes, logged out and left the terminal.

The following morning, after Dinka had moved Elio's effects onto *The Queen's Pleasure*, the prince joined Duke Steren and the other officers at the military bay. King Lorne was also present to officially see the delegation off.

The Queen's Pleasure was inside the hangar, ready for takeoff, next to the Diplomatic vessel.

Duke Steren's round face turned towards the king in surprise. "Your Grace, it was my understanding that I would travel with the royal delegation."

The king shrugged. "I don't write the manifests, Rod."

The duke stroked his black hair, revealing a nervous

tell. For supposedly being a political expert, Steren was not very adept at concealing his emotions. Elio knew arriving at their destination in a separate ship from a royal family member would instantly show the welcoming committee on Tor that the duke was not on the same social level as the prince.

"Well, shall we be off?" Elio asked.

Steren was still trying to conceal his frustration. King Lorne tried to conceal a smirk as he briefly made eye contact with his son. Elio knew this unspoken gesture of approval would be the only way his father would praise him. This was the closest thing in his thirty years that Elio had gotten to an "I'm proud of you, son." It was evident the king still wished Elio would do something more patriotic or political with his life, but Elio was still his son, his only son. And even the king himself couldn't resist being proud of his son's... strategic move.

"Thank you again, father." Elio bowed his head. "We will return in good time."

Elio turned and walked towards his ship. Duke Steren could do nothing other than say his goodbyes and go to his own generic diplomatic vessel.

"Good morning, my prince," Kyla, the ship's AI said as he entered the flight deck. "I hope you're having a pleasant day."

"Very much so, Kyla," Elio replied. "Bring up the systems, if you please."

The ship trembled slightly as it came to life. A dome-shaped hologram of the star systems and the proposed route to Tor appeared between the command chair and the one usually occupied by a copilot, in this case, Dinka.

"Take us out, Kyla," Elio said. "No, better wait for the duke. I don't need to make him any angrier than he already is."

He watched as the diplomatic vessel lifted on its grav drives and moved slowly out of the hangar.

"Now you can take us out," Elio said.

"Rendezvous with cruiser *Vanguard* in seventeen minutes and fifty-four seconds," Kyla said.

Twenty minutes later, the three ships were already out of the atmosphere and on their way towards the Slipstream. The military cruiser took the point of their V-shaped standard formation: Steren's ship on the left and Elio's on the right.

Elio checked the speed of the Cruiser ahead of him and manually typed it into the navigation computer.

"Is there anything you would like me to get for you, sir?" Dinka asked as he looked at the prince from the co-pilot's chair.

"No, thank you, Dinka."

"As you wish, sir."

"Would you like to take the controls, my prince?" Kyla asked.

"Yes, thank you." Elio placed his hands on the yoke, adjusted the thrusters, then sat back in his seat. He enjoyed the power of the ship and the mental challenge of putting his piloting skills to use. He wasn't too excited about the trip, but at least he could pilot his own craft and not have the duke breathing down his neck the entire time.

Some twenty-seven minutes later, traveling at one-tenth light speed, the tiny fleet was on vector to the Slipstream Control Center. They reduced speed. The massive wormhole grew in size as they approached. If it wasn't for the semi-purple haze around the edge of the wormhole, it would be almost impossible to see the Slipstream. The Slipstream refracted light differently inside of its borders than in normal space, resulting in the haze.

Elio never got tired of watching the phenomenon. He wondered what the ancients must have thought about these massive wormholes when they were first discovered more than a millennia ago. He wondered what life was like before the Slipstreams—before interstellar travel. There was little recorded history about life in those primordial times, when humans were confined to Earth's solar system, prior to the first traversable wormhole—now called a Slipstream—being discovered way back in 2047. It had been another five years before physicist Mark Holder developed the Slipstream drive that gave humanity access to the network of wormholes.

Elio was suddenly jerked out of his reverie by the warning buzz and a voice in his ear that told him they were approaching the gateway, the white and gray control station floating some ten thousand kilometers from the mouth of the wormhole.

His communicator came to life. "This is Slipstream control. You are approaching the gateway. Please identify yourself."

Elio jumped to hit the comm screen before either of the other two ships could answer.

"Slipstream control, this is Queen's Pleasure One on route to the Pricus System requesting Slipstream access," he said, then sat back and grinned at the thought that

Steren must be beside himself with rage, because once the formation had been defined, the ident would be locked in for their entire journey, there and back. The Pricus System receiving station would ask for Queen's Pleasure One, not the call sign of Steren's ship, another jab at the duke. Elio smiled.

"Roger, Queen's Pleasure One. Please activate your drive and send coordinates when ready." The female voice from the control station was calm and even.

Elio turned on his ship's Slip Drive, then tapped several times on the screen in front of him, The terminal lit up, and lines of digits and characters scrolled across the screen until finally they settled on the current Slipstream frequency.

"Sending coordinates now." Elio hit the "execute" icon.

"Coordinates received, Queen's Pleasure One. You are approved for Slipstream approach. Proceed on heading 325."

"Roger, control. 325." Elio tapped the heading into the ship's vectoring computer.

"Cruiser FH29 *Vanguard* here. Roger, Queen's Pleasure. Heading 325," the captain of the cruiser confirmed for his own computer.

Elio waited for Steren, enjoying how the duke would have to confirm the same.

"This is diplomatic vessel Orso Five. I am also confirming heading 325." Steren tried to sound like he was actually doing something, but Elio knew the duke's ship would be on autopilot. But the duke wanted to make sure the control station knew it was a diplomatic mission.

He never missed a chance to impress. Even if it was a simple comms confirmation.

Once all three ships had locked in the same coordinates, they would move as one through the Slipstream. The thrusters of all three ships worked in unison and positioned the formation at the correct angle facing the wormhole. Then they waited for the control station to confirm the headings.

"Roger that," the female voice said without emotion. "Queen's Pleasure One, you are go for Slipstream access. Good luck."

"Thank you, control." Elio switched off the comm and placed his hand on the Slip Drive control screen, looked over at Dinka and said, "Here we go."

The bot nodded its metal head in approval.

Elio engaged the Slip Drive, and the familiar sensation of being pulling into the wormhole washed over him. The stars disappeared as the ship entered the black mass of the Slipstream.

Chapter Three

Call to Arms

Military Controlled Space
Orso System
The weapons system of the F32A fighter blared a warning. Danis Morian, call sign "Domino," hauled back on the yoke and slammed it hard over to the left, sending her fighter into a sharp, sliding turn to face the oncoming missile six seconds from impact.

Without thinking, Danis re-centered her targeting computer and the outline of the missile blinked red on her screen. A beeping sound confirmed the lock. She thumbed the trigger button and her DEW lasers released two five-terawatt beams at the oncoming missile, destroying it two seconds before it reached her.

"Nice shot, Domino," her brother, Captain Richard Morian, said over the comm.

"Thanks, Avenger. Why don't you program a real challenge next time?" Danis hit the throttle and turned to face the gunship that had been launching missiles at her. "These outdated programs are too predictable."

The gunship was a USF training drone. On the outside, it looked like the standard drone used in all academy training. But this particular gunship had some of the most advanced programming and weapons systems in the entire fleet. And it had been launched from the *Avenger*.

"Don't get too cocky, Domino," Richard said.

Her fighter shifted, rolled and slewed to face the massive ship. The *Avenger*, a Defender C-class ship and one of the oldest of its kind in the USF, was now off her port bow facing its bridge. "I'm uploading module seventeen. This exercise is brand new. The gunship is now in AI mode."

An AI-commanded gunship? she thought. *All for a training exercise? Maybe this was going to be a challenge after all.*

"Okay, Zilvo," she said, more to herself than to the robot. "Heads up this time. Let's see what they have for us now."

"Shields are at one hundred percent and targeting array is ready." Zilvo, her robot co-pilot, was seated behind her. She was humanoid in form and size, which made her perfect for operating controls made for human hands. She'd been with Danis for a long time. They had completed many missions together. If it wasn't for the bot's blue and white paint scheme, Danis could almost forget she was a bot—and sometimes did.

The screen flashed a notification and beeped, indicating the gunship drone was commencing its attack.

Danis hit the thrusters and turned into a roll, moving away from the gunship—just in time—as it fired its lasers. It missed, slewed to starboard, half-rolled and came after her.

The AI gunship was almost twice the size of Danis's fighter, and it was faster. But, due to the fighter's four diametrically opposed thrusters—each arranged at the tip of a short strut and able to independently rotate a full thee-hundred-sixty degrees—the F32A was almost infinitely maneuverable. Not an easy craft to fly, it had the ability to spin, yaw and even rotate on its central axis.

The gunship continued to fire its lasers, but Danis easily avoided them, more by instinct than with the aid of her battle computers.

"Incoming," Zilvo said in her monotone female voice. "Four missiles. Two are locked on. Impact in thirty-two seconds."

Danis dodged several more bursts of laser fire then rotated the fighter to face the incoming missiles.

"Two more missiles launched," Zilvo announced.

"Damn." Danis locked onto the first two missiles, fired her DEW guns, then sped away before the missiles exploded.

"Impact in sixteen seconds," Zilvo said quietly.

Danis increased her speed. These two new missiles were approaching much faster than the first four, two of which she'd destroyed.

She rotated again and turned to face the new missiles and destroyed them both with just seconds to spare, but before she could take countermeasures, the final two missiles impacted her fighter. They were non-explosive training weapons of course, but a false detonation registered on her computer, temporarily shutting down her systems.

"Damn it," she snapped.

She waited the obligatory ten seconds for her systems to come online, then reset the nav computer and sped off before the gunship could launch any more missiles.

"Gotcha, Domino," Richard's voice rubbed it in. "You'll have to be quicker than that if you want to survive."

"Let's see," she replied. "That's one hit for you and fourteen for me. Overall, I'm sitting pretty good."

"Not for long," Richard said and laughed.

The gunship fired four more missiles as it continued to fire its DEW lasers. The lasers were easy enough to avoid, but the smart missiles were tricky, especially when there were so many.

"Impact in thirty seconds," Zilvo said.

She knew what Richard and the other officers were on the *Avenger's* bridge, watching, trying to get inside her head, trying to make her fail. It was almost as if she knew what her brother was thinking, and she decided she was having none of it. *I didn't go through all those years of training just lose at some silly game. Game on, brother.*

An AI was controlling the gunship, but the original programming had been done by humans. The barrage of missiles in the last exercise made Danis think it might try a similar tactic: launch four missiles at her and then two more on a different vector that would impact her while she was dealing with the others. *Not this time,* she thought. *What is it they say? Once bitten... Time to go with your gut, Danis.*

Danis reversed thrust, flipped the fighter end-over-end, then aligned the craft so that she could see the incoming missiles while her fighter continued moving away. She glanced at her targeting screens, noted the range, then said. "Zilvo, on my mark, reverse our vector and kill the thrusters."

"Kill the thrusters?"

"Don't question my orders. Just do it."

"Yes, ma'am. Impact in fifteen seconds."

Danis targeted the missiles and locked on, but she didn't fire; she let them get closer.

"Twelve seconds."

Just a little more.

"Two missiles at eight seconds, two at ten. Ma'am, but don't you want to—?"

"I know what I'm doing. Just be ready."

"Understood. Five seconds and seven seconds."

Danis breathed out and watched as the two pairs of missiles hurtled towards her.

"Three seconds."

"Now!" she shouted and fired the DEW guns and took out all four missiles.

As Zilvo reversed the vector and killed the thrusters, Danis opened a radiation pattern from her outgoing broadcast. The sudden reversal allowed the fighter to remain relatively in place amidst the missile debris. All of this activity plus the radiation patter would confuse the gunship's sensor sweep. The AI would have to sort through the data and calculate the chances of the fighter's survival before launching more missiles. Danis was gambling that the AI wouldn't fire any unnecessary missiles if it didn't have to whereas a human pilot probably would.

In the five to six seconds she had while the AI was calculating, Danis fired up her thrusters and raced towards the gunship. Once she was in range, she fired everything she had. The DEW lasers hit home on the gunship, tearing a smoking hole where the cockpit had been.

Danis continued to fly past the now-defunct drone and did a victory fly-by of the *Avenger*'s bridge. She could see several officers cheering while others were yelling in frustration. *Hah,* she thought, *they must have had a bet going.*

"Well done, Domino," Richard said over the comm. "End exercise. Report to bay three."

"Roger, Avenger. Bay three it is."

She maneuvered her fighter to the port side of the *Avenger* and slowed to match its speed.

"May I inquire?" Zilvo asked. "Are you planning to use that move in real combat?"

"Perhaps. Why?" she replied.

"I just wanted to know so that I can back it up to my CPU."

"What, you don't trust me?" she asked.

"I do not have the luxury of trust, ma'am," the robot replied. "But I do excel in probability."

Danis laughed. "Don't worry. I'm not planning on it being my go-to move. I did want to try it, though. And for the record, it did work."

"That it did, ma'am. Good flying."

Danis increased her speed, circled around *Avenger's* bow, rolled the F32A in front of the bridge and did a victory lap around the ship. The Defender-C class ship was longer than a jet ball field. Its smooth dutrinium armored hull bristled with weapons turrets and gun ports. The off-bore positioning of these guns was one of its trademark designs, allowing the gunners to fire in multiple directions independent of the direction of the ship. Eight massive Regeneron sixteen-point thrusters were positioned on each of its main "corners" if one would say it had corners. The bulk of the hangar protruded from the keel, its blast doors open and waiting for her. She dropped below the great ship and approached the hangar, matched her speed with that of the battle cruiser and, manipulating her thrusters with both hands, eased the F32A inside, settled it gently down on the deck and cut the drives.

* * *

Knight Captain Richard Morian watched Domino roll the fighter in front of the bridge, gave her a mocking wave and smiled to himself. She was good and getting better. If only his other pilots had the instincts she did. She always seemed to do better when he was controlling the exercise, something he'd never been able to understand.

Morian, a tall, dark-skinned man of forty-two was on the bridge at the command rail, facing the forward view screens. The command deck with the captain's chair was slightly elevated above the bridge deck, the helm, navigation, weapons and the battle control stations. This provided him an elevated view of the entire bridge and, if he needed to, he could see any and all screens and holograms.

As the captain of the *Avenger*, Morian didn't have as much time to train his pilots as he wanted. *Maybe*, he thought, *I should promote Danis to squadron commander and have her take over pilot training. Hmmm, that might cause morale problems among the pilots, but it could also be the quickest way for them to qualify.*

"I told you she could do it, Captain," Lieutenant Commander Michael Jadern, Morian's executive officer, said stepping up to join him at the rail.

"Yes." Richard nodded. "Yes, you did." The other handful of officers on the bridge were making the credit transfers on their data screens. They'd lost the bet to Jadern and Morian.

"I'll be in Bay 3 if you need me," Morian said to Jadern.

Jadern nodded.

"Ensign Quynn," Morian said.

"Yes, Captain." The young ensign stood up.

"Make sure that last exercise is uploaded into the training reviews."

"Aye, sir," Quynn said as Morian turned and headed for the door. "And forward Lieutenant Morian's stats from the exercise to my data screen."

"Yes, sir."

Morian entered the bridge elevator and tapped the icon for Deck 2. After a couple of seconds, the door opened and he walked to the gravrail, stepped into the car and tapped the icon for the hangar. The short ride to the hangar took less than three minutes. He exited the car, put his eye to the scanner and waited for the door to open—two more minutes while the hangar pressurized—then the door opened and he stepped into the massive bay just as the canopy of Danis's fighter opened.

The fighter moved slowly across the hangar on its grav drives until Danis finally set it down at the end of a row of five other fighters, filling the last spot in the two ranks of six, making a complete squadron of twelve. The hangar was just big enough for the full squadron plus two transport shuttles with four more spots reserved for visitors.

Richard stood on the floor with his hands clasped behind his back, waiting for the engines to shut down, then Danis took off her helmet and reached for the exit ladder. She descended easily with Zilvo right behind her.

"A radiation pattern? Really?" Morian asked.

Danis hopped off the final rung, pushed her hair out of her eyes and said, "What?"

"You know that would never work against a real pilot, right?"

"Come on, Richard," Danis said, wiping a bead of sweat off her brow as she checked the data screen on her forearm. "When are we ever going to have to face a 'real' pilot in a fight? That hasn't happened in more than... two hundred years. So, what was my hit factor?" She tapped an icon and swiped the screen away, searching for the stats.

"My point remains," Morian said, frowning. "A real

pilot would have a visual and would see you still in one piece."

Morian knew Danis was damn good, but he still had to keep her from becoming cocky. "An AI's computer has to compute data," he continued, "which it did. A real pilot wouldn't have had to. So, you win because you... cheated."

Danis feigned an offensive gesture with her mouth open. "Me, cheat?" she scoffed. "Never. Faking out the enemy is a perfectly legitimate part of war. Haven't you read your 'Haxtrum' lately?" she asked as she walked past him towards the down bay.

He smiled. Of course, they all had to read Haxtrum in the academy, but that was one of the least beneficial tomes.

"Colonel Boyd Haxtrum's *Treatise on the Theory of Combat*," he said as he turned to follow her, "is over 500 years old and was written about ground fighting."

"Fighting is fighting," she said.

Richard nodded. She was right, but he didn't want to admit it.

"So," she said. "How much did that run improve my rating?"

Richard smiled and checked the data screen on his forearm, then read off her latest stats. "Your hit factor improved by two-point-six percent. MOA remains in the top ten reaction times. Your overall rating is now... point six-forty-eight. Well done."

Danis nodded in satisfaction.

"I've been meaning to tell you," Richard said matter

of factly. "I'm recommending you for an instructor's slot back at the academy."

"What? Why?" she asked, taken aback.

"What do you mean, why? You clearly have the skills. You know that F32A fighter better than any pilot in the fleet. And you're due for some time on the ground. You've been out here for almost eight months now."

Danis crossed her arms and frowned. She, too was tall, but slim, fit, her brilliant blue eyes a stark contrast to her dark-colored skin.

Richard ran his hand over his hair and to the back of his neck. "Besides, we'll have a multi-system jump coming up soon. New systems, new colonies, not sure what we'll find."

"Young systems?" she asked. "That's where the squadron will be needed most. That's a better chance of getting real-world missions."

"Which means there are too many unknown variables. It could be dangerous."

Danis scoffed. "Oh, I get it," she said.

"What?"

"Are you doing this because you're my captain or because you're my brother?" she said.

"The fact that I'm your brother has nothing to do with it. The fact that I am your older brother and I promised our parents I'd take care of you is the issue."

She turned to face him, standing with her feet apart, her arms folded across the chest.

He'd known she wasn't going to like it, but there was nothing she could do about it.

"You're good, sis," he said. "But the problem is, you

know it. You have to be careful not to create bad habits and pull stunts like the one you just pulled… in case we do ever run across a real combat situation."

"I'll keep that in mind, *Captain*," she replied. "I'll also keep in mind that the USF has not been engaged in a real combat situation for… how many generations now?" She tapped her chin and continued, "Oh, that's right, all of them."

"That's not true—" he began.

"Oh, come on, big brother," she said, interrupting him. "If there was a threat to the USF, we would have rattled it loose long ago. Humankind has been colonizing systems for almost a thousand years, and not one single sentient species has been found, not one."

Richard glared at her and said, "That doesn't mean a threat from another human system couldn't rise up at any moment, you know that. That's what the USF is for."

"Unlikely, Captain," she snapped back at him. "You know as well as I do, there hasn't been a war between kingdoms for generations. Face it, our time in the military will be about nothing but peace. Drones and AI are all we'll ever be shooting at."

"Don't become complacent," Richard said. The only reason he was allowing her to be so informal was because they were alone. She was a pilot, one of his pilots, but she was still his sister, his twin sister. "The USF has notified us of our pending mission, and we could be called upon anytime. Just because nothing has happened in… a long time, doesn't mean our services couldn't be needed soon."

"Okay," Danis said, nodding. "Then I'll be ready."

"I can't fault you for winning," he said, "but you have

to remember the whole squadron of pilots was watching you, learning. I don't want them getting any bad habits either. You're not our best pilot for no reason, you know."

"Let them watch." Danis rotated her neck and stretched it to one side. "I think all of our pilots should be creative. They have to learn to think on their feet, solve problems in real time. That's what I was doing out there."

Richard couldn't argue with that. He shook his head. "I suppose you're right."

Danis walked to the door, stopped and waited for a moment before hitting the open icon. "Besides, you know what they taught us in flight school, remember?" she said.

"What?"

"If you find yourself in a fair fight, you're losing." She hit the open icon and the door to the down bay slid open. "I need a drink. Come on, let's debrief." She waved her brother through.

"I'm afraid I can't, sis," he replied. "I have uh... duties."

"Suit yourself, bro," Danis said as she walked away and the door slid shut behind her.

Zilvo stepped to Richard's side.

"Watch her back, would you, Zilvo?" he said.

"Always do, Captain." Zilvo's robotic arm gave a half salute as she walked into the down bay.

Richard smiled to himself. If he could figure out what made Danis such an instinctually good fighter, he could replicate it and feed it to the other pilots like a recipe. They had examined, measured, quantified and calculated every stat and training standard they could come up with, and nothing was particularly outstanding in Danis's record. But it appeared that piloting fighter ships in 3D space was just as much art as it was science. Some had it, and some didn't. Most didn't even come close to the art that Danis possessed.

He headed back to the gravrail. Maybe he would have to read Haxtrum again after all, but he wouldn't let Danis know that.

Chapter Four

Felder and Company

The hangar's orange lights began to flash and the high-pitched alarm sounded. Four crewmen hustled out of their nearby quarters. Another ship was entering the airlock. Morian, almost at the gravrail, tapped his data screen and called the bridge.

"Yes, Captain?" Lieutenant Sandra Lowry, his communications officer, said.

"Who is approaching?" he asked.

"Shuttle V-17, sir," Lowry said. "Dispatched from Gern in the Alastor System. Prince Padric Felder is on board. He's here for his tour of the *Avenger*. It's on your schedule, sir."

Morian rolled his eyes and said, "That's today? Well, never mind. I'll be in Hangar Bay 3 if I'm needed."

"Aye, sir," Lowry replied.

Morian had plenty of other things to do with his time than show his ship to a prince from another system. Some admiral with political ambitions thought it was a great idea to build a relationship between the two systems. He tapped his data screen to call his sister.

"Yes?" Danis answered.

"We have a special envoy arriving. It would be the perfect time for the fleet's number one pilot to greet them."

"When?" she asked.

"Right now."

"O-kay... I'll be right there," she replied.

"And Danis?"

"Yes?"

"Please use proper protocol. You never know who's listening in on these calls?"

"You bet, bro—I mean, yes, sir."

Morian ended the call as a gravrail car arrived and Commander Jadern stepped out followed by the senior navigation officer Simon DeLong and the chief engineer Maxim Volkov. Jadern saluted.

Morian returned the salute and said, "So, who exactly do we have here, Commander?"

Jadern checked his forearm data screen as, even through the closed door, the sound of the shuttle's thrusters filled the hangar. "On board is Prince Padric Felder of the Alastor System. His first assistant Tenilo Barum and... a journalist." He had to almost yell to be heard over the high-pitched whine of the shuttle's engines.

Morian turned, looked through the glass panel as one of the flight crewmen held an illuminated baton over his head and made a large circle, indicating the landing base was clear and the somewhat ornate shuttle touched down.

"Command didn't say anything about a journalist," Morian said as they waited for the hangar to pressurize. The touch panel turned green and Morian opened the door and led the small group over to the receiving area.

Jadern tapped his screen again and talked as they walked. "It looks like the journalist was added to the itinerary yesterday, Captain."

Morian stood in position and straightened his jacket. "What kind of journalist are we talking about?" he asked.

The other officers positioned themselves in a semicircle behind him.

"Her name is... April Badeaux," Jadern replied. "She's a Tier One reporter for an e-zine called *The Quantum Examiner*."

"An e-zine, are you kidding?"

"Afraid not, sir," Jadern said.

The engines died and the ramp lowered. "I've never even heard of *The Quantum Examiner*, have you?" Morian asked.

"No, sir," Jadern replied, shaking his head.

"And for how long are we hosting the prince and his entourage?" Morian asked without looking at Jadern.

"Thirty-six hours, sir. The shuttle is scheduled to depart at 1600 tomorrow."

Danis joined the line and stood at attention beside the chief engineer.

The shuttle's ramp clanked down onto the deck and three figures strode down into the hangar. Prince Felder couldn't be missed. Not only was he first, but he was a head taller than anyone else and wearing a pristine white uniform and cloak. Even his boots were white.

They surely won't be white when he leaves, Morian thought, *not if he intends to walk around this old hull.*

Prince Felder smiled widely as he made eye contact with Morian.

"Ah, Captain Morian," he said. "How splendid to see you again."

The prince opened his arms wide as he approached, as if they were long-lost friends. Morian forced a smile and pretended he was just as excited to see the prince. They had only met once before, and that had been years ago.

"Prince Felder," Morian said as he stepped forward and bowed his head in greeting. Jadern, Danis and the others behind him did the same. "Welcome aboard the *Avenger*," he continued. "We are honored to have you here."

Felder bowed his head, tilted slightly to the right, in return. "Thank you, Captain."

"May I introduce my Executive Officer, Commander Jadern?" Morian said. "He'll be your liaison during your stay. And this is Lieutenant Danis Morian." He motioned to Danis.

The prince's eyes lit up. "Ah, Danis 'Domino' Morian. Winner of the Orso Fighter's Cup three years in a row. Your reputation precedes you."

Danis bowed her head. "Thank you, my prince."

The tall, blond prince turned to the two people behind him. "This is my first assistant Tenilo Barum and April Badeaux, a reporter for *The Quantum Examiner*."

Tenilo was short and portly. His brown hair was styled in a way that was popular with royalty, but his did not have the volume or length of the prince's wavy locks.

April Badeaux was much younger than Richard anticipated. She was about thirty, slim with long red hair. She ceased tapping on her data screen just in time to look up when she was introduced.

The usual formalities and pleasantries were exchanged, and then Felder and Morian walked together, side by side, to the gravrail. The three visitors, Morian and Jadern, took the first car.

"I understand you're doing a story about the *Avenger*'s history?" Richard asked April.

The reporter looked up from her data screen again. "Oh, it's uh... not so much a history as a... chronicling of its retirement."

Richard tried to hold back a visible flinch. "Retirement?"

April looked surprised. "Yes, it's a historic ship, and the system wants to document its final days in service."

That didn't make any sense. "I'm sorry, Ms. Badeaux. I don't follow," Richard said and turned to face the reporter. "You're talking about my ship as if she's being decommissioned."

April looked back and forth between Richard and Felder, her mouth open.

"What Ms. Badeaux is trying to say, Captain," Felder said quietly, "is that King Lorne has decided to retire all Defender class ships by the end of the month." Prince Felder straightened his cape and turned to face Morian. "My father and King Lorne made the agreement during their last meeting. The Alastor System will be implementing a new class of warship. Progress, you do understand? Since our system has no ships of this age, we've been sent here to document the story."

Morian gritted his teeth. It was all he could do to refrain from lashing out at the prince. "Of course," he said, "but orders to retire an entire ship would have to come down through the admiral of the fleet. And there has been no such order."

Felder frowned and made an exaggerated gesture of trying to look sad. "Oh, I'm terribly sorry if the communication has not made its way to you yet. I'm afraid I may have said too much. I'm sure it's nothing but an administrative error."

Good sovereign stars, Morian thought angrily. *Who the hell does this royal brat think he is? Coming onto my ship and dropping a bomb like that so flippantly.*

Felder was a reminder of why Morian despised royalty, especially the princes. They had no respect for others. The railcar stopped.

"Jadern will show you to your quarters," Morian said. "Once you are settled in, he will escort you to the briefing room. I'll meet you there."

"Splendid, Captain Morian," Prince Felder said. "I'll look forward to our meeting."

Morian stepped out of the car and watched as it moved on to the elevator door to the residence level.

Morian sighed and shook his head. *Retire the Avenger? Not if I have anything to do with it... I don't have time for this. I'm not a damn tour guide. I have a ship to run. And what the hell was that about? Do they think Avenger is an antique?*

He shook his head and decided to send a message to Jadern to get to the bottom of it, and to assign Danis to show them around the ship. *Damned if I'm going to do it!*

* * *

"As you'll see in here, next to the main hangar bay is the port-side auxiliary armament magazine." Danis opened the door to a vast compartment filled with massive vac-locked crates and large cylindrical tanks stacked from floor to ceiling.

Prince Felder, Tenilo and April looked around in amazement. While playing tour guide, Danis counted the ways she would get back at her brother for giving her the assignment.

April pointed to one of the large tanks and said, "And these are power cells for the Direct Energy Lasers?"

"They are the backup power cells," Danis corrected. "And in the fleet, the correct nomenclature is Direct Energy Weapon. But we just call them lasers."

"Aren't all weapons on USF ships Direct Energy-based?" April asked.

"On most ships, yes," Mr. Tenilo said as he hurried to keep up with them. "Direct Energy Weaponry technology became the USF standard exactly twenty-three standard years ago, in 3255."

"The *Avenger* has the same armament as all USF ships—DEW lasers, DEW cannons and even DEW blasters," Danis said and then pointed to the sealed chambers that lined the walls. "And in those are our inventory of cruise missiles," she continued, "including Mark 47s and Mark 59s. Those containers over there contain railgun projectiles."

"Railguns?" Felder asked, somewhat surprised. "I was not aware that any USF ships still used railguns."

Danis nodded. "Yes, with the *Avenger* being one of the older ships in the fleet, it is one of the only C-class ships that still has them, point defense and offensive."

Tenilo pushed his spectacles up onto the bridge of his nose and said, "That's right. Most ships have replaced railgun space with DEW weapons. Very few railguns remain in service. Might I ask, can we see the generators and rails?"

"Yes, we can go there next," Danis replied, heaving a silent sigh.

Tenilo smiled and said, "Fascinating."

April typed on her data screen and began talking before she looked up. "So, why has the rest of the fleet moved away from railguns, but *Avenger* has been allowed to keep them?"

Danis kept walking and everyone automatically followed her, their boots clanging on the expanded metal walkway. "It's a matter of weight mostly," she replied without looking back. "An entire power cell weighs the same as only fifty main railgun projectiles and can power the DEW cannons with thousands of blasts."

"Then why does *Avenger* keep them?"

Danis shrugged and said, "Captain Morian is kind of... old school, I guess you could say. He respects the concepts of the projectiles."

"And the *Avenger* really is the oldest ship in the fleet?"

"Not exactly," Danis said. "It's one of the oldest, one of the few Defender class Type C ships still on active duty. There are several other D and F class Defender ships around, but nothing as big as *Avenger*." They had crossed the hall and Danis opened another door and stepped inside. The others followed one behind the other, Prince Felder leading.

"My sovereign stars," Tenilo said, stepping up to the protective railing, getting as close as he could to the long, open track just below them. "I have only read about these. It is quite something to see one in person. Look at this." He pointed down it.

"So, this rail shoots missiles just like the other launchers?" April asked.

"Not quite," Danis said. "What you're looking at here is the linear track, twin conductive rails that drive the kinetic projectile. The projectiles are fed automatically onto the track back there." She pointed to the right. "Electromagnetic force is generated to launch the projectile at extremely high velocities. We also have mini railguns that can fire up to eight hundred projectiles per minute."

"So, the projectiles explode?" April asked again. For being a reporter, April couldn't get exploding missiles off of her mind. Danis restrained her frustration.

"No, railguns are *kinetic* weapons," Danis said. "The projectile is merely a slug of depleted uranium. A standard cruise missile is about six meters long and a meter in diameter. The railgun projectiles are only a meter long and half a meter in diameter."

"That must be why the fleet has moved away from them," Prince Felder said. "They are way smaller than one of the missiles."

"They are," Danis replied, "but even with the smaller projectile, the rail generates a force that is exponentially greater in kinetic energy. A hit from a twenty-kilogram railgun projectile traveling at one-tenth light speed on an asteroid of say, half a kilometer in diameter, will shatter it. They are still very deadly weapons."

"Amazing, simply amazing," Tenilo said.

"So will a nuclear missile," April said.

"But at a much greater cost," Danis replied, her sarcasm barely hidden.

Felder and April were beginning to look a little bored. Danis decided to show them the fighter squadron in Bay 3.

"Very well," she said. "I think you've seen enough here. Why don't we go and take a look at something I think you'll find more interesting?"

She led the party back the way they came, talking to them as they walked. "The Defender C-class ships have a balance of missiles, DEW weapons, railguns, a full squadron of twelve F32A fighters and two shuttles. They were designed this way to act either as a support vessel in the fleet or to act independently on single-ship missions.

"Avenger, as you know, is one of the older ships in the Orso fleet, but she's a mighty ship, a heavy battle cruiser: fourteen-hundred meters long, two-hundred meters wide at the bow, one-hundred-and-fifty meters at the stern and two-hundred from topside to keel. She's fitted with up to two meters of Dutrinium armor and is equipped with twelve heavy DEW cannons, twenty-four point defense DEW lasers, twenty-four .50 caliber railguns firing explosive and non-explosive rounds and a single, fixed railgun capable of firing a range of projectiles from depleted uranium to nuclear. She also carries Mark 47 Saber nuclear torpedoes and Mark 59 Lance missiles. The ship's hangar can accommodate up to four shuttles and twelve fighters, a full squadron."

"Extraordinary! Quite extraordinary," Tenilo said.

Chapter Five

First Contact

Captain Richard Morian was seated at his desk in his stateroom, the only quiet place on the ship. He loved the *Avenger* and its crew, but he hated unwanted, unscheduled intrusions that were almost always beyond his control, like Felder and his entourage.

There was a knock at the door. *What now?* he thought as he hit the button on his desk and the door slid open to reveal Prince Felder. *Oh great. That's all I need. Well, at least this time his assistant and that reporter aren't with him.* Morian stood and composed himself.

"Prince Felder," he said, "please come in."

The prince stepped inside, ducking his head to avoid hitting the doorframe. They looked at each other. A moment of awkward silence passed between them. It was Morian's ship and he was in command. Although Felder was of the royal class, he was still considered a civilian.

Even so, because of his royal status, Morian couldn't order him around like a crew member. He had to respect the prince. Felder, too, was obviously trying to figure out the dynamic.

"Captain Morian," he said, "I just wanted to offer you my personal appreciation and thanks for allowing me and my staff to tour your ship."

Morian nodded, knowing that there was more to this meeting than a thank-you. "You're welcome, my prince. We hope you enjoy your stay."

Felder looked past Morian to the wall. Then he stepped forward and examined a few of the wall hangings. One of them that seemed to attract his attention was a framed copy of his captain's commission. The real record was in the ship's data banks, but Morian liked something hanging on the wall.

Felder leaned close to it to read. "Amazing, simply amazing."

"What is, my prince?"

Felder looked back at him and said, "The pride you must feel to have your own ship. I have always admired anyone serving in the fleet. You are brave people and worthy of our respect."

Morian wasn't exactly sure where he was going with this.

"Did you come from a military family, Captain?" Felder asked conversationally.

"No, my father worked as a technician in the carbon plants in the Brynn System. He designed Rayon shielding."

"Ah, Brynn, quite a ways from Orso, then?"

"Yes."

"May I ask," Felder continued, "how someone from Brynn came to be a Captain in the USF? Was it a goal of yours early on?"

"No," he replied. "I enlisted straight out of high school to pay for a university education. I did my three years, went back to school and graduated. Then realized I enjoyed life in the fleet so much, I decided to reenlist as an officer."

Felder nodded and said, "I see." And then turned again to continue eyeing the wall hangings. He stopped on a 3D-printed replica of the plaque proclaiming that Morian had graduated from the USF Marine School of Strategic Combat. A six-week course of fieldwork on the ice planet Tauntric Four.

"I myself wanted to purchase a commission in the fleet," Felder said and looked around again. "But my father would have none of it. He thought political experience would be better for me than the military."

So, that's it, Morian thought. *He thinks he's missing out. He'd rather be serving. Interesting. Hmm, so that's why he wanted to visit a fleet ship.* "Really?" Morian said. "So I assume you went straight into the senate?"

"No, I did go to university first," Felder replied. "I have a PhD in astrophysics."

"And you regret not entering the service?"

Felder frowned, hesitated, then said, "As I said, Captain. My father... My father the king is not an easy man. He and I... We did not necessarily... see eye to eye in all things."

Morian nodded and said, "I understand. Many times, fathers and sons don't see eye to eye. My own father made it very clear that I should not join the fleet, but instead, should stay on Brynn and get a stable job with Rayon, like himself."

"Interesting," Felder said thoughtfully. "Neither of our fathers wanted us to join the military, yet you did. What gave you the courage to go against your father's wishes?"

Morian shrugged one shoulder and said, "I don't know. It was many years ago. I just did what I wanted to do. That's all I can tell you. Perhaps the fact that my father wasn't king had something to do with it."

"Yes, I suppose so," the prince said and stepped closer to him. "You are a brave man, Captain Marion. I like you."

Morian had it in his head that the prince was faking, insincere, but why?

"What's it like, Captain?" Felder asked. "The military? Being a soldier? Being a warrior?"

"Well, it isn't quite like that," Morian replied. "Not with the way things are now, with how the... universe is now, now that mankind has settled so many star systems. There doesn't seem to be much need for the military these days. There hasn't been a real conflict for generations. There's no need for war. There are enough resources to go around. Those of us in the fleet today have never fought... not even a skirmish, and the situation isn't likely to change. Life in the fleet, and I hate to say it, can often be a little humdrum."

"Yes, but you still train?" Felder said. "You still live by the military code, do you not?"

"That, we do," Morian replied, "but it's all more formality than necessity. And much of what we do is mere tradition, the original meaning of which has been long forgotten."

"But tradition does connect you with the past, correct?" Felder asked. "To the warriors who've served before you?"

"Yes, I suppose, in a way." Morian could tell the prince wanted to get to something, but either was afraid to or didn't know how to bring it up.

"With all due respect, my prince," Morian said. "Do you regret not joining?"

Felder looked at him and smiled out of the corner of his mouth. His eyes said it all. He gave a little shake of his head and looked back at the wall. "Yes, I suppose I do."

The silence lingered. Morian didn't know what to say. Did the prince need encouragement or consoling? What was this conversation about?

"I don't know much about war, Captain Morian," Felder said, eventually, "but I do know about our societies. And even though you have not fought, I can assure you that the presence of the fleet is what holds the star systems together. It is the single institution that binds the worlds and allows our different governments to work together. Even more so than politics."

This surprised Morian. He expected an arrogant royal to say the opposite. "I hope we do our part well," was all he could say in reply.

"I know I'm only technically a visitor here on the

Avenger, Captain," Felder said. "But if you need anything, anything at all, please do not hesitate to call on me to help."

Morian couldn't think of a single thing he would ever need a prince to help with. "I will, my prince," he said, quietly.

"Do you think I'm too old to join?" Felder asked.

Morian was surprised by the question. "I think the age regulations depend on which branch one joins," he said. "But I think the bigger problem would be your royal lineage. Officers would find it difficult to give you orders."

"Do you find it difficult, Captain?"

"Not at all," Morian replied with a smile, "but then, I have no need to order you around."

"Do you ever wish there was a battle?" Felder asked. "Do you ever wish you could command your ship in mortal combat? After all, isn't that what you train for?"

"No, Your Highness," Morian said, "and I don't think it's wise to wish for war. War costs lives, and that should be avoided at all costs. The military we enjoy today provides services, regulation, jobs and structure to the systems and, above all, it provides a deterrent to those who might wish to cross the line. Even the pirates out on the tip of the galactic arm respect us and squabble only among themselves. I am just fine doing this job without the horror of war."

"But wouldn't a battle be exciting?" Felder said, his eyes lit up. "Wouldn't the thrill of the ultimate test of man against man be... exhilarating?"

Felder had the energy of a child now. He had a naïve view of the military and no understanding of what war was really like. Not that Morian did either, since he'd never experienced it, but at least he'd studied it. *Why would a prince think combat is good?* he wondered. *How can I disagree with him and his simple view of an insupportable situation and not insult him?*

"I suppose that's possible, yes," he replied cautiously. "But not for me. I'm happy to remain here and enjoy my career in a peacetime military."

Felder looked away and said, "I think it would be the very epitome of existence, of living, to face another man, staring down the barrel of a DEW blaster, being faced with death and fighting and living to tell the tale." Felder looked almost as if he was dreaming. "To make the right decision in the face of impossible odds. To receive a salute from your leader, from an older warrior." His eyes gleamed like he half expected Morian to give him a salute.

The prince seemed to be lost in space. *What the hell is going on?* Morian thought. *A spoiled kid who wants to feel like a man by wearing a uniform. I must end this, now!*

"Your words are inspiring, my prince," he said.

Felder nodded and smiled. He seemed to get a sense of confidence from Morian's appreciation. *Maybe that's all he needed,* he thought. *Some sort of validation from another man, someone other than his father.*

Morian's data screen beeped: a call from the bridge. Thank the stars, maybe this will give me an excuse to end this conversation. He tapped the screen and said, "Morian."

"Captain, you have an emergency call from Orso. You're required to jack into a USF meeting."

He gave the prince a look and Felder understood. The prince bowed his head slightly and left.

"Thank you," Morian said. "I'll take it in my stateroom."

He closed the door, donned his halo, tapped the link, jacked into the meeting and found himself in a large virtual room where all the commanders and captains of the Orso Carrier Group were waiting. Most of them were out among the stars at various points in the Orso System. King Lorne himself was in attendance along with several prominent dukes and Marshal Ugo Tan, the commander in chief of all of Orso's military forces. Morian couldn't remember the last time he was part of a meeting with all of these faces. The quietness of the room was unsettling.

Something was going on. Something was wrong. Morian peered at the faces trying to read what they were thinking, but no luck. Even the king looked troubled. Marshal Tan stood, ran his hand over his beard and brought the meeting to order. He looked... nervous. Something else Morian hadn't seen before.

The marshal cleared his throat and began. "Now that we are all here, I would like to start by thanking King Lorne for his leadership thus far." He looked at the king, who bowed his head. "Today, we received some unsettling news of an unprecedented event and sadly, a deadly one. Over the last forty-eight hours, several fringe settlements have disappeared from the Slipstream network.

Several members of the meeting murmured and

looked at each other. Eyebrows were raised. Someone coughed.

"At first," Tan continued, "we assumed it was a software crash somewhere in the communications systems and several ships were dispatched to investigate. A destroyer, the *Lisbon*, sent a holo feed from the Persei System. Before I play the holo, let me preface it; what you are about to see is shocking and verified. Today marks a grave and historic day for humanity.

"As you know, for hundreds of years we have been colonizing the star systems, pushing our boundaries further and further into the unknown. In all of those years, we have not encountered another sentient species, not one... Until today that is. An alien species has made contact with us."

There was a murmur around the room.

Ugo held up his hand, waited for silence, and then continued, "As I said, the holo you are about to watch comes from Typhon in the Persei System and, again, I warn you, it's disturbing." He tapped an icon on his data pad and a hologram appeared above the center of the table. It showed more than a dozen USF ships engaged in what at first appeared to be a battle among themselves. DEW lasers and missiles were being fired in all directions. Then it became clear what was actually happening. The ships were not fighting among themselves. They were fighting an enemy.

The enemy ships were small, not quite round in shape, almost an ellipse but slightly flattened, with sweptback, sickle-shaped wings. Each of the alien ships was surrounded by what appeared to be a pale blue aura, and they were fast, so fast Morian couldn't make out any other details. That is until one of them fired what appeared to be an immensely powerful blue laser blast into one of the fighters. Everyone watched in silence as the USF ships were destroyed one after the other. The level of destruction was almost beyond belief.

"Not only was the entire crew of the *Lisbon* destroyed," Ugo continued, "but this enemy destroyed the entire Persei System fleet." The room was deathly silent.

"Along with this footage, the Lisbon was able to transmit a limited amount of information about this new enemy. Their ships are small, at least those we've seen so far, and seem to be identical in size, a little more than twice the size of a USF F32A fighter but not as big as a Class D frigate. They have exhibited a devastating array of firepower. The technology does not appear to be human, although no lifeforms were observed. Their craft are fast, faster than the F32A but, so it seems, such speed comes at a price. They are not as maneuverable as the F32A."

"How do we know it's another sentient species?" one of the captains asked.

Ugo Tan nodded and replied, "We're making the determination based on the advanced technology of the craft. More disturbing is that they seem to have appeared in the Persei by using what appears to be a manufactured wormhole independent of the Slipstream network."

Several gasps could be heard among the members of the meeting. and people began to murmur again.

Again, Tan held up his hand for silence, then continued, "Captains, Commanders, as of this moment you're to consider yourselves and the fleet at DEFCON one. We have been the victims of an unprovoked attack by an alien force of unknown origin and potential. We have no idea where they will attack next, or when. We must be ready to defend our systems."

Chapter Six

Freedom Fighters

Pricus City Governor's Mansion
Planet Tor's Surface
Pricus System

Twenty-year-old Andra Graynir crept silently down the stairs. Even in complete darkness, she knew every inch of her parents' mansion by heart. She glanced at the data screen on her forearm and brought up the home's security system. Finding the back door icon, she turned off the intrusion detection and slipped out.

Andra enjoyed nights like this. To be alone under the stars was to be... free. Her father never understood her and was always overly protective. *When is he going to learn that I'm not a child anymore?* she wondered as she kept to the shadows, staying out of view of the security screens until she finally made it to the street to find them waiting for her. Gian and his two friends were beside their gravcars. Gian, a couple of years older than Andra, waved and smiled. He was tall, stocky, almost six-two, with blond hair and blue eyes. His biceps bulged under the white T-shirt as he held out his arms. They embraced and kissed. His shoulders were so broad she could barely reach around them.

Norryn and Declan joined them. "Hey, Andra," Declan said.

She waved at both of Gian's friends.

"Gian, check this out." Norryn pointed to his car's rear compartment. Everyone gathered around as Norryn opened the compartment, and Andra's jaw dropped when she saw its contents: three railgun rifles lay on a blanket inside.

"Whoa," Gian said. "Where did you get those?"

"The black market in Bellville," Norryn replied.

"Nice," Gian said, running his fingers along one of the barrels.

Andra couldn't believe it. "Guys, firearms are totally illegal here," she said. "We're not security forces. What are you doing?"

"Relax." Gian held up a hand. "It's all part of the plan. We're not doing anything with them. We're just collecting for the rebels. They pay high prices for railguns."

"What?" Andra gasped. "You're gun running?" She knew Gian was politically rebellious, as she was herself, but so far, their politics had remained mostly theoretical. It certainly didn't include illegal weapons for sale. "If my father finds out—"

"He won't find out," Gian interrupted her as he closed the compartment. "Not as long as we don't stay out here in the street." He pointed at Declan. "You guys take these and add them to the cache at the cabin, right after we see Hamel. I don't want to be riding around with these things all night."

Declan nodded and said, "No problem, G."

Gian hopped into his gravcar and thumbed the starter, bringing the gravs and thrusters online. The car rose silently until it was hovering some twelve centimeters above the pavement. "You ready?" he asked Andra.

"Absolutely," Andra said as she settled into the passenger seat.

"Then let's go!" Declan said as he fired up his thrusters and took off, with Gian and Norryn right behind him.

Andra loved the freedom of the wind in her hair. The gravcars were almost silent as Gian took the turns at high speed. At night, past curfew, without her parents managing every minute of her schedule or guards carefully watching her every move, was one of the few times she could really be herself.

"So, where is he tonight?" she asked.

Gian turned, looked at her, smiled at her and said, "He's at the Lookout."

She nodded. They hadn't been up there for a while, so it would be nice to go again; the view from the top was stunning, especially at night. *How many will there be this time?* she wondered.

Once they were out of the city, it only took a few minutes to reach the road to the Lookout. Pricus City was the largest settlement on planet Tor, but that wasn't saying much. It was still a very small city.

When they arrived at their destination, Andra was surprised to see at least another two-dozen cars already parked there, a lot more than she'd expected.

Gian parked and they hopped out, Norryn and Declan right behind them. *It's a perfect night to be outside*, Andra thought as she looked out over the lights of Pricus City, then she looked up at the stars that filled the sky and couldn't help but wonder at the expanse.

The Pricus System itself was massive: six gas giants, thirty-seven minor planets and an as yet unknown number of moons circling a star slightly larger that Sol. She tried to imagine the scale of the universe, the other worlds across the galaxy all connected to one another by the Slipstream, but she couldn't grasp the enormity of it all. She'd never been through the Slipstream, but one day she knew she would. She longed to visit those far-off systems and planets, especially captaining her own ship, and she knew nothing could stop her, not even her father.

People were still arriving. It was one of the largest crowds of rebels and supporters she had seen in one place. Only her three friends knew she was the royal governor's daughter, for which she was glad. These people would have avoided her like a plague if they'd known. They would've despised her political lineage. It wasn't as if the Graynirs were royalty, but out here it was close enough. The political families were despised by this group. And she wanted to be accepted by them.

"There he is," Gian said suddenly, pointing into the crowd.

Hamel was walking through the crowd, nodding this way and that, accepting high fives. The poet had become popular in the last six months. He was always traveling and never stayed in one place too long. The local authorities couldn't decide if he was a rebel terrorist or just a dumb kid who was just trying to get likes on his data screen.

Hamel was in his late twenties, tall and skinny and wore a light brown bushy beard with an unruly head of hair. Andra and Gian joined the rest of the crowd in front of the row of parked gravcars. Hamel turned his back to the cliff's edge so the city lights could be seen behind him. He held up his arm and tapped his data screen to enable a livestream.

He held out his hands and began, "Friends and citizens of Pricus City." His voice resonated. "I am honored to be here to speak to you tonight, and I appreciate you foregoing sleep and choosing to see me, for my words have no power if they fall upon deaf ears. Deaf ears you are not!" He raised his voice and the crowd seemed to follow in his excitement. "Who are you?"

"The people!" the crowd chanted in unison.

"Yes, you are the people," Hamel continued. "So, tonight, not only lend me your ears, but also lend me your mind and your will. Tonight, there are no rules, no bosses, no parents, no teachers or schools. Lend me your mind and learn at the feet of a fool."

Andra checked her own data screen. Sure enough, Hamel was streaming his speech. The data showed that more than six thousand people on Tor were watching his performance.

The crowd laughed. His words were delivered almost

poetically. The way he spoke was as entertaining as his oratory.

"I am humbled, good people of Pricus City, that you would come to listen to me. I travel and must keep moving so the authorities will not nab me, nor will they stop me, watch me, catch me or grab me." He jumped up and hugged himself with his knees to his chest and landed in a curled-up ball on the ground. Then before anyone could react, he sprang up, leaned back and performed a perfect back handspring. He stuck the landing and held out his arms for applause. The group clapped. Andra blew a whistle.

"Good people, listen to me. Tonight, I will tell you tales of the predicament we are in. We on Tor are locked in a tremendous battle, a battle we are losing. A battle we must fight with all our might against the tyrant, and who is that?" He cupped his ear with his hand, prompting the crowd to answer.

"King Lorne!" everyone shouted.

Hamel leapt into the air and spun three hundred and sixty degrees, sticking the landing. "Yes," he yelled. "King Lorne. King Lorne is he who wants to take our precious Tor, our precious city, our precious planet and our precious system and turn it into nothing more than a simple, small, meek and modest..." He lowered his voice, "...mining colony."

Andra booed along with the rest of the crowd.

"I know, I know." Hamel balled his fists on his hips and marched back and forth, moving closer to the crowd. "Biomium. That's what they want. Our planet is over-flowing with it and therefore, it should be, and will be, ours to do with as we wish. What good are we if we allow them to steal our precious Biomium and ship it to King Lorne and his fleet? What right does he have to take it? What right does he have to ship it? What right does he have to make us his slaves?"

He did a cartwheel to more hoots and hollers from the crowd.

"People of Pricus City, you are not alone. Hear me, I beg you. You are here tonight not because I forced you to come or coerced you. You are here because you want to be here. Because there is something deep within you that speaks to you, that yearns, that cries out for freedom from oppression. Do not deny those feelings. They are alive, living within you. Can you feel them?"

"Yes!" the crowd yelled.

Andra felt her stomach tingle. She had never heard anyone speak the way Hamel did, and she was both alarmed and exhilarated. He was calling for rebellion, a crime that could get him locked up for the rest of his life, and the thought of a hundred and fifty years behind bars frightened her. *Does he not know this?* she wondered. But there was something about what he was saying, something that excited her, made her feel... alive. She had no idea what it was, but she loved it.

"That feeling inside of you," Hamel continued, his expression serious as he pointed a dominant finger at first one member of the crowd, then another and another. "That sense of hope and love that is in you, all of you." His voice grew louder. "That consciousness I see within you and self-awareness that lives within you." He paused, pointed at Andra and stared into her eyes. "That very tingle within your breast... That is the call of freedom... and I call upon you to heed it and follow your heart."

Andra was stunned. It was as if he could read her mind. He stood like a statue, tall, strong, quiet, and continued staring directly at Andra. Then he smiled and slowly looked away.

"So, if you feel freedom's call," he said to the crowd. "If your heart longs to be set free from the oppressive hand of a king who cares nothing for you, who wants only to exploit you. If you hope one day to see Pricus City free... then follow me to... FREEDOM." He shouted that last word and raised his hands high above his head, then continued, "Listen to your heart when I sing that word. Freedom. Take note of how your body stirs when you hear it... Freedom."

Andra could feel something inside. A longing growing within her. She wanted to hear more, to know more. She wanted to know what to do. Her life, her school, her parents, they were no longer important to her. But what Hamel said was.

"Long ago," Hamel said quietly, "centuries ago our ancestors fought one another. They fought when the Slipstream was new, and humanity battled for control over it." He paused, smiled, and held up a finger. "Then... then, the tyrants took control. Those that survived The Purge were those with the Gifts. It was the Gifts, you see, that allowed them to win. Those certain men and women who were somehow endowed with the awesome gifts of telekinesis and telepathy... It was those special powers that allowed them to win and survive The Purge. It was those special powers that enabled them to get the upper hand. May we never forget it."

He paused and looked around the crowd, now silent, hanging on his every word. "BUT!" he shouted, his hand held high. "Not only did they win, they subjugated the losers. They used their Gifts to become the ruling class. They became the Royal class and those same abilities, those Gifts, are still in their blood."

At least that part, Andra knew, was an exaggeration. There were no Gifts anymore. Everyone knew that. But Hamel did have a flair about him.

"Even to this day, those Royals lord it over you, my dear people. But... we are not here to talk, to merely talk. No, we are here to act. Yes, action is what will make us free. To do or not do. To act or not act. To live or to die. For yes or for no. Those are the questions we must answer. And the answer is... Yes! We must act. We must take action, for action brings freedom and only with freedom can we truly come alive."

Andra wanted to act. She wanted to do something, but just what, she didn't know.

"King Lorne rules from afar," Hamel continued. "He sits on the throne not in Pricus City, not amongst us but many systems away on Orso. He sits there and gives orders, takes his taxes and tells us what to do. Nay," he shouted. "I say, nay... He is not our elected leader. We gave no consent to be governed by Lorne or anyone else. We had no vote. We signed no contract with this tyrant. We made no accord, no agreement or treaty. Why does he speak for us? For what is he?"

"Tyrant!" someone called out.

"Lazy!" someone else said.

"Oppressor!" Gian yelled as he smiled at Andra.

"Yes, yes, you are correct," Hamel shouted. "Your words are gentle, loving music to my ears. Your words write the notes of which my heart sings, and I love you for it." He folded his hands over his chest and made a loving gesture. "But we must not stop here. We have a duty to ourselves. We cannot let the tyrant king control us any longer. So, if what I am saying makes sense to you, if the words I preach ring true for you, then I welcome you all to come join me and, with that, I bid you adieu." He gave a sweeping bow to a roar of applause and cheers and turned away.

The crowd was ecstatic. They rushed forward and Hamel gave a huge high five to the first person that reached him. Others patted him on the back. Gian rushed to meet him and they hugged each other. Then Gian wrapped his arm around his shoulder and said something in his ear Andra couldn't hear.

She hung back. Declan brought her a bottle of brew, and she thanked him. The rest of the group began breaking up into their own little cliques. Most of them broke out their data screens and began spreading Hamel's new holo.

Once the commotion had died down, Gian came and found her. "Come on," he shouted. "Come with me." He grabbed her hand and led her back behind the parked gravcars where, to her surprise, Norryn and Declan were talking animatedly with Hamel.

"Hamel," Gian said as they joined the small group, "this is Andra. I told you about her."

"Gian, I can't say thank you enough," Hamel said after greeting Andra. His voice was low. He was no longer in front of a crowd or being recorded. But his tone was serious, and Andra was fascinated by how quickly he'd changed.

"So, the intel I have says that tomorrow," Hamel said, "a representative from King Lorne is coming to Tor to seal the deal on the Biomium mines."

"And?" Gian asked.

"I think our time to strike is now," Hamel replied and then took a drink from his bottle. "I think it would be a strategic move. We get very few chances like this, and I think with Andra's help, we can do something really significant this time."

"What are you talking about?" Andra asked.

Hamel turned to her. "I'm talking about kidnapping the king's representative and holding him hostage until Lorne agrees to give us our independence."

Andra caught her breath. She had no idea he was planning something like that. He was talking and planning treason, and that could get them executed.

"But what about the authorities?" Declan asked.

"Don't worry about them," Hamel said. "They can't do anything to us out here. And besides, if they turn up the heat, we'll just let him go. That's the whole point of these harassing tactics." The poet took another drink.

"He's right," Gian said. "If they press us, we just let him go."

"No," Andra said. "You don't know my father. They'll hunt us down. What then?"

Hamel shrugged. "Remember, we can't win a military battle, but we can show them how the people of Tor won't be ruled and won't stand for this tyranny. Just by merely kidnapping the representative, we'll show them that the king has no power here. Even if we only hold him for a short time." Hamel looked around. "So, are we all in?"

Andra looked at them. They were young, between the ages of twenty and twenty-five. At twenty, she was one of the youngest.

Gian looked at Norryn, then Declan, then her and said, "We're in, Andra."

"I'm in," Andra said quietly. "But how exactly do I come in?"

Hamel smiled. "You're the key to this whole thing, Andra. Tomorrow that representative will be staying at your house. Your father's house. The governor of Tor."

Chapter Seven

Pricus City Governor's Mansion
Planet Tor
Plan of Action

The following day, Andra stood on the veranda with her mother and her father, Governor Raymar Graynir. She was no longer dressed in the fashionable style of her friends as she had been the night before. Instead, she wore the formal attire required for the occasion. It had taken her forever to dress. The body-hugging white gown with its extravagant gold embroidery seemed, to her at least, more than a little too much but, she supposed, one had to look the part when meeting an emissary of another system. She would much rather have been wearing the commoner's pants and in style V-neck top she wore the night before.

The greenspace behind their mansion was wide and open. A large circular landing pad occupied much of the space between the rear of the mansion and the tree line several hundred meters away. The gray concrete of the landing pad seemed so out of place among the field of long grass and flowers.

Andra's father stood next to her and checked the data screen on his forearm, then said, "The diplomat's ship is three minutes out. I'm told it's Duke Steren himself."

Governor Graynir was of medium build, balding, with an uncharacteristic paunch around his middle. He was in his late sixties and had a habit of constantly fiddling with and twirling the ends of his gray mustache. He pulled on his white leather gloves, clasped his hands behind his back and pushed his shoulders back. His belly stuck out farther than his chest, although it used to be the other way around.

"A duke, how exciting," Andra's mother said, just as ready to play the role of host as her husband. She turned to the governor and said, "Do you think sending a duke means the Pricus System is progressing faster on the sovereign track than we think?"

"It's possible," Graynir replied. He looked around and flicked something off his lapel, then he glanced at Andra and said, "Daughter, please stand up straight."

"They aren't even here yet," she replied.

"No matter, you need to act like royalty even when no one is watching."

"We're not royalty," Andra said, frustrated.

Graynir sighed. "I know we do not officially meet the standards of the royal class, but you are a member of the house of Graynir, governor of Pricus City. Families all over this city look up to us. And therefore, here, in Pricus City, you are royalty, and I need you to act the part."

Andra wanted desperately to roll her eyes but

restrained herself. She pushed back her shoulders and flattened her stomach. It was not the time or the place to argue with her father. She would do as she was told, for now. But hopefully, in less than twenty-four standard hours, she would be acting out her defiance in a way her father could never comprehend.

"Yes, Father," she said quietly.

Every critique her father spat out was one more motivation for her to help with Hamel and Gian's plan.

Am I really going to go through with this? she wondered. *He'll not only disown me, but he's also fanatical enough to have me arrested, even imprisoned. So what? He's a pig!*

The thought that she could get back at her father made her want to kidnap this duke even more. The feelings of freedom, expression and choice that Hamel had spoken about welled up inside her. There was something about his cause that made her feel... alive.

The high-pitched whine of a shuttle's engines brought her out of her reverie. She looked to the east. *There it is,* she thought, *the duke's shuttle...* Then a second ship appeared. *Two ships? That's odd.*

Six of the governor's security guards marched out from their posts by the deck to greet the guests on the landing pad. Each guard wore the standard black and gray uniform of the Tor Defense Forces. Each carried a DEW rifle. Her father was trying to impress his guests. Those six guards were assigned to the governor's mansion at all times. Andra had never liked them. Between them they managed to be everywhere, so it seemed. As the governor's daughter and only child, she was watched constantly, never really alone.

The first ship looked like one of the regular diplomatic USF ships she'd seen a dozen times before. The second ship flew closer to the ground, then sped up and passed the USF shuttle. *Hmm. Interesting.*

Both ships were on their final approach to the landing pad. The faster ship was obviously a yacht of some kind. It was tricked out with duel grav converters on each side forward of its engines. *Hmmm*, Andra thought. *A newer model.* The sleek reflective black stripe on the side was definitely a custom job.

The yacht touched down first, the USF ship shortly after. The ships' engines powered down and the ramps opened.

A moment later, an extremely tall young man appeared on the yacht's ramp. He stood for a moment and looked around. His blond hair was the shoulder-length of a royal, but his dress was different. He was wearing a navy-blue jumpsuit with gold trim. He had high cheekbones and broad shoulders. *Who* is *that?* she wondered. His hair and face told her pretty much everything she needed to know. He was a typical royal, spoiled and most likely exceedingly boring to talk to.

The young man spotted the governor right away and walked quickly toward him. By then, a portly, older man with a worried look on his face had exited the USF shuttle. He spotted the young man and tried to catch up with him, but the royal was already making eye contact with the governor, his arms spread wide in greeting.

"Governor Graynir, I presume. If I may, I would like

to request my yacht be placed in your underground hangar for protection. Is that an option?"

"Of course." Her father waved to one of the guards.

Andra didn't like the prince already. They had barely greeted each other, and he was already concerned about his fancy ship.

Everyone exchanged the customary political pleasantries on the landing pad, and Governor Graynir led the group to the mansion's patio, where Andra and her mother waited.

Her father introduced the two men. He gestured to the young man first. "I would like to present Crown Prince Elio of the Orso system, the son of King Lorne."

Andra's mother bowed her head. "A great honor to welcome you here, my prince."

"And this is my eldest daughter, Andra."

Prince Elio turned his blue eyes to Andra and smiled. Andra was intrigued by the genuine expression of pleasure on his face. Her mother elbowed her in the side, reminding her to bow and speak. Andra lowered her head.

"It's an honor to meet you, my prince."

"And I am delighted to be here," the young man said.

"And this is...?" her father asked.

"And this is Duke Steren of my father's court." Prince Elio's introduction took the duke by surprise. The chubby little man had obviously wanted to introduce himself with all pomp due to his rank and position, and he didn't like the prince getting the upper hand in the exchange, and it showed.

The prince, on the other hand, was amused by the

look on Steren's face and the corner of his mouth turned up in a half-smile. He looked at Andra and winked. She, too, was taken by surprise and, much to her chagrin, blushed furiously. Fortunately, the prince had turned his head and didn't see her reaction. Much as she hated to, she had to admit to herself that Prince Elio was extremely handsome with a commanding presence. *But a bit smug, perhaps?* she thought.

"Shall we go inside?" Governor Graynir asked.

"By all means," Elio replied. "I'm parched. You do have something good to drink, I assume, Governor?"

"Indeed, we do. If you'll allow me to escort you, my prince."

Once inside the governor's parlor, his attendants began to circulate carrying trays loaded with glasses of water, spark tea and brandy. Duke Steren, the consummate politician, went straight for the brandy.

"Do you have any caff cola by any chance?" Elio asked no one in particular.

"Of course." Andra's mother beckoned one of the attendants.

Caff cola? What was he? A child? Andra thought. She'd watched her parents entertain hundreds of important political guests and never once had anyone asked for caff cola, a drink served to the masses in common cafés, not to royal princes. The drinks were only customary anyway, a necessary formality.

Before long, the governor politely asked Andra and her mother to leave while he and his guests "talked shop."

Her mother led her into the kitchen, grabbed her arm

and said, "Isn't this exciting?" She smiled and raised her shoulders.

"What? What's exciting?" Andra asked.

"The king sending his very own son here to visit us."

Her mother gripped her arm tighter. "The timing is amazing. Now, I want you to know that your father and I have been in talks with representatives from Orso for a long time. We know that if you married Prince Elio one day, it would accelerate Pricus City's path to sovereign status."

"Mother!" Andra jerked her arm away, stunned. "What are you talking about? I'm not going to marry him. He's a self-opinionated... boor. I don't even know him."

Her mother rolled her eyes. "I know, I know, it all sounds so old-fashioned. We would never arrange anything you didn't agree with, but your father and I have wanted you to meet Prince Elio for many years, and here he is, right under our own roof."

Andra crossed her arms and walked away. "Well, I think he's rude and arrogant."

"Oh, come on, Andra. You don't even know him. You've barely met him."

Andra didn't like where this was going. Her conflict of emotions, her commitment to Gian and Hamel and their plan clashed with her parent's expectations. She'd known it wasn't going to be easy. But now, the situation had suddenly grown more complex. She shook her head and forced herself not to argue with her mother. It didn't matter anyway. She would pretend to go through the motions like everything was normal and move on with the plan.

Andra made an excuse to her mother, rushed upstairs to her room, and closed the door behind her. Then she flipped open her data screen and typed a message to Gian.

ANDRA: Duke arrived. Prince Elio with him.

GIAN: Hamel says plan is a go. We'll get two for the price of one.

ANDRA: Both?

GIAN: Yes, we'll take both.

ANDRA: Are you sure?

GIAN: Yes, plan is still a go.

Andra sat back on her window seat and tried to absorb what was happening. She was still supportive of the plan. She knew it meant a lot to Gian, but kidnapping a sovereign prince was taking things to a whole new level. What they were planning was treason. No doubt about it. And it was going to be tricky to kidnap one person. Now two? And the prince was no old, fat politician. He was young and looked strong. It might not be so easy. But she couldn't get cold feet now. It was too late. The plan was already in motion.

She looked out of her window. She could see the custom yacht still on the pad. It was an impressive ship, she had to admit. *What would it be like to fly that thing, I wonder?* Time and time again she'd asked her father if she could learn to fly, but he would have none of it. He said it was not acceptable for a governor's daughter to do anything of the sort. But still, ships and flying were her passion. She'd do it, someday.

Chapter Eight

Enemy Contact

ilitary Controlled Space
Orso System

Richard Morian walked onto the bridge, looked around, spotted Jadern at his station and said, "Commander, we've just received orders to move to the Pallas System. Set a course to the Slipstream."

"Yes, sir," Jadern said and pointed to the helmsman. Haltar Sen nodded his acknowledgment, having already heard the order.

Chief Science Officer Herrick Tobbs, Chief Weapons Officer Corin Fargo, Chief Medical Officer Jyra Dowd, and his sister Danis stood on the captain's deck awaiting orders.

"Tobbs, Dowd," Morian said quietly, "prepare your

staff for emergency operations. Dismissed." The two nodded and left. "Corin, I need an up-to-the-minute status report."

"All weapons and shields are online and functioning at one hundred percent, sir," she replied, "and the magazines are at capacity. We have two-hundred ten nukes, three hundred Mark 59s, three hundred Mark 57s and one thousand depleted uranium projectiles and two million fifty caliber mini-railgun rounds. Fighter armament is at one hundred percent. We're good to go, Captain."

Morian nodded, then turned to Danis and said, "As of today, Lieutenant, you're promoted to lieutenant commander and as such are now Commander Air Group. I have confirmation of your promotion from Fleet Command. What is the status of the squadron?"

Danis's mouth dropped open and closed again. What had just happened was unprecedented. "Er... um..."

"Spit it out, Commander," Morian snapped.

"Yessir," she said and quickly gathered herself together. "We're short two pilots. Nine ships are fully serviceable, two are undergoing routine maintenance, and a third is undergoing a reactor replacement. The nine serviceable ships are armed and ready for deployment..." She tailed off, still stunned by the enormity of what had just happened.

"I want those three ships serviceable and ready to fight ASAP," Morian snapped. "See to it. Dismissed."

Danis nodded, snapped a half-hearted salute and left the bridge, wondering how in the name of Hades the rest of the pilots would take the news of her elevation to CAG.

"Navigation, give me an ETA to the Slipstream," Morian said.

"Yes, sir." Navigations Officer Lieutenant Simon DeLong turned to his console and began inputting the coordinates.

Officers began moving around the bridge from station to station. Morian didn't have to micromanage his crew. Everyone on the bridge could hear the urgency in his voice.

He stepped closer to the command rail and looked at the giant curved screen that served as the forward view port, offering a one-hundred-twenty-degree view of the starfield. He could see the minor planet Otak off the starboard bow begin to move away as the ship began to turn. He felt the inertia dampeners kick as the four fusion engines deep within the bowels of *Avenger* came online. He took an involuntary step backward as the main thrusters engaged and the dampeners effectively eliminated the crushing G-forces as they pushed the ship to one-tenth light speed.

"Main engines at twenty-five percent," Haltar Sen said without looking up from his station. "ETA to the Orso Slip Station two-hours-seven-minutes standard."

Morian nodded, then said, "Go to point two light. I want to be there within the hour... Attention on deck!" Everyone turned to look at him. "I have just received orders to deploy to the Pallas System. Military Command on Orso has received information that the system is under attack. Be ready to go to battle stations as we exit the Slip."

"What about the Pallas Fleet, sir?" Jadern asked.

"The Pallas fleet is already engaged. Time is of the essence—"

The bridge door behind him opened with a whoosh, interrupting him. He turned and was surprised to see Danis and Prince Felder enter. *Oh terrific*, he thought. *This is all I need.* He'd almost forgotten about the prince and his field trip.

"I tried to tell him—" Danis began.

Morian held up his hand to silence her.

Felder stepped forward to join him, Tenilo and April trailing along behind. "I have been informed that King Lorne has ordered your ship to the Pallas System. Is this true?"

"It is," Morian said quietly, not wanting to give out any sensitive information while Tenilo and April were within earshot, but a prince was a prince. "The system is under attack, and we've been dispatched to assist."

"Under attack?" Felder asked and frowned. "By whom?"

"We don't have that information."

"There hasn't been an inter-system conflict in generations," Felder said skeptically. "What in the sovereign stars is going on?"

"As I said, we don't have that information yet." Morian looked around. The prince and his entourage were staring at him, waiting for answers. Danis, Jadern and the other bridge officers were staring at him, too, wondering what he was going to say. He said nothing, maintaining eye contact with Felder.

"Captain Morian," Felder said, not to be put off, especially in front of Tenilo and Badeaux. "I demand you tell me precisely what's going on."

"And I can't tell you," he replied. "The USF isn't sure if it's an inter-system conflict or... something else," he finished lamely.

The prince shook his head in frustration. "Something else? What? What do you mean by that?"

Morian sighed. "There's reason to believe the attackers are non-human. A sentient species; from where we don't know."

"What?" Prince Felder's mouth hung open. "You can't be serious?"

"Oh, we're serious, my prince." Morian pointed to Lt. Lowry and said, "Comms, replay the feed for Prince Felder."

"Yes, sir." Lowry rolled her chair to the adjacent console and began tapping on the screen.

As the feed came up, April opened her data screen and began typing. Morian glanced at her and pursed his lips. The last thing he needed was for a two-bit reporter to broadcast sensitive material. He opened his own data screen and hit the emergency override key to block any unauthorized communications from leaving the ship.

April wrinkled her forehead and shook her forearm in confusion. "My data pad just died," she said.

"Sorry, standard protocol. No communications will be allowed to leave the ship from now on," Morian said in a tone that brooked no arguments. "I'm already pushing the boundaries of USF regulations by allowing any of you on the bridge."

"Oh, come now, Captain," Felder said. "There's no need for... well, let's see, shall we?"

Morian bit his tongue. If this arrogant prince thought he was going to order him around, he had another thing coming. He had to get him and his little gang off his ship.

There was a moment of silence as they watched the holo of the fighting in the Pallas System.

"Slipstream ETA in fourteen minutes, Captain," Lieutenant DeLong called out as he rolled his chair back to his main station.

Morian let the prince and his crew absorb what they were seeing. They were all speechless.

"Prince Felder, I'm afraid we are going to need to move you off ship within the next fourteen minutes. We will be engaging an unknown enemy, and I can't risk endangering you by letting you remain on this ship."

"Nonsense." Felder turned to face him. "I will not be going anywhere, Captain, and you do not have the rank to order me otherwise."

Damn royals, Morian thought angrily. He was about to engage an unknown and possibly superior enemy, to go into battle for the first time in his career, and he was not going to do it with a sight-seeing wanna-be soldier of a prince on board.

Morian took a deep breath, then said, "My prince, I do not presume to challenge your position. However, a battle zone against an unknown enemy is unpredictable, chaotic. I cannot be responsible—"

"Am I not on the *Avenger*?" Felder shot back, interrupting him. "You are the great Knight Captain Richard Morian. Since I first set foot on the *Avenger*, I have been bombarded with chatter about how great this ship is. What is there to fear?"

"With all due respect, *sir*. There is everything to fear. We know nothing about our enemy, only what we've seen." He waved his hand in the direction of the frozen holo and the image of an exploding Pallas System cruiser. "They have already destroyed the entire Persei fleet, and now they are attacking Pallas. That, I think, tells us that we're not invincible, far from it. I cannot allow you to remain aboard. Your safety is paramount, my prince."

"Captain," Lowry said. "Four Angel Class ships are also en route to the Pallas System. They will enter the Slipstream eight minutes after we do."

"ETA to the Slipstream?" Morian asked.

"ETA twelve minutes, Captain," DeLong replied.

"It appears to me, Captain, that we're out of time." Felder stood with his legs apart, hands behind his back, chin held high in what he assumed was a power stance

Morian didn't have time to argue with him. Tenilo and April stood stock-still, waiting to see how he would react. They didn't have to wait long. If the prince was refusing to leave the ship, there was little Morian could do about it other than have him arrested and forcibly removed. That, however, would cause an untenable political incident, and he wasn't prepared to go that far.

Instead, he activated his data pad and said, "Captain's log," then he gave the date and time and continued, "I have requested that Prince Padric Felder and his entourage leave the ship immediately. Prince Felder has refused to do so and will now confirm that he has been made aware that we are about to engage the enemy and insists on remaining aboard. Prince Felder, please officially confirm that you do indeed insist on remaining aboard the *Avenger* as we embark upon hazardous duty."

He held his arm out to Felder, who glared at him then confirmed his intentions.

"Captain's log closed at," and again Morian stated the time and date.

"Captain," Commander Jadern's voice came from across the bridge. "There's new intel coming in from the Pallas Fleet."

"What orders do you have for the fighter squadron, sir?" Danis asked.

"Stand fast," he replied.

First, he thought, *I have to take care of Felder.*

"Prince Felder." Morian faced the prince, drew himself up to his full height and said, "You were given the option to leave this ship before we enter the Slipstream. You refused to do so, and your refusal was entered into the official record. You are correct in that I cannot directly order you off my ship. However, the *Avenger* is about to enter a battle zone and, as captain of this ship, and according to sovereign law, I outrank you and will expect your compliance at all times. You are not to talk to my officers or interfere with the running of the ship in any way. Do you understand, sir?"

Felder raised his chin. He knew Morian was right.

"Your understanding of sovereign law is impressive, Captain. I will submit to your leadership while on board. However, by having a royal diplomat on board your vessel, you are duty-bound to protect myself and my staff." He pointed to Tenilo and April.

Morian's hands were tied. The prince was right, but there was no time to debate the finer points of sovereign law. So, not only was he going to take his ship into battle for the first time, he was going to have to make all of his decisions knowing that he must protect his passengers. As the captain, he would, of course, do all he could to protect his crew anyway, so, technically, protecting the prince should not be too much of a problem, he hoped.

"ETA to Slipstream eight minutes," DeLong said.

"Captain," Jadern said.

"What is it, Commander?" Morian asked Jadern.

"New holo feed, sir." Jadern turned the monitor towards his captain. "This is the last transmission sent from the battle, from the *Minstrel*, an Angel class light carrier. It's the best footage of one of the enemy so far."

Morian leaned forward.

Jadern pointed to the side of the image. "Shortly, you will see an enemy vessel fly in from the left. It will fire, then keep moving."

From out of the frame, a bird-like craft appeared. It was almost egg-shaped, but flattened, with short, stubby swept-back appendages that came to a point at the tips, not exactly wings. The craft itself was a glistening caramel color surrounded by a light-blue glow. It had no visible view ports, hatches or, as far as he could tell, cockpit. It was simple in its design, utilitarian, even. On each wing he could see something that resembled an articulated arm, facing forward, joined to the wing by a short, stubby mount. There were four of them: two above the wings and two below.

"What in the sovereign stars is that?" Morian asked.

"I... I don't know, sir," Jadern replied.

As they watched, one of the arms rotated some sixty degrees to port, elevated slightly and fired a bolt of brilliant blue light from its tip. Then, the same arm rotated again, some twenty degrees in the opposite direction and fired a bolt of brilliant, continuous white light at something they couldn't see. The craft turned slowly to starboard, the beam of white light tracking its target and then the craft was gone.

"Replay it," Morian said. "I want to see that again."

"This is Slipstream control. Please identify yourself," the Slipstream control station communications officer's voice echoed throughout the bridge.

Sandra Lowry replied, "Slipstream control, this is USF2918C Avenger, requesting Slipstream access."

"Roger, Avenger. Send coordinates when ready."

"Sending coordinates for the Pallas System." Sandra punched the final button.

"Coordinates received, Avenger. You are approved for Slipstream approach. Proceed on heading 217.92."

"Roger, control. 217.92."

"Thank you, Avenger, you are go for Slipstream access. Good luck."

"Thank you, control."

"ETA to Slipstream five minutes," DeLong said.

"Very well, Prince Felder," Morian said, "since we'll be entering the Slipstream and the battle zone shortly, I suggest you go to your quarters and secure yourselves.

Commander Morian will show you the way." Then, before Felder could respond, he turned his back on him, effectively dismissing him.

"Commander," Morian said to Danis as he strode over to Jadern. "Get our passengers secured away then get down to the hangar and prepare your squadron."

"Yes, sir," he heard his sister say as he turned again to Jadern.

Chapter Nine

The Slipstream

Morian looked up at the forward viewing screen again. It had already turned black, indicating they were approaching the Slipstream.

Commander Jadern looked at Haltar Sen and nodded. Sen nodded back and tapped his screen several times, then flipped the cover off the key that would activate the Slip Drive.

"Slipstream engaged in three, two, one," and Sen turned the key.

Morian felt the subtle rush in the pit of his stomach as the drive engaged, and then they were inside the Slipstream. No sound and no visual. Nothing but blackness surrounded them.

"Navigation, ETA to Slipstream exit?" Morian said.

"ETA to Slipstream exit is... twenty-three minutes and seven seconds standard, sir," DeLong replied.

"Roger, that," Morian replied. Now he had time to study the footage.

He had Jadern replay the holo in slow motion, then loop it. This strange craft that flew into the frame was like nothing he had ever seen before. The arms—the weapons —moved fluidly and seemed to attain target lock instantly.

"See that?" Morian said, more to himself than to Jadern. "See how those arms move?"

"Yes, sir," Jadern responded. "It appears to be firing some type of DEW weapons. Like ours."

"But theirs seem much more powerful. See how slowly it turns?"

Jadern didn't answer. He knew the captain was talking to himself.

Morian gave up. There was little he could learn from the holo feed, and he had to prepare the vessel for whatever might lie ahead.

"All stations report status," Morian commanded.

"Fuel cells at ninety-seven percent, Captain."

"Weapons on line and ready, Captain."

"Emergency protocols engaged, Captain."

He nodded as each voice rang out from around the bridge.

Morian's heartbeat quickened. He was exhilarated and apprehensive. His thoughts raced ahead, but his outward appearance remained stoic as he watched his crew come together.

He looked around the bridge and inwardly smiled. He knew they all had feelings similar to his own, of stress, uncertainty. Most of them, he knew, must be wondering if they were going to die. His job as captain was to project calm and confidence. He slowed his breathing and narrowed his eyes as the enormity of what was happening washed over him. *An unknown enemy, combat for the first time, an entire ship depending on me. Am I up to it? I have to be.* He pushed away the feelings of self-doubt and focused on his training and experience.

"Commander Jadern," he said. "My ready room, let's see if we can figure out how we are going to defeat them."

* * *

Danis Morian, her charges safely stowed away in the section of the ship reserved for VIPs and other guests, ran to the elevator and descended quickly to the hangar, glad that she could finally climb into her familiar cockpit and do what she was born to do, fight.

Stars, she thought as she looked around the hangar. The deck crew was scrambling to arm and ready the nine serviceable F32As. All nine of her fighter pilots were on deck in various stages of readiness. Some were struggling into their flight suits, some were berating their mechanics, two were sitting together talking quietly.

I suppose I'd better say something. "Attention, please, everybody!" The words came out of her mouth, but nobody heard them.

She closed her eyes, took a deep breath and shouted, "Attention on deck!"

That got their attention.

"Gather round, please, and listen up."

She waited until the semi-circle formed around her then began.

"Look, I know you've all heard about my promotion." She was wearing a dark blue flight suit with the gold leaves of her new rank on the epaulets. "I didn't ask for it, but I'm not going to apologize for it either. It is what it is, and I'm going to do my damnedest to do the best job I can. If any of you have anything to say about it, say it now. It's the only chance you'll get." She paused, then looked at each of them in turn. No one said a word. They all maintained eye contact with her.

She nodded. "Good. In twenty minutes, we'll exit the Slip and launch. We'll be facing what we believe to be an unknown alien force. We've trained for this. You're good at what you do, but this is..." She shook her head. "This is something none of us has ever experienced before. So how do we handle it?" She looked around. No one spoke. "We rely on our training, our skills," she continued, "our machines and... above all, each other. Any questions?"

There were none.

She nodded and continued, "We'll fly in three flights of three. I'll lead Ranger One, Lieutenant Beshear will lead Ranger Two, and Lieutenant Chen will lead Ranger three. That's it. We learn as we go. Do not take any unnecessary risks. Protect one another. Good Luck. Now go to it."

She turned and walked to her F32A, leaving them staring after her, then did a quick walk around the machine and began to climb the ladder. "Zilvo, fire up the engines and initiate launch sequence," she said as she slipped into the cockpit.

"Yes, ma'am." The bot was already in the back seat at the controls.

Danis secured her harness, checked her inertia dampeners, and verified her instruments and weapons. She flipped on the targeting systems and stared at the triple screens, not really seeing them, lost in thought.

She held out her hands. They were steady, not a hint of a tremor, which surprised her. *Combat!* The thought terrified her as much as it excited her. *Who or what is this unknown enemy? Where did they come from? How advanced are they? Stars! Can I really handle this?* Her pulse raced. She was sweating. She had to calm down. Then something came over her. She didn't know what it was, but suddenly she felt a sense of calm and awareness she'd never felt before. She concentrated on her rapidly beating heart, willing it to slow down, and it did. Gradually her heart rate slowed to its normal fifty-two beats per second.

Something had told her to focus on her breathing. She could control that. She knew she couldn't control the enemy, or how her squadron would perform, or who would die. All that was out of her hands now.

Danis sat still, her hands resting on her knees, her eyes closed, enjoying the moment of supreme calm. She didn't know what was happening to her, but whatever it was, it was comforting. Was it some untapped reserve of... she didn't know what, but she embraced it, reveled in it.

She breathed out—slowly through pursed lips—and opened her eyes. She no longer felt overwhelmed or nervous. The simple steps she needed to take were clear.

She was focused. She clipped the chin strap of her helmet and turned on the comm link. "Avenger Squadron, this is Ranger Leader, all ships report in."

"Ranger Two here, good to go."

"Ranger Three here. I'm ready."

All eight pilots confirmed their readiness. They all sounded calm, but who could tell what they were really feeling.

"And now we wait," she said. "When we receive the order to deploy, you'll adhere to your default attack formations unless the situation dictates otherwise. Other than that, I have nothing much to add. You know almost as much as I do."

"What's their firepower, boss?" It was Ranger Three.

"It appears they have some sort of DEW laser. Power factor unknown. Be careful out there. Stay sharp and watch your six. Remember your training."

"Morian to Domino. Domino, do you copy?" Morian's voice came over her personal channel.

"Domino here, go ahead, Captain."

"Danis," Morian said, "we'll be exiting the Slipstream in five minutes. You are to hold until we are able to assess the situation, copy?"

"Copy that, Captain."

The comms clicked in her ear. He was gone.

She changed channels. "Ranger One to all units. We are on indefinite hold. Relax. Take it easy. We'll go soon enough." Then she settled back in her seat, closed her eyes, and let the deep feeling of calm envelop her.

Chapter Ten

Exit Strategy

Morian and Jadern were seated at the table in Morian's ready room. Morian was quiet for a moment, then said, "I don't know about you, Michael, but I could do with a drink. How about you?"

Jadern's eyes opened wide. "I... er... I..." he stuttered. This was something new, and he didn't know what to say.

Morian smiled and said, "Yes, it's true. I am, no matter what you may have heard, human." He opened one of the drawers and removed a bottle of Camrien Bourbon and two glasses.

"Just a small one," he said as he poured. "We need to remain sharp." He handed one of the glasses to Jadern, lifted his own and said, "To victory." Then he downed the drink in a single swallow.

"To victory," Jadern said and followed suit.

Morian took a deep breath and forced it quickly out

through his mouth, then looked at Jadern and said... nothing.

Jadern looked back at him, not sure how to proceed, then took the bull by the horns and said, "So, Captain, how *are* we going to defeat them?"

Morian looked at him for a long moment, then replied, "The truth is, Michael, I don't know."

Again, Jadern was stunned by his captain's forthrightness.

"Then... What?"

"I guess we'll just have to play it by ear. We don't know the specifics of what they are, or their capabilities. That being so, we have to assume, until we know different, that they are superior to us in every possible way. Yes, I know, that's not what you wanted to hear, but there's nothing else I can tell you."

"So," Jadern said, "you must have a plan?"

Morian shrugged, seemingly at peace with himself, the situation, and the inevitability of it all, and said, "We have no idea of what we'll find when we exit the Slip. So, we'll take a look around—if we're not attacked on sight— and assess the situation. When we do exit, I want you at my side. We'll make what decisions we have to then but, my friend, we need to be ready for anything and everything. Now, let's get back to it."

Morian and Jadern returned to the bridge, and he settled easily into the command seat and relaxed. Jadern remained standing just to his left and rear.

"ETA please, Simon."

DeLong, shocked at the informality, turned and looked at him. He raised his eyebrows at him and smiled. *Anything to alleviate the doom and gloom,* he thought.

DeLong turned again to his console and, without looking round, said, "ETA six minutes and forty-one seconds."

Morian nodded, thumbed his data pad and called Danis.

The next five minutes passed slowly until, "ETA one minute and counting," DeLong said.

Morian sat up in his chair and said, "Battle stations on my mark, Mr. Jadern."

There was a slight shudder as the ship exited the Slipstream into normal space.

"Mark!" Morian said loudly, more loudly than he intended. *Damn it!* "Active scan. Report."

"Now hear this, now hear this. All hands to battle stations. I repeat, all hands to battle stations," Jadern's order echoed in every corner of the ship then... nothing.

"I said report, damn it," Morian snapped.

"There's nothing to report, Captain," Lowry said.

"I want to see," he snapped. "Put it on the forward screens and the hologram."

She was right. The starfield ahead was clear, or was it?

He rose from his chair and stepped up to the command rail and stared first at the giant screens and then at the globe-shaped hologram hovering just above the center of the lower bridge deck. He walked back and forth along the rail, once, twice, then stopped, just to the right of center and stared at a point on the screen.

"What's that?" he asked, pointing at a faint red glow.

"The scanners are unable to resolve that anomaly, Captain," Lowry said. "It's too far out."

"How far out?"

She ran her fingers over her console, then looked up at him and said, "I can't be precise, Captain, but—"

"Oh, for God's sake," he said, interrupting her, "give me something I can work with."

"I... It's more than four-hundred-million kilometers, sir."

"That's where they are," Morian said. "I know it. I can feel it. Navigation. How long will it take us to get there?"

"Eighty-nine standard minutes at one-quarter light speed, sir," Delong answered without hesitation.

Morian bared his teeth and sucked in a huge breath. Point-two-five light was the maximum speed *Avenger* was rated for.

"Too long," he snapped. He turned to Maxim Volkov, the ship's chief engineer. "How much can you give me? I need to be there in an hour, no more." He waved his hand at the dim red glow on the screen.

Volkov looked at him and shook his head. "That's not possible, Captain."

"Well, what is possible, damn it?"

The chief engineer nodded his head from side to side, the corners of his mouth turned down in a furious frown, then said, "One-hundred-ten percent is the best I can do."

"I want one-hundred-twenty and I want it now."

"That's not possible, Captain," Volkov said. "The reactor will melt down."

Morian sucked in a deep breath breath, stared at Volkov, narrowed his eyes, then nodded and said, "Very well, Mr. Volkov, one-hundred-ten it is. Helm, go to maximum thrust. Mr. Volkov, go see to your reactors. I want an update on the quarter-hour. Navigation, set a course for the anomaly." *Ninety minutes,* he thought savagely, *ninety minutes, ninety minutes... It's too damn long.*

As it turned out, Lowry's guess at the distance to the anomaly was off by almost twenty percent, something Morian would never have forgiven had he not known she'd made her estimate without the help of the ship's long-range scanners, which had an effective range of something less than three-hundred-million kilometers. That being so, they arrived within range some fifty-six minutes after exiting the Slip.

The battlefield was vast, spread over many millions of cubic kilometers, and Morian was stunned to see it was littered with the remains of dozens of USF ships, large and small. The burned-out hulks of once-great ships were drifting, dead in space, some reduced to little more than debris. In the distance, he could see flashes of brilliant blue and white light.

So, it's not yet over, he thought.

"Thrusters at ten percent," he said quietly. "Take us in, Mr. Sen."

Chapter Eleven

Enemy Engaged

Morian's voice in her ear sounded calm. "Two minutes to launch, Danis. Good luck and stay safe."

Danis did not know quite how to respond to that. There was a resonance in her brother's voice she hadn't heard before. She swallowed and took a deep breath and said, "Copy that, Captain. We'll be fine. Just make sure we have a ship to return to when we're done with this little mission. Domino out."

Orange lights flashed. The hangar lights dimmed, signaling they were approved to launch. Danis looked down the line and watched as the closest fighter to the hangar bay door lifted off and headed out into the black. The rest of the ships followed in order. Danis, as squadron leader, was last to take off.

She killed the ship's docking gravs and the fighter lifted off the deck. She increased power to the thrusters, turned her head slightly to look at the black expanse of space beyond the bay door, eased the throttle forward and the F32A exited the hangar. Then she turned to starboard to meet her two wingmen.

"Ranger Leader to Rangers Two and Three. Report?" she said as she scanned the vastness around her.

"This is Ranger Two," Sheva Beshear said. "Multiple targets off *Avenger*'s starboard bow, range seven hundred kilometers."

"Engage," Danis said, her voice elevated but calm. "Let's go."

"Ranger Two moving to engage at heading zero six zero."

So, Team Two and Danis's command team had targets, but there was still nothing from Lucy Chen and Ranger Three. Danis flipped the fighter, aligning herself with *Avenger*'s massive hull, and then she saw it.

The battle was spread out in front of her. She was stunned by its enormity. Nothing had prepared her for anything remotely like this.

She knew the entire Pallas fleet was engaged, but it was not until she actually saw the number of dead and damaged craft and the vast debris field that she began to grasp the scale of the carnage. Away in the distance, off *Avenger*'s starboard bow, she could see a handful of the enemy ships, each of them surrounded by a blue halo, engaged with several fighters from an unidentified Pallas ship, and they weren't doing well.

"Domino to Gladiator and Swordsman," she said to her wingmen. "Stay on me as we engage."

The three fighters of her attack formation moved

towards the battle. Danis's scanners lit up and her targeting computers began tracking potential targets. Between her screens and her visual, she could see there were at least a dozen targets.

As she closed with her targets, she noticed a much larger ship—an Angel Class cruiser—in the middle of the fray, its weapons blazing as it fired bolt after bolt of laser fire at the enemy craft. The smaller USF fighters—she counted eight—had it surrounded and appeared to be trying to protect it, but to little effect.

Stars! Danis thought. *That ship carries two squadrons. Where the hell are the rest of them?*

One of the enemy craft flew across the field and fired a long burst of brilliant blue light from one of its appendages. It struck one of the fighters and sliced it in two, like a knife chopping through a tin can.

They must be firing some sort of plasma weapon, Danis thought as she watched the two halves of the fighter spinning slowly as they drifted away. The enemy craft fired another bolt of blue light from all four of its weapons. The blast struck the side of the Angel Class cruiser, tearing a hole almost the entire length of her hull. Then all four of the enemy craft's appendages moved together toward the rear. The craft slowed, made a gentle, looping turn and vectored away toward another section of the battle.

Why? she asked herself. *Why did it leave? It could have, should have, gone in for the kill.* It was a question to which she had no answer.

Another of the strange craft flew in from a different direction. It crossed the Angel's bow and headed toward her. Danis slammed the throttle to the max, spun the F32A and made a hard left turn. Her inertia dampeners tightened around her body, alleviating the crushing force of the thirty-five-G turn. She adjusted her thrusters and brought the fighter out of its spin and, for the first time, was able to see her enemy close up as it flashed by.

It was difficult to figure it out, especially as she saw it for no more than two or three seconds. It was as if the thing was playing tricks on her eyes. She couldn't focus. The blue halo shimmered and flowed around it and the way—how—the craft was moving didn't make any sense. It was bigger than an F32, almost three times bigger, but there were no thrusters, no identifiable means of propulsion, no cockpit, windows or doors. It did have those strange, swept-back sickle-shaped wings upon which the four articulated arms were mounted, but there was nothing aerodynamic about them, or the craft.

The alien ships still engaging the Angel and her fighters had slowed to match her speed and were pounding the stars out of them. The Angel appeared to be dying. Fire from her weapons had died away almost to nothing, and her eight remaining fighters were now down to five. It was a massacre.

"Enemy in range, engaging," Ranger Two said conversationally.

"Watch those weapons," Danis called. She was several seconds behind Ranger Two—Sheva Beshear— who by then was engaging one of the enemy craft. All three of her fighters opened fire with DEW lasers. Multiple blasts slammed into the alien ship. Its blue halo shone brightly for a moment as it absorbed the energy.

The craft slowed and appeared to veer off course slightly, but it wasn't disabled and recovered quickly.

Another enemy ship flashed by in front of her. They were close enough to engage. Two more flew slowly, side by side, along the length of the USF cruiser, firing long blasts into its hull, effectively carving it in two. She could see life pods leaving the dying ship as it began to break apart. Then, in one vast and all-encompassing explosion as the electromagnetic containment fields of its six fusion reactors collapsed, it was gone, leaving only a few life pods and a rapidly spreading debris field.

"Look out, look out!" Lucy Chen, commanding Ranger Three, shouted.

Where she was exactly, Danis couldn't tell, but something was obviously wrong. She wanted to confirm Chen's position, but one of the enemy craft was heading toward her. The proximity alarm buzzed in her ears. Her targeting computers lit up. Her screens showed multiple targets, all moving fast. *Too much frickin' information, damn it!*

Breathe. Danis shoved the throttle forward, jinked left, down, up, right, changing her trajectory, buying herself precious seconds. She let out another deep breath and moved away from the enemy fighter. Again, she experienced the feeling of infinite calm as her training kicked in and, for a moment, she was ashamed of herself for letting her emotions run away with her.

Read the data. Confirm with visual. Maneuver to a superior position. Engage. The enemy craft was still approaching.

"Gladiator, Swordsman, follow my lead," she shouted.

She couldn't see them, but she knew from her screens they were behind her. She jinked to the right, then up, moving quickly to what looked like the top of the craft. And she watched as its two upper arms tracked after her.

Danis modified her course, the F32's four thrusters working independently for maximum maneuverability as she jinked and closed in. All of this took only fractions of a second and then she was in range. Her targeting computers locked on and she fired four bursts. Four blasts from each of her two two-terabyte DEW canons hit home. Eight more slammed into it from her two wing-men. And then... instead of the massive bolts of energy tearing the craft apart as she expected, the blasts impacted the ship and barely jolted it off its trajectory. The halo glowed an eye-searing blue as it absorbed the more than ten trillion watts of power generated by the three F32s.

For a moment, it seemed to stall, but as far as Danis could see, the craft had not sustained any visible damage, although the arms seemed to have stopped moving. She put full power to her thrusters as they swiveled and came around again in a hard, forty-two-G turn and fired three more times as she flew by. Again, her lasers had little to no effect.

"Gladiator, Swordsman, with me," she ordered, and she punched it and flew out of range.

It was at that point that Lucy Chen, Ranger Three leader, appeared on her port side.

"Domino, are you alright?" Chen asked.

"Yes, I'm fine. We just hit one of the eggs full-on with multiple DEWs, but it's still moving."

"Ranger Three, look out!" someone shouted.

Danis instinctively looked up. Chen's fighter was several thousands of meters away above her and to her left with an enemy craft closing on her fast.

Danis watched as all four of the craft's arms turned and locked onto Chen's ship.

Chen spotted it, changed direction, jinked in a classic evasive maneuver, but the arms tracked her and then all four fired. Four massive bolts of directed energy hit Chen's fighter and, for what could only have been a nanosecond, the F32 glowed brilliant blue and then exploded.

"No!" Danis shouted. She'd spent many hours sparring hand-to-hand with Lucy, who was like a sister to everyone on the team.

From that point on, things seemed to move in slow motion. Pieces of Chen's fighter floated by in front of her. Of Lucy Chen herself there was no sign; she must have died instantly.

Get it together, Danis. Don't panic. Read. Confirm. Maneuver. Engage. The targeting computer lit up again, showing multiple targets.

"Sword, Gladiator, get the hell out of here. Go back to *Avenger*. They're going to need all the help they can get."

"What about you, Domino?" Gladiator asked.

"Just go. I'll be fine. Look out for yourselves."

Danis jerked the yoke to port and pushed it forward, putting the F32 into a spinning, turning dive, chasing the ship that had killed her friend. The target centered on her screen. She pulled out of the spin but held the turn and fired a long burst at the enemy. Again, the craft lit up and glowed brighter blue as it absorbed the energy, but this time Danis did not let up. She kept firing, burst after burst, as she moved closer, focusing her fire on the center of the craft. The craft faltered, seemed to stall... and then she was on top of it. She turned hard to starboard, her thrusters at full power, to avoid colliding with she was sure was a stricken ship... only it wasn't. As she came out of the turn, she could see it was undamaged.

"Sovereign stars," she yelled at herself. "What in God's name do I have to do to kill this thing?"

"May I suggest we deploy missiles next time?" Zilvo said, her voice devoid of emotion.

It was so ludicrous, the monotone sound of the bot's voice, that Danis found it funny, but it did serve to calm her down.

"Good idea, Zilvo. Why the hell didn't I think of that? Arm one and two!"

The F32A was armed with six Rapier, five-megaton cruise missiles: small compared to the fifty-megaton Lance missiles the *Avenger* carried.

Danis stopped firing. She was slightly more than a thousand meters out as she continued to circle the stalled enemy ship, watching as it quickly returned to functionality and its arms began to turn toward her.

"One and two armed and locked," Zilvo intoned.

"Fire!" she shouted, then watched the enemy ship. The blue craft's arms were pointed almost directly at her. She dropped the nose of her ship, reversed her thrusters and rocked upward and away, her eyes still on the target. It was close. The two upper arms of the enemy craft continued to track her. How close she didn't know. Both missiles slammed into the target and exploded in a brilliant flash of white light. The light subsided. The ship's arms had stopped moving. The blue halo dimmed. The missiles obviously weren't effective enough. The enemy craft was still intact.

"Ranger Leader, I'm coming in. Get out of my way."

Danis jinked to port. Sheva Beshear swooped in, DEW lasers firing. Danis checked her scanners to make sure no other craft were bearing down on their position.

"Use missiles, Sheva," Danis called as she moved away.

"Roger that!" Sheva replied and fired two more missiles at the slowly recovering enemy. The craft was definitely stunned but still intact. Danis couldn't believe the resiliency of these enemy ships.

"Disengage, Ranger Two. What the hell *are* these things? Watch out for those arms."

I've got to do something, she thought, her mind in a whirl. *I have to try to figure out how to destroy them.*

Danis sucked her bottom lip, closed her eyes and quickly opened them again. It was no time to be daydreaming. She had to do something, and quickly. She checked her screens. Except for the enemy craft and Ranger Two, the immediate sky was relatively clear. The enemy craft was now more than a thousand kilometers off and moving slowly, but it was moving, its halo pulsating from white light to dark blue. It appeared to be recovering.

"Not happening, you son of a bitch," she muttered to herself. "You killed my friend."

"What was that, Domino?" Sheva Beshear in Ranger Two asked.

"Nothing," Danis replied. "Watch my six. I'm going in."

She closed in to two hundred kilometers. *Too close,* she thought, *but what the hell.* Her targeting computers were locked on. She thumbed the firing button on the yoke, fired two more missiles, made a sharp turn to starboard, slammed the throttle forward pushing the F32 to maximum thrust and hurtled away from the blast. The sky behind her lit up as her missiles slammed into the strange craft, exploding in a single ball of white-hot fire. Her ship shuddered but continued its mad dash. The explosion subsided. She reversed thrust and spun the fighter so she could see the target. The enemy craft was spinning, drifting away from the impact zone, but it was still intact.

"I think we got it," Sheva said.

"Not yet," Danis said, "I want to destroy the damn thing. I'm going in for another run."

"Two coming in, six o'clock."

Danis checked the screen. Two more enemy craft were approaching fast. She shook her head. Two against one and they'd barely damaged it. Two on two would be suicide. "Disengage, Sheva," Danis said. "We're done here. Return to *Avenger*. Maybe we can do some good there."

"Copy."

"Punch it, Sheva. Get out of here, NOW!"

She glanced at her screens. The enemy craft were closing fast. She tracked their speed and knew instantly that they couldn't outrun them.

"Stay close to me, Sheva. On my mark we'll make a hard, eighty-degree turn to port."

"Copy."

Danis watched her screens, mentally counting down. *Seven thousand kilometers... five... four... Damn, they're fast, two thousand, one,* "MARK!"

The two F32s, their thrusters at one hundred percent, cut hard left then straightened, streaking away from the two enemy craft.

"They're overshooting," Sheva shouted.

Danis glanced at her screens. Sheva was right. The two enemy craft were turning, but not nearly as tight as the F32s.

"Let them go," Danis said. "Resume course for the *Avenger*." She switched to the open channel. "Ranger Squadron report in and return to *Avenger* to regroup."

"Ranger Eight, copy."

"Ranger Seven, copy that."

The *Avenger* was fighting hard. Six enemy craft were attacking her from all directions. There seemed to be no design or strategy to their attack, each enemy fighter operating independently. *Avenger*'s twenty-four-point defense laser cannons, drawing their immense power from the ship's six fusion reactors, were doing their best to hold the aliens off.

Danis watched in horror as one of the fighters closed and fired two massive bolts of blue energy at *Avenger*'s keel. From what she'd seen of the destruction of the

Pallas Angel class cruiser, she expected to see *Avenger*'s hull ripped open, but it wasn't. The blasts penetrated the shields and seared the hull, damaging it but not punching through. *Avenger*'s two-meters-thick, Dutrinium armor was damaged but holding.

* * *

On the bridge, Morian felt Avenger shudder as her hull took the full impact of the enemy's lasers.

"What the hell was that?" he shouted.

"We sustained a major hit to the hull, Captain," Science Officer Herrick Tobbs yelled.

"Hull breach?" Morian shouted.

"No, sir," Tobbs replied.

"Damage report?" Morian said, a little less loudly.

"We've lost turrets four, twelve, fourteen, sixteen and seventeen," Tobbs shouted. "Engines are undamaged. Reactors are holding at ninety-three percent."

* * *

"Ranger Four, here. Coming up on your six, Domino."

"Where is everyone?" Danis asked. "All fighters report in, NOW!"

Two, Four, Seven and Eight reported, then... silence.

"That's it?" she said, unable to believe what she knew to be true. "Five of us? No one else?" *Gladiator's gone!* Gladiator was, had been, Ranger Five. Her other wingman, Swordsman, was Ranger four.

No one answered.

Sovereign Stars. Gladiator, and almost half the squadron, gone. Danis swallowed. She couldn't believe it. She shook her head, trying to focus on the task at hand.

"Alright, stay together. We attack as a group. Use missiles first. The enemy ships are fast and those off-bore arms are deadly. But we can outmaneuver them, so use that to our advantage. Fire and move. I have two missiles left. Report your status."

"I have four," Ranger Two said.

"Ranger Four; six."

"Ranger Seven; six."

"Ranger Eight; four."

"On me then," Danis said. "We'll go in line astern; take them out one at a time."

"Copy, Ranger Leader. We're right behind you."

Danis's targeting computer locked on to a target. It was coming right for her. All four of its appendages pointed in her direction. She reacted instantly, without thinking, slammed the yoke hard to port and shoved it forward, sending the F32 into a spinning, looping dive. The enemy ship fired, faster than she expected. The bolts of blue fire seared past her, missing her ship by no more than a couple of meters.

The enemy craft continued moving rapidly in the same direction, its weapons tracking her but, due to her erratic trajectory, seemingly unable to lock on. She flipped the fighter end over end. Her missile targeting locked on. She fired her last two missiles and veered away to starboard.

"Go, go, go," she shouted as her missiles slammed into

the target and exploded in a gigantic ball of white fire. "Don't give it time to recover."

She watched as Sheva's missiles slammed home even before the first explosions had subsided. Sheva was followed in by Ranger Four, who was followed by Ranger Seven.

"Ranger Leader to Ranger Eight. Abort. Let's see if we've done any damage."

They all watched as the ball of fire that engulfed the enemy ship quickly subsided into nothing. The enemy craft was still in one piece, but its blue halo was rapidly fading, turning white and then it was gone. The craft itself drifted onward, dead in space. The fact that it was still in one piece was amazing, but Danis had no time to dwell on it.

"Enemy craft approaching," Zilvo said. "Vector one, one two zero."

"I'm out of weapons," Danis said. "Sheva, you take the lead. Wait 'till I get its attention. Four, Seven and Eight follow him in, line astern."

She flew straight towards the incoming enemy, her DEWs blazing. Two hundred kilometers out, she hauled back on the yoke and slammed it over to the right, putting the fighter into a twisting, looping climb to starboard. Behind her the sky lit up as Sheva's last two missiles found their target. Danis righted her ship and turned to watch. During that single maneuver, she'd traveled more than a thousand kilometers, but the ball of fire around the enemy ship was easy to spot as the rest of what was left of her squadron engaged, one after another. The enemy ship died quickly but remained intact, dead in space.

Danis glanced at her ship's chron and was surprised to see that only thirteen minutes had passed since the squadron had launched. In that small amount of time, she'd lost four pilots and disabled two enemy craft.

She found it hard to believe, but she knew that things move quickly in battle, especially in the vast expanse of space.

Chapter Twelve

Avenger

Some fifteen minutes after Avenger Squadron had launched, Captain Morian was standing on the bridge with his hands gripping the command rail while he monitored the progress of the battle. The giant forward screen was lit up like a Christmas tree. To his right, three smaller screens offered views to starboard, below and to the rear. To his left, three similar screens offered views to port, above and again to the rear. Slightly below the elevated platform upon which he was standing, in the center of the lower command deck, hovering above a circular holo generator, three meters in diameter, the giant hologram offered a real-time view of the entire battlefield. And what he could see alarmed him.

There weren't as many enemy ships as he'd expected. The constantly changing numbers on the data net above the holo informed him there were fifty-four active enemy ships and seven disabled.

Of the Pallas fleet, only two Angel Class cruisers remained, along with three D-class destroyers and seven E-class frigates.

Stars, he thought. *Four Angels destroyed along with most of the rest of the fleet. How many lives has it cost? Four, five thousand?*

"DEW cannons are ineffective, Captain," Commander Jadern said. "Even with direct hits."

Morian pursed his lips and rolled his shoulders. The Avenger's DEW cannons emitted massive amounts of firepower, but the enemy ships seemed virtually impervious to them.

"Domino to Captain Morian," Danis's voice came over the comm.

Morian stepped back to his command chair and took the call on his private channel.

"Go ahead, Danis." He was relieved to hear from her. He knew she'd lost four pilots, but he didn't know which ones.

"You need to know that DEW lasers are useless against these ships, but we were able to take out a couple using our Rapiers, but you're not going to believe this... It takes eight hits to disable them. As far as I can tell, they're impossible to destroy completely."

"Give me a minute, Danis." He switched back to the open channel and said, "Lieutenant Fargo. Switch to Lance missiles, Lance missiles, Commander, and fire at will."

"Yes, Captain."

He switched channels again and said, "Eight missiles just to take out one of them? What are these things made of?"

"You got it, and I don't know," Danis replied. "They recover quickly. You have to hit them again and again. *Avenger*'s fifty-mega-ton Lances should do better than our five megaton rapiers. Richard, we're all out. We need to come in and rearm."

"Do it, and then get back out there as soon as you can. How many of your squadron do you have left?"

"Five."

"Roger that." He paused for a second. "Get them rearmed and back in the air. I want all remaining fighters to stay within missile range of *Avenger*. Understood?"

"Understood, Captain."

By the time Danis and her remaining fighters had entered the hangar, the four Angel Class ships had engaged and launched their fighter squadrons.

"Captain." Commander Jadern turned away from the weapons console. "We've taken out one of the enemy craft."

"Excellent. Talk to me. How many missiles?"

"Four, sir."

"FOUR?" Richard asked, stunned. As soon as the word left his mouth, he realized the crew could hear the frustration in his voice. He could have kicked himself for responding with so much emotion.

"Good," he said calmly. "That's very good. Now we know what it takes to stop them. Continue coordinating fire with Ranger Squadron and relay that information to the fleet."

"Yes, sir."

Four Mark 59 Lances to take out one little ship? he thought. *What are these things? Where do they come from?*

Morian stood, stepped back to the command rail and stared down at the giant holo. The *Avenger* and what was left of the Pallas fleet were beginning to take a toll on the enemy. One by one, their ships flared brilliant and disappeared from the holo.

"Target numbers are dropping, sir," Jadern said without looking up from the weapons console.

"How many?" Morian asked, looking up at the net above the holo.

"Sixteen confirmed."

Morian nodded. It matched the numbers on the net.

The fleet was gaining the upper hand, finally. The atmosphere on the command deck began to change from one of impending doom to optimism.

"Stay calm, everyone," Morian said. "Solve one problem at a time." He stared up at the net. Two more alien craft disappeared. "They appear to be leaving, but stay sharp. We're not out of this yet."

"Domino to Avenger."

"Go, Domino," Morian said. "You're on an open channel."

"The enemy ships are retreating."

"Talk to me. If they're heading for the Slip, we need to stop them."

"They're not," Danis replied. "They seem to be heading off in a dozen different directions."

Morian looked down at the holo. She was right.

"What about the ones we've killed?" he asked, and as he did so, he spotted one of the disabled craft drifting across the forward view screen.

"I have one," he said before Danis could answer. "Morian out." He closed the channel and said, "Commander Jadern, I want that ship. Let's go get it. Navigation, plot the course."

"Aye, sir," the two officers said in unison.

But before they could even begin to move, a blue halo traveling at what was later determined to be slightly more than one-tenth light speed came streaking across the screen. A single blast of blue light and the dead ship was no more.

"The retreating ships are cleaning house," Danis said over the open channel.

Morian nodded. "They're protecting their tech," he said. "Interesting."

"They're leaving," Danis said, "but not through the Slipstream."

"*What?* How can that be possible?" Morian asked no one in particular.

"Confirmed, Captain," Commander Herrick Tobbs, *Avenger*'s chief science officer, said. "The enemy ships are not entering the Slipstream. They are just... heading out into open space."

"Captain," Lowry said loudly. "The four USF Angel Class vessels and their support ships are twelve thousand kilometers out. ETA four minutes."

"Finally," he said, more to himself than his command crew. "Stream everything we have to them and advise them only nuclear weapons are effective."

"Yes, sir."

"Who's leading the fleet?"

Lowry studied the screen. "Captain Paris of the *Mariposa.*"

Hmm... he thought. *Interesting. She has quite a reputation.*

"Morian to Domino. Bring your squadron in when ready. As soon as you've accounted for your people, I want all recorded imagery and intel from your fighters forwarded to the bridge data net. That includes all tactical imagery, data, camera, radar, lidar, and FLIR footage. All of it."

"Roger that, Captain."

Chapter Thirteen

Meeting of the minds

Morian slumped down in his command chair, a wave of exhaustion rushing over him. His adrenaline was dissipating. He couldn't tell exactly how long the battle had lasted. *Forty minutes? An hour? Or an hour and a half?* He checked his chron and was surprised to see that only thirty-seven minutes had passed since *Avenger* had entered the battle.

He looked around. The bridge was silent. He stood and said, "Well done, everyone. Not a bad outcome for our first engagement. We've learned a lot. Now we just have to figure out what to do with it. Lieutenant Lowry?"

"Sir!"

"Establish a link to the *Mariposa.* Let me know when they're ready to debrief."

"Aye, sir!"

"Commander Jadern," Morian continued, "I want a full damage report, casualty count, IMS and ordnance status reports right away. If you need me, I'll be in the hangar."

"Aye, sir."

Morian nodded, then turned, walked off the bridge and headed for the elevators. He needed to speak to Danis.

Before he could make it to the elevator, however, the data screen on his forearm lit up and alerted him with a mild electric shock, indicating a priority communication. He checked the notification. He was being summoned to a level one meeting, which meant he had no option but to attend along with the USF Fleet Admiral and the rest of the Orso fleet captains. He took the elevator to Deck 9 and went to the briefing room, where he found Prince Felder and his entourage outside the door waiting for him.

Oh no! He'd completely forgotten about the prince. Felder was red-faced and wide-eyed. Tenilo and April Badeaux were standing behind him.

"Captain Morian," Felder said. "It's so good to see you. I've been waiting for you. I've—"

Morian held up a hand to silence him. He had yet to assess the number of casualties, the damage to his ship, and establish comms with the rest of the fleet. Until then, the battle wasn't over and he had no time for the prince.

"I'm sorry, Prince Felder, you'll have to excuse me. I'm being called to a Command debriefing. I'll come for you when we're done."

"That's why I'm here, Captain." Felder held up his forearm screen. "I've also been summoned to the meeting."

Morian clenched his jaw. He knew it was more likely that the prince had forced his way in. This was not the time or place for royals or politics.

His data pad alerted him that the meeting had already begun. He shook his head, knowing he couldn't stop the prince from attending, and Felder knew he knew it.

Morian smiled wryly, tapped the screen on his pad and the door slid open. "After you, my prince."

"Thank you," Felder said loftily and stepped inside, with Tenilo and Badeaux stepping forward to follow.

Morian stepped into the doorway, blocking their entrance. "I'm sorry," he said, smiling, "command level clearance only." Tenilo looked shocked and Badeaux crossed her arms with attitude.

"They are my personal staff," Felder said. "Wherever I go, they are permitted to go too."

Morian sighed to himself. Prince or no prince, there was no way in hell he was going to let unvetted personnel into a command level meeting, especially when one of them was a reporter. He paused for a moment before speaking, and suddenly he experienced a feeling of almost infinite calm, and he no longer cared about Felder and his influence. It was his ship and his call to make. It was his hill to die on if he had to. He'd just won a major battle, the first in modern history—to hell with royal protocols.

"Fleet law," he said, "states that combat is not over until after the debrief. Your staff will remain outside the briefing room until we're done. Until then, everyone aboard this ship is still under my command. Now get 'em the hell out of here. They're waiting for us." He turned and stepped inside without waiting for any response.

Felder was stunned. He said nothing. And Morian didn't care. His universe had changed almost in an instant. He'd just lost half his squadron, and God only knew how many of his crew were either dead or wounded, and he didn't know the state of his ship, and here was this jumped-up son of a... acting like a spoiled child. Could Felder have him fired? He doubted it, but even if he could, Morian didn't give a shit, not at that moment, anyway.

Morian took the halo off its rack and sat down at the head of the table. He gestured to the open chair next to him and said, "You are welcome to take the halo there, my prince."

Commander Jadern walked in and took his place opposite Felder. Morian slipped his halo onto his head, activated it, felt the familiar tingle of the nerve jack and found himself sitting at a large conference table in the same virtual room he'd been in prior to the battle. This time, though, there were fewer people in attendance: Felder, Jadern, Captain Paris and the three fleet captains, one of the Pallas fleet captains, USF Fleet Admiral Hammond, King Jurak of the Pallas System, one of his generals, and King Orson Lorne, which surprised Morian. Lorne's image was fuzzy and flickering, disrupted by the Slipstream through which his signal was being relayed.

"Are we all here now?" Fleet Admiral Hammond said dryly, looking at Morian. "Good! Thank you." Hammond paused, stroked his white mustache, cleared his throat and began. "First, I would like to take a moment to congratulate all of you on your victory, especially you, Captain Morian, for answering the call and executing a swift and brave rescue of..." He paused again and looked around the room.

It was clear that when he woke that morning, the Admiral did not expect to be chairing, let alone attending, such a meeting. None of them had.

"...rescue of the remains of the Pallas fleet," he continued. "Although, I am sad to say, much of it has been lost. We are still awaiting casualty and damage reports."

Morian nodded and glanced around the virtual room. The attendees, for the most part, stared stoically ahead. Even King Orson was silent, motionless. Only Paris was looking at him, smirking.

"Captain Keevo," Hammond continued, "your fleet fought valiantly. We are sorry for your unexpected losses, but you served the USF bravely. I know the loss is... difficult, most difficult. But you must put it behind you, secure in the knowledge that you saved the citizens of your system."

Keevo nodded, his face deathly pale.

"Captain Paris, you came a little late to the conflict, but..." Paris's face fell and she glared at Morian. "Well done and thank you for answering the call so swiftly." The Admiral cleared his throat again and shifted in his chair.

Morian's screen buzzed on his arm. The data was in: the damage report and the imagery from Danis's fighters, along with Danis's assessment of the tactics and capabilities of the enemy craft. He forwarded the intel to Fleet

Admiral Hammond's command ship. He'd lost four fighters and seven of his twenty-four-point defense lasers. Casualties included seventeen dead, including the four fighter pilots and sixty-three wounded. Most of the casualties were sustained in the seven point defense turrets. The loss of any of his crew was a tragedy. *Still, not quite as bad as I thought.*

"Today was historic in any number of ways," the admiral continued, and then he went on to list them. "You have won the first major battle in more than three hundred years. You have taken on an alien invader of superior numbers and firepower, and you've defeated him. You are the first of a new generation of combat survivors. The experience and learning you have gained today in the Pallas System is... unprecedented in our history. I understand that at this moment, everyone is in various states of acceptance and awareness, but we must proceed slowly. And since we don't know when this unknown enemy will return, we must be ready to fight at any moment. I would like to begin by telling you what we know. I'll turn the table over to General Gara." He turned to look at him.

General Gara, commander of the Pallas home planet defense force, leaned forward on the table and clasped his hands together in front of him. He was obese, tired-looking and flustered.

"Today," he began, "at 1426 standard time, our scanners detected the first enemy ships entering the system. The Pallas fleet was dispatched and made contact. We did not know the nature of the threat at that time." The general was reading from the screen on his forearm. "At

1437, the first enemy ships entered the Pallas home planet atmosphere. Marine and Air units were deployed. The enemy attacked three locations: BesTown, Durameen and Epilon. The military and security units put up a valiant defense, but I'm afraid the toll was... catastrophic." He looked around, obviously motioning to someone beside him who was not visible on the holo. "Footage of the enemy, of the fighting in and around Epilon, can be seen here."

The holo generator at the center of the table lit up. The feed was a mix of static security footage and someone recording on their personal data screen. Buildings were on fire. People were running in all directions. Several of the blue haloed ships came streaking in, flying low, firing blue bolts of energy at the fleeing people and the surrounding buildings. Then the feed switched and what Morian saw next stunned him.

Walking down the street were what appeared to be three tall, stocky beings clad in some kind of battle armor. They, too, were surrounded by the same pale blue halo as the enemy craft. Overall, they were humanoid in shape, but oddly and terrifyingly inhuman. They looked alike, but it was hard to tell because of the armor. Each carried a weapon, a rifle that fired bolts of blue, but it was like no rifle that Morian had ever seen: short, bulky and seemingly an integral part of the right arm of the battle armor. The entire room was silent. The carnage on the screen seemed to be forgotten as they watched the images of the alien soldiers.

"We don't know where they first made landfall," Gara continued. "My staff is still trying to make sense of the data. Much of Epilon is under the control of the emergency management response teams. Having said that, there are two things I would like to point out. One is these weapons, these appendages, appear to be firing some kind of plasma energy. The second point is that after Captain Morian and the rest of the supporting fleet fought off the main assault, they ceased the ground attack."

"What do you mean?" King Orson asked.

"The enemy began its retreat from Pallas space at 1742. At 1743, the enemy ceased all ground operations, boarded their craft and left."

"What of the enemy casualties?" Morian asked. "How many were killed? Were any of their craft damaged? Did they abandon any?"

"There are no reports of any enemy casualties," Gara said, shaking his head. "No enemy bodies have been found. Our field commanders are reporting that their weapons have little to no effect on the aliens."

The room was silent.

"I'm told these craft did not enter or leave our system via the Slipstream," King Jurak said. "If that's true, I want to know how they were able to do that and where the hell they came from." He paused, then said, "They must have used the Slipstream. The alternative is impossible."

"As of yet, we have no answers for you, Your Grace," Admiral Hammond replied. "We, too, are still compiling the data, but it appears unlikely they entered or left the Pallas System via the Slipstream."

"Then how did they do it?" Morian asked, receiving no answer. "And where did they go? Are they still somewhere in the system? We can't let our guard down. Until we know for sure they're gone, we must consider the Pallas System unsecured."

"The enemy's technology is what we need to be talking about," one of Paris's captains said.

"We'll know nothing of their technology until we can capture either one of the beings or their ships," King Jurak said. "I want to know how much of my system... how many of my citizens have died."

"But what about—" someone else started to say.

"Please, please." Admiral Hammond raised his hands and his voice and quieted everyone. It was clear that an overwhelming sense of confusion, anger, surprise, and pure dread was boiling up among the officers at the table. "Please," Admiral Hammond said, "I know you have many questions; we all do, but let's stick to the narrative. Let's get back to—"

"I'm sorry, Admiral," Prince Felder said and rose to his feet.

Here we go, Morian thought, wanting to bury his face in his hands, but he didn't.

"Being one of the three royals present here today, and the highest-ranking representative of the Alastor System, I must say I think we're all missing the point."

The perfect royal politician's way of introducing your-self. Morian thought.

"It's obvious we know nothing about these... these beings. And I have already heard multiple comments around this table referring to them as *enemies*. We know nothing about them! Today was a historic event, and we were blessed to witness it. Yes, the attack was terrible, catastrophic even, but for the first time in recorded history, we have confirmed the existence of alien life, intelligent life with technology beyond our understanding. This is—"

"With all due respect, my prince," Gara said, interrupting him, something unprecedented in diplomatic circles, "they *are* the enemy. They carried out an unprovoked attack, not only on this system but also the Persei System. They attacked and murdered unarmed civilians."

"I'm not minimizing that fact, General," Felder said, unperturbed by the interruption. "I'm just saying the science and history of today cannot be overshadowed."

Here it comes. This royal's out to lunch. Morian couldn't contain himself. "The science of whatever happened today is not the priority. The safety of our people is."

Felder slowly turned his head and glared down at Morian with a look that promised repercussions.

"The science and history of today will be acknowledged, Prince Felder," King Orson said testily. "However, now is not the time to discuss it. There are more immediate needs to be dealt with. Please sit down."

Felder frowned and did as he was told.

"Captain Morian," Gara said. "You arrived on the field at 1655. What did you observe?"

"I observed the Pallas fleet taking heavy casualties," Morian replied. "That being so, I immediately launched our fighter squadron and they engaged the enemy, as did *Avenger*, to little effect, I might add. They are virtually impervious to directed energy weapons. Unfortunately, the same cannot be said for us. Had it not been for our Dutrinium armor, I would not be sitting here now."

Admiral Hammond nodded and said, "You're being modest, Captain. What can you tell us about their tactics, speeds, firepower?"

Morian nodded and said, "If I could direct your attention to the hologram." He turned his head and nodded to Jadern. "We've not had time to fully analyze the data yet, but I do have some footage to show you."

Selected footage from Danis's fighter began looping on the hologram. "As you can see, the enemy craft are roughly two and a half times the size of an F32A fighter. They are... elliptical... somewhat oval in shape, with no apparent windows, doors, hatches or drives. The craft's only other features are the blueish halo and the wings, if you can call them that, which seem to have no other purpose than to support the articulated weapons. Freeze, please, Mr. Jadern."

The hologram froze and Morian continued, "The craft has four of these appendages. They can operate in unison or independently in any direction. Each weapon can fire what appears to be an extremely powerful laser, almost always blue, but sometimes white. They're fast, faster than our F32s, but they're not as maneuverable. Our fighters were easily able to outmaneuver them. Unfortunately, avoiding their weapons was not so easy. Their weapons tracking systems are extremely effective."

Morian paused, looked around the table, then continued, "As I previously stated, they are impervious to our directed energy weapons, though repeated hits do slow them down, but they recover quickly. Again, note the blue halo. We think it's some kind of shielding. It appears to absorb the energy from even our most powerful lasers, leaving the craft unharmed. It also absorbs the energy from a nuclear blast, but not quite as effectively. In fact, the *Avenger,* along with our fighters, were able to disable seventeen of them but at great cost: it takes no less than eight Rapiers or four Mark 59s to kill one of them."

"How are they powered?" King Orson asked.

"We don't know," Morian replied.

"What about their energy weapons?" King Jurak asked. "What sort of technology are we dealing with?"

"I'm afraid we don't know that either," Morian replied, frowning.

"But surely you were able to capture some of the disabled craft?" Jurak asked.

"No, Your Grace. They were all destroyed by the retreating craft. They left nothing behind."

"If I may," General Gara said. "Thank you, Captain Morian, but how were these small craft able to take down so many of the fleet's largest ships so quickly and so easily?"

"You'll find this painful to watch," Morian said and nodded to Jadern. The hologram began to play again. "As you can see, a single direct hit from all four of the enemy craft's weapons is enough to destroy an Angel Class cruiser."

Morian paused and watched them as they stared at the holo, the enemy's lasers raking the Angel-class cruiser almost from stern to bow, resulting in a catastrophic, all-consuming explosion and a debris field that covered many cubic kilometers. Then the scene changed, and they were looking at a wide field view of *Avenger*.

"And, as you can see," Morian continued, "we were raked by a similar blast along our keel, but our armor held. It was damaged—I'm told the trench it scoured out of the hull is, in places, more than seventy centimeters deep—but it held. *Avenger*'s Dutrinium armor, in its most vulnerable locations, such as her keel, is in excess of two meters thick. The Angel Class ship has a reduced, reflective armor designed to deflect laser fire which, from what you've seen, appears to be inadequate. It's my recommendation, therefore, that all Angel Class ships be immediately withdrawn from service and refitted with Dutrinium armor."

"That's impossible, ludicrous," Captain Paris snapped.

"Not impossible," Morian retorted, "and better than the alternative. If we don't, we'll lose the fleet."

"I don't believe it," Paris said.

"You don't believe your own eyes?" Morian replied. "Then what will it take to convince you, Captain? The loss of your ship and crew?"

Paris opened her mouth to speak again, but before she could, "That's enough, Captain Paris!" King Orson said, his voice raised. "This kind of exchange is disruptive and unhelpful."

Paris nodded but continued to glare at Morian. "My apologies, Your Grace," she said with a noticeable edge to her voice.

"So, Captain Morian, this... this swarm of blue ships," King Jurak said thoughtfully, "came from another system.

If so, they *must* have come through the Slipstream, and if they did the control station must have the data. Is that not true, Captain?"

Morian looked at Admiral Hammond. Hammond nodded his agreement to take the question and said, "I'm afraid we don't know. As far as we know, this enemy, this swarm as you call it, did not arrive through the Slipstream."

"That's impossible!" Jurak snapped.

"I'm afraid not, Your Grace. It appears they have FTL capability."

"Impossible," King Orson said. "Faster than light travel outside of the Slipstream is... impossible."

"I would agree with you, Your Grace," Hammond said, "except that they seem to be able to do it."

No one spoke. Each person at the table seemingly trying to digest not only the reality but also the enormity of what they were being asked to accept.

But Morian's thoughts were suddenly elsewhere, with his sister, Danis. He had the distinct feeling that she was taking the loss of her pilots hard. *What?* It was as if he knew her exact thoughts. He squeezed the bridge of his nose and shook his head. How could he know what she was thinking? It wasn't possible. It was as if he was inside her head, listening to her thoughts. They were twins, so they were close, yes, and he'd always had an affinity for her, but this; this was different. He needed to get out of the meeting so he could find her.

"In summary," General Gara broke the silence, "the Persei System and the Pallas System will recover from these attacks. But we must be diligent. If what we're thinking is true, that they do indeed have FTL capability, then we can expect another attack, anytime, anywhere."

"I want this data sent to every ship in the fleet," Hammond said, nodding at the now frozen hologram.

"I'm afraid that might not be possible," King Orson said, his image flickering. "Most of the communication systems are down. We've been trying to reach the outer systems all day with no success."

"But what of our system?" King Jurak asked. "Our fleet has been destroyed. Who will protect us?"

"The *Avenger* and the four remaining USF ships will have to assume that role, for now," Hammond said.

King Orson sat up, held up a finger, looked around at somebody, spoke for a moment, then turned back again and said, "I'm afraid that won't work, Admiral." Everyone looked at the fuzzy image of the king. "I have just been informed that communications to and from the Pricus System have ceased, and it appears likely that Planet Tor was already under attack."

"I'll make contact with the Tor fleet immediately," Admiral Hammond said.

"I'm afraid I have a... personal need," King Orson said. "My son, Elio, is currently on a diplomatic mission to Tor. And I intend to dispatch a ship immediately to ensure his safety and return him to Orso."

Admiral Hammond began. "I can alert the fleet to this need—"

"That will not be necessary, or even possible," Orson raised his voice, interrupting the admiral. "All communications are down. Tor is cut off." The king looked at Morian and said, "Captain?"

"Yes, Your Grace?"

"I am assigning you and the *Avenger* to the Pricus system. Captain Paris and the *Mariposa* will accompany you. You are to leave immediately. You are to retrieve my son and transport him back to Orso with the utmost haste."

The *Avenger* needed repairs and rearming; his inventory of Mark 59 Lances had been depleted by more than twenty-five percent, but he had no option but to comply with the king's orders.

Captain Sheela Paris sat up in her seat. Her face brightened at the prospect of a special mission. She opened her mouth as if to say something, but the king beat her to it.

"Captain Morian. Please save my son."

Morian bowed his head. "It will be my honor, Your Grace."

Hammond looked annoyed, but there was nothing he could do either. He was duty-bound to support the king. "Captain Morian. Captain Paris," he said. "This is a Tier One mission, top priority. Captain Morian, you will assume the role of task force commander with the acting rank of commodore, for this mission only."

Paris tried to hide her scowl, but Morian saw the change in the alignment of her eyebrows. She was angry.

"Very well," Hammond continued. "The rest of the USF ships will remain here in Pallas."

"One more thing, Admiral," Morian said. "Prince Felder and his staff are still aboard the *Avenger*. For his safety and that of his entourage, I request he be removed to another ship."

"No, no, no." Felder was on his feet and arguing almost before Morian had finished speaking. "It is clear," he almost shouted the words, then calmed down a little, "that with its armored hull, Captain Morian's ship is, without doubt, the safest ship in the fleet. I demand, therefore, that we be allowed to remain aboard the *Avenger*."

Morian looked at King Orson, an unspoken request for help. But the king only shrugged. The wayward prince of Alastor was of no concern to him.

Admiral Hammond also looked at the king and received the same message. "Request denied, Captain," Hammond said. "There are no other ships available. Retrieve Prince Elio and return both of them safely to Orso."

The room turned dark as one by one they turned off their halos, leaving Morian, Jadern and a smiling Prince Felder sitting together at the table. Morian took off his halo and stood.

Jadern also stood, saying, "I'll inform the bridge to prepare to get underway, Captain."

Morian nodded and went to find his sister.

Chapter Fourteen

The Plan in Action

Pricus System
Planet Tor's Surface
Pricus City Governor's Mansion

Andra Graynir walked quickly across the large room in the basement of the mansion. It was just after midnight; one of Tor's two moons was up and she knew everyone would be sleeping. Prince Elio and Duke Steren were in the guest wing. It was, she knew, their best chance to pull off the kidnapping, the first night before the royals began their official duties. Both the prince and the duke had been tired from their journey, so they'd gone to bed early and would by now be sleeping soundly.

She was nervous and felt jittery all the way down to the pit of her stomach. This level of deceit was unlike anything she'd participated in before. She knew what she was about to do was a serious crime, but she trusted Gian and badly wanted to impress Hamel. She could do it. She had to do it. The desire to see the truth exposed propelled her forward.

The data pad on her forearm buzzed. She flinched and glanced at it; Gian was outside with Hamel. *Right on time,* she thought nervously.

She hurried as light-footed as possible to the control pad on the basement door and entered her code, silencing the alarm on the exterior doors. She unlocked the door and peered out. Nothing. Then she heard something, saw movement, and sucked in her breath as she spied Gian, Hamel, Norryn and Declan running across the back lawn toward her.

She ushered them in, took one last look around, then closed the door behind them but didn't lock it. Gian, his face flushed, his eyes wide, grabbed her and wrapped her up in a hug.

"Thank you, Andra," Hamel said. "You're so brave. You will not be forgotten."

Andra felt the heat of embarrassment and pride on her face, then asked, "Are you really going to take both of them, the prince and Duke Steren?"

Hamel smiled and said, "Even better. We'll gladly take two as one." He slapped Gian on the shoulder. "Andra, where do we go from here?"

Andra breathed out a long shuddering breath, straightened her shoulders, pulled back her hair and said, "Follow me. There's a tunnel that leads from here to the guest wing where they're staying. It's an emergency escape route."

"Good," Hamel said and looked at everyone. "This is it, then. Lead the way, Andra."

Andra, still nervous but feeling better now that Gian was there, led the group through the dimly lit tunnel until they came to an intersection with two flights of stone steps leading upward in different directions.

"The prince's suite is that way," Andra said, pointing to the right. "That's the way to the duke's room." She pointed in the other direction. "I've disarmed the alarm systems on both doors."

Hamel nodded to Gian, and they ascended the steps to the prince's room, Norryn and Declan to the duke's room. Andra waited below, biting her nails.

Elio was seated cross-legged on the bed with his halo on, trying to log on. It was late, and he was tired, but he'd been trying to get on the net ever since he and Dinka had touched down. He was sure the problem was the small rock they were on out in the middle of nowhere. *Their tech must be older than I am,* he thought savagely.

Dinka, suddenly alarmed, tried to get Elio's attention, but he was totally focused on what he was doing. He tapped the halo to turn it off and then back on again, but there was still no signal. He flicked it off again and tore the halo off his head in frustration. *What was that?*

He turned his head. Too late. He started to get up and opened his mouth to speak, but before he could they were on him, two of them. One of them grabbed his arm, wrenched it up his back and shoved him face down on the bed while the other, the bigger of the two, put a hand in the middle of his back and pushed him deeper into the soft bed covering.

Elio didn't resist. He said nothing.

"Don't struggle, Prince," one of them said. "You're coming with us."

He felt something hard and metallic clamp over his wrists. And then he was jerked off the bed onto his feet.

"Don't worry, Prince," the man holding his arms behind him said. "Just do as you're told and you won't get hurt.

He nodded. *Amateurs.* Elio tried to figure out which one of them was the mastermind, but he couldn't. They were undisciplined, arguing with each other as they pushed him toward the door.

He smiled to himself and played along as they led him down the stone steps to the tunnel. They ran along the tunnel, into the basement and to a door where they stopped and turned, startled by something buzzing behind them.

Dinka was following his master.

"Shoot it," the larger of the two men said.

"No, don't shoot it," the girl said. "We're not shooting a royal bot. Plus, the blast in this confined space will blow out our eardrums."

Hmm, the girl has spirit and is smart, Elio thought. *Maybe she's the one in charge.*

"Too bad," the big man said. "We have to destroy it. It's probably recording."

"No, please," Elio said. "I'll cooperate. Just... please

don't destroy Dinka. He's been with me since I was six years old. I'm not resisting. I'll go with you quietly."

They looked at each other. The girl stood firmly between the two men and the robot. They didn't like it, but the big one nodded and together they left the basement, Dinka following.

Chapter Fifteen

The Swarm

Pricus System

Tor controlled space

Morian was at the command rail when the *Avenger* dropped out of the Slipstream into the Pricus System, the crew already at battle stations. He stared intently at the main view screen, hoping for nothing but ready for anything. Again, at first glance he saw nothing.

"How far to Tor atmosphere?" Richard called out.

"Approximately three hundred million kilometers, sir," Commander Jadern said.

"Take us in, Mr. Sen," Morian said. "Flank speed. Lieutenant Lowry, send to *Mariposa*: follow *Avenger*, line astern. Flank speed."

When they reached the battle, as prepared as he was, Morian was still astounded by the number of enemy ships that were swarming around the USF ships. The battle was clearly already underway, and the USF fleet wasn't doing well. Between the *Avenger* and the home planet of Tor, a massive struggle was taking place.

"Straight into the battle, or are we going to bypass?" Jadern asked. "Pricus City is on the southern hemisphere."

Of course it had to be. Nothing was ever easy. Their mission was to make contact with Prince Elio, and Morian couldn't help but remember the image of the three alien soldiers stalking the streets of Epsilon. Every minute was precious. If he decided to avoid the battle raging above the planet, it would add drastically to the time and distance. If he decided to take the direct route... Well, there was a chance he might not get there at all. His priority was the prince's safety, so the correct option was clear. He opted for the indirect route.

"Set course for Pricus City, Mr. DeLong. We'll reassess when we get closer. Lieutenant Lowry, send to *Mariposa*: follow us in."

"Yes, sir."

Morian sat down in his command chair and thoughtfully rubbed his chin. What he'd hoped would be a quick and easy rescue mission had just turned into something much larger.

He stood again, stepped to the rail and stared down at the hologram, then at the forward view screen, then at the data net above the holo. The numbers were staggering. The combined Tor/USF fleet numbered in the hundreds, from two A-class carriers to more than ninety D-class destroyers and everything in between. The enemy, however, had some thirteen hundred of their small, blue haloed ships. The USF fleet was outnumbered almost four to one.

Morian shook his head. *This is about to become an unmitigated disaster*, he thought.

"Are we going to engage, sir?" Jadern asked as he joined Morian at the command rail.

Morian shook his head. "Not if I can help it. Our mission is to locate the prince and get him safely out of here, but they do need some help," he said, nodding down at the holo. "Who's the fleet admiral commanding, do we know?"

"Yes, sir," Jadern said. "Fleet Admiral Lucian Moreau on the carrier *Juno*."

Morian nodded. "He's a good man. Lieutenant Lowry, open a channel to Admiral Moreau."

"Aye, sir."

"Morian?" the admiral's voice was gruff, tense. "Is that really you? Where the hell are you? Good to see you, man. I need all the damn help I can get."

"I'm sorry, Admiral. I'm on a priority one mission to Tor. Prince Elio is down there."

"Then what the hell are you bothering me for? Get the hell off this channel and go do your duty."

"I will, sir, but first I have some information that will help."

"Well, go ahead, man. Tell me."

And Morian did. He told him about his experience during the Battle of Pallas and that he should stop trying to kill the enemy with lasers and use missiles. And that got him into more trouble.

"D'you think I'm stupid, Morian? I figured that out

nearly an hour ago. We're holding them, but it's touch and go because we're vastly outnumbered, but we're going to pull it off. Now go do your job and leave me to do mine."

"Aye, sir. Morian out," he said as he looked at the holo of the massive carrier. The *Juno* was four thousand meters long with fifteen decks. She carried ten squadrons of F32A fighters and four squadrons of B29 fighter bombers.

Morian looked at Jadern and grinned. Jadern stared back at him wide-eyed.

"I had to give it a shot. If anyone can pull it off, Moreau can. Now, back to the task at hand. Any suggestions?"

Jadern recovered his composure almost instantly. "We could enter the atmosphere on the far side of the planet and approach out of the sun."

"That would take too long," Morian said. "If the Swarm is fighting here, they'll already be engaged on the surface."

"How do you know that, Captain? How do you know they already have boots on the ground?"

"I don't, but if the MO is the same as it was in the Pallas and Persei Systems, it's a good bet they'll do the same here."

"Do you think this is the same group as the one that attacked the other systems?" Jadern asked. "Or are these different fleets?"

"I wish I knew," Morian said. "For now, though, it's not something I can worry about. Right now, our mission is to ensure the safety of Prince Elio. We'll bypass this battle and get planetside. Continue on course. If we're engaged, we'll deal with it. In the meantime, I need you to keep an eye on *Mariposa*. I don't trust that woman."

"Aye, sir." Jadern nodded, then turned and walked away, down into the well of the bridge.

Morian keyed his data screen to call Danis and asked her to join him on the bridge.

"Mariposa to Avenger."

"Go ahead, Mariposa," Morian said as he returned to his chair.

"Captain," Paris said. "The Tor fleet is in trouble. We should engage with them first."

She did not even phrase it as a request.

"Negative, Captain Paris. We'll proceed on our mission to Pricus City. If we are attacked, we'll deal with it. Other than that, we'll maintain our present heading."

There was a pause before Paris responded. "I am officially requesting permission to join the fleet. One ship should be more than sufficient for the Pricus City mission."

Paris was now directly challenging his authority in front of his entire bridge, and she knew it too.

"Understood, Mariposa. Request denied. Stay on course."

If she continued pushing the issue, Morian would have to turn up the heat. He had enough to worry about and didn't need a rogue captain to deal with. *At least Felder's secure and staying out of my way,* he thought.

Danis stepped out of the elevator onto the bridge, and Morian motioned Jadern and Lowry to join him. They stood together in a small circle. Morian studied his sister.

He still hadn't had time to talk to her, but she appeared calm and professional.

Morian addressed Danis while the others in the small circle listened. "I've already briefed Captain Paris of the plan. We are on course to bypass the battle and head for Pricus City. As soon as we're in range, Commander, you'll launch your squadron and a shuttle with a squad of marines—under the command of First Lieutenant Van der Veen—and lead *Mariposa*'s First Squadron to the surface, to Pricus City. You will establish comms with us and then locate Prince Elio. The *Avenger* and the *Mariposa* will provide cover for your exit. Understood?"

"Yes, sir," she replied. "I reviewed the intel packet and the op orders."

"Lieutenant Lowry." He turned to his communications officer. "Communications from the planet are down. I want you to continuously scan all frequencies: X-ray, digital, shortwave, even analog, everything."

"Yes, sir."

"How long until we're in range, Mr. Jadern?"

Jadern checked the data screen on his arm. "Fourteen minutes until we have to make the course change."

"Outstanding. Thank you, everyone, and good luck."

Everyone departed to their stations and Morian to his command chair. Minutes ticked by. And then...

"Mariposa to Avenger, we are being engaged," Paris's voice said on the open channel.

What the hell?

"Looks like they are attacking," Paris said. "Multiple craft vectoring one nine zero."

Morian stood, moved to the rail and scanned the holo. *Damn it. They're not even close.*

"Mariposa leaving formation to engage," Paris said.

Morian saw heads turn to look at him. He was furious, but he couldn't show it.

"Negative, Mariposa. Stay in formation."

No reply. He watched as Captain Paris blatantly disobeyed and began to turn the *Mariposa* away to port. The enemy ships must have noticed the movement because they turned toward the *Mariposa*.

"Avenger to Mariposa. Belay that! Return to formation immediately."

"The enemy is closing, sir," Jadern said. "Five ships. Contact in less than three minutes."

"Domino," Morian said, more calmly than he felt, "launch now. We're being engaged."

"Roger. Ranger Squadron deploying."

"More craft approaching, Captain," Jadern said. "Ten... no, twelve altogether."

"Ready all guns," Morian called out. "Fire as they come to bear. Fighters stay close. Point defense explosive rounds. Provide support."

"Starboard DEW cannons in range in ten seconds."

"Belay that!" Morian snapped. "Deploy cruise missiles. Mark 47s and 59s."

"Roger that, sir," Jadern said. "The Mark 47 Sabers are only twenty-five m—"

"I know that, Commander," Morian snapped. "Just do it! We need all the firepower we have."

"Aye, sir. 47s and 59s it is," Jadern replied. "Stand by. Enemy contact in ten, nine, eight..."

Chapter Sixteen

Hostile Intentions

Pricus City
Tor Planet's Surface
Pricus System

Prince Elio sat in the back of the gravcar, next to Dinka. Duke Steren sat on Elio's other side. The duke was completely freaked out, looking like he thought he was going to die. But it was obvious to Elio that these were just kids. Not that they were much younger than himself, but they were inexperienced. He figured they were likely a small group of idealists, fed up with being stuck in a small town in a backwater system and wanting to do something big to prove themselves. *Kidnapping me isn't it*, he thought.

"You do know you could all be executed for what you're doing?" he asked.

Elio could tell by the distress on the girl's face that

she was nervous. The big man was confident, but it seemed to him that the leader was the older, tall one.

"They'll hunt you down," Elio said lightly. "All of you."

"We're not going to hurt you," the girl said. "We just want our demands listened to."

"You realize what those sirens mean, don't you?" Elio asked. "It means they've already missed us."

"Doubtful," the tall one said.

The girl looked at the big man and mouthed something unintelligible.

The big man checked his data screen. "There's no signal," he said, frowning. "How could that be?"

The female checked her screen with the same result.

"Dinka." Elio turned to his bot. "Check the government's emergency frequencies."

"No!" The tall one turned and reached toward the robot, pulling the gravcar to one side.

"Keep your eyes on the road, damn it," the big man yelled. "You'll kill us all."

"Relax," Elio said. "We need to know what's going on. In case you haven't noticed, I'm not exactly the biggest fan of my father, or the sovereign government in general. I didn't even want to come on this stupid diplomatic trip."

"What?" the girl asked.

"I'm not sure who you are or where we're going," Elio said. "But it's kind of exciting. The best part of the trip so far." He swept his hair out of his eyes and smiled.

The girl frowned, confused. "Maybe he's right, Gian," she said.

So, his name's Gian.

"Sir," Dinka said. "I have connected to the planet's data grid. It appears the USF fleet is engaged with an enemy beyond the planet's atmosphere, and the Sovereign Defense Force Command has issued an alert of an imminent attack on Pricus City."

"What?" the girl asked.

"An attack by who?" Gian asked. "I don't believe it. There hasn't been a war in decades."

"The enemy is unknown," Dinka said.

The tall man turned the gravcar onto a smaller road and parked under the trees in front of an old and weathered cabin. The cabin overlooked Pricus City, its lights sparkling in the distance. It was a beautiful night.

"Doesn't look like an attack to me," Gian said. "What do you think, Hamel?"

"I don't hear anything," the tall one replied.

Elio made eye contact with the girl, tilted his head to one side and raised his eyebrows in question.

"Maybe he's right," she said. "We should listen to him."

"Andra, he's one of them," Gian said. "He represents the reason we're here. You can't trust them, any of them. Come on. Let's get them inside." He jumped out of the gravcar and was quickly followed by the others.

"I insist you stop this foolery immediately," Duke Steren said as Gian grabbed him by the arm and helped him out. "I insist you take us back to Pricus City. I'll personally see that they go easy on you."

"Shut up, old man," Hamel said, "and do as you're

told and keep your mouth shut. Nobody's going anywhere... What the hell? What's that noise?"

They all turned to look out across the escarpment toward the city. The humming sound grew louder and more intense. Andra, now frightened, spun around, looking for the source of the sound. It was all-encompassing. She couldn't tell from which direction it was coming.

Then she saw it. They all saw it: blue lights descending from the sky. The glowing lights descended slowly, eight of them, with more of the lights way off in the distance, until they were clearly small spacecrafts hovering over the city.

Suddenly, two beams of brilliant blue light shot from the underside of one of them at one of the tall buildings. The structure exploded in a shower of fire and debris.

"Oh, my God," Gian whispered.

"Oh yes," Elio said, almost conversationally, "we're definitely under attack."

"What the hell's happening?" Gian shouted as he swung around and grabbed Elio by the front of his shirt. "You're a prince; you must know what's happening. You follow the politics. Is this why you're here? What have we done to deserve this?" He let go of Elio's shirt and pointed at Duke Steren. "You! You're the diplomat. What have you done?" He took a step toward the duke. Steren took several steps back.

The duke was speechless. His mouth was working, but nothing came out.

"He doesn't know, and neither do I," Elio said. "Now. How about you take these damn things off so I can think. Him too." He nodded in the duke's direction and held out his hands. "I think you can agree that they are more of a threat than we are."

Gian looked at Hamel. Hamel nodded, and Gian released them.

"They're obviously some sort of secret military weapon," Hamel said. "Typical of the sovereign government."

Elio shook his head, still watching in awe as the shimmering blue craft continued to rain havoc down on the city. "Not likely," he said. "If it was, I would know about it. Trust me. This is bad, very bad."

They watched in silence as the strange craft continued to attack the city until finally, the carnage slowed and then stopped altogether. For several minutes, all was quiet, then several of them began to descend slowly to the ground.

"We have to go," Elio said. "Those things are landing. Your people need help."

"No!" Hamel snapped. "We stay here, where we're safe."

"NO!" the girl shouted. "My family is down there. We have to help them."

"She's right," Elio said. "We need to go. The concept of safety in numbers is real. We need to get down there and help them."

"By doing what?" Hamel snarled.

"For one, you can take me back to my yacht."

The girl stared at him. She seemed to be the only one who was truly listening. The other four men were just standing there, staring down at the burning city and the strange blue craft hovering above it.

"Look," Elio said. "You wannabe revolutionaries need to get it together. Your petty grievances mean nothing now. Your planet, your cities, your friends, families, your way of life, they are all gone... or they soon will be. Nobody gives a damn about us or is worried about where we are. But we can help."

Hamel narrowed his eyes and squinted at Elio.

"He's right," Andra shouted. "My family's down there. We need to go. What are you thinking, all of you?" She was crying now. "*Please!*"

"We're not going anywhere," Hamel said.

The ground began to shake beneath their feet. The humming sound was all around them, vibrating inside them, all the way down to their bones.

They looked up, hands over their ears, squinting in the blue light that seemed to encompass the enemy craft.

"COME ON!" Elio shouted, grabbing Andra's hand and beginning to run toward the trees.

He looked back as he ran and watched as the weapons, on the underside of what he took to be wings, turned quickly and fired two brilliant beams of blue light into the cabin. The cabin burst apart in one single, mighty explosion. One minute it was there, the next it was gone, gone in a flash of light, leaving only a few smoking embers.

Someone cried out. Elio and Andra were flung to the ground by the force of the explosion. He rolled and looked up. One of the other men—he thought his name was Declan—had been injured by a piece of flying wood. The other man, whose name he didn't know, stooped to help him. A beam of blue light shot out of one of the ship's weapons and vaporized them both.

Andra, on her knees, screamed and screamed. Elio grabbed her hand and hauled her to her feet, still screaming.

"Come on!" Gian shouted as he and Hamel ran toward the gravcar. A gibbering Duke Steren beat them to it by several meters and scrambled into the back seats. The gravcar was already moving when Elio shoved the sobbing Andra in beside the robot and fell in after them.

Gian took off down the trail away from the cabin, pushing the gravcar as hard as it could go.

"Go, go, go!" Hamel yelled frantically as the enemy craft began to follow them.

"Look out!" Elio shouted. "It's going to shoot!"

Gian jerked the yoke hard over to the left. The gravcar veered off the road as a bolt of blue splashed onto the road behind them, tearing a three-meter-wide, four-meter-deep groove that extended for more than fifty meters. The power of the weapon was immense.

"Go left, go left!" Elio shouted.

Gian turned, and again the bolt of blue energy tore past them, vaporizing trees and vegetation, even rocks.

"Hold on!" Gian yelled and pulled a hard right turn. The enemy craft continued onward and then began to turn, slowly, in a wide arc.

"Go, go go," Elio yelled to Gian.

"What?"

"Get the hell out of here," Elio shouted as another bolt of blue energy shot towards them, but Gian was jinking wildly, like a fighter pilot, and it missed.

"Keep an eye on that thing and tell me what it's doing," Gian yelled. "I have an idea."

Gian reversed the gravcar's thrusters, turned violently onto a smaller dirt road and reversed his thrusters again, heading away at full speed. Elio was flung sideways and smashed into Dinka. Again, the enemy craft overshot and continued onward before making a wide, looping course correction.

"Where are you going?" Andra shrieked.

"Lookout Bluffs," Gian said as he craned his neck behind them, trying to see the craft.

"The Bluffs? Are you crazy?" Andra yelled.

"Don't worry," Gian shouted as he steered the gravcar up and over a hill and down and around a tight curve.

"Enemy at six o'clock," Elio said.

"How far back?"

"Two... no, three hundred meters and gaining fast."

Gian hit the throttle and Elio was slammed back in his seat as the gravcar rocketed forward, swaying, jinking from side to side. The trees thinned and then were gone as they entered a canyon. Steep rock walls towered above them on both sides and the space between them was getting narrower by the second. A bolt of blue exploded behind them, showering them with shards of rock. The gravcar trembled. Gian fought to maintain control. The car rocketed onward at speeds Elio wouldn't have thought possible.

"No!" Andra yelled. "Gian, no. You can't. You won't make it."

"Just hold on," he shouted.

"It's getting closer," Elio shouted, glancing back over

his shoulder, hanging onto his seat for dear life. The enemy craft was less than a hundred meters behind them.

"I got it," Gian shouted. "Hang on."

Elio glanced sideways and cringed. The canyon walls were a blur and closing in. There was barely enough room to dodge the energy blasts.

"Almost there," Gian yelled. "One more minute.

That one more minute was the longest in Elio's thirty-year lifetime.

The enemy craft slowly closed the distance, firing bolt after bolt. Gian was somehow able to dodge them all, but Elio knew it was over. He clenched his teeth and gripped the sides of his seat with both hands, expecting imminent death.

"Grab onto something," Gian yelled. "This is going to be tight."

The gravcar's headlights lit up a wall of solid rock in front of them. Elio felt his heart spasm as Gian reversed the thrusters and hauled the yoke as far as it would go to the right. The gravcar slowed, turned onto its side and veered to the right, flinging Elio to the left hard against Dinka, who seemed to be anchored to the seat. Gian reversed the thrusters and the gravcar sped away down the trail.

Behind them an almighty explosion blasted into the air as the enemy craft slammed into the canyon wall. The flash of blue energy lit up the night sky. Pieces of the craft flew in all directions. Beams and bursts of blue and white light lit up the canyon walls.

Andra and Hamel jumped up and down in their seats, yelling and waving their arms in excitement. Elio couldn't help it. He raised his arms and yelled with them.

Gian slowed the gravcar and spun it around so they could see what was left of the enemy craft. There was nothing but the seared face of the canyon wall.

"Whew," Elio said. "Now that... that was intense. Well done, Gian."

"Thanks," Gian said, wiping the sweat, dust and grime from his brow. "Do you see any more of them?"

"No," Elio replied. "I think we're clear, for now anyway." He took a deep breath, trying to slow his heart rate.

Gian killed the engines and the gravcar slowly sank to the ground.

For a moment, no one spoke. They all just looked at each other, their faces pale.

"My scanners show no airborne craft in our immediate vicinity," Dinka said.

"That's... good," Gian said as he released his iron grip on the yoke, flexed his fingers, and sat back in his seat. "Now what?"

Chapter Seventeen

Death of a Giant

Pricus System

Tor controlled space

Morian watched the screens as multiple Swarm craft came into range, and he smiled at the thought that the nickname King Jurak had given them at the meeting was going to stick.

He watched and listened as Danis corralled her small squadron into a tight group and stayed close below *Avenger*'s keel. Her point defense gunners were already lighting up the sky around the great ship. Her fifty caliber rails were firing thousands of rounds of explosive shells, and her forward tubes fired salvo after salvo of Mark 47 torpedoes, all to little effect. Jadern had been right. The twenty-megaton warheads were having little effect.

More than a thousand kilometers ahead of the *Avenger*, Morian could see the *Mariposa* hurtling into battle, her twenty-four F32 fighters spread out in a vast fan-shaped formation ahead of her.

"Avenger to Mariposa," he said, trying to keep his anger contained.

"Go ahead, Avenger."

"Captain Paris, draw your fighters in close under the protection of your missile batteries and reduce speed. We'll cover each other and reduce casualties."

A long pause then, "Received and understood, Avenger. I trust my pilots to adjust tactics as the situation requires."

Morian shook his head. *Mariposa* had already lost one fighter. He focused on his breathing. There was only so much he could control, and Captain Paris was apparently not one of them, but he had to try.

"Morian to Mariposa," he said, his voice calm, regulated. "This is a direct order. You are to fall back on my starboard flank immediately. Acknowledge."

Paris didn't respond.

Danis was coordinating her squadron's fire with *Avenger*'s gunners, and it was working, but for every Swarm ship that was disabled, two more appeared. Her shields were holding, barely, but her armored hull was doing better. Her fifty cals were virtually useless, the explosive projectiles flaring briefly as they exploded against the enemy's shields.

Morian continued to watch as Paris lost five more of her fighters and the *Mariposa* began taking damage. She had shields, but her armor was light, reflective, and designed to deflect laser weapons, offering little protection against the advanced weaponry of the aliens.

"Mariposa," Morian shouted. "Disengage and draw back on our starboard side. We'll protect you."

No response.

"Mr. Sen," he said as he rose up on his toes and then down again, his knuckles white as he gripped the rail and stared at the screen. "Take us to *Mariposa*'s port flank." The helmsman nodded, changed course and the ship began to move toward *Mariposa*.

Morian staggered as *Avenger* was rocked by a massive hit forward of her number four starboard engine.

They were closing in on *Mariposa* and he could clearly see that the ship was taking heavy damage, yet she was still firing her laser cannons instead of missiles. *What the hell is Paris thinking?* he thought savagely

"Missiles down to forty-four percent, Captain," Lieutenant Fargo said without looking up from her console.

"Engine four losing power," Volkov shouted. "Shields at seventy-two percent."

"Mr. Sen," Morian said, "Get us within range of the *Mariposa*, now! We can't afford to lose her."

* * *

Danis reversed her thrusters, flipped the F32A end-over-end, rammed the throttle to maximum thrust and dodged an energy blast that was close enough to sear the skin of her craft.

"Lookout, Domino," someone yelled. "You've another coming in at five o'clock."

"Roger." Danis checked her screens and, sure enough, there it was. She kicked the fighter hard to port, reversed her thrusters, hit the throttle and brought her craft almost to a dead stop. The incoming enemy craft overshot and continued on, making a long looping turn to port. Again she reversed her thrusters and took off after it.

"Target locked," Zilvo said, her monotone voice barely audible in her ear.

Danis fired two missiles and watched as both hit home and exploded. The enemy craft seemed to shudder, then pick up speed, moving too fast for her to catch it.

She glanced at her screens. *Damn it!* She had only two missiles left.

"Ranger Squadron," she said. "Report status."

"Ranger Seven, here. I'm out of missiles."

"Then get the hell out of here back to the *Avenger* and rearm. Then rejoin the squadron," Danis ordered.

"Ranger Two, here. I have four left."

Danis glanced to her right. Sheva Beshear was on her starboard wing. He raised two fingers to his helmet and smiled at her.

"Good, stay close," Danis replied. "How about you, Five?"

"Only two."

"Ranger Eight, here. Four left."

"Morian to Domino."

"Yes, Captain."

"The *Mariposa*'s in trouble. I need you to do what you can. We can't afford to lose her."

"Roger. Where is she?"

"Eight hundred sixty clicks to your starboard."

"Domino out!" Danis replied. "Two, Five and Eight, on me. Stay close. Stay in formation."

She made a hard turn to starboard, spotted the wounded *Mariposa* and hit the thrusters.

What the hell are they doing? she wondered. The sky around *Mariposa* was lit up. It looked like all of her laser cannons were firing at once. *Why is she not using missiles?*

Mariposa's fighters, what was left of them, were swarming all around her, flying in singles instead of protective formation. Not only that, but they were also too far out from their mother ship.

She spotted two enemy craft closing on one lone *Mariposa* fighter. *Only twelve missiles between the four of us,* she thought. *Not enough to kill 'em, but maybe we can save the fighter.*

"Follow me, guys. Line astern. You know the drill. Sheva, we'll take the one to the left. I go in first. You follow and hit it with all four missiles. Five, you and Eight take the one to the right."

"Copy, Domino."

Danis looped in behind the enemy craft. She could tell it had seen her because its two upper weapons began to turn toward her. She was within two hundred meters and locked. She fired her missiles, watched them hit, then banked away to port. Sheva was less than two seconds behind her. He fired all four of his missiles, made a tight turn and followed Danis.

Almost simultaneously, Five and Eight released all six of their missiles, closed up on Danis and Sheva and reformed.

Together they watched as *Mariposa*'s fighter hurtled away, heading back to her ship.

The two enemy ships appeared to be stalled, their blue halos had faded almost to nothing, but Danis could see they were already recovering.

"Good job, everyone," she said. "Now let's get the hell out of here and rearm."

"Copy that," Sheva said. "We're right behind you."

She glanced at *Mariposa*. She was losing. One by one, her fighters were being destroyed. Then she saw them. Three Swarm fighters came hurtling in on the *Mariposa*.

Two of the Swarm ships fired all four of their weapons at one of *Mariposa*'s main engines. The third fired at a second engine. For a moment her shields held, then failed. The two damaged engines flared, then shut down, and *Mariposa* began to veer off course.

There was nothing more Danis could do except watch as her fighters entered the hangar. She entered last, shut down her engines and waited for the hangar to pressurize before opening her canopy.

"Zilvo," she said. "You stay put. We'll be leaving as soon as we've rearmed."

"Of course, Commander," the robot replied.

"Morian to Domino."

"Domino here, Captain. We're in the bay rearming."

"How long before you can re-deploy?"

"Ten minutes... fifteen."

"Captain Paris is preparing to abandon ship. I need you to escort their escape pods and any surviving fighters to *Avenger*."

"Copy that, Captain." Danis looked over at Ranger

Seven, her eyebrows raised in question. Seven nodded. He'd understood the transmission.

"Domino to Ranger Squadron," she transmitted. "You heard that. Same rules apply. You stay on me. Tight formation. Watch each other's backs."

Ten minutes later they were back in space, heading toward the *Mariposa* as the remainder of her crew prepared to abandon ship. She was dead in space, drifting away from the main Swarm attack which was now far off in the distance.

"Morian to Domino."

"Captain?" Danis replied.

"Captain Paris has left the bridge. Her escape pod is about to launch."

"Copy, we'll bring them in."

She increased speed. "Stay with me, Rangers. And stay sharp. Watch for enemy fighters."

But for now, at least, it seemed they were alone, not a Swarm ship anywhere in sight. *Where the hell are they?* she wondered. *At their speeds they could come out of anywhere, from any direction.* "Keep your eyes open," she said. "Watch your screens. If they come, they'll come in fast. Be ready."

A small, minimal-looking ship shot out of *Mariposa*'s upper deck just aft of the bridge. It was the escape pod. It was quickly joined on its port flank by a lone fighter.

Is that it? Danis thought, stunned. *Only one fighter left out of twenty-four?*

The *Mariposa* was still in one piece, barely. All four of her engines were destroyed. Her hull was holed in a dozen different places. Fires were burning inside her, but without oxygen they'd burn out quickly, leaving the once-great ship a hulk drifting on the solar winds.

The escape pod was about twice the size of a fighter. It had minimal engines and no weapons, making it a slow-moving target.

"Stay with me," Danis said as she joined the pod on its starboard side and reversed thrust to match its speed. They formed a semi-circle around the pod and its lone fighter, and together the six fighters and the pod slowly approached *Avenger*'s open hangar doors.

Danis, ever watchful, continually scanned the surrounding space for enemy fighters, but there were none, except for the battle still raging some three-thousand kilometers away in the distance.

Why did they leave? she wondered. *Where did they go?* She shook her head. There were no answers. *Maybe they think we're not worth the bother.*

She took one last look at *Mariposa*. It was difficult to see her against the black of space. *It couldn't have been easy for Captain Paris to leave her,* she couldn't help but think.

"Avenger, this is Ranger Leader. We're ready to dock. Prepare to receive *Mariposa*'s escape pod and one fighter."

"We have you, Ranger Leader. You're clear to dock."

Danis reversed thrust and spun her fighter to cover the docking squadron and their charges. All was clear and Danis, the last to enter the hangar, breathed a sigh of relief as her F32A touched gently down.

Chapter Eighteen

No Escape

Pricus City outskirts
Planet Tor's Surface
Pricus System

Elio watched as the three friends tried to make sense of what they'd just been through. Andra tried to call her father, but nothing would go through.

"I don't have a signal either," Hamel said as he tapped his data screen.

"They must have taken out the Comm towers," Gian said.

"What about you, Prince?" Hamel turned in the seat to face Elio and the duke. "Don't you royals have some super-expensive updated service that will work out here?"

The duke, still in shock, said nothing. Elio slowly

shook his head, his eyebrows raised and smiled mockingly. "No. I don't but..." He turned to his bot and said, "Dinka?"

"I'm afraid not, sir," the robot replied. "All of the towers are down. This means they have either been destroyed or the power has been cut off. Clearly the strategy of the enemy."

"There hasn't been an inter-system war for generations," Andra said. "Why would someone want to attack Pricus City?"

"I don't think this is an inter-system conflict," Elio said.

"What?" Hamel asked.

"That ship was like nothing I've ever seen before," Elio said.

Hamel rolled his eyes and said, "Are you serious? Are you saying it was an alien ship?"

Elio shrugged and said, "If you have a better explanation, let's hear it."

Hamel sneered. "You royals make me sick. We've explored the entire galactic arm almost to the center. Never once in more than a thousand years have we encountered non-human intelligent life. Do you know that—"

"He's right," Andra said. Everyone turned to look at her, even the duke. "It makes perfect sense. You're right about inter-system conflict. What do we have to fight over? Why would some other system attack any of us? That ship... the technology... Just because we haven't found them yet doesn't mean they aren't out there. I don't see how non-human sentient life is out of the question."

"It's more likely these big government royals have some secret weapons program they've been hiding from us," Hamel snapped, irritated at being interrupted; something he wasn't used to.

Duke Steren seemed to gather himself together. He sat up straight in his seat and said, "If you're insinuating the government is behind this, then—"

"Shut up, old man," Hamel snapped, interrupting him. "You think we don't know that you people have all kinds of secret technology you never tell us about? What about the Gestar Nova incident? It's common knowledge now that the USF attacked that transport just to incite a war."

So, Elio thought grimly, *Hamel's a conspiracy theorist. That makes perfect sense. He's a rebel trying to incite an insurrection.*

"I don't think it matters who or what they are," Gian said, turning his head slightly to look at Andra. "All that matters is that they were trying to kill us. They killed Norryn and Declan back there, and we got lucky."

Everyone fell silent as they remembered what had happened to Hamel's two accomplices.

Gian shook his head and turned his attention back to the road.

"The militia is probably fighting right now," he muttered to himself

"Where are we going?" Andra asked.

"Back to town."

* * *

Andra was in a state of almost total disbelief. *This can't be happening,* she thought as the gravcar rocketed toward the burning city, her hair flying in the wind. *An attack? From where? And why? What are these things?*

Gian slowed as they approached the city limits, then pulled over and stopped under the cover of a small stand of trees and turned off the lights. The view was terrifying. Buildings all over the city were burning or had been reduced to rubble. Several of the blue-haloed craft could still be seen in the sky above the city center.

"Where are the rest of them, I wonder?" Elio said.

"How many are there even?" Gian said.

"We need to go to the mansion," Andra said. "My father will know what to do."

"Game Theory suggests," Dinka said, "that whatever enemy is attacking us would already have attacked and occupied the governor's house."

Elio shook his head and glared at the enigmatic robot, but he said nothing.

"That's even more reason for us to go there," Andra said. "I need to know where my family is and if they're... still alive."

"Andra," Gian said. "I don't think—"

"She's right," Elio said. "My ship's there. It has an X-ray communications system. We can use it to call for help."

Gian nodded. "Some weapons would be good."

"If your ship is still in one piece," Hamel said.

Elio nodded. "So let's go find out."

Gian nodded, put the gravcar's thrusters into drive and pulled slowly out onto the road, with the headlights off. They were on the north side of town in a major residential district, driving slowly. It was almost pitch-black. All of the lights were off. Andra had never seen anything like it. Her stomach churned as she thought about what might have happened to her family. She swallowed hard.

"I..." she began to speak.

There was a brilliant flash of blue light, an almighty explosion and Andra felt herself hurtling through the air. She hit the ground rolling. Her head hit something and white light flashed before her eyes. For a moment she lay there on her back, stunned. Then her vision cleared and the ground stopped spinning. Her ears were ringing. She struggled up onto her elbows and looked around. Dinka, just a couple of meters away, was staring back at her. He wasn't moving. He was lying on his side, crumpled, his left leg missing. She watched open-mouthed as the yellow light in his eyes slowly faded away to nothing.

She rolled over onto her knees. The gravcar was in pieces. Prince Elio lay just to its right, unmoving. The duke's body lay motionless next to him.

Gian? Where's Gian? She looked frantically around. Her eyes widened. Her mouth opened. She felt the hair on the back of her neck rise. Terrified, she watched the two humanoid figures walking purposefully towards them. They were tall, heavily built and were surrounded by the same blue-white halo as the craft they'd destroyed.

She looked wildly around and spotted Gian some twenty meters away to her left. He was sitting up, his shirt red with blood. He was injured.

Hamel, just a few meters away to Gian's right, was on his knees. He spotted the two beings, scrambled to his feet, yelled something, began waving his arms in the air, and started half walking half staggering toward them, shouting something Andra couldn't make out. Gian rose to one knee then stood up.

One of the beings raised its arm. At first, she thought it was a hand, or something it was holding—something short and stubby. The alien pointed it at Hamel. A bolt of blue energy hit him. Hamel blew apart in an explosion of noise and blue light. One of his hands, spinning like a top, arched through the air and landed at her feet. She screamed.

She heard Gian's voice. He was on his feet, yelling and running towards the blue beings. "No, no, no," she screamed.

Both beings turned to face him and lifted their weapons. But Gian was close, too close. His massive fist swiped at the nearest being's weapon, knocking it sideways, half spinning the being around. Gian kept going and slammed his shoulder into the second being, knocking it off its feet. He grabbed at its weapon with both hands, forcing it upward. He tried to punch it, but his fist hit nothing but air. Something hit him hard on the side of his head, sending him spinning several meters to land hard on his back. He was stunned but still conscious. He tried to get up. He couldn't. He tried to look around. His vision was blurred, but not so much he couldn't see the being bringing its weapon to bear on him.

He closed his eyes, but before the alien could fire, Elio slammed into its side, sending it staggering sideways, its arms waving as it tried to maintain balance.

Andra, still on her knees, tried to get to her feet, but

her knees buckled and she found herself on all fours, watching Gian on top of the second being, swinging punches like he was out of his mind. One of his punches landed hard on the side of its head and, much to Gian's surprise, it went limp.

The other being, having recovered from Elio's charge, was still on its feet and walking purposely towards Gian, its weapon raised.

Elio charged again, wrapping his arms around the alien's waist. The alien simply swatted him off and continued walking toward Gian, who was still sitting astride the downed alien.

Why doesn't it shoot him? Andra wondered.

Gian rolled off the alien and staggered to his feet, blood pouring from his nose.

The alien raised its weapon, but before it could fire, Elio crashed into it from behind. The being staggered slightly. Elio swung at it with something but missed. He swung again, and this time Andra could see he was holding a large rock. His hand looped toward the alien's head. The alien blocked it with its weapon and the rock flew out of Elio's hand. Elio went down hard and lay there, barely moving.

The alien turned again to Gian who, still barely conscious, was standing over its partner and again brought its weapon to bear.

Andra panicked and willed her body to move. *I have to help.*

"Hey!" she screamed.

The alien stopped, turned its head to look at her, paused, then turned its attention back to Gian.

Elio staggered to his feet, grabbed another rock and threw it at the alien. It missed, landing short by more than a dozen meters.

Andra's head tingled and she became light-headed.

The rock! she thought. And at that moment something happened to her, something strange, something monumental, and she knew exactly what she had to do.

She focused on the rock Elio had thrown. She closed her eyes. Her body went rigid. In her mind's eye, she could still see the rock. She screamed, a primal yell, like a war cry, that rose up inside her and burst forth. The rock flew into the air, straight at the alien as if it had been fired from a railgun. It smashed into the side of its head. The alien went limp, fell to its knees and pitched forward on what was left of its face.

Andra also dropped to her knees, covered her face with her hands, toppled over sideways and then... nothing. Only darkness.

Chapter Nineteen

This is no Lady

Pricus System
Tor controlled space

Captain Morian was at the command rail when the door opened behind him and Captain Paris stormed in with two of her crew members behind her.

Morian had hoped they could meet in the briefing room, but... "Captain Paris, welcome aboard, we—"

"What kind of battle d'you think you were fighting out there, Morian?" she snapped, interrupting him, her face red.

"Excuse me?" he said.

"We were clearly under attack," Paris snarled as she strode up to him.

Every member of the bridge crew froze.

"Captain Paris, if you have something to say to me, I suggest we move to the briefing room where we can—"

Again, she interrupted him. "I have just lost my ship, Morian." She crossed her arms over her chest, her feet apart. "My entire ship. Thirteen of my crew are all that survived. Thirteen. They attacked us both from starboard. You saw them. I told you. Why didn't you help us?" she said, her voice rising.

"You left formation, Captain Paris. Against my express orders. I ordered you to return. You did not. I was appointed commander of this task force and, as you seem to have forgotten, I still am, and you are aboard my ship."

"Don't you dare lecture me, Morian." Paris's voice rose another octave. "You left us out there unprotected."

"I did exactly the opposite," Morian snapped. "If you'd obeyed my orders, we could have helped one another. Instead, you decided to go off on your own, and it cost you your ship, two squadrons of fighters and the lives of more than six hundred of your crew."

"At least I did something—"

"And how did that turn out for you?" his sharp response cut her off. "This enemy cannot be fought one on one. If they separate us, we're done for. We have to work together. Now, I'll ask you once more, may we continue this conversation in the briefing room?"

Paris clenched her teeth, opened her mouth to say something, then changed her mind, nodded, turned and walked off the bridge. Her two crew members looked at one another, then at Morian, then turned and followed her.

"The bridge is yours, Commander Jadern," Morian

said as he too walked off the bridge into the corridor where he met Danis, who was still in her flight suit and somewhat out of breath, with a sheen of perspiration glistening on her dark skin.

Morian jerked his head toward the briefing room, and together they entered to find Paris and what was left of her crew already waiting for them.

They were angry, sullen, ashen-faced and obviously in shock. Danis froze, surprised by the assembly and unprepared for it; she stood back and tried to gather her thoughts.

"Please sit down," Morian said, taking his seat at the head of the table. Danis took the seat next to him. "Welcome aboard the *Avenger*. I'm sorry for your loss and cannot begin to imagine how you must feel."

He's so calm, Danis thought, *but I bet he's seething inside.*

"The Swarm has left our immediate area but is still engaged with the fleet," Morian continued. "Apparently, they think we are also disabled. Fortunately, that gives us some time to complete our mission. We'll just have to make the most of what we have."

Paris glared at him, leaned forward and spread her arms out across the table.

"Members of *Mariposa*'s crew," she said, her eyes locked on Morian's. "I am proud of you. You fought bravely today. Our vessel and our crewmates may be gone, but we still live. This enemy will be defeated. We have merely lost a battle."

Morian maintained eye contact. *She may be spoiled and petty,* he thought, *but at least she knows the right words to say to her crew in their time of need. Whether she actually believes those words or not is something we'll probably never know.*

"Captain Paris, if I may?" Morian said without emotion. "Commander Morian will escort your crew to the passenger deck if they wish. There are refreshments, clean uniforms, food, and anything else you may need."

Paris looked at her crew and nodded.

"If you'll follow me, then," Danis said and rose to her feet.

Once the last of *Mariposa*'s crew had left, Morian closed the door and returned to his seat and opened his mouth to speak, but Paris beat him to it. "You pulled back and left us to fight alone. You are responsible for the destruction of my ship."

"Ridiculous. That is an insane accusation, Captain. You broke formation. Had you followed my command and stayed with us, you would still have your ship."

Paris's face turned redder than ever. She leaned forward in her chair, clasped her hands together in front of her, and said, "Captain Morian. I heard what Fleet Commander Hammond said when he placed you in charge. But on the battlefield, sometimes such decisions are made when there are conditions of which the Fleet Commander is unaware. Your elevation to command was one of them, and he was wrong."

"What the hell are you talking about?" Morian snapped.

Paris smiled, leaned back and folded her arms. It was as if she knew she had an ace up her sleeve.

What's her game? he wondered.

"You forget, Captain Morian, that my ID number is in the three-hundreds. Three twenty-nine, to be exact."

Morian shook his head. "So?"

"Yours is four zero five and even though we are the same rank, as captains, USF Incident Command SOP, paragraph seventeen A says that, during a time of war, if an emergency ranking decision needs to be made, the chain of command automatically falls to the senior officer. That would be me."

Morian was stunned. "What?"

"That's right, Captain Morian. I am senior to you. And therefore, I will be assuming command of this mission and of the *Avenger*. You are dismissed, Captain."

This lady's completely out of her mind, he thought.

The very idea of someone taking over the *Avenger* took him right to the edge, but he restrained himself from erupting. *If Paris thinks she's going to walk onto this ship and tell me to stand down, she has another thing coming.*

She taunted him by raising her eyebrows, thinking he had nothing to say. She thought she'd won but, in reality, she had no idea he wasn't even going to play her game. He leaned forward, narrowed his eyes and stared at her.

"Dismissed, am I?" he said quietly. "Captain Paris. I recommend you be extremely careful with your words. My cam is on at all times." He touched his forearm screen. "It's been recording since our first battle. All briefing room conversations are recorded. If you speak treason in time of war again, if you undermine or threaten my command in any way, I will have you arrested and removed to the brig. And when this is all over, I will have the evidence, your words, not mine, to have you locked away for the rest of your life."

Her smile disappeared. "But I—"

"This is not some game, Paris. This is not some academy tabletop exercise. We're not out there shooting target drones. People died today, your people and mine. Get your head out of your ass and drop the ego."

"But the manual states—"

"Shove the manual, Paris," he said so loudly she blinked in surprise. "The manual was written decades ago by someone who'd never been to war. That manual gets thrown out into space if it doesn't help us beat the enemy, and it doesn't. Screw the manual. We have to survive. You lost your ship; that's on you whether you like it or not. So, just because your academy graduation number happens to come before mine, it means nothing. We're both captains. The day I lose my ship and take to my escape pod and you rescue me, I'll follow your lead. Until then, we'll operate in today's reality. And in that reality, Fleet Admiral Hammond assigned me as the Task Force Commander, and you will obey my orders or face a court-martial.

"The *Avenger* is my ship," he continued, "and you are merely a passenger. If it hadn't been for me and my crew, you would be a frozen corpse floating in the vacuum of space. I don't need your thanks, nor do I want them. But if you want to remain on my ship and out of the brig, you will not challenge my command again. Regardless of our personal differences, I want you to know I am truly sorry for your loss. I tried to help, but there is much we cannot control in battle. Whatever differences we may have about tactics, they can wait. I am happy to debrief the incident whenever you are, but on my ship, it will be done professionally and according to the book."

Morian stopped talking as he realized he was running out of breath. No one had ever made him so angry.

Paris stood and stuck out her chin. "Very well, *Commodore*." She said his acting title with sarcastic disdain, and Morian realized that how she conducted herself in person-to-person conversation was clearly a representation of how she commanded her ship, which made her loss no surprise. Bad leadership kills.

"If you can get your massive ego out of the way," Morian said, "you might remember that we still have a Tier One mission to complete. I will gladly accept your help if you can work with me and my crew. We need a new plan, and I am willing to forgive your comments and allow you back on my bridge."

He waited for a response. None came. She tried to hide her anger.

"I don't know how you run your ship, Captain Paris," Morian said. "But aboard the *Avenger*, an officer does not storm onto the captain's bridge and lecture him on battle-field failures. Especially when that captain is the one and only reason you're standing there. Is that clear?"

"Very well, Captain Morian. Thank you for your rescue. I would like to remain with my crew." She moved to the door.

Morian watched her leave, relieved by her decision. His data pad buzzed. He glanced at it, tapped it and said, "I'll be there in just a minute, Commander."

Chapter Twenty

Chain of Command

Pricus System

Tor controlled space

Morian was seated in his command chair, watching the planet Tor grow larger on the view screen. He glanced left and right and inwardly shook his head. All of his screens were clear—not an enemy ship within a thousand kilometers.

"Long-range scanners, Lieutenant Fargo," he said.

"Aye, sir," the weapons officer replied.

"How long to deployment, Mr. Jadern?" he asked.

"We'll be entering the planet's exosphere in twelve-minutes-forty-two-seconds," Jadern replied.

"Good. Thank you. Have Captain Paris and Commander Morian join us in the briefing room. Let's go."

Morian stood, turned and left the bridge. Jadern hurried after him, talking into his data pad.

Paris, Morian knew, had decided to pout and confine herself to the passenger quarters, which suited him fine. But he did want to follow Admiral Hammond's orders, which meant he had to include her in the strategic planning of the mission, which is why he'd had Jadern send her an invitation, hoping she'd refuse.

He was disappointed. Not only was she there, so was Prince Felder. He closed his eyes and muttered a curse. Getting rid of Felder would be a hassle he just didn't have the time for.

He took his seat at the table and began, without acknowledging Felder.

"We don't have much time," he said. "We'll be entering Tor's atmosphere in less than ten minutes. Domino, what do you have?" He looked at his sister.

"Since we have no support ships or transports, our only choice is to go in with fighters and a shuttle. I have six functional fighters standing by along with shuttlecraft 2. Five pilots from *Avenger*, including me, and one from *Mariposa*."

Danis tapped the screen on her forearm. A satellite view of Pricus City replaced the view of the planet on the hologram.

"If we launch on our current heading," Danis continued, "the shortest route to Pricus City is vector three five two, which will bring us in... here." She tapped the screen again and the route was displayed on the hologram as a looping yellow line. "We should be able to make visual contact with Pricus City within twenty-two minutes of deployment. We'll land the marines and they'll recon the town and try to establish comms. We haven't heard from the planet in more than thirty-seven hours, so there's no way of telling what's happening down there."

"What if you encounter those things down there?" Paris asked.

"We'll stay in tight formation and establish a synchronous orbit over the city," Danis replied. "We can fight in the atmosphere, but we have no idea of the Swarm ship's capabilities. We'll just have to play it as we find it."

"What about the prince?" Jadern asked.

"Our plan is to locate the prince as soon as possible and fly him out on the shuttle," Danis replied. "If we need to do more, we'll have to try to coordinate with the USF fleet. It's not perfect, but it's all we can do with what little time we have. Captain, we have to go now."

"If you can't establish comms down there, we won't be able to help you," Morian said. "You'll be on your own."

Danis nodded and said, "Understood, Captain. Our first goal will be to link up with the Pricus City defense forces and start from there."

"Our last intel from the Orso system," Morian said, "is that Prince Elio was traveling with Duke Steren. So, your mission is to extract two royals. Elio should have activated his emergency beacon. If so, it should give the marines his location."

"If he's still with his ship," Paris said, leaning back in her seat, her arms folded across her chest.

Morian looked at Jadern and nodded.

"*Avenger*'s role will be to maintain synchronous orbit at thirty-thousand kilometers," Jadern said, "just beyond the planet's exobase until Ranger Squadron and the shuttle return."

"And if we're attacked and have to move?" Morian asked.

Jadern nodded. "Alternative rendezvous locations have already been provided to Domino and her pilots and have also been uploaded to *Avenger*'s navs."

"Very well, then," Morian said, rising to his feet. "Good hunting."

"Captain." Prince Felder raised his finger in the air.

Inwardly, Morian closed his eyes and sighed. "Yes, Prince Felder."

"I feel it's important to let you know that my assistant, Mister Tenilo, has some very important news for you. He has some ideas about weaponry we can use against the Swarm ships."

"This is not the time for such a discussion," Morian snapped impatiently. "Time is of the essence. We can discuss your assistant's *ideas* later when we have more time. Now, if you don't mind, I have a ship to run and a mission to complete."

The room was silent. They were visibly shocked that Morian spoke so flippantly to the prince. Danis actually gasped.

"Captain, I can assure you, Tenilo is quite brilliant when it comes to such things—"

Morian clapped his hands, interrupting him and said, "As I said, I'll be more than happy to speak to Mister Tenilo, *later!*"

Now, not only had he given the prince attitude, but he'd literally interrupted him. And the look on Felder's face made it clear that he wasn't used to being treated that way. He looked sideways at Paris. Paris smiled at him. Morian caught both looks. *What game are they playing now?* he wondered.

"Go to your squadron, Commander," Morian said. "Mr. Jadern, please return to the bridge. I'll join you there shortly. Thank you, Captain Paris. We'll talk later."

He waited until they'd cleared the room and the door had closed behind them, then turned to Felder and said, "I feel I should apologize, my prince, but the ship and battle operations and my mission for the king are my first priorities. I apologize if I disrespected you, but I needed to deploy my fighters. We can talk once they are away."

The prince smiled and slowly nodded and said, "Apology accepted, Captain. I totally understand."

Morian brought his heels together, bowed his head slightly, then turned and walked out of the room. He'd apologized, not because he thought he'd done anything to apologize for, but purely out of a need to diffuse a potentially volatile situation.

Offending a sovereign prince wasn't something he did often—not ever, in fact—but he'd lost a lot of good people. Nor did he care about offending Paris or any other person on the ship. They were at war. Pricus City could be under enemy occupation at that very moment. If they were going to survive and complete the mission, they were going to have to listen to him and follow orders. Dealing with the Swarm was difficult enough, and he couldn't afford to let an ambitious prince and a rogue captain get in his way.

He was already at the bridge door when he became

aware of the tension deep within his mind and body. He stopped before the closed door. Why he didn't know. Something had stopped him. What it was, he couldn't tell. A feeling? Something told him to stop and relax. *What's wrong with me?* he thought. *Am I losing it? Is the stress getting to me?* He closed his eyes and took a deep breath, then another, and he felt his muscles begin to relax.

His data pad buzzed. He had a message from Danis. Two words, "Relax. Breathe."

That's... that's just too weird, he thought.

The bridge door opened to reveal Sandra Lowry. She was startled to see him standing so close to the door.

"Captain, you look pale. Is everything all right?" she asked.

"Yes, of course."

She hesitated, then said, "When was the last time you ate, sir?"

Morian was taken aback. He had to think. "I... I don't know."

"Well, can I get you something? An energy bar? Some water perhaps?"

"No, Sandra, but thank you. I'll get something when the fighters have launched and we know what we're up against."

She nodded, stepped forward and past him.

"Domino to Bridge," Danis's voice came over the comms.

Morian went to his chair, sat down, and said, "Go ahead, Domino."

"Squadron ready, awaiting launch command," she replied.

Morian turned to Jadern and lifted his chin. Jadern gave him a thumbs up.

"You're a go for launch, Domino."

"Copy that, Captain." The Comm went dead.

Morian leaned back in his chair and thoughtfully stroked his chin. The mission was in her hands now. His job was to watch her back.

Chapter Twenty-One

Royal Power

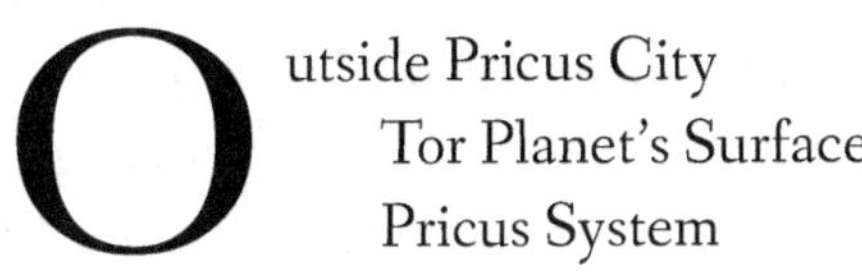

utside Pricus City
Tor Planet's Surface
Pricus System

Between them, Elio and Gian picked up the unconscious Andra and carried her to the closest house. The house was dark and appeared to be abandoned. They approached the back door and, without stopping, Gian kicked it open.

"Hello?" Elio shouted. "Hello? We need help."

Gently, they laid Andra on the floor. Elio looked at Gian and put his fingers to his lips. Gian nodded. They listened. All was quiet.

"Anybody home?" Gian shouted. Nothing.

Elio tapped his data pad. The green light from the screen did little to illuminate the small room. He looked for a light switch. After finding one by the back door, he tapped the button. Nothing.

"The power's out," he said. "We'll have to make do until morning."

He knelt down beside Andra. The green light from his data pad gave her face a ghastly, unearthly look. Gian knelt next to her and gently moved her hair away from her face.

"She's breathing," Elio said as he rose to his feet. He gasped as pain shot through his knee.

He limped into the next room, looking for the kitchen. He found it, went to the sink and turned on the tap. Nothing. He began to search the kitchen and eventually found two three-liter disposable containers of purified water—one half empty—in a cupboard. He tried the cap on the full one. The seal was intact. He rummaged through the cupboards, found a tall polymer glass, half filled it with the lukewarm water and took it to Andra.

To his surprise, she was already coming around.

"Hey, just take it easy," Gian said. "You're doing fine now. You're safe. It's just me and... It's just us."

Andra blinked, looked at Gian and said, "What happened?"

"They blew up the gravcar," Gian said.

"Here, have her drink this," Elio said and handed the glass to Gian.

Gian held the glass to Andra's lips. She took a small sip, then coughed and spit it out.

"What is that?" she asked. "It's hot, disgusting."

"It's water," Elio said. "It's warm, yes, but it will make you feel better. Try again."

She took another small sip, closed her eyes, grimaced, then swallowed. "Oh, that's nasty. I can't drink any more of it." She looked around. "Where are the others?"

"Hamel and the Duke are dead," Gian said.

"Oh no." Andra winced, closed her eyes again, licked her lips then said, "Please, I can sit up."

Gian gently helped her sit up.

"What happened?" she asked. "All I remember is watching you fighting those... whatever they were. I wanted to help, but I couldn't move. The last thing I remember is Elio throwing a rock at one of them... He was about to kill you! I must have blacked out. How did you survive?"

Elio looked at Gian. He was speechless. He just rolled his shoulders and shook his head, not knowing how to answer her.

"I don't think you were exactly... helpless," Elio said.

"What do you mean?" Andra asked.

"I can't believe you don't remember," Elio said, sucking in a breath between his teeth.

"Remember what?"

"The rock," Elio said.

"What rock?"

"The one you killed the alien with," Elio said.

She stared at him, her eyes wide, mouth open. "I killed the alien? With... the rock?" she asked hesitantly.

Elio nodded.

She looked at Gian.

He also nodded, then grinned at her.

Slowly it was coming back to her.

"The rock?" Andra asked again, squinting and

rubbing her forehead.

"Yes, the rock," Elio said, standing up. "We both saw you do it. Somehow, you caused a rock the size of Gian's fist to fly into that creature's head. Then you passed out."

Andra looked up at him, shaking her head. "How? I mean... I did that? Are you sure?"

"Yes!" Gian said. "I wouldn't be here now if you hadn't. You saved my life, Elio's, too."

"He's right," Elio said. "I know I didn't do it. I was flat out on the ground. How did you do it?"

"I... I don't know!"

"I've never seen anything like it," Gian said. "I mean, it was like... it was like it had been shot from a railgun."

"Neither have I," Elio said. "It must have been..." he paused, took a deep breath, swallowed, then continued. "It had to have been TK."

"TK?" Gian looked up at Elio, his head tilted to one side. "Are you serious? TK... as in telekinesis? Like in the old stories? That wasn't real."

"We don't know if it was real or not," Elio said.

"That was just propaganda your people used after they won The Purge," Gian said sarcastically. "Everybody knows that."

"What else could it have been, then?" Elio asked.

Gian looked at Andra. They both shook their heads in disbelief.

"Andra, your family is of a royal bloodline, is that not true?" Elio asked.

"Ye-es, but that was a long time ago—hundreds of years ago."

"It's true the stories of telekinesis are ancient legend,"

Elio said, sitting down on the floor beside her. "There are no official records, but we've all read the stories. There has to be some truth in them. They say telekinesis was used by members of the heroic families—the royal families."

"Then why don't you have it?" Gian asked skeptically.

Elio shrugged. "I don't know," he said. "Who knows who had what and when?"

"That can't be right." Andra grabbed the container, took another drink, grimaced, and said, "Maybe I just dreamed it or something. I did hit my head."

"No, Andra. We saw it." Gian rested his hand on her shoulder. "It's the craziest thing I ever saw. I mean, that rock... It just up and flew at that thing, then you passed out. It had to have been you. There's no other explanation. We'd be dead if not for you."

"Andra," Elio said, "can you remember what you were thinking? I mean, did you consciously try to move it?"

"No..." she replied hesitantly. "I was in pain. My ears were ringing. I couldn't hear anything. I saw you guys fighting and I wanted to help. That's all I know."

"And then what?" Elio asked.

Andra scrunched her face in thought, then looked at Elio and said, "I saw you throw a rock at one of the aliens, but you missed. I know I wanted to get up and help, but I couldn't move my legs." She closed her eyes and looked away, then continued.

"I saw the rock. I didn't want you to be killed. I... stared at it. Then... it just seemed to take off and fly through the air, and it hit that thing in the head. The next thing I remember is when I woke up here."

Elio stared at her, not knowing what to say or think. He thought he heard something outside and looked up, listening, but he heard nothing. "We need to go," he said and rose to his feet.

Gian nodded, poured some of the tepid water onto his hands and washed the dried blood from his face. Then he tore the sleeve off his shirt and wrapped it around the cut on his arm.

"Here, let me," Elio said and tied it for him.

"We need to get back to the mansion and find your father," Gian said, then he turned to Elio. "And your ship."

Elio nodded.

"Andra, can you walk?" Gian asked

"Yes, I think so, if you'll give me a hand."

They helped her to her feet.

"Your bot," Andra said. "I don't think he survived the crash."

Elio shrugged. "True. Duke Steren didn't make it either."

"Thank you, Elio," Gian said.

"For what?"

"For saving me back there. You saved my life. You both did. If you hadn't tackled that thing when you did, I would have been vaporized. And I'm sorry for... well, you know." He held out his hand.

Elio studied it for a second, then reached out, shook his hand, smiled and said, "Forget it. Come on. Let's get out of here."

Chapter Twenty-Two

In and Out

The Avenger
Battle Space
Pricus System

"Thank you for seeing me, Captain Morian." Tenilo pushed his glasses farther up the bridge of his nose with a forefinger. He seemed a little out of place in the captain's stateroom.

All was quiet on the *Avenger* and, Morian hoped it would remain so until they received the next location marker signal from Danis once she entered Tor's atmosphere. In the meantime, all they could do was wait. So, having put Felder and his assistant off for as long as he could, he'd decided to get it over with.

Morian was seated at his desk. The prince, Tenilo

and April sat across from him. "What do you have for me, Mister Tenilo?" he asked.

"Well, as you know, we've had plenty of spare time since we came aboard and well, your hangar bay engineer was kind enough to show me the footage from the Pallas battle."

The engineer? Morian thought. *How the hell did he get hold of that?*

Morian looked at Badeaux, hoping she hadn't already distributed the footage to the systems. Instinctively, he checked his data pad. He tapped the screen a couple of times, then inwardly nodded to himself, having confirmed the ship's comms were still locked down.

"And," Tenilo continued, "I have spent a great deal of time analyzing said footage, and I am excited to announce I have made some very interesting observations."

"And they are?" Morian asked.

"For one, I have analyzed the footage of our weaponry making hits on the enemy Swarm craft many times, and I keep reaching the same conclusion."

"And what instruments did you use to make your analysis?" Morian asked.

Tenilo smiled nervously, his forehead glistening. "I uh... well, I don't have access to the instruments I'm used to back home in my lab, so I uh... I just had to slow the footage down and watch it through frame by frame."

"I see," Morian said, folding his arms and leaning back in his chair. "So, you've just watched the footage over and over?"

"Yes, but—"

"As have I," Morian said. "I've watched that footage

dozens of times myself." *And more importantly,* he thought, *I've also replayed my own actions and reactions during the battle in my head ever since we left the Pallas System.*

"After watching the footage," Tenilo continued, "I was able to see how our directed energy weapons affected the Swarm craft."

"They are almost ineffective. We know that," Morian said.

"Yes, but—"

"I'm sorry, Mister Tenilo," Morian said. "I don't mean to interrupt, but I do have a Tier One mission just minutes away from making contact."

Morian leaned forward and rested his elbows on the table. "Remind me again of your role on Prince Felder's staff?"

"Uh... well, sir, I am the Prince's Chief Historian."

"Historian? You're not an engineer, not a weapons specialist?"

"No, sir."

"What about your standing in the Alastor System? Did you graduate in STEM, tech or statistics?"

"No, sir." Tenilo was sweating. "I graduated from the School of the Arts. My major was Inter-system History with an emphasis on the Restoration Era."

"Any service in the USF?" Morian asked, a slight smile on his lips.

"No, sir."

"I see. I'm just trying to understand your qualifications in the study of combat footage."

"Your point is well taken, Captain," Felder said.

"Mister Tenilo knows his place, and that's why he is grateful for your audience. Let me assure you, Captain, his ideas are worth listening to. Please give him a chance to explain."

"What ideas, Mister Tenilo?" Richard asked.

"In reviewing footage of the direct hits of our DEW weapons compared to those of the missiles, I noticed the reactions on the craft surface to be well... identical."

Morian smiled. "What do you mean? We know them to be completely different. DEW weapons do nothing; missiles degrade their power, their shields. That's all we know so far."

"Yes, agreed, Captain. I am not referring to the actual effect of the weaponry. I am talking specifically about the reaction of the Swarm craft's surface." Tenilo leaned in and began talking faster. He seemed happy to finally be getting into the details.

"And?" Morian asked, suddenly intrigued.

Tenilo smiled and began talking kilometers per second. "You see, after seeing the craft absorb enough direct hits by the *Avenger*'s guns, I was reminded of the post-Purge period of the Orso system."

"Why?"

"Because, Captain, during that time, the USF, as young as it was back then, ran through a period when plasma weaponry was of the utmost superiority in battle. The USF plasma weaponry was developed by refining the rare Cheloniam isotopes, first discovered in the Viox System in 2530."

Richard was already losing interest. Tenilo was smart, but he was using too many words. "You lost me," he said. "Plasma was phased out and replaced by DEW tech. How does this relate to the *Avenger*'s weapons?"

"You see, Captain. When USF vessels began using silicon plasma weapon blasts, they couldn't find a single weakness in its makeup. So, they began storing more and more of the silicon in the vessels. Silicon XD, to be precise. These were pre-numeric class ships, nothing like the *Avenger* was around at the time... But I digress... so, a certain ship, a huge, lumbering vessel, a heavy cruiser named the *Gloryberg*, was loaded with massive stores of silicon in tanks for resupplying the ships in orbit above the planet's surface."

"The captain most likely does not need to know all of the specifics, Mister Tenilo," Felder said. "Remember to stay with the relevant details."

Even Felder noticed Tenilo's mouth was running away with him. Richard looked at Felder. They shared a look that made Richard feel, for the first time, thankful Felder was there.

"Yes, yes, apologies. The *Gloryberg* blew an engine on takeoff and the extra weight prevented the backup grav engines from firing. A list of other technical components also failed, like dominos. The *Gloryberg* crash-landed on the tarmac and all aboard lost their lives."

Morian breathed deeply, trying to keep his patience.

"I am one of the few people who have seen the footage from the *Gloryberg* security cameras, from inside the vessel as it crashed. It was old digital data stored away at the Generon University Library, a fascinating find. Anyway, when the vessel crashed, obviously the silicon XD exploded. But what is key here is the footage. When those silicon tanks blew, they did not explode as one might think, like watching a normal silicon blast. When that form of silicon destabilizes, it flies apart, shattering like glass. But only for an instant. It is silicon, then glass, then light, then it's gone. It reacted like nothing I have ever seen. The very chemical nature of its makeup allows the silicon to literally turn into a solid just before explosion. But this only happens when enough silicon is stored in one mass."

"Get back to the Pallas holo," Felder said.

"Yes, the surface of the Swarm craft reacts in much the same way. It reacts exactly like the silicon on the *Gloryberg* did."

"So, you are saying the Swarm ships shoot plasma. We know this."

"No, Captain. That's the point. Well, yes, the Swarm uses plasma weapons, that's true, but what I'm telling you is that these ships are made out of silicon."

Silence.

"What did you say?" Morian asked.

"Their craft, they're constructed from silicon."

"That can't be," Morian said. "Silicon is unstable."

"Yes, silicon as we know it," Tenilo said, nodding furiously. "But, am I not correct that this is an unknown alien enemy we've not encountered before? We don't know anything about them; how they travel without using the Slipstream; where they come from... There's much we don't understand. The nature and makeup of the silicon they are using could also be new. Certainly it is impervious to DEW weaponry, nuclear energy, and explosives.

Even the explosive railgun rounds have no effect on them."

"Silicon?" Morian asked.

Tenilo nodded. "Silicon!"

Morian nodded and said, "Interesting. I'll have the science and engineering staff look into it. I'll also arrange for you to meet with our senior science officer, Dr. Tobbs."

Tenilo smiled, bowed his head slightly and said, "Thank you, Captain."

Morian's data screen buzzed. Danis was about to enter Tor's atmosphere. Richard stood to leave.

"Captain," Tenilo said, "one more minute, if you please. My point is that the silicon is weak, very weak."

"We are already using missiles, to little effect." Morian moved to the door.

"Yes, but—"

"Do please excuse me, Mister Tenilo," Morian said, "but our mission is about to enter the next phase and I'm needed on the bridge. Thank you, Prince Felder."

Chapter Twenty-Three

Overwhelmed

The Avenger
Battle Space
Pricus System

Danis had her fighters grouped together in two arrowhead formations of three, one behind the other with the shuttle following close behind. She was preparing to enter Tor's atmosphere when her screens lit up. She was flying without her co-pilot, Zilvo, as were all the other pilots, so there was no early warning.

"Three marks coming in at three five," Ranger Seven said.

"Stars, those things are fast," someone else said.

The blips appeared at the edge of her targeting screen, moving fast.

"Ranger One to Ranger Seven. Break off," Danis said. "Stay together. Divide them up. Protect the shuttle."

Danis and her two wingmen turned hard to starboard. One of the Swarm fighters broke formation and chased after her.

"On my mark," she said, "reverse thrusters and take it head-on, line astern. You know the drill."

She streaked away at full throttle, Rangers Two and Eight close on her tail, the enemy fighter following, gaining fast.

"Steady..." she said quietly, "steady... *Mark!*"

She slammed all four of her thrusters into reverse, flipped the F32A end-over-end, and slammed the throttle forward. Her targeting computer locked on and she fired her first pair of missiles almost at point-blank range. She had no time to see if they hit. She made a hard turn to port, reversed her thrusters again, spun the fighter and fell in behind Ranger Eight just as Sheva in Ranger Two fired his first salvo, and she watched as they slammed into the wallowing Swarm craft. In less than the blink of an eye, Sheva turned hard to port and Ranger Eight followed him in. Two more missiles hit the enemy craft. She gave it no time to recover. She hit it with two more. The blue craft rocked, its halo dying as it continued on like a meteor into Tor's atmosphere.

"Domino to Avenger," Danis snapped. "We're under attack. Prepare to receive the shuttle. We're heading home."

"Received and understood, Domino," the hangar chief replied.

She was down to two missiles. Her two wingmen had

four each. *One more,* she thought. *We can take one more. Five, seven and... should be able to handle the other one.*

It was only then she realized she didn't even know the *Mariposa* pilot's name.

Oh hell! she thought as three more enemy fighters appeared on her screens, then three more. *Where the hell are they coming from?*

"Rangers Two and Eight," she yelled. "Sheva, we'll take the one to the right. Ranger Seven, you take the other one, then we get the hell out of here and back to *Avenger.*"

Avenger turned, presenting her starboard side to the oncoming enemy fighters and fired a broadside of sixteen Mark 47 Saber missiles at the six incoming enemy craft.

Four of the missiles missed their targets, but twelve hit home, taking out three of the enemy fighters. A second broadside took out two more.

Sheva locked onto his target and fired his second pair of missiles. Danis throttled back, watched them hit home, then followed Seven in. She launched her final pair, turned hard to starboard, cut her thrusters, flipped the fighter, slammed the yoke hard to port, hit the thrusters and the F32 rocketed away with a Swarm ship close on her tail, but by then she was flying close to her ship's maximum speed, almost Mach 32, and turning hard to port. The enemy was faster, much faster, but not as maneuverable. It flew by, firing its weapons. She looped to starboard and reversed thrust. The twin beams of plasma flashed past in front of her, lighting up her cockpit and temporarily blinding her. She blinked twice, trying to rid herself of the white lights in front of her eyes. She shook her head. Her vision cleared.

"Domino to Ranger squadron," she shouted. "Fall back to *Avenger* and rearm. Do it *now!*"

But it wasn't that easy. More and more of the enemy craft were approaching. Her screens were lit up. She counted nineteen of them.

Danis dodged two more plasma blasts as she raced for the hangar doors.

It was at that moment when Ranger Five, at a high rate of speed, coming in from behind, flew across her field of view. Five was turning fast, coming around to fire on another ship, when a blinding flash of blue light came out of nowhere and struck Five's fighter midship. The F32 exploded in a ball of orange fire, leaving nothing but a few small pieces of twisted metal spinning wildly. Danis had no time to contemplate the death of her teammate. Enemy fighters were all around her. She had to keep moving—to reach *Avenger* and safety.

Morian was deep in thought, watching the progress of the battle from the bridge rail. It wasn't going well. *Avenger* was surrounded. He counted twenty-seven enemy craft. He'd lost two fighters, that he knew of. They were taking the enemy down but at what cost, and for how long? *As long as we have ammunition and the hull holds,* he thought. *Not long now!*

"We're running out of missiles, sir," Fargo shouted.

That's not like her, Morian thought.

"Status, please, Lieutenant?" Morian said calmly.

"Less than five percent in bays two and four. Ten percent in one and three."

Morian cursed himself. *Damn! I should have insisted on a resupply before we left.*

"Shields at twenty-three percent, Captain," Jadern said. "We're not going to be able to hold them much longer."

A blast rocked the ship.

"Hull breach aft on deck three," Jadern shouted.

"Damage control?" Morian said.

There was a moment of silence then, "Chief Master Sergeant Logan Ryan here, Captain. Hull breach in Section 3A7. We're venting atmosphere. The gun turret is gone. We have the section locked down and we're sealing the breach. We need thirty... twenty minutes."

"You have fifteen minutes, Chief."

Morian looked down at the hologram. It didn't look good. Here and there a blue dot flared and blinked out. They were killing them, but with each kill, the more their stock of missiles was further depleted. *It's just a matter of time,* he thought.

"Domino to Avenger." *She sounds stressed.*

"Talk to me, Danis," Morian said. "What's your status?"

"I'm taking heavy losses and I'm out of missiles."

"Where are you," Morian asked. "Can you make it to the hangar?"

"Coming up on your port side. Two on my tail."

Richard instinctively looked at the port side weapons officer. "Do you see her?"

"She's in view now, sir." The man spoke without taking his eyes off the screen.

"Can you provide cover?" Morian asked.

"Tubes P6 and 7 just fired their last missiles, sir. Switching to DEW cannons."

"Belay that, Lieutenant," Morian snapped. "Lasers are virtually useless. Have them switch to railguns: fifty cal' explosive rounds. Have them lay down a curtain while we get her inside."

Railguns, Morian thought savagely. *That's what we're reduced to? We might as well throw rocks at them, but it's all we have, damn it.*

"I need help, Avenger," Danis shouted. "I can't shake them."

"Railguns, *now!*" Morian shouted.

He needn't have shouted. Even before the words were out of his mouth, a stream of projectiles, thousands of rounds from P7, impacted one of the enemy craft and it exploded in a blinding flash of white light. P7 fired again at the second Swarm ship with similar results. The bridge crew, all of them, including Morian, were silent, many of them with their eyes wide and their mouths hanging open in total disbelief.

"What the hell was that, Avenger?" Danis said, obviously in shock."

"Put me through to P7," Morian said. "Do it now."

"Turret P7," a gruff voice answered.

"Who am I talking to?" Morian asked.

"Gunnery Sergeant Pavlov. Who am I talking to?"

"Captain Morian. What the hell did you do, Gunny?"

"We were all out of explosive projectiles, sir. I had to use fifty-cal' kinetic slugs."

"You're telling me you destroyed two enemy craft using steel slugs?" Morian asked incredulously.

"Well, yes, sir. No, sir. Not steel, sir. Depleted uranium."

"Lieutenant Fargo," Morian said sharply. "Belay the missiles. All turrets switch to railguns. Depleted rounds. Do it now, Lieutenant."

His order was quickly acknowledged and they made the switch. Unfortunately, only ten of his twenty-four-point defense turrets had railgun capability, and three of those were out. Only seven remained: one one-hundred-twenty-caliber gun mounted above and to the rear of the command bridge, four on the port side and two on the starboard side.

It took several minutes to change ammunition from explosive to kinetic rounds, but then, when they commenced firing, the swarm of enemy craft began to explode and die. Morian didn't understand it, but he didn't care. All he knew was that he was beginning to win. How and why he could figure out later.

* * *

Railguns? Danis thought when she heard the news. *Are you kidding me?* She looked around as her F32 approached *Avenger*'s hangar door. Not only were the railguns taking out the enemy craft, but those that remained were leaving.

"Domino to Avenger. The enemy is... retreating."

"We see it, Domino," Morian replied.

Danis, slowly approaching the hangar doors, suddenly remembered Ranger Five's destruction, right in front of her.

"Domino to Ranger Squadron. Report in."

"Ranger Eight. I'm right behind you."

"Ranger Seven. Me, too."

Danis waited for a moment, then said, "That it? Just two?"

"Looks like it," Seven said.

Danis checked her screens to make sure she was clear, then veered away from the open hangar doors, a sick feeling boiling in her gut. *They're all gone? Just me, Seven and Eight left? Oh m'God! It can't be.*

"Seven and Eight check visuals," Danis said. "I want to know who else is out there. Maybe their comms are down."

"Copy, Domino."

Danis circled around *Avenger* looking for disabled fighters, but she found none; neither did Seven and Eight. *Sheva gone? Only three of us left.* Tears ran down her cheeks, but there was nothing she could do about it; she was sealed inside her inertia suit.

She set the F32 down inside the empty hangar, empty but for the three fighters still undergoing maintenance, Prince Felder's ship and the ship's two shuttles. The hangar seemed vast, an empty cave, a sad reminder of lost friends.

Seven and Eight touched down beside her, the doors closed and they waited for the hangar to pressurize. The green lights flashed, and Danis opened her canopy and removed her helmet. She quickly wiped the sweat from her forehead and the tears from her cheeks. A crew member clamped a ladder to the edge of her cockpit, then climbed up and handed her a fresh hydro pack. She replaced her half-empty pack, checked the fighter's power cells and nodded to herself; they were at eighty-three percent. The crew was already reloading her six missile pods.

"If only it could hold about twenty more of those," she muttered to herself.

"It appears railguns will be enough to do the job," she heard someone say. Morian reached the top of the ladder, smiled at her, then leaned in and kissed her on her forehead.

"Hey," Danis said. "Railguns, huh?"

Richard nodded. "Apparently, yes."

"How's that possible?" Danis asked. "Nothing can get through their shields. Well, not missiles."

"We don't know," Morian replied. "Tobbs and his people are on it, though. I'm hoping they'll be able to figure it out... Danis, are you all right? You lost a lot of pilots today."

"I'm fine," she said, looking away so her brother wouldn't see the tears starting to well in her eyes. "It was... It was not easy out there. Sheva's gone. Five... I saw Five go..." She swiped at the tears. "Look, they're almost done. I need to go. Too bad you can't come with us."

"Yes, I know." Morian reached in, took her gloved hand and squeezed it. "We'll do what we can to cover you from here, which won't be much. Just get in, get the prince, and get the hell out."

She nodded, looked him in the eye, smiled at him and said, "Sounds good, bro."

"You good to go?" Morian asked.

"Yes, sir." A buzzer sounded inside the cockpit, letting her know she was cleared for takeoff. "Good to go, Captain."

"Be safe," Morian said as he descended the steps.

"Always," she replied.

Chapter Twenty-Four

Revelations

The Avenger
Battle Space
Pricus System

Morian rode the elevator to the bridge deck, his mind in a whirl. He didn't like Danis's chances of staying alive down there, much less completing the mission, but there was nothing he could do about it. She had only two fighters for protection and God only knew what she'd find waiting for her.

He shook off the sense of impending doom that was threatening to overwhelm him and sent a message to his Chief Science Officer, Dr. Herrick Tobbs, to meet him on the bridge. The elevator door opened, and Richard stepped out to find Jadern waiting for him.

"Is everything all right, Captain?" Jadern said as he matched Morian's fast pace.

Morian stopped walking and said, "Yes. Danis is fine. Michael, I want you to ready a Search and Rescue Drone."

"An SRD? Why? Do we have missing people out there?"

"No, but we do have the chance to study those things. Come on."

Morian strode onto the bridge and focused his attention on the forward view screen.

"What do you mean?" Jadern asked.

"Look! There." Morian pointed. "What's that?"

It was white in color, spinning, but too far away and too small to make out its exact shape.

"A piece of one of the enemy ships?" Jadern asked.

"Exactly," Morian said. "I want it, and as many more pieces as we can find. It's moving quickly away from us. Get the drone out there before it's all gone."

Jadern nodded and smiled. "On it, Captain. I'll see to it personally." Then he turned and hurried away.

Morian stood with his hands behind his back, staring at the tiny piece of debris. *Who the hell are these... things?* he wondered. *Where did they come from? Why are they attacking us? We need to know.*

"Captain," Dr. Tobbs said as he stepped out of the elevator. He was older than Richard by almost sixty years. His hair was gray, but he was fit and strong and looked not a day older than fifty. His navy-blue USF uniform was a size too big for him and bloused out around his waist. "You wanted to see me?"

"Yes, doctor, thank you for coming." Richard waved him onto the bridge. "Tell me what you and your team have come up with so far."

"Not much, I'm afraid, Captain," he said, stepping up to the rail beside him. "After examining all of the available footage, we have a couple of hypotheses and one or two guesses."

"And those are?"

"Let's start with the propulsion of the craft. Each craft has four appendages, weapons, if you will, but we think they might also be part of the propulsion system."

Morian made a fist, put it to his mouth and gently chewed the side of his forefinger.

"I don't understand, doctor," he said, "We know they're weapons. How can they serve two functions?"

"We don't know, Captain," Tobbs replied. "We don't even know that they do. It's just an observation, an... uneducated guess. There are no other visible forms of propulsion. So, what else could there be?"

Morian had no answer.

"XO to Captain Morian."

Morian tapped his data pad and said, "What is it, Commander?"

"The drone is ready to deploy, sir."

"Good! Deploy," Morian said. "I want as many pieces of those alien craft as we can get."

"Aye, sir. Deploying... now."

Dr. Tobbs touched Morian's arm and said, "We have debris? We'll have physical evidence to study?"

Morian smiled. The science officer was ecstatic. "Yes, doctor, we will."

"Outstanding, sir. Thank you."

"What about the weapons? Plasma based?" Morian asked.

Tobbs nodded. "Yes, I think some form of plasma is a good starting point. From the heat signatures, we think they're either a plasma-based technology we're unfamiliar with or some kind of electrothermal-chemical technology."

Morian nodded. "I see," he said, frowning.

Tobbs shrugged. "Or it could very well be some sort of derivative of both. There's no telling what sort of technology they're using. I would very much like to see inside of one of those craft."

"And the craft themselves?" Morian asked. "Prince Felder's assistant seems to think they're made from a sort of silicon. Is that even possible?"

"Yes, anything is possible, but without samples to study, I can only hazard a guess. But I would concur with Mr. Tenilo. It's possible the enemy craft are constructed from some kind of silicon-based material."

"But—"

"Yes," Tobbs interrupted him. "I understand how difficult it is to accept such a concept, but silicon—not to be confused with silicone—is the fourteenth element on the periodic table, a metalloid with properties both metal and nonmetal, and it's the second most abundant element in the universe. Synthetic materials—polymers —with a chemical structure based on chains of alternate silicon and oxygen atoms, are typically resistant to chemical attack and insensitive to temperature changes, properties we've seen in these strange craft, which seem impervious to our DEW and explosive weaponry."

Morian stared at him, then said, "Silicone? Silicon?" He shook his head and continued. "I'll take your word for it, doctor, but isn't silicon basically glass?"

"No," Tobbs replied. "You're thinking of 'silicate glasses' based on the chemical compound silica—silicon dioxide, or quartz—the primary constituent of sand. Glass comes in many forms, some of them formed naturally in volcanos, for example. Silica glass is used where high temperatures, high thermal shock resistance, high chemical durability, very low electrical conductivity are... desired..." Seeing the look on Morian's face, he tailed off.

"So they're made of glass, then?" Morian asked.

Tobbs pulled a face, rolled his shoulders, spread his arms, and said, "I don't know. All I can do is guess. We, our universe, are carbon-based. It could be that these entities are..." Tobbs cleared his throat. "It could be these entities are from a... silicon-based universe. In which case, anything and everything is possible."

Morian stared at him in disbelief. "You can't be serious, doctor."

Tobbs merely shrugged and held his gaze.

"You are serious," Morian said, stunned by the enormity of what the doctor had said. "You're saying these things are from another dimension!"

"I'm not saying anything—yet. I just don't know, and I won't until I've had a chance to study them in detail. What I can tell you is that they appear to be bound by the same laws of physics as we are."

"S and R coming in, sir," Jadern's voice emanated from his data pad.

Morian continued to stare at Tobbs. Tobbs stared back, unflinching.

"Well, doctor," Morian said, "it looks like you're about to get your chance. The first samples are being delivered as we speak."

Chapter Twenty-Five

Domino

Planet Tor's Atmosphere
Pricus System

Danis, her two wingmen, and the shuttle descended into the exosphere, slowed their descent, and she punched in her location code that relayed her position back to *Avenger*.

"Clear skies, Domino," Eight said. "Not an enemy in sight."

"Copy that, Eight," Danis said as she began to run the numbers. She was tired. *Three battles in two days?* she thought. *It seems like a lifetime. Twenty-seven minutes! Hmm.* She missed Zilvo. Not that Zilvo was much comfort in a stressful situation; she wasn't, but she was reliable. *Can't be helped. I may need her seat for a passenger.*

"Navs to Domino." It was the *Avenger*'s controller.

"Go ahead, Navs."

"Your last location marker was received and confirmed. We'll expect an update in... nine-minutes-twenty seconds. You may find comms unstable on the surface, but we'll do what we can to stay in touch."

"Copy that, Navs."

"Captain Morian wants to speak to you. Go ahead, Captain."

"Danis?" Morian said.

"Yes, Captain."

"I've just been talking to Tobbs. He's of the opinion that the enemy craft are constructed from some sort of silicon-based material." He didn't mention Tobbs' hypothesis about them coming from an alternate universe. That was too much even for him to contemplate, much less Danis minutes out from a dangerous mission.

"Isn't that what Prince Felder's assistant said?" Danis said.

"Not in so many words, but yes, I guess he did. Maybe the little man's not the fool he appears to be after all."

"Copy that," Danis said and laughed. "Ask Tobbs what he's going to name the silicon-based material. Tell him not to name the discovery after himself."

"Will do, Domino. Good Hunting."

"Thanks, bro."

Danis checked her computers, then said, "Domino to

Ranger Squadron. Three minutes to retro burn. Stay sharp. Especially you, Shuttle Two. And remember, we go in fast, stay low, find the prince and get out again as quickly as possible. Stay together. No one flies alone."

Three minutes later, the tight little formation was less than six hundred kilometers out and streaking down through the thermosphere. Danis slowed the F32 and switched her thrusters to gravity mode. The F32 would not be quite as maneuverable, but it would still have the edge in a fight with the enemy. At least she hoped it would.

Dawn was breaking as they approached Pricus City from the southwest at a little more than Mach 2. She could see the city skyline in the distance. She checked her comms. Nothing. She eased the throttle back, adjusted her thrusters, slowed to two-hundred seventy knots, and activated her automatic scanners to search for any open transmissions, emergency signals or a signal generated by the prince's personal beacon. Again, nothing. The airwaves were dead. All she could hear was a faint static.

Again, she throttled back.

"Domino to Ranger Squadron. Stay sharp. Maintain altitude at eight-thousand meters. I'm going to take a look."

She descended to fifteen hundred meters, flew over the city, slowed her speed and circled to the east, into the sun. Her forward shields dimmed. The cockpit darkened. She turned north, skirting the city limits. As far as she could tell, the city was deserted. Many of the tall buildings had been destroyed, reduced to rubble, though the governor's mansion and much of the downtown area appeared to be intact. Smoke was rising here and there, but there were no signs of life—no sign of enemy craft.

"Domino to Ranger Squadron. All clear. Shuttle Two. You're go for the palace. Seven and Eight, stay with Two."

"This is Two. Copy that."

She reached the northern city limits and circled to the west, the sun at her back. Her forward shields cleared, and the cockpit brightened.

What the hell is that? Something rose from behind one of the buildings, something blue, and it was heading straight for her at an unbelievable speed. Then another, and another, and another.

"Watch out!" she yelled. "Multiple enemy craft incoming from the west... Oh shit. Here we go!"

She rotated her thrusters and streaked away to the east with four enemy fighters on her tail and a half-dozen more going for the shuttle and her two wingmen.

"Rangers Six and Seven..." she yelled but was unable to finish the warning. She was twisting and turning, jinking up and down, as the enemy closed on her.

She flipped the F32 end over end in a desperate attempt to give herself some space and, in so doing, was able to see that Seven and Eight were both able to get missiles away before they were hit. Plasma bolts from six enemy fighters destroyed the two fighters in less than the blink of an eye. Danis gasped.

The shuttle was almost on the ground when it was hit by a long, raking blast of blue that left nothing but a few pieces of debris smoldering on the mansion's forecourt.

And just like that, they were gone, all of them: three pilots and twelve marines. Her heart clenched.

Oh shit! Here they come!

Danis hauled back on the yoke, slammed it hard left and put the F32 into a spiraling, looping climb, then turned and headed north at a speed she didn't think the fighter capable of in the atmosphere. She checked her screens, wishing Zilvo was there to do it for her. Her thrusters were at maximum burn, but the enemy craft were still gaining on her.

Danis, shocked to her core by the loss of the last of her squadron and the shuttle, turned northeast and put her craft into a steep dive, trying for more speed.

Her proximity alarms began to shriek. She gritted her teeth. Glanced again at the screens. An enemy craft was coming at her from her eleven o'clock and closing fast. She put the F32 into a spiral dive to the right. Two bolts of blue passed over her canopy so close she was sure she could feel the heat. The enemy fighter, unable to match the F32's maneuver, continued onward in a long looping turn.

A spear of pain flashed through her frontal lobe. *A headache? Oh hell, not now.*

Holy crap. What is it? Is my suit failing? G-forces? She squinted in pain, shook her head, to no avail. *What the hell?*

"Danis?"

"Richard?" She looked at her screens. Her comms were dead. *What?*

"Danis, can you hear me?" Richard's voice said.

"Yes. I hear you. Seven and Eight are down, so's the

shuttle, and I've got three of them on my tail. It's not looking good."

"Where are you?"

What does he mean, where am I? "Pricus City, right where I'm supposed to be. I can't talk. I'm trying to lose them, but I can't."

Another bolt of blue slashed in front of her. She cut the drives and dropped like a stone just in time to avoid another lightning bolt. She hit the throttle and pulled up less than ten meters from the ground. She banked left, climbed, and performed a perfect Immelmann loop, placing her on the enemy craft's tail. She locked on and fired all six of her missiles, then turned away as yet another plasma bolt seared the paint on her upper starboard engine.

"Danis, you're in trouble," the voice in her head said.

"No shit, Captain!" she screamed back at him. He wasn't helping. "My position is—" It was at that moment she realized she could see him. Everything around her went quiet. She could hear nothing, not even the engines.

She could see him. He looked confused.

"Richard?"

"I know. I don't know how but I can see you, too. Just get out of there. Now!"

She glanced at the comms panel. The indicator was still blinking red. *No comms. Oh my God. What's happening to me?*

She put the F32 into a vertical climb at a speed that almost defied the laws of physics, dodged two more bolts of plasma, and watched as all three enemy craft flashed by below her.

"Danis," Richard said, slowly shaking his head. "You have to eject. There are too many of them."

"Oh my God, Richard. What the hell's happening? My comms are down, but I can see and hear you."

All three of her proximity alarms began to sound. She dodged one blast, then another and then another. The blasts were coming fast, too fast.

"Richard," she screamed, "help!"

She lost focus. She managed to dodge another blast. She put the F32 into a steep dive, pulled out at zero feet, almost scraping the desert floor, then pulled up into another Immelmann. This time it didn't work. The enemy had learned quickly and anticipated her. A bolt of blue plasma hit her upper port engine. The engine exploded, taking part of the wing with it, and the fighter flipped over, spinning out of control.

Danis hauled back on the yoke, adjusted her three remaining thrusters and tried to correct the spin, but all she managed to do was slow it down.

"I'm going down. I'm going down!" she yelled into the dead comms.

Chapter Twenty-Six

All is lost

The Avenger
Battle space
Pricus System

Morian stood on the bridge, disoriented, confused by what was happening. He could see and hear his sister as if she was standing next to him; he could feel her fear, her desperation. Her thoughts were flashing through his mind too fast for him to grasp. Suddenly, he could see everything that was happening through her eyes. He gripped the rail in front of him so hard his knuckles turned white. She was in a half-controlled panic, trying to outrun the Swarm craft. He flinched when she pulled up her F32 just meters from crashing into the ground, and again as the bolts of blue flashed over her canopy. She was barely holding her own, and he knew it was only a matter of time before she...

"Danis," he shouted. "You have to eject! There are too many of them."

"Captain?" Jadern's voice came from behind him. "Do you have Domino on comms? I've got nothing. I think her comms must be down."

"No... uh, yes." Morian closed his eyes and shook his head. "I... I can hear her. I can see her. She's going down. We've got to help her!"

Morian's head spun. He clamped his fists to his temples, trying to hold back the pain. He staggered back, away from the rail.

"Captain?" someone shouted.

He fell back and landed in his command chair, his head swimming. He opened his eyes. All he could see was a spinning blackness. Faintly, seemingly far, far away, he heard her scream, "I'm going down!"

Slowly, his head began to clear. He sat still. Willing himself to hear her voice, see her face, but there was nothing.

He looked up. Jadern was standing over him.

"Captain? What's wrong? What is it?" Jadern waved his hand in front of Morian's eyes, trying to get his attention. "Someone get him some water. Captain, can you hear me?" Jadern asked.

Morian took a deep breath, struggled to sit up straight, blinked several times, then said, "Yes."

"What happened?" Jadern asked, offering him the hydropack. "You passed out."

"No. No, I didn't," Morian said before taking a sip of water. He could still feel the sensations: the exhilaration, fear, sadness, anger, desperation, but the emotions weren't his. They belonged to Danis.

"She's gone," he said bitterly, "shot down."

"Who?"

"Danis. They're all gone," Morian replied quietly. "They'd just made it to Pricus City when they were attacked by an overwhelming force of Swarm ships. They were all shot down."

Jadern looked confused. "Sir, you can't know that. Domino hasn't transmitted her location code yet. We've received no transmissions from her at all. Her comms are down."

"No, she's gone. They're all gone," Morian said and took a long drink and then handed the hydro pack to Jadern. "And she will not be sending her location code. Is she dead? I don't know. I do know Rangers Seven and Eight are dead, and so is everyone aboard the shuttle. Try to link with one of the satellites. We need to find something that will work."

Jadern gave the order, then turned again to Morian and said, "Richard, I need to get you out of here. You need medical attention."

Morian looked up at him, shook his head and said, "I'm all right, Michael. It was just... I don't know what it was, but my sister was reaching out to me."

"Sir, you almost passed out. I insist you take a few minutes and visit with Doctor Dowd."

Morian glared up at him, his head pounding. Jadern

tilted his head slightly to one side, his face set, determined. Morian's expression softened. He smiled and nodded.

Chapter Twenty-Seven

It's all in the mind

The Avenger
Battle space
Pricus System

Morian was seated in the diagnostic chair in the med bay, waiting for the scan to finish. Chief Medical Officer Dr. Jyra Dowd was seated next to him consulting her data pad.

Dowd was almost eighty years old, approaching middle age, though she didn't look a day older than thirty. Her auburn hair showed no signs of gray, And her brown eyes were clear and full of life. She had amber skin, without blemish or wrinkle. Her mind was quick, intuitive and, so Morian had always thought, all-seeing.

The scanner beeped, indicating it was finished.

"How you feeling, Captain?" Dowd asked.

"I still have a headache, but much better, thank you."

"Your BP is normal—one-fifteen over sixty-two—pulse fifty-eight. Your vitals are..." She looked at him and shrugged. "...normal, for someone who's fought three battles in the last thirty-six hours." She crossed her arms, stared at him and said, "So tell me, how are you really feeling?"

Richard sat up and removed the sensor from his upper arm. "Like a captain who has been in three battles in the last thirty-six hours. Who has an interfering prince as a passenger and another captain on board who wants to take his ship. Oh, and my sister is probably dead. Other than that, I feel just fine."

Dowd unplugged his biometrics feed and nodded. "I'm sorry about Danis. If we were anywhere else, I'd say you need a week of shore leave, but since we're in the middle of a war, I suggest you drink more fluids and get as much sleep as you can."

"Thanks, doc," Morian said and started to rise from the seat.

"Before you go, Captain," Dowd said.

"Yes."

"I had a chat with Commander Jadern. He told me what happened. Why do you believe your sister's dead?"

Morian shrugged. "It's just a feeling. I can't explain it."

"Can't or won't?" Dowd said. "Commander Jadern's account of what happened is a little more than that. He's of the opinion that it's more than just a feeling. He said you grabbed your head, collapsed in your chair, and shouted, 'I'm going down.' Then you told him

Commander Morian and the entire away team had been shot down. Those are strange things to say, things you couldn't possibly know. Tell me about it, Captain."

"I told you. I can't explain it. I just... know. I'm very close to my sister. We're twins. We've always been close."

"Captain, if I may," Dowd said, "have you experienced anything like this before?"

Morian thought for a moment, then said, "No. Not that I can remember."

"Any headaches or dizziness?"

"No."

"Any other thoughts or feelings that suddenly came into your head, seemingly out of nowhere?"

"What do you mean?"

Dowd shrugged. "Just what it sounds like."

Morian had no idea what she was trying to get at, but he figured he might as well tell her.

"It was probably nothing," he said, "but earlier today, Danis and her squadron were about to launch. I'd just left the hangar after a... somewhat strained conversation with Prince Felder and was on my way back to the bridge when I suddenly had the urge to stop. Something told me to breathe and relax."

Dowd slowly nodded. Her forehead wrinkled in concentration.

"But the weird thing was, just after that I got a text from Danis that said, 'breathe, relax.'"

"Captain, I know this may sound a bit... odd, but what you're describing and what just happened to you on the bridge—your out-of-body communication with Danis —sounds a lot like telepathy to me."

He was shocked. "You're talking about Psy? That's not possible. It's part of the legend: just one of the stories."

She nodded. "That's true. They are stories, ancient tales, but the condition is still taught in the universities. We covered it, although not in any great depth. I've never studied it with actual people who have the condition, but I do know something about it. From what you've just told me, I think it's a real possibility that you and your sister share something very special."

He looked at her thoughtfully. What she said made sense, sort of, but...

"I need to get back to the bridge," he said. "Thank you. You've given me something to think about."

"Captain," she said. "Don't be shy. If you have any more of these experiences, I need to know."

"Of course, doctor," Morian said. "If it happens again, you'll be the first to know."

Chapter Twenty-Eight

Old Tech

The Avenger
Battle space
Pricus System

Morian stepped onto the bridge to find everyone calm and quietly monitoring their stations. Commander Jadern was standing at the rail, staring down at the hologram.

"What's the situation, Commander?" Morian asked as he stepped up beside him.

"Ah, Captain. You're back," Jadern said. "The situation is calm. Nothing on the scanners. Nothing on the Holo. You're feeling better, I hope?"

"Yes, thank you, much better," Morian replied. "Anything from the surface?"

"No, sir. Nothing. We haven't received any signals of

any kind from the planet's surface. Everything is dead... Oh, sorry, Captain. Poor choice of words."

Morian shook his head and said, "Not a problem, Commander. Have you tried the other cities?" *Stupid question. Of course he has.*

"Yes, sir. We're monitoring everything on this hemisphere," Jadern replied. "All frequencies. Nothing."

Morian cupped his chin in his hand and scowled at the comms monitor.

"The good news is that the USF fleet is continuing to make progress," Jadern said. "We've told them about the railguns, but none of the ships have them."

"Old tech." Richard nodded. "I guess that's another win for *Avenger* and her antiquated weaponry."

Jadern smiled. "It would appear so. The fleet consists mostly of B and C Angel Class ships and E-class Destroyers. All modern ships. None of them have railguns."

Jadern's data pad buzzed. He glanced down at the screen, then said, "Sir, your presence is being requested on Deck Two, in the Armory."

Morian frowned. "The Armory? What for?"

Jadern finished reading the message, then turned to Morian, took a deep breath and said, "While you were in the med bay, I followed up with our friend, Mister Tenilo. It seems he's discovered something I think you'll want to hear."

"And he's in the Armory?" Morian asked.

Jadern nodded.

"Then let's go," Morian replied. "I just hope he doesn't have another history lesson for us."

They rode the elevator to Deck 2 and then took the

gravtrack aft to the Armory, where they found April Badeaux and Prince Felder at the rail looking down at Tenilo who, along with two senior armorers, was bent over an open Mark 47 Saber nuclear torpedo container.

The two armorers snapped to attention when they saw Morian.

"As you were," Morian said, and the two men relaxed.

"What's going on here?" Morian asked.

"Ah, Captain," Felder said, bowing his head slightly. "Thank you for joining us."

"My prince," Morian replied dryly. "So, Mister Tenilo," he raised his voice so he could be heard over the hum of the loading machinery, "what's this all about?"

Tenilo looked up at him. His eyes widened and he smiled, then stood upright and turned to face him.

"Ah, Captain. Captain Morian. Thank you. Please, I must show you." His voice was pitched an octave higher than usual. It was obvious the little man was excited.

Morian leaned on the rail overlooking Tenilo and the open missile container and said, "I know things are somewhat... fluid, the situation being what it is, Mister Tenilo. Even so, it's rather disconcerting to find a passenger in my armory fiddling with a live Mark 47 torpedo."

"I... er... approved it, Captain," Jadern said. "I think he may be onto something. Please listen to what he has to say."

"Thank you, Commander." Tenilo wiped his hands on a rag and stepped away from the torpedo, patting the sweat off his forehead with the same dirty rag. "Captain, as you see here, with the help of your two very competent engineers, we have disarmed this torpedo."

"You did *what?*"

"Yes, it was quite easy. These two fine gentlemen seem to know exactly what they're doing."

The two fine gentlemen looked decidedly uneasy.

"And how, exactly, did you manage to access the USF codes?"

Tenilo looked guilty. "I hacked the unit's command board. It was quite simple, really and, by the way, did you know that one access code fits all? That's not very secure, Captain. May I recommend—"

"No, you may not recommend anything, sir," Morian said. "Now, please tell me why, exactly, would we want to disarm a cruise missile in the middle of a war?"

Tenilo smiled widely and said, "Ah, yes. Good question, sir. Because, Captain... Well, you see, I had an idea. I remembered from the final battle for the Hyron System in 2632—"

Prince Felder cleared his throat.

Tenilo glanced at Felder, blinked rapidly, then said, "Ah, yes, apologies, Captain. The point is, you know how effective your railguns were against the enemy ships, yes?"

"Yes."

"It's exactly that principle that will make a disarmed cruise missile just as effective, actually more effective, because of its guidance systems. You see, railguns are notoriously inaccurate and..." He saw the look on Morian's face and quickly changed track. "When something strikes high-density silicon, such as silicon XD, the material undergoes an instantaneous change at the molecular level; it solidifies and explodes. I'm not saying these ships are constructed from XD; we don't know that. But from what we've seen, they do react to a kinetic impact in much the same way.

"You see, it is not the explosion of the cruise missile that damages them. They seem to be impervious to chemical and nuclear explosions. So what we now have here," Tenilo said and pointed at the missile, "is a *smart,* kinetic projectile that will punch into an enemy craft and destroy it, just like the railgun... only better." He smiled even wider.

Morian nodded slowly, smiled at the historian and said, "Like the *Gloryberg?*"

"Yes, Captain. The same principle as the *Gloryberg* disaster."

"You're a smart man, Mister Tenilo."

"Thank you, sir."

Morian turned to Felder and said, "Thank you, my prince."

Felder lowered his head and said, "As always."

Morian again looked down at Tenilo and said, "You say the codes you hacked will work for the rest of the fleet?"

"I think so, Captain."

"Well, we'll soon see," Morian said skeptically.

"Commander," Morian said to Jadern, "get his information to the rest of the USF fleet and have our engineers disarm every missile we have left."

Prince Felder joined Morian and Jadern on the gravtrack back to the elevator. April Badeaux checked her data pad and then went off in another direction.

"Tenilo is a strange little man," Felder said as the elevator door closed behind them, "but very clever. I'm pleased my staff have turned out to be of some value to you."

"They have indeed, and again, I thank you for it," Morian said. "Now, if you'll excuse me, I'm needed on the bridge."

"Of course, Captain. I'll be in my quarters if you need me."

The elevator doors opened and the prince walked quickly out into the corridor, his hands clasped together behind his back.

Morian and Jadern had started toward the bridge when Jadern received a message that he was needed in Engineering. The two of them stood together for a few moments, talking about what had happened to Danis and the status of the mission.

"The mission continues, Michael," Morian said. "Regardless of my sister, until we can determine Prince Elio's status, we are duty bound to do all we can to find him and bring him home. If Danis is alive or dead, it makes no difference. The prince is our priority."

Jadern nodded and said, "I understand, sir, but I can't imagine how you must be feeling."

"That's of no consequence, Michael," Morian replied. "We're in a state of war. My feelings don't matter. Now, you're needed in Engineering."

Jadern nodded, saluted, then reentered the elevator.

Morian continued on along the corridor, past the open briefing room door toward the bridge.

"Captain Morian?" someone shouted from inside the briefing room. "A moment of your time, if you please."

Paris! he thought. *Damn it. That's all I need.*

He stepped into the briefing room to find Paris and April Badeaux standing together behind the conference table.

"Yes, Captain Paris?" he said, his voice revealing his irritation.

Paris walked around the table. "I've just been informed that you have new information. Information that needs to be transmitted to the rest of the fleet."

"To what are you referring exactly?"

"To what am I referring? Are you serious? The conversion of nuclear weapons to kinetic projectiles and the perceived makeup of the enemy craft. This is crucial intelligence. D'you not agree, Captain Morian?"

"I do agree, Captain, but, as you know, we have a Tier One mission to complete. That's our priority. The intelligence has been sent to the Tor Fleet and to USF Fleet Admiral Moreau but, as of three minutes ago, they have not yet acknowledged our transmission."

"I'm not talking about the Tor Fleet," Paris snapped. "I'm talking about the entire USF. Who knows which systems are being attacked right now or will be attacked tomorrow or the next day or next week? They have to be informed."

"Captain, please," Morian said, his head aching. "Let's agree that you do not want to be aboard this ship any more than I want you here. You've made your position abundantly clear. Yet here we are, and we cannot change it. As you well know, we cannot make that transmission unless we are within range of the Slipstream. The Swarm has taken out the Tor control station, and we are more than half a billion kilometers from the nearest active station."

"Then why are we not moving to the Slipstream right now?" Paris said, her face flushed.

It was at that point that Morian realized something. "Captain Paris. How did you learn of this intelligence?"

"I learned of it because I need to know." She put her hands on her hips.

It was then that April Badeaux lowered her eyes, raised her data pad and walked out of the briefing room, away along the corridor.

The journalist, Morian thought. *Of course. I should have known. I'll have to deal with that later.*

He looked Paris in the eye and said, "I see."

She held his gaze, defiant, but said nothing.

"As you know, Captain," he continued when Badeaux was out of earshot. "We still have a Tier One mission to complete. The king's son is still down there."

Paris stuck her chin out and sucked in a deep breath through her nose. "I see. So you're putting the mission before the safety of the entire USF?"

"What else would you have me do?"

"I would have you do your duty. As a Captain in the USF, I am trained to see the battlefield as it is, not as I wish it to be?"

"Which means what?"

"Logic dictates, Captain Morian, that Ranger

Squadron has failed, that they are all dead, including Commander Morian—the prince, too. As captain of the *Avenger*, you know that as well as I do."

"That is yet to be confirmed, Captain. My sister and the prince are still alive until I have proof otherwise."

His data pad buzzed. He ignored it.

"And how do you propose to confirm it? Fly this... great lumbering craft down there and peek out of the window—"

"*STOP!*" Morian shouted. "You will not speak so flippantly about this ship or my crew. You seem to forget, Captain, that had it not been for this great lumbering craft, you would not be standing here."

"That's still no answer as to how you propose to confirm the status of your crew."

"That, Captain Paris, is for me to decide. So, if you'll excuse me." Morian turned to walk away.

"Captain Morian?"

Morian turned on his heel. "Yes, Captain Paris?"

She smiled out of one side of her mouth. "Are you sure you're not putting family feelings before the safety of the greater USF?"

Morian opened his mouth to speak, but before he could answer her, the door leading to the bridge opened and Lieutenant Sandra Lowry walked into the briefing room. "Captain, I tried to reach you. You're needed on the bridge. We've just received a transmission from the surface, from Prince Elio."

He looked back at Paris.

The look on her face was priceless.

Chapter Twenty-Nine

Signal into Darkness

Pricus City
Planet Tor's Surface
Pricus System

Prince Elio was sitting on the floor in a dimly lit room of an abandoned home some five or six kilometers from the mansion, working on what was left of the home's satellite system. The upper torso of his bot, Dinka, lay on the ground beside him, surrounded by wires and microchips. He was trying to get Dinka's emergency power cell to link the bot's programming to the satellite system's transmitter.

"How do you know how to do that?" Andra asked.

Elio shrugged. "It's just something I've always been able to do. I don't even have to think about it."

Gian walked into the room and sat down next to

Andra. "You're sure those were USF fighters that were shot down?" he asked.

"Yes," Elio replied. "I'm sure. I assume they're from the Tor Fleet, but they were definitely USF."

"We should go to that last crash site," Gian said. "The pilot may have survived."

"I agree," Andra said.

Elio nodded. "Yes, but let me finish here first." He paused what he was doing and looked thoughtfully at Gian. "I'm thinking it's not just the city that's under attack. I think it's the entire Pricus System."

He bent back over the remains of his bot, made a couple of final adjustments, then leaned back, stared down at the maze of chips and motherboards and said, "Here we go." Then he touched the power button, held it for a moment, then let go. The screen flashed, lit up for a brief second and then dimmed.

"It's working," Andra said.

Elio grabbed the mic and began speaking. "Mayday, mayday mayday. This is Prince Elio Lorne of the Orso System. I am located just to the north of Pricus City central. We are under attack. Repeat, we are under attack by an unknown enemy—"

Before he could say anymore, something sparked deep within the bot's electronics and the system shut down. Elio tried the power button again, but nothing happened. He tried several more times, made several adjustments and finally sat back and said, "Well, it was worth a try."

"D'you think it got out?" Gian asked.

Elio shrugged. "Maybe, but even if it did, the signal

was extremely weak. I don't think it could have been received unless there was a ship in close orbit, and even then, only if they were scanning the right frequency. It was a very long shot." He shrugged again and continued, "But who knows? Maybe we'll get lucky. Those fighters had to have come from a big USF ship."

Andra stood up and looked out the window to the street. "It still looks clear," she said. "You know, I've been thinking: perhaps we should get back to the mansion. It's not too far."

"What about the downed fighter?" Gian asked.

"How far are we from the mansion?" Elio asked.

Andra thought for a second. "Twenty, maybe thirty minutes, if we run."

Elio put his hand to his chin, thinking, then said, "We don't know exactly where that fighter is, and we need to get to my ship. We need to get help and we need weapons. We can find the fighter later."

"What if the pilot's injured?" Andra asked.

"What if he's dead?" Gian asked. "What if we run into more of those... things?"

"How's everybody feeling?" Elio asked. "Can we make it to the palace?"

"My head feels fine," Andra said. She pointed at Elio's swollen knee. "What about you? Can you walk?"

"I can walk," he replied. "What about you, Gian? How's your arm?"

Gian grinned and flexed his muscle. "It's not great, but I don't have to walk on it, do I? Let's go."

Elio nodded and said, "You're right. Let's get moving. If we can get to *The Queen's Pleasure*, we should be safe and I can get a message out... if she's still in one piece."

* * *

Andra didn't know what time it was, only that dawn had come and gone, the sun was up in the eastern sky, and she could barely keep her eyes open. They'd been walking for what seemed like hours, but she knew it couldn't have been much more than about thirty minutes. She hadn't slept all night; none of them had. And though she'd told them her head felt fine, it still throbbed with occasional bursts of pain.

Elio was limping steadily along in front of her; Gian was at her side, his arm and shirt covered with dried blood. The bleeding had stopped, but she knew it must be painful. As to her own situation, what bothered her most was the filthy state she was in. She'd been wearing the same clothes for almost twenty-four hours, and she was covered in dirt and dried sweat.

She looked up at the sun, a great red ball some twenty degrees above the horizon. *It's going to be a hot one,* she thought. *The first thing I'm going to do when I get home is hit the hydro and then dress in some clean clothes.*

The trio hadn't had much to say to each other. *No wonder, just walking's hard enough,* she thought. *One foot in front of the other, then another, then another...* Her mind wandered back and forth, for as crazy as the last twenty-four hours had been—her discomfort, her clothes, her thirst, her grumbling stomach, the strange blue beings that had tried to kill them—she couldn't stop thinking about the possibility that she might be a telekinetic. The idea overwhelmed and... thrilled her. As hard as she tried, she just couldn't process the thought. The idea of a human having TK powers was almost... unbelievable.

It would have been completely unbelievable had they not grown up with the legendary tales about the powers the Heroics had once possessed. *Did I really do that? Did I really cause that rock to fly through the air and kill that... thing? If I'd been by myself... But I wasn't. Gian and Elio both saw it. I must have done it... but how? And why now?*

"Andra?"

Gian's voice interrupted her thoughts. They were approaching the corner of a building.

"What?" she asked.

"Are you okay?"

"Of course," she replied. "Why?"

"Because you haven't said a word for at least ten minutes, and now you were just standing there... staring off into space."

Gian stepped closer to her, took one of her hands, and said, "I said we're here. Didn't you hear me? This is the end of Creek Road. The mansion's driveway is just a few meters that way. We're going to have to make a run for it." He pointed to the familiar grove of trees that surrounded the mansion's entrance.

Gian's hand was still outstretched, pointing toward the trees, when a burst of brilliant blue energy slammed into the wall next to them, showering them with dust and debris. Andra screamed, covered her head and dropped to the ground.

"Come on! Run!" Elio yelled. "Run for the trees."

Andra jumped to her feet, her hands over her ears. Gian grabbed her arm and they began to run.

Together, they sprinted around the corner of the building, heading across the debris-littered street toward the entrance of the driveway. She glanced over her shoulder and saw three of them, line abreast, marching towards them. Another blast of energy exploded just behind her as she ran, taking out the corner of the building they'd been using for cover.

"Come on, come on! Run!" Gian had her by the arm dragging her along as she stumbled, trying to stay on her feet.

She could hardly breathe. Her heart was pounding so hard she thought it was going to burst. She found her feet, jerked her arm away from Gian and sprinted for the trees. She wanted to look back but didn't dare, knowing that to do so might cost her precious seconds, or even her life.

They reached the trees and kept running. A fornax tree in front of her exploded. The force of the blast sent Gian spinning. Andra stopped, grabbed his arm in both hands and hauled him to his feet.

She glanced back. The three aliens had cleared the corner of the building and were walking quickly toward them, shooting as they came.

Why aren't they running? she wondered.

Gian, now on his feet, staggered forward unsteadily. She grabbed his arm, steadying him.

"I'm alright," he whispered. "Let's go." And together they began to run after Elio through the trees.

Their pursuers were now almost at the entrance to the driveway. On they ran, the trees exploding around them as blast after blast streaked after them, some so close they could feel the heat.

Elio, out in front, stopped, turned, ran back and grabbed Gian's other arm. "Come on!" he shouted. "They can't shoot at what they can't see." And they took off together into the deep cover of the trees.

"Why aren't they running?" Andra gasped.

"Who knows," Elio said, breathing hard. "Who cares? We've got to find somewhere to hide. We need to get to my ship. Where is it, Andra?"

"You asked them to put it in the hangar." She gasped, trying to stay on her feet. "That's on the far side of the mansion."

"How do we get there?" he asked.

"That way. Across the lawn. See?"

They were almost through the trees and Andra could see the mansion.

They reached the edge of the trees and stopped. Andra dropped to her knees, her hands on the ground in front of her, breathing hard. Gian's face was pale. His breath coming in quick gasps. Elio leaned back against one of the trees, put his head back against the trunk, closed his eyes and breathed deeply.

The moment lasted no more than a few seconds before Gian said, "That's a lot of open ground we're going to have to cover. I don't think I can make it."

"Is there another way?" Elio asked, breathing a little easier. "Can we stay in the trees and go around? We're dead meat if we go out there. *Oh shit!* Here they come. *Run!*"

A bolt of energy slammed into the tree just above his head. A meter of the tree trunk exploded with an earsplitting bang and disappeared, bringing down the rest of the tree in a shower of leaves, limbs and branches. If they hadn't moved when they did, they would have gone down under the deluge of falling wood.

"That way," Andra shouted, looking back. "They're out of the trees. They're coming. Run!"

"Follow me," Elio shouted and took off running, limping, across the lawn toward the great front door.

Andra and Gian followed, the hair on the back of her neck prickling. She just knew she was going to be shot in the back.

They were just over halfway across the lawn when the front door of the mansion burst open and four of her father's security guards rushed out onto the patio, rifles shouldered, and began shooting at the aliens. Andra ducked and kept running. Unfortunately, their DEW rifles had little effect on the aliens. They absorbed hit after hit. Their shields, if that's what they were, seemed to absorb the energy. The aliens slowed; their blue halos flickered, lost some of their color, then seemed to reenergize.

"This way! Come on, come on," one of the security guards shouted.

Andra cleared the lawn and hit the driveway running, took the stone steps three at a time, up onto the patio and in through the open door, Elio and Gian close on her heels.

The four security guards began to back up toward the door, shooting bolt after bolt of laser fire at the oncoming aliens. The last guard was at the door when a bolt of blue plasma hit him just above the belt. The man's chest exploded, vaporized in a flash of blue light as the door slammed behind them.

Chapter Thirty

The great door slammed behind them. Andra leaned her backside against the wall, bent over, her hands on her knees, her chest heaving, Gian and Elio beside her, both gasping for air, all three filthy, covered in dust, sweat and grime.

"That door won't hold them," Andra said between gasps.

"Move! Follow me," one of the three remaining guards said. "Now! Let's go, let's go." Then he turned and ran through the Great Hall, the other two guards and Andra's little group right behind him.

They followed him through the private quarters to the back of the house and then down a flight of stone steps to the basement into a large, sparsely furnished concrete room.

"We should be safe here for now," the security guard said, laying his rifle down on the table.

"Do you have another one of those?" Elio pointed to the security guard's rifle.

"Yes, over there." The guard pointed to several DEW rifles in a rack on the far wall. "Not that it will do you much good. They're virtually useless against those... creatures."

Elio and Gian each grabbed a rifle.

"Where's my family?" Andra asked. "Why are you here?"

"Your father and mother and the rest of his staff are off-site in a safe location," the guard replied. "We were ordered to remain here in case you came back. Your father's been trying to find you. He wouldn't leave without you."

"Then shouldn't we be leaving? Those things are going to blast right through the walls."

The guard shook his head. "They haven't come inside yet. Why, we don't know."

"So, you think we're safe in here?" she asked.

The guard shrugged and pulled a face, wiped the sweat from his brow with the back of his hand, then grabbed a commlink attached to his belt and spoke into it. "Team One to Bunker. D'you copy?"

"Go ahead, One."

"This is Mac," the guard said. "I have Miss Andra plus two civilians. My team is down to three, me, Carl and Petra. We're coming to link up with you."

"That's great news, Mac. Take the secondary route and we'll meet you outside."

"Tell him I'm with Prince Elio," Andra said.

Mac looked at Gian and Elio and said, "What?"

"Prince Elio," she said. "Tell him."

"Miss Andra says one of the civilians is Prince Elio."

There was a moment of silence, then the voice on comms said, "Copy. We'll be waiting for you."

He turned to Andra, looked again at the trio and said, "Which one of you is the prince?"

"That would be me," Elio said.

Mac nodded, then said, "Let's go."

"Wait, where's the bunker?" Andra asked.

"About a half a kilometer south of here. We need to go now."

"No! We should go to my ship," Elio said.

"Your ship?" Mac said. "Where the hell is it?"

Elio looked at Andra. "It should be in the hangar," she said. "We can get there from here."

"No! No, we can't," Mac said. "We have to go to the bunker. Now!"

"You mean the tunnels are down?" Andra asked.

"No, not that," Mac replied. "You can't fly. The minute you lift off, those things will destroy you. They've destroyed every shuttlecraft we have. They own the sky. Now come on. We don't have much time."

"What about those outside?" Elio asked. "Surely they have the place surrounded."

Again Mac shrugged. "Maybe, maybe not. They're strange, unpredictable. They've been watching this place ever since they landed... maybe because they know it's an important building, a government building, but never once have they tried to come inside. Most of the fighting has been out on the streets. Look, we have to go."

"Do they have comms? How do they talk to each other?" Elio asked.

"We don't know," Mac replied. "We haven't heard them. And we haven't picked up any transmissions."

"What about our transmissions?" Elio asked. "Have you contacted the fleet?"

"All comms, except these short-range units," he said, tapping the communicator on his belt, "are down. No off-planet transmissions get through. We're on our own. Now, are you ready to go, or do you want to talk us all to death?"

"We're ready." Elio held up his rifle, thumbed the power button, and the weapon whined as it powered up. "I don't feel quite so helpless now that I have this."

"You might as well be carrying a stick for all the good it will do you," Mac said. "If you hit them enough times it will slow them down, but that's all. Their battle armor seems to absorb the energy."

"They're not invulnerable," Gian said. "We managed to kill two of them and destroy one of their ships."

Mac's mouth dropped open. "You killed one?"

"Yes, but not one; two of them. Andra—" Elio stopped when he saw the look she was giving him. He got it. She didn't want him to mention TK. "Andra threw a rock at one of them. It hit it in the head. Cracked it wide open. The thing dropped dead. Gian punched one of them in the head, same result."

"What?"

"Yes," Gian said. "It's true. And we ran one of their ships into a rock wall at Lookout Point, and it exploded."

"That doesn't make any sense. Our DEW rifles don't hurt them, but you brought one down with a rock and a... punch in the head? That's unbelievable."

"Well, it was a hard punch," Gian replied, grinning at him.

"What about the other star systems?" Elio asked. "Have you heard from any of them, or our fleet? Are we offering any resistance?"

Mac shook his head and said, "As far as I know, there hasn't been any communications with anyone since the initial attack. We're cut off. Look, we need to go. Now." Mac slung his rifle over his shoulder. "Follow me. We'll use the tunnels. Stay close."

Andra went to the racks, grabbed a rifle and thumbed the power button. The weapon whined as it powered up, then she followed Mac out into the tunnel with Gian and Elio close behind.

"Hah, I remember this place," Elio muttered with a chuckle.

"What?" Mac asked.

"Nothing," Elio said as he pulled the door closed behind him, smiling to himself.

Chapter Thirty-One

Broken Bird

Pricus City
    Planet's Surface
    Pricus System

Danis opened her eyes to the feel of the warm early morning sunshine on her face. She blinked and stared up at the cloudless sky, wondering where the hell she was.

As she struggled up onto her elbows, pain seared through her temples. She clamped her eyes shut, trying to overcome the pain. Why did she ache... everywhere? It was as if every bone in her body was broken. She rolled over in the tall grass, totally disoriented. Then she struggled up onto her hands and knees, blinked several times and shook her head. The headache seemed to ease a little. She sat back on her heels, unbuckled the chin strap, removed her helmet and looked around.

Her wrecked ejection seat lay on its side entangled in a nest of guides and cords some fifty meters away on the edge of the clearing to her right. What was left of its nanofiber parachute was hanging in ribbons from the tree branches. The remains of her F32 fighter were scattered over a wide area beyond the trees nearly a half kilometer to her left. The cockpit—its canopy missing—lay smoldering on its side.

And then she shuddered as the memories came flooding back. She remembered seeing Seven and Eight going down together, the shuttle and its contingent of marines exploding just a few meters above the surface, and she remembered losing one of her starboard engines and spinning out of control toward the ground. What she didn't remember was activating the ejection seat. *It must have deployed automatically*, she thought as she struggled to her feet.

She stood for a moment, trying to control her trembling legs. She rubbed the back of her aching neck. *Whiplash? No!* She rotated her left shoulder and winced as the pain reached all the way down to her fingertips. Hesitantly, she took a step, then another. The pain in her lower body was almost unbearable. She reached into a pocket on the breast of her flight suit, took out a small med kit, broke the seal, opened it and removed a package of four painkillers. She tore it open, put all four tabs into her mouth and chewed, grimacing at the bitter taste. Then she leaned back against the trunk of a tree, closed her eyes and waited. Within minutes, she felt the pain throughout her body begin to subside.

She took a deep breath, pushed herself upright from the tree, took several tentative steps, nodded, breathed deeply several times, then headed slowly across the clearing toward her wrecked fighter.

There wasn't much of it left, nothing useful to salvage from the wreckage. All she had was what was in her flight suit and the data pad on her arm. She tapped the screen. It lit up. It seemed to be intact, but it wasn't receiving anything. She turned on her beacon. It flashed red. *Damn! Comms must be down.*

She knew Avenger Search and Rescue would be scanning the planet's surface, looking for the beacon, but without a signal from her data pad, they'd never find her. *I guess I'm on my own, then,* she thought and looked around.

She sat down on a rock to think. She had no idea where she was. She tapped the data screen to bring up her GPS. Nothing!

She sighed, shook her head and looked at the wrecked fighter. Something jogged her memory. She stood, stepped over to the wreck, crouched down and looked into the cockpit. She leaned inside and tapped one of the screens. Nothing! It was dead. She stared at the darkened screens... *Richard? He was talking to me right before the crash, but the comms were down. I know they were. I checked, but I could hear him. He told me to eject... then I could see him. I could hear his voice, but that's not possible.*

She stood up and stepped away from the downed fighter, staring wide-eyed at the open cockpit. She shook her head in disbelief. She took several more steps back, then turned and looked around, trying to get her bearings. *Where the hell am I?*

She looked up at the sun, squinted and shook her head. *Damn it! How am I supposed to rescue the prince now?*

She started walking, heading what she thought must be east, keeping a close eye on her surroundings and the sky.

There were no enemy ships in the sky, not that she could see anyway. She thought they must be scanning the area, looking for her, especially over her crash site. She had no idea of how long she had been unconscious but figured it couldn't have been long.

I need to find the city. I need to figure out where the hell I am.

She stopped walking, turned around and looked back the way she'd come. She could see the trees in the distance and a tiny plume of smoke rising from the wrecked fighter. She turned again to face the east. She looked to the north, more trees. Same to the south. She started walking east again.

She'd been walking for more than an hour when she spotted something in the distance. *Buildings?* She began to run. The buildings grew larger. There were lots of them. *Pricus City?*

Danis stopped running and dropped to her knees, gasping for breath. She froze and listened; she heard nothing. The silence was palpable. Many of the buildings had been reduced to rubble. *Where are the people?* she wondered.

For a long moment, she knelt there, listening, wondering. Finally, she made up her mind, rose to her feet and headed for the nearest large, single-story building. *Must be some sort of repair shop*, she thought, *judging by the doors.*

The side door was open. She stepped inside and looked around. She counted three gravcars in various states of repair. The lights were off. A little light was coming in from four skylights high above in the roof.

The place was deserted. She walked across the shop to another open door into a much smaller room lit by two large windows. She spotted a sink, went to it, turned on the tap and watched the water flow. She licked her lips, looking around for something to drink from. There was nothing. She cupped her hands and filled them with water and drank, and drank, and drank. Finally, she splashed water on her face and then dried off using the sleeve of her flight suit.

She returned to the front door, poked her head out and looked up and down the rubble-covered street. All was quiet. Nothing was moving.

Chapter Thirty-Two

Pricus City

Planet Tor's Surface
Pricus System

For several moments, Danis stood still, looking up and down the street, but more than that, wondering what to do next. She'd never felt quite so alone.

I need to find a terminal. Maybe I can check the data net for emergency transmissions. Maybe they issued evacuation routes. Ugh, no power... Damn! It's hopeless. Where did all the people go? They can't all be dead... can they? Well, I can't stay here, that's for sure.

Again, she looked both ways up and down the street. Nothing. All was quiet. Disturbingly quiet. She looked up at the cloudless sky. Nothing. She looked to her left. A dust devil, some seventy-five meters from where she was standing, sucked up a tiny tornado of dust and whirled away down the street, and eventually disappeared. She took a deep breath, then stepped out into the street and started walking. Part of her wanted to run, but the better part of her told her not to draw attention to herself. She reached the corner of the four-way intersection, stopped, looked in all four directions and saw... nothing.

She walked out into the road and had almost reached the far side when she heard something. She stopped dead, stood still, barely breathing, then looked around and, at the far end of the street, she saw it. An enemy ship appeared above and beyond the ruined buildings, perhaps five hundred meters from where she was standing, its blue halo pulsing, flying low and slow, barely moving. And the humming; it seemed to penetrate her very soul. It was a sound she knew well: *anti-grav drive,* she thought. *It hasn't seen me. Maybe if I don't move, it'll go away. Fat chance. Go, go, go! No wait. It stopped moving.*

The ship had stopped, hovering over an intersection at the far end of the street, slowly rotating. Its two upper weapons pointed at the sky, the lower ones pointing straight down at the ground. It began to descend, slowly, still rotating.

Twenty meters above the street, four arms extended from the underside of the craft. As it got closer to the ground, the dust and debris began to swirl beneath it. The humming noise increased. Its descent slowed almost to nothing as it settled gently onto its landing pads. Its four weapons began to rotate, as if looking for a target.

And then she ran. She covered the ten or fifteen

meters to the side of the street in seconds, into the open doorway of a demolished building only to find her way blocked by an insurmountable pile of rubble. She was trapped. She spun around, huddled against the wall, and looked out into the street toward the enemy craft.

A large section of the underside had opened and was lowering toward the ground, forming a ramp. The edge of the ramp gently touched down and three humanoid forms appeared, walking slowly down onto the street, each carrying what appeared to be a short, blocky-looking gadget she guessed must be some kind of weapon.

She watched, fascinated, her heart in her mouth as they stepped down. They stood for a moment. They were tall, slightly more than two meters. They appeared to be wearing smooth, one-piece suits of battle armor, and they were surrounded by the same shimmering, pale blue halo as the enemy craft.

What was that? She heard it first, then, out of the corner of her eye, on the other side of the street, perhaps one-hundred-twenty meters away to the west, she saw it: another of the blue-clad beings, and this one had seen her. She couldn't see its eyes, but she could tell by the angle of its head it was looking right at her. And, for a second, she froze.

It raised its weapon. She dropped to the floor just as a flash of brilliant blue light slammed into the rubble behind her. The pile disintegrated in a shower of dust.

She scrambled to her feet and took off running as hard as she could down the street. The three beings from the ship joined the fourth and began walking quickly after her. She took the first turn to the right and ran.

Another bolt of blue that barely missed her exploded into the wall on the far side of the street.

Danis was calm now, her head clear. She was sprinting for all she was worth, knowing they were close behind and that she needed to find cover, and quickly.

She ran to the next building and threw herself sideways into the doorway just as another blast of blue seared the pavement behind her. She slammed into the door with her shoulder. The door burst open and she fell into the building, crying out from the pain in her shoulder.

She staggered to her feet, looking wildly around. She was in some kind of office. It looked as if the occupants had left in a hurry. The desks were covered with papers, drink containers and holo generators. She went to the window. The Blues were only meters away from the door.

She turned and ran through the office, down a long hall to a door that looked like it might open to the outside. It was locked. Desperately, she looked around, ran through a side door into a small storage room and out through another door onto a narrow street between two buildings.

She glanced both ways. All was clear. She turned right out of the door and began to run toward the next building, only to be confronted by more of the blue-clad beings, at least six of them. She skidded to a stop, turned, dropped and rolled as a bolt of blue hit the door of the building she'd just exited. The force of the blast knocked her sideways, shards of concrete ripping into her flight suit. She could feel blood—or was it tears—rolling down her cheeks, and she knew it was over. There was no way she could outrun so many of them.

"Stay down," a voice shouted. "We've got you." And a massive volley of DEW laser fire flew over her head.

She looked up and saw a group of men and women, some in uniforms firing at the beings. *Oh, my God. They're Tor Defense Force, but how?*

"Come on," one of them shouted. "This way, quickly."

She scrambled to her feet and ran. The soldiers laid down a continuous barrage of laser fire. Someone grabbed her arm and dragged her into the building to join a small group of five civilians huddled together at the far end of the room.

One by one the uniformed soldiers backed in through the door maintaining a constant stream of fire. Once they were all inside, they slammed the door and backed away from it, their weapons at the ready.

"You're lucky we found you, Commander," a soldier wearing the insignia of a first lieutenant said, smiling at her. "Welcome to Pricus City, though there's not much of it left, I'm afraid."

"Commander Danis Morian, *Avenger* Fighter Squadron," Danis said, dusting the front of her pants with her hands. "Thank you. You saved my life. What are you doing here?"

The lieutenant raised his eyebrows, nodded in the direction of the civilians and said, "We're trying to get them to safety. What about you? What were you doing out there alone?"

"I was trying to stay alive. I was shot down east of the

city. I was looking for... I was looking for a way to contact my ship. I've been walking for hours. I need to find a comms center. You don't have..." She saw the look on his face and tailed off. "That's what I thought," she said and sighed. "So, what exactly is your situation?"

He shrugged and said, "I just got here myself. I'm Lieutenant Kolb, TDF Third Platoon, Company C... what's left of it. I've lost more than thirty of my men in less than an hour. We were posted at Station B, in a bunker, when I got the word to abandon the post and rescue these guys, get them to safety." He pointed to the civilians. "We need to get out of here." Then he turned and said, "Everybody, follow me, quickly now." And he headed to a staircase.

Danis followed him. She was followed by the civilians. The four members of Kolb's platoon formed a rearguard position covering their exit.

"You say you were shot down east of town?" Kolb asked as they mounted the stairs.

"Unfortunately, yes," Danis replied.

"We saw it. Three to one. I'm surprised you made it out alive."

"No more than I am," she said.

"What about the others?" he asked. "There were more of you, surely."

She nodded. "There were three of us and a shuttle with a detachment of marines. The enemy took us by surprise. We were outnumbered. My wingmen didn't have a chance. The shuttle was almost on the ground when they... no one could have survived. I tried to make a run for it. My weapons were virtually useless."

"Same here," Kolb replied. "Our DEW rifles have little effect on them. We keep hitting them and they just keep coming. But they're slow."

"What about their ships?" Danis asked.

"There are still plenty of them around, though we don't see much of them now that they've taken out all of our ships."

"Railguns!" Danis said and stopped dead as she suddenly remembered what had happened just before she left *Avenger*.

"What about them?" Kolb said.

"Railguns," she repeated and continued on up the stairs. "They worked against their ships."

By then they'd reached the second floor and Kolb waited until everyone was gathered together, then turned again to Danis.

"What are you talking about?" he asked.

Danis explained how the gunners on the *Avenger* had discovered that old-world kinetic projectiles worked against the enemy ships when nothing else did. The soldier listened to her in silence.

"Are you kidding?" Kolb asked when she finished.

"No. Not at all," she replied. "I'm no scientist, but apparently it has something to do with their molecular structure. From what I was told, they're a silicon-based lifeform. We're carbon-based. When their ships sustain a high-velocity impact, the silicon—or whatever it is— instantly hardens and... shatters. My guess is that the same thing will happen to the Blues."

"The Blues?"

Danis shrugged. "They have that blue halo. Seems like a good name for them."

"Yes, well, we don't have railguns, and we can't stay here," Kolb said. "Let's go. Follow me."

He turned and trotted to a door at the far end of the room that opened onto a flight of stone steps.

"You have a plan, then?" Danis asked as she followed him down into the darkness.

He nodded and said, "We're trying to get these people to safety; him especially." He nodded in the direction of a portly, older man dressed in formal attire.

"Who is he?" Danis asked, noticing him for the first time.

"That's the governor, Governor Graynir. He used to run things around here. Not anymore, though. We've been picking up survivors along the way. It seems there aren't too many of us left."

"I heard that, Lieutenant," Graynir said. "Until the king formally removes me from office, I am still, as you so aptly put it, running things around here. My daughter will be headed to the bunker. I keep telling you that we must find her before she gets there."

"We're moving as fast as we can, Governor." Kolb's face was covered in sweat and dirt. He was angry. "We can only go as fast as the slowest man, which is you."

The governor's mouth opened and shut. He took a deep breath and drew himself up to his full height—still six inches shorter than Kolb—and said, "How dare you, sir? Never, I say never, has anyone ever spoken to me like that—"

"And we've never been attacked by a hostile alien

race armed with tech we can't even begin to dent," Kolb said, interrupting him. He took a step closer to the governor. The governor took two steps back. "Welcome to reality, Governor," Kolb snarled. "What are you going to do? Fire me? Court-martial me? You need me to get you out of here, so stop your whining and let's do this."

Danis smiled to herself and couldn't help but wonder what would happen to the frustrated lieutenant if they did manage to get out of it.

"We need railguns, Lieutenant," Danis said.

"Who the hell are you?" a soldier wearing sergeant's stripes asked.

"Commander Morian, *Avenger* Fighter Squadron. And you are?"

"A fighter pilot?" the governor asked before the sergeant could answer. "How the stars did you get down here?"

"I was shot down on the outskirts of the city. My mission was... is to locate and rescue Prince Elio Lorne. Our last intel is that he's here in Pricus City. That's all I know."

The governor did a double take, looked at the sergeant, then at Kolb and said, "He is. He's with my daughter. We were en route to meet her, until we ran into you, that is." He glared at her, then at Kolb.

Danis stared at him. "How d'you know that? Where are they?"

The governor frowned, then said, "That, Commander, is the problem. We had to abandon the bunker and, in so doing, we lost contact with them. They were on their way to join us. We had no way to warn them."

The sergeant grunted, flicked the safety on his rifle and slung it over his shoulder.

"So, what are we going to do?" Danis asked, looking around. The sergeant shrugged and looked away. The governor frowned and shook his head. Kolb looked impatient. No one spoke. Everyone in the room was quiet, staring at her.

"*What?*" she said.

"You're the ranking officer," Kolb said, smiling at her.

"I'm a pilot, not a damn soldier," she snapped, "and take that silly grin off your face, Lieutenant, and think of something."

"We have to find a ship and get out of here," the sergeant said and spat on the floor.

"That's enough of that, Sergeant," Kolb said. "Show a little respect."

"No, he's right," Graynir said, "but we have to find my daughter first."

"And how do you suggest we do that?" the sergeant asked.

The governor had no response.

The sergeant lifted his chin towards Danis and said, "The lieutenant's right. You have the rank. There has to be a way to contact your ship. What about that thing on your arm?"

She shook her head, raised her arm and tapped the screen. The indicator blinked red. "Either it's damaged or I have no comms. We need to find a terminal that's working."

The sergeant cursed. "Fat frickin' chance. The power's out all over the city. We did have low-frequency comms, but we lost that when we left the bunker. It's on you, honey. You'd better come up with something, and soon, or we'll all be dead."

Danis looked at Kolb.

"What he said," Kolb said.

"You can't be serious," she said.

"You're a squadron leader," Kolb said. "This is no different. We're in a tight spot. What would you do?"

"I'd call for backup, damn it," she replied.

"What if you can't call for backup?" Kolb asked. "What would you do then?"

"What d'you think?" she asked angrily. "I'd fight to the last man... I am the last man, damn it."

"Then—" Kolb began.

"Oh, shut the hell up and let me think," she snapped. "And stop grinning at me."

Kolb raised his hands and backed away. "You're the boss," he said.

She glared at him. Then quite suddenly she realized the mess she was in. She was indeed the ranking officer, and protocol demanded that she take command of the situation, something she knew she wasn't qualified to do. Leading a squadron into battle was one thing; leading a ragtag band of soldiers and civilians to safety through an enemy-occupied city was quite another.

I need to find the daughter, the prince and a ship, she thought. *Oh, my God. I have to get these people out of here. What am I going to do?*

She looked around the room. Everyone was quiet. The soldiers were at the windows, weapons at the ready.

The five civilians were grouped together, all staring at her. Kolb was seated on the edge of a desk, watching her.

She turned her back to him. *What am I going to do?* she thought. *We can't just stay here... We can't go anywhere. I don't know where to go.* She looked over her shoulder at Kolb. He looked back at her, his face set, expressionless.

She looked away and closed her eyes, trying to come up with an answer. Nothing. She thought back over the last thirty-six hours. Nothing... and then she remembered something. She remembered going down under fire. She remembered her flash of connection to her brother telling her to eject.

But that wasn't real, was it? Just stress. Imagination. Whatever it was, she couldn't shake the feeling that Richard had somehow reached out to her. *If only... Could she do it again?* She opened her eyes and then closed them again, concentrated and whispered, "Richard? Can you hear me? It's me, Danis." A deep feeling of total calm flooded her mind. "Richard, if you can hear me... I need you. I need you more now than I ever have. Richard, are you there?" The image of a man's face began to form in front of her. It was him. She could almost see him.

"Hello?"

"You can hear me. Oh, thank God," Danis whispered.

Slowly, the face materialized, but it wasn't Richard. The man was young, perhaps in his early thirties, with shoulder-length blond hair and a small, hook-shaped scar at the corner of his left eye. It was a face she'd seen once before, in the intel file that was sent to her F32A just before she launched. It was Prince Elio.

"Who are you?" The prince had his eyes closed and was holding his closed fists to his temples.

"Prince Elio?" she asked.

"Yes. Who are you? How are you doing this?"

"I don't know how. It... It just happened. I'm Commander Danis Morian, squadron leader on the *Avenger*. I was sent to find you. Where are you?"

"I... I can see you, Commander. Holy stars. This is amazing. Are you using a halo? I don't have one. How are you doing this?"

"No. No halo," she said. "Prince Elio. I need to know where you are, and I need to know now."

"We're... somewhere north of the city, in the woods, close to... there's a water tower just north of city limits, but—"

"You're to stay exactly where you are," she said. "We're coming to you." Danis opened her eyes and Prince Elio's face faded away.

She turned to face the room. Everyone was staring at her.

"What the hell was that?" the sergeant asked.

"Never mind," Danis said, then looked at the governor. "I know where your daughter and the prince are."

Chapter Thirty-Three

Command Decisions

The Avenger
Battle space
Pricus System

Captain Morian entered the briefing room, tapped the display on his forearm, called Paris and asked her to join him. Then he waited, something he wasn't used to doing, and something that irritated him immensely.

He was still waiting for confirmation that Danis was alive. He was still waiting for Dr. Tobbs's research on the enemy ships. And now he was waiting for Paris, whom he knew was keeping him waiting on purpose, something he never would have tolerated from anyone else, not even his sister.

It was some ten minutes later when the briefing room door slid open and Paris walked in.

"How can I help you now, Captain Morian?" she asked as her two senior officers strode in behind her.

"This meeting is for captains only," he said with authority. "Please ask your officers to leave."

Paris stood for a moment, trying unsuccessfully to stare him down, then she turned and nodded to her officers. They saluted, turned on their heels and left the room. The door closed silently behind them.

"Please, Captain, sit down," Morian said.

She did as she was asked, and Morian sat down opposite her.

"What d'you want of me, Captain Morian?" Paris asked.

"I need your help, Captain Paris," he replied. "We have a need for missiles with neutralized warheads."

"I'm aware of that," she replied, unable to hide the disdain in her voice.

"You abandoned your ship early in the battle," Morian said, more to annoy her than confirm the fact.

She crossed her arms, her face creased in anger. She narrowed her eyes and said, "I did not abandon my ship, Captain Morian. I followed protocol to save my crew."

What a stupid thing to say, Morian thought.

"I'm not interested in your reasoning as to why you left your ship. What I am interested in is the ordnance still on board."

"Ordnance?"

"Yes. Your ship was not destroyed by the Swarm, nor was it boarded. So, it still holds an almost full inventory of missiles. Is that not correct, Captain?"

"Yes. That's correct."

"How many missiles are there left on board the *Mariposa*?"

Paris bit her lower lip and said, "Are you suggesting that you intend to ransack the *Mariposa*?"

"I'm not suggesting anything," Morian replied. "I asked a simple question. How many missiles are still on board?"

"I have no idea, Captain," Paris said. "I had the safety of my crew in mind when we took to the life pod. The inventory of my armory was the last thing on my mind."

"I need those missiles," Morian said, sitting up higher in his chair. "The *Mariposa* is still pretty much intact, but she's out of the fight, her engines destroyed. She's dead in space. She has missiles aboard and I need them. That being so, I'm sending a detachment to retrieve them."

"You can't be serious," Paris scoffed. "To do that, you'd need an Ordnance Recovery Vessel with pilot ships, front and back. USF regulations state—"

"Oh, for God's sake, wake up, Paris. We're at war and I need armament. No one could have predicted this. The fleet is still engaged out there. God only knows if they're winning or not. There are no regulations out here. We can't even transmit to the Slipstream control tower because there is no damn tower. The enemy has taken it out. They think the *Avenger* is disabled. When they figure out that it's not, we can expect them to return and finish us off."

He waited for her to reply. She didn't. She simply sat there, her arms folded across her chest, her face set, her eyebrows raised, with just the tiniest hint of a smile on her lips.

What the hell is she cooking up now? Morian wondered.

"Once we complete the mission," Morian said, "and Prince Elio is on board, then we'll have to fly to the Slipstream. The Swarm is not going to allow us to do that, not without a fight. They have the entrance to the Slipstream surrounded. I need those missiles, Captain Paris. We'll perform a battlefield pick up of inventory from a dead ship. We do not need an ORV, nor do we need pilot ships. We're in a war, ma'am."

"Then please tell me how you propose to transport them," Paris said in a deceptively gentle voice.

"I propose to use my remaining shuttle. The seats have already been removed. There's enough space to hold at least fourteen crates of Mark 59s."

Paris inhaled, tilted her head to one side and smiled at him, showing her teeth. He was reminded of a hungry creenfish. The idea that Morian was going to ransack her ship, dead in space or not, must only have added insult to the injury of her losing it.

"It will take some time to transfer the log data over to your command bridge," she said. "Then I will have to—"

"You don't have to do anything, Captain," Morian said. "I'm not asking your permission, and you don't need to transfer anything. I'm making the call. I'll ask you once more, how many missiles d'you have left, either in the armory or in storage? I need to know so that we can determine where we dock the transport vessel. You should have the number in your ship's log."

"I'll have to get back to you, Captain," she said, still smiling mockingly at him.

"You have it in your log. You can look it up right now on your data screen. Do it. I'll wait."

Morian sat back in his seat, folded his arms and stared at her, knowing there was nothing she could do about it, that she had to comply.

"Is this some kind of stalling tactic, Captain?" she asked.

"*What?*" Morian asked, stunned by the question. "Why in the name of the Almighty would you ask such a question?"

"Because you know as well as I do that the mission to Tor is over and that we must leave. We have crucial intelligence that must be disseminated to the rest of the USF fleet. It could save thousands of lives, if not entire systems. Are you willing to risk all of that for one person who we don't even know is alive?"

Morian didn't know if she was referring to Prince Elio or Danis, or both, but she still had a way of cutting directly to what infuriated him the most. This time, however, he was prepared. He was determined not to react to whatever taunt Paris might throw at him.

"We do know that the prince is alive, or he was less than an hour ago, and until we can confirm Prince Elio is dead or rescued, our mission will continue. That's the basic parameter of USF mission protocols."

"I see," she said and lifted her arm and began typing on the data screen. The log, he knew, should be easy enough to access, but she was obviously playing one of her games. Morian refused to bite and waited patiently.

"I'm documenting this, of course," Paris said. "I do not intend to be held accountable for misappropriated USF ordnance when and if we arrive back at base."

"If I don't get those missiles, there may not be any base to return to."

Paris looked up, raised her eyebrows and said, "That's a little overdramatic, don't you think, Captain?"

"What part of losing your ship and most of your crew in combat makes you think I am being overdramatic?"

She clenched her jaw. *That last one may have been a little too much,* Morian thought, smiling to himself, *but what the hell. I'm not going to waste time worrying about stepping on the woman's toes.*

"I would also like to request you allow the members of your crew to help my team make the transfer," he said. "They know the *Mariposa* and will be able to guide them while on board, and they know your access codes."

"And if I refuse," she said, "I suppose you will just spout some sort of dramatic wartime power that gives you the right to order my crew members to do your bidding?"

"Something like that, yes."

Paris knew she was losing the battle, and she hated it just as much as Morian was loving every second of it.

Paris nodded and sighed. "Yes, I will allow my crew to join your team. I will inform Lieutenant Haarac immediately." Paris glanced at her data screen and said, "*Mariposa*'s missile magazines are at eighty-two percent, and all reload canisters are full."

Richard nodded. "Good. We can dock at the weapon's bay. Thank you, Captain Paris."

He didn't wait for a response. He stood, nodded, turned and opened the door, surprised she had nothing sarcastic to say as he left the room.

Chapter Thirty-Four

North of Pricus City

Planet Tor's Surface
Pricus System

Elio collapsed to his knees, clutching his head, and then rolled over onto his back, his eyes shut tight. The pain was intense. He couldn't see or hear anything.

"Elio, what happened? What was that?" Gian said as he dropped to his knees beside him.

"Elio, are you all right?" Andra asked.

The pain began to subside. His vision started to clear.

"Elio, say something," Gian said.

"Yes. I'm all right," Elio said and opened his eyes. "Sorry."

"Who were you talking to?" Gian asked.

"Yes, what was that?" Mac turned and looked at him over his shoulder.

Elio sat up and pinched the bridge of his nose. "Someone was talking to me. I must have imagined it, but it was so real. I could see her."

"There was no one here," Andra said. "Just us. You were talking to yourself."

"No, I wasn't." Elio looked at her. "I was talking to a woman, a USF officer. I could see her, hear her. It was real, I tell you. It was as if I was talking to you."

Elio struggled to his feet.

"D'you know who she was?" Gian asked, staring at him with a worried look on his face.

"No. I've never seen her before, but she knew who I was. She said she's a commander with the USF fleet and that we're to stay here, that she's coming to get us. She said she's been sent to find me."

"So we're just supposed to stay put?" Mac asked skeptically.

Elio leaned forward, lowered his head, rested his hands on his knees and said, "Stars, that was intense. I feel like I just ran a marathon. Yes, that's what she said."

"Here, you need to drink." Andra offered him her hydro pack. "Your face, it's white as a sheet."

"So, what you're telling me," Mac said, staring at him, "is that you have TK or Psy abilities? I don't believe it. You're just stressed, scared, imagining things. I've seen it before. It's called PTSD. You need help, all three of you. I need to get you out of here. Get you somewhere safe."

"We're going nowhere," Elio said and handed the

hydro pack back to Andra. "I'm not stressed or scared, and I don't have PTSD. What just happened to me was real. You can leave if you want to. You all can, but I intend to remain here and wait for the commander."

Mac looked at him for a long moment, seemed to make up his mind, then nodded and said, "I apologize, my prince."

Elio nodded and said, "Apology accepted."

"He's telling you the truth," Andra said. "It happened to me too. I didn't just throw that rock at the alien."

Mac froze. "You, too? What the hell's going on?"

"Beats me," Andra said and rested her rifle against the trunk of a tree. "I can't explain it either."

Mac just shook his head, apparently unable to believe what he was hearing.

Elio took a deep breath, let it out slowly, sat down with his back against a tree and said, "So, we stay here and wait for the commander?"

Mac nodded slowly. "If that's what you want. But what if it is some kind of trick?"

Elio turned his head to look at him and said, "You're doing it again."

"I'm doing what?" Mac asked.

"You're insinuating that I'm out of my mind," Elio said dryly.

"No, my Prince," Mac replied. "Not at all. It's just that... Maybe it's the aliens. We don't know anything about them. Maybe they can mess with our heads. Stars, I don't know." Mac just shook his head in frustration.

"It's all right," Elio said. "I understand.

* * *

Danis tried again to reach out to her brother but to no avail, so she tried to link with Prince Elio again, but that didn't work either. By the time they'd reached the northern edge of the city limits, she was beginning to wonder if maybe it was just a one-time thing. Or perhaps it was something that happened only in moments of extreme stress.

Kolb and the sergeant led the small group northeast keeping to the side roads, out of sight of the enemy, so they hoped. Even so, they spotted several small groups of Blues but were able to bypass them without being seen.

They'd been walking for almost an hour when the sergeant who claimed he knew the area took the lead.

"We're getting close now," he said, calling a halt. "The water tower's over that way." He pointed. "Stay here while I take a look. Stay out of sight, and for God's sake, keep quiet." And with that he slipped silently away through the trees.

It must have been some ten minutes later when Danis heard a twig snap somewhere off to her left. She looked at Kolb. He'd heard it too. He nodded. She raised her rifle. Kolb raised a hand, dropped to one knee and raised his rifle. His men did the same.

The sounds grew louder, closer. Someone or something was approaching.

"Don't shoot," the sergeant shouted. "It's me. I found them. They're with me."

Danis lowered her rifle and rose to her feet.

The sergeant appeared, brushing away the low-hanging branches. There were six other people with him: three security guards, a heavily muscled civilian man, a young woman, and a tall young man who Danis recognized instantly as the prince.

Elio spotted her immediately. "You must be Commander Danis Morian," he said.

"Yes, and you're Prince Elio Lorne?"

"I am," he replied. "You're here to get me out of this mess?"

"That was the plan," Danis replied.

"The best-laid plans of mice and men oft go astray," he said. "Who said that, d'you know?"

"I believe it was a pre-Purge Scottish poet by the name of Robert Burns, sir," she replied.

"Do you, now?" Elio said. "Then you know more than I do. It is apt, though, don't you think? Seeing as we seem to be trapped here on this godforsaken planet. But I do thank you for trying." He looked down at her, held her gaze for an unusually long moment, then bowed his head slightly and offered her his hand.

Danis shook his hand. More than a little confused and quite unsure of what to do next. A royal prince bowing his head to her was a first.

"Thank you, my prince."

"Call me Elio," he said smiling. "Everyone does. Well, almost everyone. You have no idea what my father calls me sometimes."

She smiled up at him. "Sir, what happened? How were we able to... connect?"

"I have no idea, Danis. I assume it's all right for me to call you Danis?"

"Yes, of course, my prince." She caught his frown and said, "Sorry. Elio." She almost choked as she said his name. "People like me... well, we just don't call a crown prince by his first name."

"Well, now you do," he said, then continued, "and, as I said, I don't know how we were able to do what we did. I was hoping you could tell me. We should talk about it, but later. Now's not the time, I think. Why don't you introduce us to your friends?"

The introductions were quickly made and Governor Graynir, crying tears of joy, was quickly reunited with his daughter.

"Where's your mother?" Graynir asked, clasping her to him.

Andra pushed herself away from him, looked at him open-mouthed and said, "I thought she was with you?"

Graynir's face fell. He looked at Mac. Mac shook his head.

"But..." Graynir said. "But..." Then he turned, walked away, sat down and put his head in his hands. There was nothing anyone could say.

It took a few minutes, but Graynir, ever the professional politician, gathered himself together, stood, stared at the trees for a moment, took a deep breath then turned to the group and said, "Now that my daughter's safe, we must find transport off of the planet."

"The only possible transports, if there are any left, are in the town's central hub," the sergeant said.

"That's out of the question," Elio said. "We'd never

make it, not with this many people. The city must be swarming with the creatures. What about my ship? It's still in your hangar." He looked at Graynir.

"It is," Graynir said, "but even if it's undamaged, and even if we could get there, you'd never get it out. The doors are closed and the power's out."

"But protocol demands that there must be emergency power for just such a situation," Elio said. "Stars! You can't have the most important hangar on the planet locked down because of a power cut."

Graynir looked at him, realized his omission and said, "Of course. What you say is true." He turned to the sergeant, his eyebrows raised in question.

"It's true," the sergeant said. "In fact, there are two backup systems for the hangar; two one-hundred-thousand-watt generators. That's not the problem. The problem is getting to the hangar."

"We could make it easily if we had kinetic weapons," Danis said. "The Blues' weapons are powerful, but they themselves are slow. If we can shoot and move quickly, we can take them out."

"I hear you," the sergeant said, "but we haven't used K-rifles in more than twenty years."

Danis turned to look at him and said, "But you must have a stockpile of those weapons somewhere?"

The sergeant frowned and shook his head. "As I said, we replaced all our K's with DEWs more than twenty years ago, just as we did all of our obsolete systems. The last of the old railguns went into storage over in Bellville. That's half a day's ride from here by gravcar, and we don't have one."

Gian looked at Andra and raised his eyebrows. She bit her lower lip and nodded.

"That's... not entirely true," Gian said quietly.

Everyone turned to look at him. He smiled self-consciously.

"What are you talking about?" the sergeant asked.

"I know where there are some railguns... and ammo," Gian said.

"Oh yeah?" the sergeant said. "Where? And how d'you know that?"

"There's a cabin not far from here, where we... that is a group of us... Look, we need railguns. I know where they are, all right?"

"Illegal weapons?" Governor Graynir scoffed. "How? Who would—"

"Rebels, that's who," the sergeant interrupted him and took a step forward closer to Gian.

"Rebels?" the governor asked, his eyes wide in disbelief. "What are you talking about, sergeant?"

"Yes, rebels." The sergeant smiled. "We've known about them for quite a while, an underground group led by a firebrand they call Hamel. We didn't know they had weapons, though. You're one of them!" He took another step forward. Gian took a step back and raised his hands, palms out as if to ward him off.

"Whoa," Gian said. "Hamel's dead. You want the weapons or not? If so, back off, sergeant. You're not big enough. You'd have to kill me, and then you'd never find them."

The governor, again in a state of shock, looked first at

Gian, then his daughter and said, "Andra, did you know about this?"

Andra nodded and looked away, her face pale.

"None of that matters now," Danis said. "We can deal with it later. For now, we need to get our hands on those weapons."

Chapter Thirty-Five

Turn of Events

The Avenger
Battle space
Pricus System

Captain Richard Morian, wearing a halo, was seated at the briefing room table. Seated around the table with him were holographic representations of Fleet Admiral Lucien Moreau on the carrier *Juno*, Rear Admiral Johnathan "Jack" Lassiter on the carrier *Halcion* and all three captains of the remaining Angel Class cruisers, the *Caesar*, the *Guardian* and the *Valiant*. They were the major players still engaged in the battle against the Swarm.

"Good day to you, Commodore Morian," Moreau said by way of opening the meeting. "I called this meeting for two reasons. One, to thank you for your help.

We've deactivated the warheads on all of our missiles and the tide is beginning to turn. Why the hell we didn't think of it ourselves is a mystery to me." He looked around at the rest of his commanders, all of whom looked suitably embarrassed. "And two," he continued, "to find out the status of your mission. What the hell are you still doing there? Captain Paris has informed me you refuse to leave. Where is she, by the way?"

"Captain Paris is involved in other duties," Morian said, "namely the recovery of ordnance from the wreck of the *Mariposa*."

"Well, she's right," Moreau continued, "the rest of the USF fleet needs this information. I'd send one of my ships, but I need every one I have to defeat these monsters. What do you have to say for yourself, sir?"

So, Paris went over my head, he thought. *Why am I not surprised?*

"Why am I still here?" Morian said. "I've received a communique from the Crown Prince Elio of Orso. He's still alive, and I am under direct orders from my king to retrieve him. As you well know, Admiral, I'm duty-bound to do exactly that. I anticipate having him aboard the *Avenger* within the next six to eight hours, possibly even sooner." *That's a bit of a stretch, but what the hell?*

Moreau nodded and said, "You have the king's orders in writing, I assume?"

"I do, Admiral."

"Then you must do your duty, sir," Moreau said, then leaned forward and clasped his hands together on the table. "But for God's sake, don't take too long about it," he said earnestly.

"As soon as we have him, sir," Morian replied. "If I may, Admiral. What's your status? How are you doing?"

"Swarm ship numbers are dwindling, but there are still too many of them to count." He looked at Rear Admiral Lassiter and said, "Jack?"

"We're holding our own, just," Lassiter replied. "They're quick, very quick. If they get through, they strike hard. And they learn fast. They seem to be concentrating on our smaller ships, staying away from the capital ships. Our fighters can do little but slow them down. If we can hit the enemy with the deactivated cruise missiles, we can take them out. Unfortunately, their weapons and targeting are better than ours, so they intercept many of our missiles. As I said, they learn quickly. Fortunately, we have plenty of missiles, but how long that will last is anybody's guess."

"And the Swarm is still not using the Slipstream?" Morian asked.

"Not that we know of," Moreau said, "but they're getting reinforcements from somewhere."

"So they have true FTL, then?" Morian asked.

"We don't know that," Lassiter said, "but it does seem likely."

"That would be a total game-changer," Moreau said, "so let's hope not."

"It's possible they're generating wormholes independent of the Slipstream," Captain Danner of the *Valiant* said.

"That, too, would be an unthinkable disaster," Moreau said.

"But we do know they've taken out the Slipstream control station," Captain Garcon of the *Caesar* said.

Morian sat back in his chair and pursed his lips. His data pad buzzed. He glanced at the screen. It was Jadern.

"If you'll excuse me, Admiral," he said. "My XO needs me on the bridge."

"Of course, Commodore," Moreau said, rising to his feet. "Good hunting, sir, but remember what I said. Don't take too long."

Morian removed his halo and tapped his data pad. Jadern's face appeared.

"What's so urgent, Commander, that you deemed it necessary to interrupt a Command Meeting?" Morian asked.

"Captain, the transport has returned from the *Mariposa* with the cruise missiles."

"Outstanding, no issues?"

"No issues, sir, they are good to go. We are transporting the crates to the armory now. They also brought an F32A fighter with them."

"That's good, Commander," Morian replied, "but I say again, what's so urgent?"

"The problem, Captain, is the crew. I just received the vessel with the crew debarking."

"And?" Morian asked impatiently.

"And the problem is that none of the *Mariposa* crew was with them."

"What? You mean they stayed behind on the *Mariposa*?"

"No, sir. I mean they never left the *Avenger*."

Morian didn't answer. His mind was in a whirl. *What the hell?*

"Captain?"

"Please continue, Michael," Morian said quietly.

"I heard you give the order for the *Mariposa* crew to accompany the recovery team," Jadern continued. "But I was talking to the senior transport pilot just now, and he said Captain Paris oversaw the staffing and approved the crew, but none of them were from the *Mariposa*."

Paris, he thought. *What the hell is she up to now? Once again, she's disobeyed a direct order.*

His data pad alerted him to another incoming message. It was Dr. Dowd. She wanted to see him in her office immediately.

"I'll follow up with Captain Paris later," he said. "Return to the bridge. I'll join you there shortly."

"Yes, sir."

By the time he reached the med bay, he'd received three more alerts on his data pad and had ignored them all, promising himself that he'd check them later.

Dr. Jyra Dowd was standing in front of a trio of slowly rotating holograms of a CT scan.

"You wanted to see me, doctor?"

She looked up, surprised. "Captain Morian? No? It's nice to see you, but no. How are you feeling?"

"I'm fine. I received a message that you want to see me," he said testily, "so here I am."

Dowd cocked her head to one side, frowned and said, "You must be mistaken, Captain. I sent no such message, but I'm happy to visit for a few minutes, if that's what you need."

Morian scowled, frustrated, and checked his screen.

"See," he said. "Right here." He held up his arm for her to see.

Dowd looked at the message, narrowed her eyes, looked up and him and said, "I didn't send it, Captain." She took his hand, brought his forearm closer to her face, tapped on the message to highlight it, then tapped "history" and then "details," bringing up another screen. "This message was forwarded from someone in the Captains' net."

"Why does it show your name?" he asked.

"As you know, Captain, only officers of command rank or higher have access to our profiles." Dowd shrugged. "Either it was a mistake, or someone wanted the message to look like it came from me."

Morian felt uneasy. This was, he knew, more than just a simple mistake. It was a deliberate attempt to divert him, but from what? He wasn't sure, but he was beginning to suspect he knew the answer.

"Thank you, doctor," he said. "I'm sorry to have troubled you." He turned and walked to the door.

"No trouble, Captain."

The med bay door closed behind him. He tapped his screen as he walked to the elevator. "Morian to Jadern." No response. "Captain Morian to Commander Jadern." Still no response.

The elevator door opened, and Morian stepped out to find Dr. Tobbs running down the corridor towards the bridge.

What in the stars? Morian presented his eye to the scanner. The bridge door opened and he froze, stunned to see the bridge filled with twice as many people as usual. Voices were raised. People were talking over one another.

All of his bridge officers were standing awkwardly at their positions. Commander Jadern was standing by the captain's chair, waving his arms and yelling something at none other than Captain Paris, the members of her crew behind her in a rough semi-circle. Even Tenilo and April were there.

"What's going on here?" Morian shouted.

The room went quiet. Everyone turned to look at him.

"Captain," Jadern said. "I've been trying to reach you. Paris is trying to take over—"

"Not quite, Commander, and it's *Captain* Paris," she said, loud enough for all to hear. "I have made a command decision in the best interests of safety and for the common good of the USF. I am taking command of this ship."

Morian smiled at her. Not exactly the reaction she was expecting.

"So," he said, "it was you who sent the message. You decided to separate me from my bridge and my crew. Nicely done, ma'am."

"You can't do this!" Jadern moved a step closer to her.

"Oh, but I already have," Paris said, smiling as she reached around her back and produced a DEW pistol. Three of her other officers did the same.

"Paris," Morian said quietly. "Are you mad? Have you gone out of your mind?"

Paris pointed the gun at him. He slowly raised his

hands, tilted his head to one side and smiled benignly at her. Again, not the reaction she was expecting.

"Captain Morian. You have been found in dereliction of your duty. Therefore, I am relieving you of your command."

"Found by whom?" Morian asked.

"By me," she replied. "This fool's mission to save the prince and your devotion to your sister is costing lives. This nepotism demonstrates a clear conflict of interest. Since you refuse to depart to the Slipstream to communicate vital intelligence to the rest of the fleet, I will do it."

Morian already knew Paris was stubborn and carried a chip on her shoulder, but mutiny? *Apparently, the stress of her first battle,* he thought, *and the loss of her ship has pushed her over the edge. Better tread carefully. The state she's in, she's liable to shoot first and ask questions after.*

"So, you resorted to treason?" he asked reasonably. "Not a good idea."

Paris scoffed. "No, no. Not treason. It is my duty to the fleet that warrants this action."

"You're only duty is to yourself and your pride," Morian said. "This, Captain Paris, is mutiny plain and simple and, in time of war, is punishable by death."

I need to keep her talking, he thought, *buy some time.*

"It's not mutiny if the action taken is to relieve a derelict officer of his command, especially when lives are at stake." Paris quoted the policy almost word for word from the manual. "And lives are at stake, Captain Morian."

"You don't know that, Paris," Morian said. "We have no idea what is going on outside of this system."

"Yes, and that's why we must leave immediately, to the Slipstream. And we're leaving now. Navigation, set a course—"

"*Stop!*" Morian shouted so loud that everyone, including Paris, jumped. "Nobody move! That's an order." He took a step forward. "No one gives orders on my ship other than me."

Paris raised the DEW pistol and said, "You clearly don't understand who's in charge here."

Morian focused his attention on the pistol, amazed at how big it looked pointed directly at him. His adrenaline was pumping. He could see the white knuckles of Paris's hand, the sweat on Jadern's face, and he could feel the tension in the air.

They're right, he couldn't help but think, *when they say war makes people do crazy things. Now I have a half-crazy officer threatening to kill me. It shouldn't have come to this. I knew she was suffering. I should have seen this coming.*

For a moment, he held her gaze. Then he nodded and glanced around the bridge. Everyone was stock-still, quiet, except for April Badeaux and Tenilo, who was cowering down behind one of the consoles. Badeaux was typing something on her data screen. *Quite a scoop for her,* he thought.

Morian put his hands down but kept them in sight.

"Sheela," he said to Paris, "I know we don't see things quite the same way, but trust me, you don't want to do this."

"I've made my decision, Morian. Just as you made

yours. You've decided to sacrifice the entire USF in favor of your family."

"That's not true," Morian said. "I am under direct orders from the king of Orso to save the prince. Such orders supersede all others, and you know that. You cannot countermand such orders under *any* circumstance."

"You're out of line, Paris," Jadern growled.

"Am I?" Paris turned and pointed the weapon at him. "I don't think so."

Morian looked to Paris's officers and men standing behind her and said, "Officers and men of the *Mariposa*, you don't want to do this. You know it's wrong. The Sovereign Systems are at war. We can't just decide to call our own shots—"

"Quiet!" Paris shouted, turning the gun on Morian once more.

"Paris, I'm sorry about the *Mariposa*," Morian said gently.

"I said quiet," Paris snapped. "Don't you dare try to placate me, Morian. You have nothing to offer me. I know exactly what I'm doing. I'm doing what you wouldn't. I'm officially calling an end to the mission to Tor."

"What are you going to do, shoot all of us?" Morian raised his arms to encompass the entire bridge. "You're just going to murder us all and take over, is that it? That won't work, and you know it. How're you going to fly the ship with just three officers?"

He was interrupted by the bridge door opening and was surprised to see Prince Felder striding confidently in, his hands clasped behind his back.

"Captain Paris, what is the meaning of this?" Felder's voice boomed across the bridge. He sounded like the king he would one day become.

The only person more surprised to see him than Paris, was Morian.

"Prince Felder." Paris gasped. "I—"

"I was under the impression that I was traveling in the safest ship in the fleet," Felder said as he strode past the command chair, placed both hands on the command rail, stared down at the hologram, then turned again and stepped between Morian and Paris. Paris's weapon was now pointed directly at his chest.

"I came here to check in with Captain Morian," Felder continued, "and what do I find? I find you and your crew holding him at gunpoint, threatening his life. I demand an explanation." His voice was calm but threatening.

Paris got the point. Felder may have never been an officer, but his royal upbringing had trained him to command, and there was no denying him. His presence was overpowering.

"My prince," Paris stuttered. "I am sorry to inform you that... that I... I have been made aware that Captain Morian is unfit for command."

"On what grounds?"

"I... well..."

"Stop driveling, Captain," Felder said. "And put down your weapon. All of you. Put down your weapons." No one moved.

"Are you all insane?" Felder shouted. "You are threatening the life of a royal prince. That's treason and punishable by death. Put them down, *NOW!*" The word reverberated around the bridge.

Paris's officers began to see the reality of what was happening to them, and slowly they lowered their pistols. Paris, too, but only a few inches. She was still committed.

Paris began talking again, "I am relieving Captain Morian of his command due to—"

"You will do no such thing," Felder snapped. "Now stand down, Captain."

To everyone's surprise, Paris actually raised the pistol and gritted her teeth. Jadern and several of the others flinched, anticipating a blast of energy and a dead prince.

Felder didn't flinch, nor did he move an inch.

Morian was impressed by the prince's poise and bravery as he watched him staring down the barrel of a pistol.

"Captain Paris," Felder said. "I'm giving you one last chance to lower your weapon and cease this disastrous attempt at a mutiny. If you do not, I will have you arrested and held for treason on the Alastor System. You will also be charged with the attempted murder of a royal prince and violating USF orders from your commanding officer, Captain Morian. I know your intentions and motives are good, and that you were just doing what you think is right. So, if you cease this silliness now, you will be allowed to remain peacefully in the guest quarters until we dock and nothing more will be said of the matter. What do you say, Captain? Stop it now, and all will be well."

"But... but it's too late," Paris stuttered.

"Nothing is ever too late, Captain. My father and I

will make sure that nothing comes of it. Now, please. You are a worthy captain, and captains are desperately needed in the USF, especially after today when we have lost so many good officers. We need you, Captain Paris. Please, give me your weapon." He held out his hand to her.

Paris slowly lowered the weapon. "Forgive me, my prince. I was just..." She stared down at the pistol, looked up at Felder, smiled and said, "Thank you for your support, my prince." Then handed him the weapon.

"Thank you," Felder said as he took it from her, obviously relieved. Then he turned to Jadern and said, "You, sir. Take the rest of their weapons."

Paris looked around at Morian's bridge crew, then at Morian, her eyes narrowed. He couldn't tell if she was angry or embarrassed. She gripped the bottom edge of her uniform jacket and tugged it down, sharpening her look as if it was the last shred of dignity she had left. She looked back at her officers and men and nodded. Then she straightened her back and walked purposefully toward the bridge door, her supporters at her heels.

Morian was stunned. *Surely, Felder isn't really going to let her get away with this,* he thought. *I can't... The woman's a loose cannon. Who knows what she'll do next?*

He opened his mouth to speak, but before he could, Felder turned to Jadern and said loudly, "Commander. You will arrest these rebels, all of them."

Paris stopped, turned, and looked back at him, her face drained of its color. The rest of *Mariposa's* crew froze.

"Captain Paris," Prince Felder said, "you and these

members of your crew are hereby under arrest for mutiny and sedition under royal order of the Alastor System and the United Sovereign Fleet. You will be confined to the brig until we dock at Gern." He put his hand out toward Richard. "Captain Morian, these prisoners are now under your command."

"But, Prince Felder, you promised," Paris said, a look of utter betrayal flashing across her ashen face.

"Sorry, Paris. I said what I had to in order to get you to stand down. You've been an unruly influence ever since you joined the *Avenger,* and you're lucky that Captain Morian has extended you the grace that he already has. No one attempts a mutiny without grounds, and you have none. Captain Morian is acting under the lawful orders of his king. Such orders are inviolate. You'll be given a fair trial, I assure you." Felder clasped his hands behind his back and turned to stand next to Morian.

Paris started forward, reaching out to him. Jadern and Chief Engineer Volkov stepped in front of her.

"It's over, Paris," Morian said. "You and the rest of your mutineers will be escorted immediately to the brig by Commander Jadern. If you do not comply, I will have the marines forcibly remove you."

Paris looked at Jadern. His face was set, determined. He was holding one of the pistols he'd taken from her officers. Volkov was holding another.

Slowly, Paris nodded. She knew she was defeated, and the reality, the enormity of her predicament was beginning to sink in. Paris suddenly looked old beyond her years, but she still managed to retain a modicum of pride. She lifted her chin, straightened her back, stuck out her chest, and with one last gesture of defiance, she saluted, first Felder, then Morian, then looked into Jadern's eyes and said, "We agree to be moved to the brig, Commander. Please show us the way."

The door closed behind them. Morian turned to Felder and said, "Thank you, my prince. That was... trying, to say the least."

Felder, his hands still behind his back and a bland look on his face, looked at him and smiled, "The pleasure is all mine, Captain Morian."

"My prince," Morian said. "I can't thank you enough."

"Oh, I'm sure you would have worked it out," Felder said. "You were doing just fine when I showed up."

"Why *did* you show up, may I ask?" Morian said. "How did you know?"

"A little bird told me," Felder said, smiling, and nodded in the direction of April Badeaux, who was standing beside Tenilo looking a little embarrassed.

So, that's what she was doing in that corner, Morian thought. *I need to thank her. She saved my ship.*

"I must commend you for your bravery, my prince," Morian said. "It's not every day that one stares down the barrel of a gun and lives to tell about it, much less win the day. I am proud to know you, sir." Morian took a step back, came to attention and saluted the prince.

Felder, his face now showing his embarrassment, put his heels together and clumsily returned the salute. It was clear he'd never performed the gesture before, but Morian could tell by the serious look on his face that his heart was fully into it. Morian relaxed, smiled, nodded, and offered the prince his hand.

Felder smiled, took his hand, covered it with his other hand, shook it and said, "Thank you, Captain, but that's enough. I am truly honored to call you my friend, but now I must get out of your way and let you continue your mission."

And with that, Felder put his hands behind his back once more, nodded to Badeaux and Tenilo, and together they marched to the door and out into the corridor, leaving Morian at the command rail, deep in thought.

The mission. Where are you, Danis?

No sooner had he finished the thought when the pain speared through his frontal lobe. He put his clenched fists to his temples and closed his eyes.

"Captain?" Weapons Officer Lieutenant Fargo rushed to his side and grabbed his arm to steady him. "What's wrong? Are you all right?"

Chapter Thirty-Six

Weapons of War

Planet Tor's Surface
Pricus System

Andra could tell her father was more than a little disappointed by what she'd done, but there was nothing she could do about it now. Yesterday her biggest problem was trying to figure out how to be herself and live her own life, out from under her father's thumb. Today, none of that seemed to matter. Now her main objective was simply to stay alive and get off the planet.

And, while her father was still her father, he was also the governor of the entire Pricus System. He'd lost his home and was in imminent danger of losing his home planet. So, while he was disappointed at his daughter's rebellious behavior, he made no comment, but that did nothing to allay Andra's guilty feelings.

It was almost midday when the ragtag group arrived at the cabin, and it was hot. It was hot inside and out, and about as inviting as a gollo rat's den. It was filthy, sparsely furnished, and in an overall state of disrepair; not at all what Elio and Governor Graynir had been expecting.

Kolb, Mac and the sergeant entered first, clearing the interior while the rest of the group waited outside. Then they called them inside, leaving a guard outside at the door as a lookout.

"So," Graynir said, "we're here. Now where are the weapons?"

Gian walked to the far wall and a row of built-in wooden benches beneath the window. He lifted one of the seats and then stepped away so Kolb could see inside.

Kolb leaned over, reached inside the cavity and brought out what appeared to be a rifle, but what a rifle. Including the barrel it was almost a meter long, and looked like it weighed a ton. The stock was short, stubby. The chamber a black, rectangular box-like structure about the size of a small shoebox. The barrel, supported by a black metal forestock, was about seventy centimeters long with a cross section shaped like a flattened ellipse with a tiny hole at its center.

Kolb hefted the rifle, looked again inside the cavity, extracted a bulky magazine, and locked it in place below the chamber.

"Heavenly stars," he said. "I haven't seen one of these since... Hell, it's been so long I can't remember. It's old... really old. This is a Z9 railgun; we used to call them needle guns. Wow." He tapped a button on the left side of the chamber with his forefinger. There was a high-pitched whine as the weapon powered up. A light flashed red then turned green. Two slim strips of white light ran the length of the barrel several times and then stayed on.

Kolb checked the meter below the power switch and said, "And it's fully charged. Amazing."

The sergeant stepped forward, reached into the seat cavity and took out another rifle. "I remember these," he said. "Heavy as hell, a real man-killer. How many slugs per mag?" He slung his DEW rifle on his back and powered up the Z9.

Kolb looked at the side of the magazine and said, "Two hundred eighty rounds."

"That sounds about right. How many of these do we have?" the sergeant asked Gian.

Gian shrugged, opened two more benches and grabbed one for himself.

Andra set her DEW rifle down, stepped forward and also took one, feeling self-conscious about doing so in front of her father and the rest of the group. Not more than twenty-four hours ago, she'd been afraid to be in the same room as a weapon, but no more. She grabbed a magazine, slammed it into the port as she'd seen Kolb do, and, holding the weapon in both hands, glanced at her father.

"Andra," Graynir snapped. "What do you think you're doing? Put that thing down before you hurt yourself."

"No, Father! I know you're concerned about me, but I'm protecting us," she said, not wanting to admit the weapon was so heavy she could barely hold it, much less that she had no idea how the thing worked. But, after tapping the button with her finger, as she'd seen Kolb and the sergeant do, she was rewarded. The weapon vibrated in her hands and whined comfortingly. She looked at the magazine. *Two hundred eighty rounds,* she thought. *No wonder it's so heavy. No wonder the military switched to DEWs all those years ago. This old thing must weigh as much as four DEW rifles, and there's no sling.* She turned the rifle over and looked at it. The grip and the trigger were in the same place, but the barrel of the railgun, with the slits along each side, each lit up with white light, was like nothing she'd ever seen before.

Kolb picked up another of the rifles and held it out towards the man nearest to him, a tall thin man, a civilian. The man looked around, surprised, then pointed at himself and said, "Me?"

"Yes, you," Kolb said. "Take it. The sergeant will show you how to use it in a minute." He shoved it at the man's chest. The man had no option but to grab it. It was obvious he'd never held a rifle before.

"Lieutenant Kolb," Graynir said. "What are you doing? You can't issue military grade weaponry to civilians."

Andra looked away, embarrassed. Clearly her father had no sense of what had happened to them, or the danger they were in.

"Yes, he can, Governor," Danis said quietly. "This is war. Peacetime regulations no longer apply and, with all due respect, sir, I'm in charge here. I have to make the decisions that will keep us all alive." She turned to Kolb and the sergeant and said, "Carry on, Lieutenant, and give me one of those things."

Kolb nodded, handed her one of the Z9s, then turned to the group and said, "You don't have to take one of these rifles if you don't want to, but if you want to stay alive, I suggest you do."

Five minutes later, with the exception of Governor Graynir, all six soldiers, five civilians, Danis, Andra, Gian and Elio were armed with what Andra had no doubt were antique railguns.

"Everyone, pay attention," the sergeant said loudly, holding his Z9 above his head with one hand.

How can he do that? Andra wondered. *I can hardly hold mine at all.*

"This here is your pistol grip," the sergeant said. "This is the forestock. Your left hand goes here, and you shoulder the weapon like this." He pulled the butt of the gun into his shoulder. "This here is your power switch. This is your ammo counter and this button here—look at it. It's important. This is your safety. You must turn it off before the weapon will fire. This switch here is your fire selector. Flip it forward for semi-automatic, which means it will fire one projectile every time you pull the trigger. Flip it to the rear and the weapon is fully automatic, which means it's a machine gun. On fully automatic, the weapon will fire at a rate of seven-hundred-fifty rounds a minute. As long as you are pulling the trigger it will keep firing. Just make sure that the red dot of your optics is on your target before you pull the trigger. This button here is how you chamber a round and cock the weapon. It will not work if the safety is on."

Andra heaved the weapon to her shoulder, leveled the weapon, laid her cheek on the stock and squinted at the hologram hovering above the chamber. She looked up; the hologram disappeared. She lowered her cheek to the stock again. The hologram reappeared. It could only be seen from the shooting position. *Amazing.*

"These sights are Yezzin N7os. Similar to those we use in the military today. The holographic sight does all the work for you. It calculates distance, windage and angles. The smaller the dot, the farther away your target is. If your target is out of range, the dot will disappear. The weapon fires projectiles the size of small nails, six centimeters long, two millimeters thick; that's why we used to call them needle guns. As I said, the projectiles are small, but their velocity is—if I remember rightly—in excess of fifteen hundred meters per second, and the impact is deadly." He paused and looked at Andra.

"This weapon will not fire if there's another Z9 within its target window. This helps reduce death by friendly fire. Even so, this weapon is a killer and you are the operator, and therefore, responsible for it. You WILL NOT, I say you WILL NOT, under any circumstances point it at anyone other than an enemy. If your weapon is not pointed at a Blue, it had better be pointed at the ground. Does everyone understand that?"

The group murmured, most of them nodding. The sergeant shook his head and then nodded to the soldiers who handed out magazines.

The sergeant turned to Kolb and Andra heard him say, "I think the old man's right. There's no way these people should have their hands on these Z9s. It's a disaster waiting to happen."

Kolb nodded and said, "I agree, but we have no choice. They're all we have... Hey, Commander, where are you going?"

Danis, half-way out the back door, turned and said, "I'm going to try this thing out. I'd hate to carry the damn thing very far only to find out it doesn't work."

Kolb looked at her for a long moment, then nodded, looked around and said, "Everyone outside. Let's see if these things work."

Danis stepped out into what once had been quite a large back yard bounded by tall trees, now untended and overgrown.

She stood for a moment, the heavy weapon hanging from her hands in front of her thighs. She took a stance, feet apart, her right foot slightly to the rear, heaved the Z9 to her shoulder, touched the power button, then flipped off the safety, took a deep breath and touched the button to chamber a round. The weapon whirred, then clicked, then whined, then went quiet.

She looked around at Kolb. The entire group was gathered behind him, watching her.

Kolb nodded.

She flipped the fire selector to full auto, put her cheek to the stock, looked at the hologram, swept the weapon sideways and then back again, watching the red dot in the hologram floating above the chamber. She selected a tall young tree, its trunk maybe thirty centimeters in diameter, took a long slow breath in, breathed out slowly and then squeezed the trigger.

The noise of the continuous sonic boom as a stream of tiny projectiles left the weapon at more than four times the speed of sound was... devastating, earsplitting. So much so that Danis almost dropped the weapon.

She took her finger off the trigger. Her ears were ringing. There was an almighty crack as the tree fell sideways, its trunk cut through by the hail of hardened steel.

Danis flipped on the safety, lowered the weapon, took an unsteady step backward, then turned, walked to Kolb and said, "I guess the damn thing works. You'd better let everyone else shoot. It's one hell of a shock. They should know what they're in for."

"There's no time," the sergeant said, looking at Kolb. "We've a long way to go. We need to get out of here."

Danis nodded. "He's right. They can learn as they go."

She turned to Elio and said, "Your ship. How many will she carry?"

"Eighteen, plus two crew," he replied.

"Good," Danis said. "There are sixteen of us. Let's hope she's still in one piece."

Elio turned and looked at Graynir. "Last I heard, she was in the hangar behind your mansion."

"Let's hope she still is," Graynir said.

Chapter Thirty-Seven

Street Fighters

Downtown Pricus City
Planet Tor's Surface
Pricus System

It was mid-afternoon when they finally reached the city center, or close to it. They were all tired, worn out from carrying the heavy weapons. The magazines alone weighed several kilos and each carried two of them. For some, it had been too much, and they'd abandoned them along the way. The others? Knowing that the needle guns were perhaps their only chance of making it safely to the hangar where Elio's ship was stored, they'd hung onto them, swapping them from one shoulder to the other as they walked. So, by two o'clock standard time, the small group had arrived at the corner of the large, four-way intersection of 5th and Mansion House Boulevard.

Up to that point they'd seen very little of the Blues, just odd glimpses of a ship hovering over the buildings in the distance. For the most part, they'd managed to keep to the narrower side streets, but now they'd reached the section of the city where those streets joined with the major thoroughfares that converged on the city center. The buildings were tall, four to six stories, some of them intact, some of them reduced to little more than piles of concrete rubble. The streets were wide, twenty to thirty meters, some even wider, all strewn with debris.

The group was on 5th with Kolb in the lead when they reached the corner of a building. He held up his hand, halting them, and peeked around the corner. The group flattened themselves against the wall and waited. Kolb spotted two Blues some hundred meters or so to his left, on Mansion House. They had their backs to him and were walking away.

He leaned back against the wall, his rifle clamped to his chest. He looked across the street. They needed to be on Mansion House, heading in the same direction as the Blues.

He looked at Elio who was next to him, held up two fingers and mouthed the word, "Two."

Elio nodded and said quietly, "Now we'll know." He flipped off the safety, stepped forward, dropped to one knee beside Kolb and raised his rifle to his shoulder. Quiet as they were, the Blues must have heard them, because they both turned to face them.

Elio put his cheek to the stock and peered at the red targeting hologram. The heavy weapon was almost impossible to keep steady. The red dot, small because of the distance, wandered this way and that and up and down as he tried in vain to keep it on target. Finally, the dot wandered across the chest of the Blue to the right, and he pulled the trigger. The quiet was shattered by a continuous sonic boom that echoed between the buildings as a stream of needle-like projectiles hurtled down the street and stitched a line across the alien's chest.

The alien's chest exploded. It went limp and crumpled to the ground as the second alien went down under a hail of fire from Kolb's weapon.

Elio, his ears ringing, looked at Kolb, stunned, then down at his weapon and shook his head in disbelief.

"Come on, run," Kolb shouted and took off running down the street toward the two dead aliens.

Danis, Gian, Andra and the sergeant stepped to the corner beside Elio who was struggling to get to his feet and shoulder the railgun.

"So, it worked then?" Gian asked.

"Hah," Elio said. "You'd better believe it. Come on. We need to follow Kolb. Where's the governor?"

"He's back there," Danis said. "I don't think he can run anymore."

"He's got to," the sergeant said as he waved everyone out into the street. "We have to keep moving." He nodded down the street where Kolb was now some fifty meters on and still running. "We're going east. The mansion is maybe another klick, or so, farther on. Come on, everybody. Move it, move it, move it. We haven't got all day."

And, in single file, Danis leading, followed by Andra, then Gian, they followed Elio out into the street and turned east, Governor Graynir puffing and wheezing, bringing up the rear.

The sergeant grabbed the old man by the arm and together they ran after the rest of the group.

"I... can't go... on. I need... to rest," Graynir said stumbling to a stop.

"You can't," the sergeant said, dragging him into a doorway. "We have to keep moving. If we don't, we die."

"Then I'll just have to d—"

A bolt of blue flashed and exploded just fifty meters down the street in front of them, taking out one of the civilians at the rear of the line.

Graynir squealed and took off running as fast as his legs could carry him, the sergeant following close on his heels, smiling, even under such terrifying circumstances.

"Rooftop!" one of the soldiers yelled as he stopped running and raised his weapon. But before he could shoot, a bolt of blue from the rooftop cut him down.

The rest of the group ran on, spreading out in all directions, the civilians panicking.

Elio grabbed Danis by the arm and shouted, "With me!" And together they ran to the side of the road and took cover behind a pile of toppled concrete pillars, to be joined seconds later by Gian and Andra.

"Where are they?" Gian asked.

"Up there," Elio said and pointed. "On the roof. Three of them."

They looked up at the parapet four stories high on the far side of the street. The three Blues were in plain sight and preparing to fire at the leading members of the group still running toward the mansion, now just visible in the distance.

Danis, lying flat on her belly, her weapon propped on

a large chunk of concrete, fired first. The nearest Blue spun around; its arm, severed from its body at the shoulder, along with its weapon still in hand, flew into the air and spiraled down onto the sidewalk.

The other two Blues fell under a devastating volley of railgun fire from Gian, Andra and Elio who then jumped to their feet and began to run toward the mansion.

"In here," a voice shouted.

They turned and looked and saw Kolb and the sergeant beckoning them from inside an open doorway. They ran inside to find Governor Graynir cowering against the far wall, gasping for air. One of the sergeant's soldiers lay dead in the middle of the floor, his head missing, no blood. A blast of plasma had simply disintegrated it and sealed the man's neck at the shoulders. Andra ran to a corner of the room, threw up violently, then turned to face the room, leaned back against the wall and closed her eyes.

"Look!" Gian said from the open doorway, his eyes wide with panic. "There are more of them. I can see at least six and they're coming this way. We can't stay here. We have to go... Now!"

Elio ran to join Gian in the doorway. "He's right," he said. "We have to go. Follow me."

"You go," Kolb said and readied his weapon. "Take the governor and women with you. We'll stay and try to hold them off, give you some cover and time."

"Come on," Elio said with a quick look at the group, then ran out of the door.

"What about the governor?" Danis said and nodded her head in the exhausted man's direction.

"You go. I got him," Gian said as he dropped his rifle, grabbed the governor around the waist, slung him over his shoulder and began to run, with Danis, Andra, the four remaining soldiers and three civilians following close behind.

Elio waited for the others to catch up, keeping an eye on the rooftops on the far side of the street, and then he headed off at a fast clip in the direction of the distant mansion, his railgun clamped to his chest. He could see the three other civilians, weaponless, and four soldiers running hard some fifty meters ahead.

A blast of plasma from somewhere across the street exploded the wall to their right, showering them with dust and debris.

Elio stopped running, turned, spotted something in a ground floor window, and fired a long burst from the hip. Whatever it was he'd seen disappeared as more than a hundred railgun needles ripped through the glass.

Two more blasts came from somewhere behind them and one of the soldiers running up ahead literally exploded. Elio stopped running, turned, spotted two Blues at the corner of 5th and Mansion House, and dropped to one knee and fired two quick bursts. They didn't even bother to try to take cover. They just came marching toward them, weapons raised ready to fire. Elio's first burst hit one of them in the right leg just above what looked like its knee. The leg exploded. The being dropped to the ground and lay still. Elio's second burst hit the other blue in what for a human would have been its guts. Again, the result was explosive and what was left of the alien staggered sideways, then fell slowly to the concrete.

Elio checked his magazine. *Seventy-three left. Time to reload...* He felt for the spares on his belt and was about to unclip one when he had second thoughts, *No, not yet. I'm going to need all I have.*

The thought disappeared as another bolt of blue came from somewhere up ahead, taking out another of the soldiers. Everyone scattered again, ran to the walls, looking for cover.

"We've got to get off the street!" the sergeant shouted. "We have to find another way. We're never going to make it out in the open like this."

Elio stood and ran, bent almost double, to join Andra, Kolb and the sergeant now huddled together in an open doorway. Danis joined them a second later. Kolb tried the door. It was locked. He stepped back, peeked out into the street, looked up at the roofs on the far side of the street, then left, then right, and then stepped back into the shelter of the doorway.

"They're everywhere," he said. "I spotted at least ten. Where are the others?"

"The governor's in the doorway next door with the big fellow and one of the soldiers," Danis said. "I saw another of your men with several civilians a few yards farther on."

Kolb nodded and said, "We need to get everyone together and get the hell out of here while we still can."

"And how do you propose to do that?" Elio asked.

"Move out of the way," the sergeant said.

They moved to the sides, their backs against the walls. The sergeant took a half step back, lowered his railgun and fired a burst at the lock. The lock and the wood around it disintegrated, hit by more than thirty of the tiny projectiles. He gave the door a kick with the sole of his boot and it flew open.

Danis stepped to the edge of the doorway and shouted for the others to join them, then she and Elio waited and watched as one by one the rest of the group ran, bent at the waist, toward them, Gian last carrying a rifle taken from the dead soldier.

More Blues appeared at both ends of the street. There were now more than a dozen of them marching resolutely toward them, firing as they came. They dodged back as the concrete walls around them took multiple hits, chunks and shards of concrete and dust showering them as the walls disintegrated.

Elio waited for a lull, then stepped forward and emptied his magazine, taking out two more aliens. He stepped back, ejected the empty magazine, grabbed a fresh one from his belt, slammed it into the receiver, tapped the button to recock the weapon and chamber a round, and then stepped forward again, just as the last of the group ran past him into the building.

He fired two quick bursts, dropping another alien only to see six more march into view from around the corner of 5th and Mansion House. He fired a long burst in their direction and then backed quickly inside to join the others.

"We have to get out of here," he gasped. "There are dozens of them out there. There's no way we can make it to the mansion. There has to be another way."

Everyone turned to look at Andra and Graynir. The

old man said nothing. In all his years as governor, he'd never spent any time out on the streets.

"We could try the tunnels," Andra said. "There's an entrance on the south side of the building, in the Rose Garden."

"How do you know that, Andra?" Graynir snapped.

"I don't think that matters, does it?" Danis asked then looked at Andra and said, "That's good, but we still have to get to the mansion."

"We'll go through the side streets," Andra replied. "I know the way. I used to do it all the time when..." She glanced at her father and stopped talking.

Danis looked around the group. They were all white-faced, scared out of their minds, even the two remaining soldiers. Governor Graynir's face was bright red. He was leaning against the wall, his hands on his knees, trying to get his breath.

"What d'you think?" Kolb asked Danis.

"I think we have to try it," she replied. "We can't stay here. Let's hope there's a way out back."

Kolb nodded and said loudly, "Let's go, everyone. Follow me." And he turned and ran out of the room into a long hallway.

There was indeed a door at the rear of the building but, like the one at the front, it was locked. A quick burst from Kolb's rifle took care of the lock. He grabbed the handle and pulled. There was a sharp crack as the lock gave and he dragged the door open, then stepped cautiously to the opening and peered out. Nothing.

"Andra," he said. "You're with me. Stay close and give me directions. The rest of you... follow us."

Chapter Thirty-Eight

Images Past and Future

Downtown Pricus City
Planet Tor's Surface
Pricus System

"You heard what the officer said," the sergeant shouted as he checked the status of his magazine, then ejected and replaced it with a full one. "Move, move, move. Quickly now," he said as he watched them move out.

"That way," Andra said to Kolb and pointed as they jogged along the narrow street. "Then take the first right onto Deeker, then left again onto Rupid. That will take us to the Coreen roundabout. If we go straight through that, we'll have one more turn until we reach the gate to the Rose Garden."

"How far?" Danis asked.

"I'd just be guessing," she replied. "I never thought about it... Not more than a kilometer, though."

"Okay, everyone," The sergeant said, running backward, his railgun at the port across his chest, raising his voice. "We're going to follow the officers. Let's try to stay together just like we were doing before. Unarmed civilians in the middle, a railgun to front and another the rear, and watch those rooftops. Governor, how are you doing?"

The governor, already winded, didn't answer. He just shook his head and ran onward.

"Don't worry about him," Gian said. "I got him, if need be."

The sergeant nodded. There was a blinding flash of blue and he was gone. Elio flinched, looked down at what was left of the sergeant, bit his lip and flinched again as someone screamed. Another blast killed one of the civilians. Everyone dropped flat on the floor, their hands clasped over their heads.

"I see it," Gian shouted as he raised his rifle and fired a burst at a Blue marching toward them some one hundred meters ahead of them. The alien's head exploded in a flash of blue and white.

"Let's move! Let's go, let's go!" Kolb yelled as he jumped to his feet and started to run.

And they ran, and they ran until they could run no more. They made the first turn, but not before the governor went sprawling on his face. Almost without stopping, Gian dropped his weapon and, in a single fluid movement, scooped him up, flung him over his shoulder and continued running.

They reached the second turn and ran on to the

roundabout. They crossed it, then the street, then ran on to the final turn where Kolb called a halt.

"Back against the wall, everybody, while I take a look," he said.

He leaned forward, peeked around the corner. He could see the gate in the wall maybe a hundred meters away. There were four blues guarding it and two more some seventy-five meters beyond toward the end of the street.

He turned back to the group and said, "Six Blues, four at the gate."

"What are we going to do?" Andra asked.

"Is there another way into the tunnels?" Danis asked.

"Yes," Andra replied, "but it's on the north side of the mansion, more than two kilometers from here."

Kolb thought for a minute then said, "That's out of the question... If we can surprise them..." He closed his eyes, opened them again and peeked around the corner. The four Blues were standing motionless in front of the gate, weapons in hand. He backed away from the corner. "We don't have a choice," he said. "We need to do this now. Let's go." Then he looked again at the group and saw they were all just about done for. They were lined up against the wall, some of them seated on the sidewalk, their backs against the wall, most of them gasping for breath. Even Gian with the governor still draped across his massive shoulders was showing signs of fatigue. He lowered the governor gently to his feet and took a deep breath.

Kolb flattened himself against the wall, his head back, his eyes closed, his rifle across his chest, shaking his head.

"What?" Danis asked. "What is it?"

"Nothing," he replied. "Maybe we should take a quick break. Some of these people are just about done for."

Elio checked his ammo display. *Just over two hundred rounds left,* he thought, *and one mag left.* Sweat stung his eyes. He couldn't believe how many of the Blues there were.

And then he heard something; they all did. A deep humming sound that vibrated the very ground beneath them. And, slowly, it appeared, just above the rooftops maybe three hundred meters back the way they'd come, its blue halo pulsing, all four of its weapons slowly circling as if they were looking for targets. It was huge, far bigger than Danis remembered, but then she also remembered she hadn't seen one of the enemy ships up close, not like this.

"Oh wow," Andra said, her face white. "What are we going to do now?"

"We have to shoot it down," Elio said quietly.

"Are you kidding?" Kolb asked. "With these?" He looked at the railgun at his chest; they all did, and suddenly the heavy weapon looked... puny.

"We have no choice," Danis said. "If it sees us; if it hasn't already, it will wipe us all out with one blast from just one of those weapons. We have to try. The *Avenger* was able to take them out with its fifty-caliber guns."

"Fifty-cal?" Kolb said incredulously. "These things are less than two millimeters and that thing is massive. We've no chance. We have to get out of here."

"There's nowhere to go," Danis said. "We have to try. We've nothing to lose. We're dead if we don't."

"Maybe if we all fire together," Elio said, checking his mag for the third time. *Two hundred seventeen at... seven-hundred-fifty a minute. That's maybe... seventeen seconds. If that won't knock it down, nothing will.*

"No way," Kolb said.

The alien ship was now less than two hundred meters away and turning toward them.

"We don't have time for anything else," Elio said, taking charge. "You two." He pointed at the last two soldiers. "Danis, Andra, Kolb, with me, now. We fire as one at its underbelly and we keep firing until our mags are empty. On my mark."

Elio ran out into the road, dropped to one knee, looked around to make sure everyone was ready, then he raised his weapon and looked at the hologram. The red targeting dot was small, but not too small. The readout at the bottom right told him the distance was two-hundred-five meters.

He raised his left arm, shouted, "Mark!" brought his hand back to the forestock, squeezed the trigger and held onto it. The weapon fired; the noise was deafening. An almost continuous stream of needle-like projectiles moving at more than four times the speed of sound slammed into the underbelly of the enemy craft.

Elio didn't know if the others were firing or not. He kept the red dot trained on the same spot, watching the white splashes of light as the tiny projectiles impacted the ship's shields and counting off the seconds... ten, eleven... seventeen, eighteen, nineteen. The weapon clicked. The noise stopped, well the noise from his weapon did; Danis, Andra and one of the soldiers were still firing.

Elio looked up at the ship. It was now less than one-hundred fifty meters away and still moving in their direction. It's weapons turning toward them. Their plan wasn't working.

At that same instant, pieces of rubble in front of him began to rise off the ground. He looked around. Andra was standing next to him, her railgun on the ground at her feet. Her eyes were closed, her hands—balled into fists—were pressed to her temples. She grimaced in concentration. Elio watched in awe as a piece of concrete the size of his head rose into the air.

The hum of the enemy ship and the noise of railgun fire was overwhelming.

One of the ship's weapons fired. The blast of blue plasma smashed into the road no more than five meters in front of them. The road exploded, showering them with debris. Both Elio and Andra were thrown backward by the shockwave, Andra screaming. She lay on her back, unmoving, blood streaming from a cut on her head.

The ship was close now; almost overhead, its two lower weapons swinging toward them.

And then... something came over Elio, something the likes of which he'd never experienced before. He had no control over what happened next. Much later, he would recall that he'd looked at the same lump of concrete Andra had moved, and that it had instantly hurtled into the air with an ear-splitting sonic boom and smashed into the underbelly of the ship. He would also remember the gargantuan flash of blue light that blinded him. Then something hit him in the face and knocked him over backwards, and after that... Nothing.

Everything was quiet when he came around what seemed like hours later, but could actually only have been minutes.

Slowly Elio got to his knees. He looked down. His railgun was on the road in front of him. Gian was holding Andra who was barely conscious. Danis was standing beside him, bent over, her arm outstretched toward him. She was saying something; he could see her lips moving, but he couldn't hear anything. She helped him to his feet and pointed toward the corner of the building behind them.

"What?" Elio knew he'd said the word, but he didn't hear it.

"It worked!" Danis shouted.

Her voice sounded muffled, but his hearing was beginning to return.

"Look," she shouted and pointed again. "You brought it down. You did that."

"I did what?" he shouted.

"You brought it down, the ship, with a rock," Danis said, no longer shouting now that she realized Elio was getting his hearing back.

He stared at her, uncomprehending. "No, I didn't... I couldn't have—"

"Come on, we have to get out of here," Kolb said as he ran to join them. "Can you walk?" he asked Elio.

Elio nodded, grabbed his rifle, rose unsteadily to his feet, staggered sideways, blood streaming from a cut just above his left eye. He regained his balance and said, "Go. I'll follow you."

Elio half-walked, half-staggered to where Gian and Andra were standing by the wall. He looked at Andra and said, "Are you all right?"

"She's fine," Gian said as he helped her steady herself. "Here, Andra, have some water." Gian handed her what was left of his hydro pack. She took it gratefully and drank.

"Everyone ready?" Kolb asked looking around the group. They all nodded, even Graynir.

"Those of you that have them," Kolb said, "check your weapons. Make sure you have a full magazine."

He watched as they did as he asked, then he said, "There are four Blues guarding the gate and two more at the end of the street. We have to take them out, all of them."

Gian, now closest to the corner, leaned forward and looked up the street toward the gate. "Where are they? I don't see them."

"What?" Kolb asked and joined him at the corner.

The street was clear. The Blues had vanished.

"They were there," Kolb said. "I swear it."

"Well, they're not there now," Gian said. "We have to keep moving. We have to get to your ship." He looked at Elio.

Elio nodded.

"Wait," Danis said. "Look! Over there!" She pointed at the downed ship. "There's something moving," and she started to run toward the ship. "Come... Quick. Come and look at this." She was pointing her weapon at something on the ground.

Elio and Gian ran to join her. She was standing beside one of the ship's wings, its huge weapon still attached to it, though it was inanimate, pointing up at the sky. A dead alien, with no apparent signs of injury, was lying curled up in the fetal position some ten meters, or so, away. A second Blue, its halo pale, pulsing slowly, was lying on its back staring up at her.

"It's still alive," Danis said as Elio and Gian joined her.

Its eyes were elliptical, black and glass-like. Its mouth small and at first looked lipless, but on closer inspection she could see they were thin and almost colorless. It had no nose or ears, just two small holes on either side of its head. It blinked, staring up at them. Its head moved slightly to the left to look at Elio.

"What the hell?" Kolb said as he joined them.

"It's alive," Elio said and reached out and gently pushed Danis's rifle barrel down.

"I see that," Danis said, "and that's why I'm going to kill it." Danis pointed her gun at the alien again.

"So kill it and let's get out of here," Kolb said raising his weapon.

"No, wait," Elio said.

The alien blinked again and then its eyes locked on Elio's.

Elio's vision blurred. His head began to swim, to ache. He tried to look away, but he couldn't. He felt as if the alien's eyes were burning into his brain, and he knew without a doubt that the strange creature hated him with all its being. Its emotions radiated between them, pain, anger... hate.

Images began to flash through Elio's mind so fast they became a blur. Images of USF ships burning, exploding. Images of the Persei System, of New Hope burning, of hundreds of Blues marching through the streets of the city. Images of the fighting in the Pallas System, the destruction of the Pallas fleet. Images of USF ships exiting the Slipstream, then more images of them—Elio and his friends—fighting their way through Pricus City.

The images stopped. Elio's brain was awash with the alien's thoughts. It was trying to communicate with him.

Open your primitive mind and hear me. The being didn't speak, but somehow Elio knew it was talking to him.

You and your kind are an abomination of life, a disgusting mutation that must be exterminated.

You know our language, Elio thought. *How can that be?*

Ignorant fool, it replied. *We have been watching your kind for more than a thousand of what you call years. We have been watching your puny attempts to conquer your reality, and in so doing, you have caused irreparable harm to our reality and others. Your indiscriminate use of what you foolishly call the Slipstream is causing rifts in our time and space. You must be stopped before you collapse not only your own reality but ours as well. Your kind must be eradicated. What I showed you is only the beginning. Now see this and be warned.*

Images of Elio's family and friends dying flashed through his mind. Pain lanced across the back of his eyes then, more images, images of fighting in the triple star system he instantly recognized as Beta Cephei and then more images of the Orso System, of entire divisions of Blues marching through the streets, killing anything and everything that moved.

The pain in Elio's head increased. He could hear someone shouting. The images blurred, then faded and were gone, and he realized the voice he could hear shouting was his own.

He looked down at the alien. Its eyes were dull, lifeless. Its blue halo was gone. Its skin was no longer blue, but dirty white. It was dead.

It was only then that Elio realized he'd not just been seeing pictures of the past, but he'd also been seeing the alien's projections of the future, of what was to come. It was also then that he passed out.

Chapter Thirty-Nine

Ship of Fools

Governor's Mansion
    Planet Tor's Surface
    Pricus System

Danis's lungs were burning. She had her railgun in her right hand and her left around Elio's waist. Gian, on Elio's other side, was carrying most of his weight. Even so, by the time they exited the tunnel onto the mansion landing pad, she was just about all in.

The last two hundred meters to the gate that provided access to the mansion gardens had been hard going, not because of the enemy—they were nowhere to be seen—but because Elio, in good physical shape as he was, was more than a foot taller than Danis, and almost dead weight since he was unconscious. Kolb had offered to relieve her, but she'd told him no, that he was to stay out front with Andra and the governor in case they ran into any enemy soldiers. So, she and the mighty Gian had half carried, half dragged the unconscious Elio, with Kolb and Andra leading the way, along the road to the gate, across the Rose Garden, into the tunnel, under the house and out into the courtyard that connected to the landing pad, where they'd expected to find an army of Blues waiting for them. But, except for the bodies of several of the governor's staff, the courtyard was clear; not a Blue in sight.

"Where's the hangar?" Danis gasped as they emerged onto the courtyard.

"This way," Andra said. "Follow me." And she ran across the courtyard, through a gate, and onto the landing pad.

"It's over there." She pointed to a long concrete ramp that led down to a pair of hangar doors.

"It's underground?" Gian asked, stunned, "and the doors are closed. How are we going to get in, much less get the ship out of there?"

"There's a door to the left," Andra shouted. "Come on."

There was indeed a door, but it was locked.

Kolb looked at the door, then at his rifle and said, "It's steel. We can try but it's not going to work." He raised his rifle and aimed it at the electronic lock.

"Wait," Graynir shouted. "The lock is electronic. It has battery backup. I can open it."

Kolb lowered his rifle and stepped away. Graynir stepped forward and placed his thumb on the scanner.

Everyone held their breath. The scanner glowed green. The lock clicked and Graynir grabbed the handle and pulled the heavy door open.

Inside the hangar it was almost pitch black. Only the light from the open door dimly illuminated the first twenty meters, showing the outline of a small, sleek ship parked in front the hangar doors.

"You said there's a backup generator," Kolb said to Graynir. "Where is it?"

"There are two," Graynir replied. "In a small room at the far end of the hangar, that way." He pointed and Kolb nodded and then disappeared into the darkness.

Gian and Danis laid the still unconscious Elio down on the concrete floor in the light of the open door. Andra knelt down beside him, tore open a hydro pack and gently poured a little cold water onto Elio's face. His eyelids fluttered, then opened. He licked his lips, cleared his throat.

"Here," Danis said, taking the hydro pack from Andra, and, lifting his head, put the spout to his lips. "Drink. It will make you feel better."

Elio took a sip, coughed, cleared his throat again, put a hand to the hydro pack, and drank. As he did so, the color began to return to his cheeks.

"Elio," Danis said, her hand still holding the back of his head. "Are you all right?"

He handed the hydro pack to Andra and tried to sit up.

"Here, let me," Gian said, lifting him into sitting position.

"How d'you feel?" Gian asked, afraid to let go of him in case he fell back.

"Yes... I'm... all right, I think." He leaned forward. "Can you help me up, please?"

Gian stepped around behind him, put his hands under Elio's armpits and lifted him onto his feet.

"There," Gian said holding onto Elio's arm. "How's that? Can you stand on your own?"

Elio gently lifted his elbow, removing Gian's hand from his arm, looked around and said, "Yes, I think so. What happened? Where are we?"

"You passed out," Andra said. "We're in the hangar. See? There's your ship."

Where are you, Danis? The words came to her with a blinding flash of light and a stab of pain in her temples. It lasted no more than a couple of seconds and then it was gone.

"Richard?" she whispered.

"What did you say?" Elio asked, swaying slightly.

"Nothing," Danis replied. "I was just thinking out loud."

Elio narrowed his eyes and locked eyes with her. "I thought you said Richard."

"Yes. Richard's my brother," she said. "I was thinking about him."

"You said it as if he was here," Elio said.

She shook her head. "No, as I said, I was just thinking about him."

She looked at Andra and Gian and said, "Can you give us a minute?"

They nodded and stepped away leaving Danis alone with the still groggy Elio.

"How's your head? Can you think?" Danis asked him.

He nodded.

"You were communicating with that thing," she said. "I know you were, just as you communicated with me. What's happening to us?"

He stared down at her, bit his lower lip, then said, "I'm not sure. I don't remember anything, just some vague flashes... I do know it wasn't pleasant. But you, I do remember. You and I..." He put his hand to his head and closed his eyes, then opened them again. "We were able to communicate. I could see you and talk to you as if I was standing next to you. I don't... understand it, though. Just that we did it."

"What about the rock?" Danis whispered. "It took off like a missile. I mean, literally. It was as if it had been fired from a railgun, or a missile tube. How did you do that?"

Elio put a hand on her arm, looked earnestly at her and said, "Danis, I don't remember any of that."

"But you must," she said. "I saw you do it. I saw you look at it and—"

"I'm sorry," he said, shaking his head. "I don't. I don't even remember passing out."

"Are you two all right?" Andra asked as she stepped up to Elio's side and touched his arm. "Here, have some more water."

"Thank you," Elio said, taking the half-empty hydro pack from her.

He took a deep breath, coughed, closed his eyes, put

his head back, put the pack to his mouth and drank, and he didn't stop until the pack was empty.

"Thank you," he said. "I needed that. What about the Blues?"

"Gone," Danis said. "Well, we think so. We haven't seen them since you brought the ship down."

It was at that moment that the lights came on and the hangar doors began to slowly open.

"Well, then," Elio said, grateful to be able to change the subject, "let's get out of here."

Gian, the governor, the two remaining soldiers and the one remaining civilian, joined them as Kolb appeared from the far end of the hangar.

"How are you feeling, my prince?" Kolb asked as he joined. "You think you can fly that thing out of here?" He nodded toward the sleek, silver ship.

Elio looked at him and grinned. The color had returned to his face. He held up his hands, palms down, and said, "See? Steady as a r—" He caught himself, coughed and continued, "Not even a tremor."

Chapter Forty

"Once we get into the atmosphere, the Swarm ships are going to find us," Danis said as she followed Elio up the steps and into the cabin, noting the luxury appointments within.

"They won't be a problem," Elio said as he limped toward the flight deck.

"You think?" Danis said, taking the copilot's seat. "I've fought those things. They are incredibly fast. It was fairly easy to outmaneuver them in space, but not so much inside the atmosphere."

"Don't worry," Elio replied as he dropped gratefully into the plush pilot's seat. "*The Queen's Pleasure* is no normal yacht. Trust me, we'll be able to outrun them." He gave her a hint of a smile.

Hah, cute, Danis thought. *And intriguing. I guess we'll soon see how good a pilot he is.*

Elio began turning on the ships systems, his fingers flying over the data screens. "Good morning, Prince Elio," the ship's AI said, her voice soft and gentle. "I trust you're having a good day."

"Not so much, Kyla," Elio replied. "Things are a little tense, you might say."

"Might I?" Kyla asked. "And why is that?"

"It's a long story," Elio said as his fingers continued to work their magic. "Let's just say the next couple of hours could get very messy."

"Really?" the AI replied. "How can I help?"

"First, you can bring up the hologram," Elio replied. "Then you can do a deep scan for enemy craft."

"Enemy craft? I'm sorry. I don't understand. And I don't recognize your copilot. Who is she?" Kyla asked as the dome-shaped hologram appeared at eye-level between the two seats.

Elio glanced at Danis over the hologram. Danis tilted her head, raised her eyebrows and smiled at him, as if to say, "How are you going to answer those questions?"

"Kyla," Elio said, "meet Commander Danis Morian from the Battle Cruiser *Avenger*. Danis, Kyla."

"I'm pleased to meet you, Commander," Kyla said.

"Likewise," Danis said dryly.

"Danis," Elio said. "Would you mind checking to make sure everyone is comfortable and locked into their inertia suits, please? And you'd better get into one yourself."

"My pleasure, Captain," she said with no little sarcasm.

Elio turned his head and grinned at her and said, "We're in for a wild ride, Danis. Engines please, Kyla."

Danis just shook her head, stood up and walked back

to the main cabin. She'd barely reached the door when she felt a slight vibration and heard a low hum as the ship's fusion reactor came online.

There were seven of them, including one civilian and two soldiers. Gian was making sure Andra and the governor were securely settled and locked into their seats. Danis checked each of the passenger's suits and then went to the locker and took one for herself.

Seven, she thought, suddenly depressed. *Is that all that's left of the people of Pricus City, just seven? How can that be?*

She suited up, said a few words of encouragement to the people in the cabin and then returned to the flight deck where she found Elio already back in his seat dressed in a custom, silver inertia suit. *I might have known,* she thought smiling to herself.

"Everything all right back there?" he asked.

She nodded, sat down and said, "Kyla, have you found anything?"

"Yes, Commander, I have," the AI replied. "My long-range scans indicate an anomaly near the gas giant, Tarkon, two-hundred-sixty-one million seven-hundred-thirty-two thousand two-hundred kilometers out. It appears to be some kind of conflict. I have also detected a large battle cruiser I assume to be the *Avenger* in orbit just beyond the exosphere at an altitude of eleven-thousand-two-hundred-three kilometers. There are no other craft detected."

"They could be out there somewhere hiding," Danis said.

Elio pursed his lips. "Possible," he replied. "But if they are, they won't catch us."

"Kyla," Elio said. "Bring the grav engines up to two percent."

"Grav engines at two percent," she replied.

Danis heard the low-pitched hum as the grav engines came on line. She felt the familiar hollow feeling in the pit of her stomach as *The Queen's Pleasure* lifted. There was a slight clunk as the landing gear retracted.

"All right," Elio said. "Here we go. Hold onto your seats."

Slowly, the ship spun one-hundred-eighty degrees until it was facing the hangar entrance. Elio eased the ship out through the open doors, across the landing pad and then, once they were clear, he hit the thrusters, hauled back on the yoke, and Danis was pushed back against her seat as the yacht hurtled skyward at Mach six. At an altitude of five-thousand meters, he reached forward and pushed the twin levers that controlled the fusion drive forward and the ship rocketed upward in a vertical climb accelerating rapidly through Mach ten, twelve, fifteen, twenty until it reached an altitude of seven-hundred-fifty kilometers and a speed approaching twenty-five-thousand kilometers per hour. Having reached escape velocity, Elio shut down the fusion drive; the ship, now driven only by its thrusters, moved onward and upward.

"Kyla," Elio said, "Short and long range scans, please. I don't see anything," he said as he scanned the hologram. "Do we have company?"

"I am detecting no other craft in the immediate vicinity," the AI replied.

"Where did you learn to fly?" Danis asked.

"The Orso Flight Academy," he replied, his eyes still on the hologram. "Distance to *Avenger*, please, Kyla."

"*Avenger* is now at altitude eleven-thousand-four-hundred kilometers, distance sixty-one-thousand-one-hundred-thirty-two kilometers. Would you like me to plot an intercept?"

"Yes, and give me an ETA."

"ETA in seventy-nine minutes and thirty-seven seconds," Kyla replied instantly. "I have the con."

"You were in the Academy?" Danis asked as Elio let go of the controls and sat back in his seat.

"No," he said. "I was never officially enrolled. I never had to because... Well, because I'm the prince of Orso. I get to do pretty much whatever I want." He said the word prince in a way that told her he was well aware of the pomp and luxuries that came with the title. It also told her that he was more than a little irritated because of it. "I'm able to... you know..."

"What?" she asked, looking at him.

"You know... get around the bureaucratic red tape. I have some good friends in the USF and another good friend in the Marines. I learned all my flying from the top instructors in the academy—"

The hologram suddenly turned from green to red and began to pulse. The proximity alarm blared as blue dots appeared in the hologram.

"What are those?" Danis asked, unfamiliar with the holo display, but already knowing the answer.

"Enemy ships," Elio said. "And they're heading this way."

"How many?" Danis asked.

"Count them," he said, nodding at the holo.

"Six... no seven," she said.

"I have the con, Kyla," Elio said and grasped the yoke with his left hand and the throttles with his right.

Danis leaned over the hologram and said, "The closest one is eighteen-hundred kilometers out and closing fast."

"I know, that's fine. No worries. We'll be fine," Elio said as he pushed the throttles forward and again Danis was pushed back in her seat as the fusion drive kicked in and the ship rocketed upward, still gaining altitude.

"Are you sure?" Danis shouted. She so desperately wanted to grasp the second yoke in front of her. "You have no idea how fast those things are."

"You keep telling me that," Elio said. "Tell me something helpful. You say you fought them. What's the maximum distance they are able to engage?"

"I don't know," she shouted. "I had more to think about than that. I was trying to stay alive, damnit... Pretty far. Twenty, thirty kilometers, more?"

Elio leveled out the ship, still in the upper reaches of the thermosphere but no longer gaining altitude. He jammed the throttles forward. The ship responded like a horse to the spurs.

"We're going to need more than time," Danis shouted watching the blue dots converge into a tight group. "What kind of armament do you have?"

"Oh yeah, that." Elio chuckled. "I forgot to tell you. I don't have any."

"Any what?" she yelled.

"Armament! Guns," he replied.

"No guns? What the hell?"

"I've never needed them," he replied, smiling. "My father always insists I fly with an escort ship."

"Oh, that's just great," Danis said. "What the hell do we do now?"

"How far out are they?" Elio asked.

"Eight hundred kilometers and closing," Kyla said.

"I need just a little more altitude," Elio said pulling back on the yoke.

"Elio," Danis yelled. "Do something."

"Enemy contact in two minutes twenty-seven seconds," Kyla said, her voice devoid of emotion.

"Calm down, Danis. I've got this," Elio said as he turned to a small screen just to the left of his elbow and touched the screen. It brightened. His fingertips danced over it as he keyed in an access code. There was a slight click. The screen began to fill with numbers.

"What's that?" Danis asked.

"Nynox fuel boosters," Elio said. "Afterburners."

"Nynox?" Danis asked incredulously. "I thought that stuff was banned."

Elio glanced at her and smiled. "I'm a prince, remember? I have friends in the right places. The fusion drive's been modified." His hand hovered over the touch screen as he looked back at the hologram.

"Well, what the hell are you waiting for?" Danis yelled. "Hit it."

She'd been in much more tense situations in her fighter, but there was something unnerving about not being in control of this luxury, hotrod craft that made her cringe.

"Hang on. I just have to wait... for the right... moment. Now. Everyone, hold on!" He tapped the touch screen and grabbed the yoke with both hands.

Danis felt as if she'd been kicked in the back by a mule as the Nynox boosters kicked in and the ship leaped forward, its speed approaching Mach 40, almost forty-nine thousand kilometers per hour, and she hoped with all her heart that the governor and the rest of the passengers were able to handle it.

Danis glanced at the hologram. The distance between them and the blue dots was increasing. She heaved a sigh of relief and relaxed for the first time since *The Queen's Pleasure* had lifted off the hangar floor.

"Twenty-seven minutes to *Avenger* intercept," Kyla's pleasant voice said as the Nynox boosters burned out.

Chapter Forty-One

Back to reality

Battle Space
　　　Pricus System

Danis looked over the hologram at Elio and said, "Still no contact with *Avenger*?"

"Nothing," Elio replied.

They were still more than twenty minutes out from the *Avenger*. She wanted to report that Prince Elio was alive and well and that she'd completed her mission.

I wonder... She smiled at the thought. *Don't be silly!* But she couldn't help herself. The thought was there, and she couldn't get rid of it. She gave in to it, closed her eyes and began to concentrate, not knowing how to do what she was trying to do.

She tried to picture Richard's face. For several

seconds she concentrated then, everything around her went quiet. The silence was... almost palpable. Her head began to clear.

Danis? Danis is that you? Slowly, in her mind's eye, her brother's face came into focus.

"Yes, it's me," she said out loud. "Oh, my God. You can hear me."

"What?" Elio said. "What did you say?"

She held up her hand for Elio to be quiet. Then she continued talking to Richard, but by thought only.

Yes, she heard Richard say, *I can. I don't know how I can, but I can hear you and see you. Is it you doing this? Where are you?*

I don't know either, she thought, *but I can see you too. What's happening to us, Richard?*

I've been talking to Doctor Dowd about it, he replied. *She thinks... oh, never mind. We can talk about it later. Where are you?*

I'm on Prince Elio's yacht, The Queen's Pleasure, she replied. *He's safe. I also have Governor Graynir and his daughter and five more survivors. We are about twenty minutes out from Avenger. We've been trying to contact you, but the comms are down.*

That's wonderful news, Danis, Morian replied. *Well done. I'm proud of you! The comms... They're not down. I have them locked. We've had... well, I'll tell you about that later, too. I'll open limited access so you can talk to the hangar. Twenty minutes, you say? That's good, because we need to leave for the Slipstream as soon as possible... I can't believe this is happening, Danis. We need to... Just get here as fast as you can.*

But...

What is it, sis?

There's no one left, Richard, she thought. *My wing-men, the marines, they're all gone. We were attacked, taken by surprise as we approached Pricus City. I watched it happen, then I was attacked and shot down...*

Stop! Richard replied. *We're at war. It happens. It couldn't be helped. Just get here. We'll debrief later. I have to go now.*

Yes... I know, she replied as Richard's image faded. "Goodbye, brother," she said out loud.

"Sounds like you're getting your new abilities all figured out," Elio said.

Danis turned her head to look at him, tears in her eyes, and she said, "I have no idea how, but I just talked to my brother, Captain Morian. He knows we're coming."

"You must teach me how to do it," Elio said. "Or maybe I can't use it anymore."

"It was easier this time," Danis said as she relaxed in her seat, overawed by what had just happened but also supremely happy that it had.

"Let's just get there," she said. "I'll feel better once we're back aboard the *Avenger*."

* * *

Andra had been off-planet before but never off-system. Even with her father being the governor, she'd never enjoyed accompanying him on his official trips. This time, though, it was different. She was no longer his little girl. She was twenty standard years old, a woman, and she'd already made up her mind she was going to the Academy and become a fighter pilot.

Danis had already told them all about the *Avenger*, how big she was, how old she was and how, because of her age and her outdated systems and armor, she'd become the most effective ship in the USF fleet. But as they approached the ship, parallel to the hangar doors, Andra was stunned by how massive she actually was. At almost a kilometer and a half from bow to stern, she dwarfed *The Queen's Pleasure*.

Elio, thanks to Morian providing limited comms, was now able to communicate with the ship.

"Queen's Pleasure to Avenger, do you copy?"

"Copy Queen's Pleasure," the hangar crew chief replied, his voice echoing through Elio's ship, "this is Avenger. We've been expecting you."

"Oh, dear Lord, thank you," Andra muttered as her father and the rest of the passengers cheered and clapped. *It's over,* she thought. *We're finally off the planet and away from those blue monsters. Now we can get out of here.*

"Avenger, this is Kyla. We are requesting permission to dock."

"Permission granted." The crew chief's voice was calm, welcoming. "Proceed to bay three and follow the orange lights to pad fourteen."

"Copy that, Avenger," Kyla said. "We're on final approach now. I can handle it from here."

Two minutes later, *The Queen's Pleasure* touched down inside the hangar and Elio's fingers fluttered across the screens, shutting down the ship's systems.

"Everyone, stay seated, please," Elio called out over his shoulder. "They have to close the doors and pressurize the hangar before we can exit the ship."

The cabin was quiet. Andra stared out of her window, watching the activity inside the hangar. She watched the great doors slowly close, and two minutes later the orange lights turned green, and then the entire hangar was ablaze with white lights. Except for a single F32A fighter, a sleek civilian transport and a shuttle, she could see the hangar was... empty.

Andra tapped the small screen on her seat. The seat hissed as it released her. She reached up and tapped the release on her suit and then stood up.

She couldn't help but stare at Elio as he limped slowly into the cabin from the flight deck, followed by Danis. His long blond hair matted with sweat, his face and arm streaked with dried blood from the cut on his face.

"What?" he asked, catching her staring at him.

Andra looked quickly away as she suddenly realized who and what he was. Never again could he be just Elio. He was, after all, the crown prince of Orso.

"Nothing," she said. "I... You look tired, my prince."

Chapter Forty-Two

Gifts from the Gods

Avenger
Battle Space
Pricus System

Prince Elio, still sweaty and streaked with blood, was seated at the briefing table, drinking the last drop of liquid from a hydro pack. Danis was seated to his left, Andra and Gian to his right. Governor Graynir sat next to Captain Morian, who was at the head of the table. Next to him was Prince Felder and his assistant, a short, round, little man with glasses. It was the first time Elio had met the prince of the Alastor System. As time was short, none of them had been able to clean up before being called to the meeting.

Also in attendance were Commander Jadern, Dr. Jyra Dowd and Dr. Herrick Tobbs, Chief Science Officer.

"We still have about forty minutes before we reach

the Slipstream," Morian said after making the introductions. "Now that we're all here, everyone in this room is aware of the extraordinary events of the past few days and I know everyone has lots of questions, but we'll deal with one problem at a time." He paused and looked around the table, then continued, "The most pressing is the unusual abilities that some of us have begun to experience. Danis and I have, on several occasions, experienced some sort of telepathic connection, as have you, Prince Elio. Before we begin, however, I'll remind you that this is an official debriefing and as such will be recorded."

Elio crumpled his hydro pack and looked around for somewhere to dispose of it. Finding none, he set it gently on the table and looked up to find everyone staring at him, waiting for him to speak.

"Oh," he said. "Me? There's not much I can tell you. I remember very little after we crossed the roundabout in Pricus City until I woke up in the hangar. Previously, Danis was somehow able to contact me, though I think that was more by accident than design. I... I thought I was going crazy."

"That's basically how I felt when I first connected with Richard," Danis said. "I mean Captain Morian, right before I was shot down."

"But how did you know how to connect with Prince Elio?" Prince Felder asked.

"That's the point. I didn't," Danis said. "After I crashed, when I came to, I tried to contact my brother again." She looked at Morian and continued, "I was concentrating on you, and I thought it was working until I realized it was someone else, Prince Elio... There's something... I don't know why, but I can't do it on demand. I think it only works in times of great stress... Except, I was able to contact you when we were approaching *Avenger*." She looked at her brother.

"There are obviously a lot more questions than answers," Jyra Dowd said. "But, from what you're telling us, Commander, I'm wondering if the more you experience the phenomena, the easier it becomes. I think we may be in the first stages of a new discovery or... perhaps, rediscovery. With your permission, Captain, I'd like to conduct some tests on you and the commander."

"Permission granted," Morian said.

Dowd nodded and continued, "What we have here is a rare gift, something unheard of since... The Purge. The answers will not come easy. I think you three have taken the first steps—"

"Four," Elio said, interrupting her.

Dowd raised her eyebrows in question.

"Miss Graynir experienced two instances of telekinesis," Elio said.

"So did you," Danis said. "TK, I mean."

"How so?" Tobbs asked, his interest instantly piqued.

Elio looked at him, shrugged and said, "As I said, I don't remember much. I do remember some sort of contact with an alien, just flashes of... Images, its thoughts. Not pleasant."

"You still don't remember bringing the enemy ship down?" Danis asked.

"You brought down an enemy ship, a Swarm ship?" Morian asked in astonishment. "How could you not remember that? How did you do it?" He looked at Danis. "How did he do it?"

"He somehow... threw a piece of concrete at it." She rolled her shoulders and pulled a face.

"He threw a piece of concrete at it?" Tobbs repeated.

Danis nodded and said, "He didn't literally pick it up and throw it. He just... looked at it, and it took off like it had been fired from a missile tube... so fast it broke the sound barrier."

They all turned to look at Elio. He tilted his head slightly, shrugged and said, "I don't remember that."

For several seconds, no one spoke. Morian, Dowd, Jadern and Tobbs were stunned by what they'd heard.

"Andra did that, too," Gian said self-consciously.

"What did you say?" Graynir asked, bewildered.

"It's true," Andra said. "I... threw a rock at a Blue. It hit it in the head and killed it."

"What?" Governor Graynir asked. "You killed an alien? That's not possible."

"Oh, it's possible," Elio said. "Gian and I both saw it."

Morian stared at Andra and absentmindedly stroked his chin.

"Telekinesis," Dowd said. "This is extraordinary. What we are witnessing is the re-emergence of human abilities that have gone undocumented for centuries."

Andra looked at Elio as he cleared his throat and said, "Yes, Dr. Dowd, perhaps that's true, but what little we know from the old stories may or may not all be true."

"Why d'you say that?" Morian asked.

"From what I remember of the stories, the heroes of old had only one of the Gifts: either telekinesis or telepathy. Some even had the gift of sight—they could see into the future—but not both, not more than one." He paused for a second, then continued, "But I, so I'm told, was able to not only communicate but to also move inanimate objects. That, as far as I know, is unheard of."

"What you're saying is true," Dowd said, tapping her data pad.

"Well," Morian said as he leaned forward, rested his elbows on the table and clasped his hands in front of him. "It seems nothing is impossible. Dr. Dowd, we need answers, but there's little we, or you, can do now. But we do need to know what's happened to these people, including me, and I want to know if it's possible to awaken these abilities in others."

She looked up at him, nodded, and then returned to what she was doing on her data pad.

"My prince," Morian said to Elio. "You say you talked to one of these creatures. Please explain, if you can."

Elio sat back in his seat, linked his fingers together behind his head, thought for a moment, unlinked them, leaned forward and said, "I have only fleeting memories of that incident, but I'll tell you what I can."

"So you did talk to it?" Tobbs asked enthusiastically.

"Well, not exactly."

The science officer frowned and sank back into his chair.

"Because they don't talk," Elio said. "At least, I don't think they do. I remember staring down at it, at its eyes. It wasn't pleasant." Elio closed his eyes, trying to remember.

"It reached out to me. It told me to open my primitive

mind and listen... No, not listen, hear. It knew our language. I..." Elio paused.

"Please, my prince," Captain Morian said. "Continue."

"I asked it about that."

"You asked it?" Dowd said, looking up. "How did you do that?"

"I just... thought it?"

"And it responded?" Tobbs asked.

Elio nodded and said, "I remember it called me an ignorant fool."

Gian snorted and stifled a laugh with a cough.

Elio glared at him and said, "It's not funny, Gian. I was scared shi... I was scared. It told me they'd been watching us for more than a thousand years, that we're damaging our reality and theirs, and that they're here to stop us, to exterminate us."

"Their reality? Our reality?" Morian asked. "Does that mean what I think it does, Dr. Tobbs?"

Tobbs nodded and said, "Yes, possibly. The word reality, in this instance, means universe or, and I hate to say it, dimension."

"You're telling us these creatures are from another dimension?" Graynir scoffed. "Impossible. There is no such thing."

"Um," Elio said. "It's coming back to me now so, if I could continue?"

"By all means," Tobbs said.

"It told me that our use of the Slipstream is causing, and I quote, 'rifts in our time and space,' and that we must be stopped before we collapse our own reality and theirs. And then it gave me some kind of a warning, only it was all in images."

"Images? Images of what?" Morian asked.

"There were literally hundreds of them. They all flashed through my mind in seconds. I can't remember all of them, but some I do, vividly. Images of war, of destruction, people dying, our people. Many of the images were from the past, the recent past. It showed me images of us... I mean *us*." He pointed to Danis, Andra, Gian, himself and continued, "Us, running through the streets of Pricus City. But some, I know, had to be images of what's to come, what they're going to do to us. It'll take days for me to process everything that thing shoved into my head, but I got the point."

"Which is?" Morian asked.

Elio looked up, locked eyes with Morian, and said, "That we're in big trouble and we're all going to die if we don't figure it out. That these creatures are here for only one purpose: They want to exterminate all humanity, to wipe the universe clean of our very existence."

He paused for a moment as he realized the weight of what he'd just said.

"For a brief moment," Elio continued, "I had a glimpse of what it thought of us: utter contempt. It called us an abomination."

Morian pursed his lips, nodded slowly, then said, "You said some of the images you received could possibly be of... things to come. Did it provide you with any indication of what their plans might be?"

"I think..." Elio squinted in concentration. "It was as if its mind, its brain, was... more complex than mine. It's as if all the aliens share one mind. Not only could I hear its thoughts, but I could also feel its emotions, and none of them were good. They hate us, Captain. I mean, they really hate us. It showed me horrible things, things that… that I couldn't understand. But yes, I think it did. I think it wanted me to know what they intend to do to us. I think they are attacking our systems in a specific order. It showed me images of what happened in New Hope and the rest of the Persei System, then the Pallas System, then here in the Pricus System… then Beta Cephei… Then Orso."

"But they haven't attacked Beta or Orso, have they?" Danis said.

"That we know of," Morian said.

"If they're attacking us system by system," Jadern said, "and they're still here, then what Prince Elio is saying is that Beta Cephei will be next. We have to warn them."

"If what it told you is true," Felder said, speaking for the first time. "But it could have been feeding you false information. Is that not correct, Prince Elio?"

Elio nodded. "It could have been, but I don't think so. Our minds were as one. I could feel it. I could…" He closed his eyes. "It was as if its thoughts were my own. I knew what it knew. It was confident. As if it knew there was nothing we could do to stop it. They will strike the Beta Cephei System next. I'm sure of it. We have to go to Luna. We have to warn them."

Chapter Forty-Three

To go or not to go

Avenger
Battle Space
Pricus System

Only Elio's friends seemed to be listening to what he was saying. Morian and his executive officer were leaning close together, whispering. Felder and his aide were both doing something on their data pads. No one was saying anything.

Governor Graynir broke the silence. "What if they have multiple fleets and are attacking those systems already?"

Elio shook his head. "They're not. I know it. I don't know how I know it. I just do. You have to trust me. They're attacking our systems with one giant fleet."

Jadern leaned back in his seat and said skeptically, "But we defeated them at Pallas and they left."

"Yes," Elio said. "They did, and they came straight here, and they're still here. Is that not true?"

Jadern nodded thoughtfully.

Morian tapped a screen on the table and a hologram of the star systems appeared above it.

He tapped the screen again. A yellow dot that represented the Persei System turned red. "So, they began here, then Pallas." He tapped several times more, and the yellow star that was Pallas also turned red, and a curved red line joined the two stars together. "Then here in Pricus," he said and joined the three stars together.

"But why attack the Beta Cephei System, instead of going straight for the Orso System? Planet Luna in Beta Cephei is small, almost barren. The triple star system's conflicting gravitational wells make life anywhere else in the system almost impossible. It's rich in mineral planets, yes... but if what you're telling us, my prince, is true, that's not why they're here."

Elio stood up and traced his finger across the hologram from one star to the next to the next. The holo shimmered like the surface of a pond as his finger traced the route across the stars ending at the yellow triple system that was Beta Cephei.

"It's a straight shot," he said, "an almost direct route to Orso. That's how they think. They must have somehow entered our... reality, as they call it, somewhere here." He poked a spot close to the Persei star. Again, the hologram rippled. "Maybe they thought we'd be an easy conquest," he continued. "Maybe they're trying to weaken us... by attacking each system in order. If they've been studying us, as it told me they have, then they must know that Orso has the largest fleet in the USF, and that by attacking Luna next, they know Orso will deploy the fleet to help them."

Morian sat back, folded his arms and stared at the hologram, nodded and said, "It makes sense. They are trying to draw resources away from Orso, their main target."

"Good," Elio said as he sat down. "So we must go immediately to Luna and warn them. We can't transmit to them."

"No," Morian said.

"What?" Elio said, stunned. "Why not?"

"Because," Morian said, looking at Jadern, "we still have to complete our mission. Which is to return you to Orso."

"You can't be serious," Elio said, rising to his feet again.

"Prince Elio," Morian said, "I understand what you're saying. I also understand the threat, but we've lost all of our fighters, our pilots. The *Avenger* is badly damaged, half of our point defense turrets have been shot away, and we're almost out of ammunition. Your father's orders are that I get you home. The King's order is inviolate; you know that. I can't take the chance of losing my ship in another one-sided battle; more important, I can't risk losing you."

"Captain," Elio said, pulling himself up to his full height, "with all due respect—"

"Please, Your Highness," Morian cut him off. "We're

grateful for your courage and all that you've done for... your friends, and for the valuable information that you've been able to provide, but I must complete my mission."

"We still have a little time before we reach the Slipstream entry point," Jadern said, "but without the control station, we'll have to calculate the jump manually."

"But we've done that before, correct?" Morian asked.

"Yes, but it's been a long time. Even so, I believe our computers can handle it. The only threat is running into another vessel when we exit, but the probability of that is low."

"Rich—Captain," Danis said, catching herself. "I understand our commitment to King Orson and Prince Elio, but we have information now that the King and Fleet Admiral Hammond don't have. That changes things. Surely the safety of the fleet supersedes—"

Morian looked at her and shook his head. "I don't think it does." He turned to Jadern and said, "What's the Slip time from here to those two systems? Beta and Orso?"

The commander tapped on his data pad. "Twenty-five minutes to Beta, twenty-four to Orso."

"Wait, wait," Elio said. "Captain, before you say anything, just think about this for a minute. If we go straight to Orso, it will take hours to get me home. The Slip Gate is ninety minutes at point-two-five light from Caerus. Then you would have to backtrack all that way to Beta. There's no time for that. By the time you get to Beta, the fleet will have been destroyed."

"I'm sorry," Morian said stoically. "Our priority is you. You're the mission."

Elio couldn't believe what he was hearing. "What good will it do to complete the mission if it costs the lives of an entire system and the destruction of the USF fleet? We must go to Beta. As crown prince of Orso, I outrank you, Captain Morian. We go to Luna. I command it."

Danis looked at him. She knew what he was going through. She could feel it, and she was torn. No one said a word. They all understood the moral dilemma Morian was facing.

Morian smiled sympathetically at Elio. He, too, understood what the prince was saying, but his first duty was to his mission and the prince's safety.

"I'm sorry, my prince," he said, "but that's not the way things work. On a USF vessel, the captain outranks all but the king and the fleet admiral. We go to Orso."

But Elio was not about to give up. He opened his mouth to speak, but before he could, Danis said, "Captain. Ever since we left Orso, you've been reminding us that war changes things, that sometimes, in the fog of war, circumstances change, and that the regulations and the manuals have to be overridden in order to do the right thing. What Prince Elio is advocating *is* the right thing."

"I—" Morian began, but before he could complete his thought, Elio interrupted him.

"Captain Morian, you have a responsibility to preserve human life, all human life. I know without a shadow of a doubt that Beta Cephei is the Swarm's next target, and I've seen what they intend to do there. If we go to Orso, all human life in that system will be wiped out, and for what? To preserve my puny life? I don't think so. I would rather die here and now than allow that to

happen." He stood up to make his point. "I will NOT...
live with the death of the entire Beta System on my
conscience, not to mention the destruction of the fleet,
and nor should you, Captain."

Jadern glanced at his data pad, then looked at Morian
and said, "Twelve minutes to Slipstream approach,
Captain. What are your orders?"

"I know I have no jurisdiction here, Captain,"
Governor Graynir said, "but I'm afraid I must agree with
the prince. Your first duty is to the preservation of life
and the fleet. We should go to Luna."

"I agree," Prince Felder said. "We can't afford to lose
the fleet."

"We don't take votes in the USF fleet," Morian said
irritably. "The decision is mine."

"Then please, do the right thing," Danis said.

Morian clenched his teeth, stood up and began to
pace the room, his hands on his lower back as if he was
sore from sitting too long.

"I *am* thinking of the fleet and the people of Beta
Cephei," he said finally. "I'm thinking of the bigger
picture. Not only are you the sole heir to the throne of
Orso, my prince, but you have crucial intelligence that
must be delivered. You have communicated with one of
these beings. You alone know our enemy as no one else
does. You said yourself it will take even you days to fully
process the information, *and* you are apparently the only
human ever to have both TK and Psy abilities."

But Elio wasn't about to let it go. "I understand,
Captain, and I admire your dedication to your duty and
your dedication to my father's mission, but things are

different now. If my father the king were here, and if he knew what I know, he would agree with me and would change the mission. You know him as well as anyone, Captain, and you know what I'm telling you is true. He would order you to Beta and the fleet."

Morian stopped pacing and turned to look at him, his hands still on his back.

"You have to believe me," Elio said, looking around the group. They were all looking up at him. "All my life, I've been seen as weak. My grandfather thought I was weak. My father thinks I am weak. And it's true, maybe I was, but not anymore. I've learned more about myself in the last few days than in my entire life. My father would want me to go to Beta. I know now, more than ever, that it's what I'm supposed to do. This is my role. My destiny. I can help my system, the Beta Cephei System, the fleet and the rest of mankind." He paused, looked around the group once more, then said, "As you say, Captain, it's your decision. Will they live or... will they all die?"

Morian sighed, shook his head and began pacing again. He took only three steps, made up his mind, glanced at his data pad, then turned to face the group and said, "Are we all agreed, then, that we go to Beta Cephei?"

Prince Felder was the first to speak, "I, for one, agree with Prince Elio. I do believe it's for the greater good. I'm desperate to return to my own system but, if we have the ability to defeat the Swarm, then that's what we must do."

Jyra Dowd raised her hand and said, "I also think we should go to Beta."

"Beta," Gian said, and Andra nodded her agreement.

Morian looked around, his forehead creased in thought. "Governor?" he said.

"Beta."

"Dr. Tobbs?"

"Beta!" Tobbs replied, nodding.

"Michael?"

"As always," Jadern said, "I will back you whatever you decide, Captain." He checked his data screen again. "Three minutes to the gate."

The rest of the room was silent. Morian stared at the floor.

"Very well," Morian said, staring at Elio. "We go to Beta. Please calculate the jump, Commander Jadern."

"I already have," Jadern said, grinning. "Slipstream in... thirty-seven seconds."

Chapter Forty-Four

Relationships

The Avenger
The Slipstream
The *Avenger* was ten minutes into their Slipstream travel when Danis arrived on the bridge to check on her brother before she went to the hangar. She found him smiling.

"Good news?" Danis whispered to Commander Jadern.

"Good news indeed," Morian said as he left the rail and stepped back to his command chair and sat down. Either he'd overheard her or knew what she was thinking.

"The Slipstream control station at Luna is still operational," Morian continued, "and we were able to establish comms. Elio was right. There is fighting in the system, but none has yet been reported on Luna itself. And, so far, there's nothing happening in the Orso system. It seems we made the right choice."

"You made the right choice," Danis said. "What about the king? How did he take it?"

Morian sucked air in through his teeth, making a hissing sound, then said, "That's still up in space. He was unavailable, but it's of no consequence. The die's cast. We are, as they say, in it to win it! What are you doing here, Danis?"

"I thought I'd come and check on you before I head down to the hangar to fire up our entire squadron of one F32A fighter."

"No," Morian said. "You'll stay aboard *Avenger*. Without backup you'd be a sitting target. If you're here, you're one less thing I have to worry about."

"That's not what I do, Captain," she replied angrily. "What the hell am I supposed to do, sit in the canteen and twiddle my thumbs?"

Morian smiled at her. "No. I'm sure you'll find something useful to do. In the meantime, why don't you go and make sure that fighter we recovered from the *Mariposa* is space worthy. It might come in handy in an emergency."

Danis didn't like it, but she knew he was right. There was little good she could do out there on her own. "Yes, Captain." She turned on her heel and left the bridge.

Morian smiled and thought, *If we go, we go together, sister!*

Danis headed to the elevators and then down to the hangar to inspect the lone F32A as Morian had suggested. *That makes sense,* she thought as she exited the gravtrack and started toward the hangar door.

She was almost to the door and was passing by the

server rooms to her right when she heard something. *Voices?*

She stopped. One of the doors was open slightly. She listened. *Yes, voices. Who?*

Danis turned, walked back several steps, pushed the door open and stepped inside.

Three people were hunched over one of the maintenance terminals. Communications Officer Sandra Lowry, her eyes focused on her data screen, Mr. Tenilo and Prince Elio, an odd combination.

"El—" She managed to catch herself. "My prince?

All three flinched at the sound of her voice. They spun around.

"Danis," Elio said. "Hi. What are you doing here?" He rubbed his eyes.

"More to the point," Danis replied, "what are you doing here, and you, Lieutenant? Does Captain Morian know you're here with... two civilians?"

Tenilo pushed his glasses up on his round nose and said, "Um... Hello, Commander."

They all looked guilty. "I asked what you're doing," Danis said.

Sandra flipped her data screen closed and said, "It's... complicated. Captain Morian asked us to find a way to circumvent the fleet comms so that he can communicate with the entire fleet once we reach the Beta Cephei system... without being... cut off."

"Why would he want to do that?" Danis asked, only half-believing her.

Lowry shrugged and widened her eyes.

Elio took a step forward, shook his hands to loosen his

fingers, then interlaced and stretched them and said, "He asked us to find a way for him to talk to the fleet in case Fleet Admiral Hammond denies our request to do so, and for a way to make sure he can't be cut off."

Hmm. Interesting, Danis thought as she took a step further inside. "It's against fleet regulations for any one ship to override an admiral," she said. "It would be a serious breach of military protocol and would result in the court-martial of the offending captain."

Sandra Lowry looked at the other two each in turn, then said to Danis. "That's why Captain Morian gave us this assignment and asked us to keep it quiet. He doesn't want anyone else to find out. Plausible deniability, he called it."

Danis smiled, nodded and said, "I see." They all smiled back, though Lowry didn't look quite as happy about it as did the others. "So," Danis continued, "the Captain is anticipating resistance from the fleet admiral when we reach the battlefield?"

"Yes, I think so," Lowry said as she brushed a strand of hair from her face. "He's been fighting, trying to find a way around the regulations... I think he's going to get himself into serious trouble, Commander. Is there nothing you can do?"

"You've been with him a long time, Sandra," Danis said. "You know him almost as well as I do. He's stubborn, a stickler for the rules. Though he's not beyond breaking them when he thinks it's the right thing to do, and so far, he's always gotten away with it. He thinks he's... untouchable, and he may be right. But if he's wrong this time... well. Why don't you tell me what it is you're trying to do?"

Elio turned back to the terminal and said, "I just have to figure out how to bypass their codes and replace them with our own. I'm close, really close."

"And once we do that," Tenilo said excitedly, "we'll be able to upload the override codes that every vessel in the fleet can use to disarm the warheads on any ionic or fusion torpedoes—or any other type of concussion missiles."

Elio nodded and went back to tapping on the screen. "Just a few more minutes and I should have it," he said.

Danis shook her head, constantly surprised by Prince Elio's resourcefulness, never-ending skills and willingness to help. *What a difference between him and Prince Felder*, she thought.

"The tricky thing is," Lowry said, "that to be able to transmit the codes, we have to be within range of the receiving ships. We'll be transmitting a vast amount of data instead of voice. So, when we arrive in the Beta System, we'll have to maneuver to a position where we can reach as many ships as possible."

"Got it," Elio said and stepped back, his hands high in the air. "You want to give it a try, Tenny?"

"Yes, Elio. I'm ready to transmit the code to you as soon as you're ready." Tenilo stood by with a large data pad in his left hand and the forefinger of his right hovering over the screen.

Danis was amazed by this odd group of conspirators: A USF officer, a royal prince and an ordinary civilian— well, she thought he was ordinary—working together.

And the civilian had just addressed the prince by his first name.

War does strange things to people, to the societal rules and protocols developed over a thousand years, she thought. *Everything goes out of the proverbial window when lives and systems are at stake, and we tend to see things from a different perspective.*

Bye, Elio, she thought. *See you later.* And she turned and walked to the door.

"Yes, later," Elio said without looking up. "Bye."

Danis stopped at the door, stunned, turned around and looked at him.

He looked up at her, smiled, winked at her and said, "Bye, Danis." The smirk on his face was... priceless.

Danis simply shook her head and left, smiling hugely, feeling that she and Elio had just entered a new stage in their telepathic relationship.

Chapter Forty-Five

Tip of the Spear

The Avenger
The Slipstream

Morian was seated in his captain's chair, his forearms on the armrests. Commander Jadern, Lieutenant Lowry, helmsman Haltar Sen, Weapons Officer Corin Fargo, Navigations Officer Simon DeLong, and Chief Engineer Maxim Volkov were at their stations. Throughout the ship, engineers, armorers and gunners were awaiting orders. Danis, the lone fighter pilot, was in the hangar, suited up and ready to go, should she be called upon to do so. In that moment, as she looked around the empty hangar—empty except for *The Queen's Pleasure*, Prince Felder's barge and a single shuttle for which they had no pilot—she realized just how alone she was.

It's all right, Danis. I hear you. You're not alone. The voice in her head belonged to her brother.

Richard? she thought, trying to reply. Suddenly, she didn't feel so alone.

Not now, Danis. We're about to exit the Slipstream.

On the bridge, Morian gritted his teeth. In mere seconds the *Avenger* would exit the Slipstream. He was confident they'd prepared as best they could. So he took a deep breath and accepted that he had no control over what might be waiting for them on the other side. There was nothing else to do but to get on with it.

Commander Jadern's voice came over the comm, echoing around the bridge, "Slipstream exit in five, four, three, two, one."

The inertial force of the *Avenger*'s exit pulled on Richard's stomach as the vessel exited the Slipstream. The blackness of the nothing inside the Slipstream turned into a sparkling backdrop of stars dominated by the supergiant star Alfirk.

Morian stood and approached the command rail. He looked down at the giant hologram and said, "Long-range scans, Lieutenant."

"Aye, Captain." Lowry's fingers flew over the semi-circular panel in front of her. "I have the fleet, sir."

"And," he replied, leaning over the rail.

"They're seventy-three-thousand-six-hundred kilometers from the planet Luna and appear to be engaged over a battlefield of more than... one-point-four-billion cubic kilometers." She looked up at him in awe and said, "It appears the entire combined Orso and Luna fleets are engaged."

"Mr. DeLong," Morian said. "Course and ETA, if you please."

"Course seven-three-four," DeLong replied. "ETA thirty-seven minutes at flank speed."

"Take us in, Mr. Sen," Morian said. "Battle stations, Mr. Jadern.

"Aye, sir," Jadern replied. "Now here this..." His voice echoed throughout the ship.

"Ms. Lowry," Morian said, both hands grasping the rail. "I need it up on the screens and the hologram. Magnify!"

The view on the screens and hologram changed as the scanners narrowed their perspective, and quite suddenly, he could see the magnitude of what was happening, and he was awed.

Spread over a field so vast it was difficult even for him to comprehend. The nearest planets, including Luna, came into view, but instead of the silent expanse of beauty he knew so well, the space surrounding them was filled with thousands of ships, USF and Swarm. There were easily ten times as many Swarm ships as there had been in the Pricus System. Space was alive with blue and white light from the plasma weapons of the enemy and lasers from the fleet. As far as he could tell, there was little order to any of it. It seemed as if it was every man for himself, and maybe it was.

The USF combined fleet was vast but taking heavy losses. He looked up at the numbers scrolling above the hologram. He counted five A-class carriers, four B-class super battleships, seventeen light carriers, thirty-two Angel Class cruisers, forty-three D-class destroyers, more than a hundred E-class frigates and just under fourteen-hundred fighters, but the number of fighters was dropping almost by the minute. The enemy ships numbered more than three thousand.

"Shields up, Mr. Volkov."

"Aye, Captain. Shields up."

"Weapons, Ms. Fargo?"

"Weapons ready, Captain."

"Inventory?" Morian asked.

"Missiles less than ten percent," Fargo replied. "Thirty-nine Mark 59 Lances and eighty-two sabers. Fifty-caliber rails... only seven turrets are operational, but they have plenty of ammunition. We're at fifty-two percent, more than one million rounds."

"And the main railgun?" Morian asked.

"Seven-hundred-thirty-two twenty-kilogram projectiles, sir."

"ETA, please, Mr. DeLong." Morian wasted no time or words, but he didn't rush them either. "How long until we're in range of those plasma weapons?"

"Eight minutes thirty seconds, Captain."

He stared down at the hologram and shook his head. The USF force appeared to be in complete disarray. Now only minutes from contact, he could see the battlefield in real-time and in detail. He looked up at the screens. Hundreds of ships were involved and that was only the section of the battlefield he could see. He watched as four Swarm ships flew in a perfect set formation, strafing the underside of a USF frigate. Brilliant blue bursts of plasma tore into the frigate's hull, almost from stern to bow. The frigate didn't explode. It just came apart, as if it had been segmented. And he watched as the crew, what was left of them, abandoned ship; the tiny escape pods being picked off one by one by a single Swarm ship.

It was clear that none of the USF fleet would survive the battle unless they changed strategy.

"Which of those carriers is Admiral Hammond's flagship?" Morian asked of no one in particular as he watched the carnage taking place in front of him.

"The *Resilience*, Captain," Lowry answered.

"Put me through to him, please, Lieutenant," Morian said, hoping he didn't sound as depressed as he felt.

"The line is open, Captain," Lowry said. "You're good to go."

"This is Captain Morian of the battle cruiser *Avenger* for Fleet Admiral Hammond," Morian said. "Do you copy?"

There was no response.

"I repeat, this is Captain Morian to Admiral Hammond. Do you copy?"

Seconds passed and then, "This is Vice Admiral Dyne aboard the *Resilience*. Admiral Hammond is indisposed."

"Vice Admiral. I am Captain Richard Morian. We have just arrived from the battle for the Pricus System. We have information vital to the outcome of this battle and the survival of the USF. I must speak to Admiral Hammond."

"Negative, *Avenger*," Dyne said. "Admiral Hammond is engaged in Tactical and cannot be disturbed."

"I'm sorry, Vice Admiral, but I must insist you put me

through to Admiral Hammond. Whatever tactics he might be engaged... The intel I have to share with him can turn the tide of this battle in his favor. You *must* put me through to him, sir."

There was a long pause, then, "Negative, Avenger." Morian heard a metallic rattle and people screaming in the background. *Resilience* was under attack and, from the noise, it seemed things were not going well.

"We are engaged in combat," Dyne said, "and Admiral Hammond has taken command of the *Resilience* and is personally conducting our defense. He's ordered that all incoming comms traffic must wait."

"Then listen up, Admiral Dyne," Morian said, having made up his mind that if he couldn't get to Hammond, he could still get the intel out through Dyne. "We've learned the enemy ships are silicon-based and can be destroyed by kinetic weapons. Lasers and explosives are ineffective against them. Do you copy, Admiral Dyne?"

There was a long pause. "Admiral Dyne. Do... you... copy?"

"Your message is received, Captain," Dyne said finally, "but our experience is that multiple percussive missiles and torpedoes are able to take them out."

"And how's that working for you?" Morian asked, exasperated. "I just watched four enemy ships take out a frigate with a single pass. I'm telling you to disarm all of your warheads and turn your missiles into kinetic projectiles. A single direct hit will take them out."

"Negative, Avenger," Dyne said. "That won't work. Their shields are too strong for something that simple."

"What do you mean, it won't work?" Morian shouted. "Have you tried it?"

"No, no time," Dyne shouted. "Stand by, Avenger. We have incoming—" And then the connection went dead.

"Stars," Richard cursed to himself. *I thought this might happen.*

"We are in range, Captain," Jadern said.

"Enemy closing at one five two," Corin Fargo said, her voice devoid of emotion. "Three marks."

"Rotate the ship and engage with railguns only," Morian said. "Hold missiles. Reposition shields as needed."

Prince Elio entered the bridge and stepped to Morian's side at the rail. "What do you think, Captain? Is now the time to send the override?"

"No. Not yet," he replied, then tapped his data pad. He still wanted to speak to Hammond before taking the ultimate step.

"Avenger to Resilience. This is Captain Morian for Fleet Admiral Hammond. I have actionable intel that must be transmitted to him."

There was no reply. Either the Resilience was ignoring him or... he didn't even want to think of the alternative.

As the *Avenger* rotated, a USF battleship came into view on the forward screens. It was under attack by eight enemy ships. He watched as missiles and torpedoes were launched in a spray to slow the oncoming Swarm fighters. Most of them missed. The ones that did find their targets only temporarily slowed them.

But the Swarm ships swooped in one after the other, moving faster than anything Morian had seen before. Many of them got through and fired at the mighty battleship at close range. Long bursts of plasma punched through the battleship's shields and ripped into its hull. Morian knew the great ship was compartmentalized and would be able to lock down and isolate the compromised sections, but it couldn't, wouldn't last. A second wave of twelve Swarm ships was already headed towards it.

Morian clenched his fists in frustration, knowing there was nothing he could do to help the wounded ship.

He continued to watch as six F32A fighters streaked into view, their lasers flashing at the blue haloed craft to little effect, and then the blue ships began picking them off, one by one. First one fighter was destroyed in a catastrophic explosion, then a second. Clearly, they had not learned how to fight the enemy and were being slaughtered.

Morian shook his head. He could take no more. He turned to Elio and said, "Do it. Upload the codes. I'll address the fleet." And he returned to his command chair and made ready to transmit.

Elio stepped across the bridge and joined Sandra Lowry. He rested one hand on the back of her chair, leaned forward, placed his other hand on her station and gave her the override codes, knowing they were about to initiate a serious breach of fleet protocol, but also knowing they had no choice.

Sandra turned, gave Morian a double thumbs up and said, "The fleet-wide channel is open, Captain. You're good to go."

Morian took one last deep breath, swallowed, tapped his screen and said, "This is Captain Richard Morian of the *Avenger* to all USF vessels. We have critical Intel that will aid you in your fight against the Swarm. As you have already found out, conventional weapons and tactics will not work against them. My science officers have determined the enemy ships are constructed from an unknown, silicon-based substance, and the most effective way to destroy them is to attack them with kinetics. We have proved this at the Battle for Pricus. Please acknowledge and I will send emergency codes that will enable you to disarm your conventional warheads and thus convert them to kinetics."

"Captain Morian, this is Fleet Admiral Hammond. You are not authorized to issue such an order. Any operational orders must come directly from me. All vessels, you will disregard Captain Morian and continue with the present plan of operation."

"Admiral," Morian said. "This information is critical to the survival of your fleet. You must listen and implement the transformation of the fleet's weaponry."

"You will stand down, Captain Morian." Hammond's voice sounded stressed. "You've just arrived and know nothing of what's happening here. I am ordering you to proceed to Luna Sector Five and link up with the Battleship *Duster*."

"I know enough that I've just watched a Class B super battleship destroyed with more than a thousand souls aboard, and I can tell you the same fate awaits the rest of your fleet, the *Resilience* included, if you don't convert your weaponry."

"I'm ordering you to stand down, Morian," Hammond snapped. "Now obey my orders or face the—"

"Morian to all USF vessels," Morian interrupted him. "Disarm your warheads. If you can't, we can transmit a code that will allow your computers to do it automatically as they are launched. *Avenger* is navigating to a central position in order for the data transmission to reach as many of you as possible."

"Negative, Avenger," Hammond yelled. "You are ordered to proceed immediately to Luna Sector Five. Refusing to obey the order will result in loss of commission and arrest."

But Morian had already accepted the consequences of what he was doing. He would rather go to jail having saved the fleet than submit to Hammond's orders.

"I understand, Admiral, and I will obey, but not before I relay the codes that will save your fleet."

"No, you will not!" Hammond yelled. "Comms, jam his transmissions."

Morian smiled, knowing that thanks to Elio, they wouldn't be able to do that. He also knew they had to move further into the battlefield to get in range of all ships before sending the missile disarm code.

He stood, stepped up to the rail and said, "Mr. Sen, thrusters full ahead. Heading five nine zero." Then he turned to Jadern and said, "How long until we're in range to transmit, Commander?"

"Nine minutes seven seconds," Jadern replied.

"Missiles, Ms. Fargo," Morian said, "and fire at will as they come to bare."

"Aye, Captain," Fargo replied, her hands sweeping across her screens.

"What's the status of our railguns?" he asked.

"So far, so good," Fargo replied, "but ammunition is down to thirty-seven percent."

Nine minutes, he thought. *Can we survive that long?*

"We're under attack on all sides, Captain," Jadern said. "Missile reserves are under ten percent. We can't keep this up, Captain. At this rate we'll be out in less than six minutes."

"I know, Michael," Morian said. "I know."

"Avenger, reverse course now," Hammond's voice yelled through the comms, echoing around the bridge.

Morian ignored him and the heads that were staring at him in awe, knowing there was nothing he could say that would persuade the admiral to listen to him. All he could do was plow ahead and do what he had to do, even if it cost him his career, or his life and that of his crew.

"Captain Morian," Hammond shouted. "If you do not obey my order, you will be relieved of your command and arrested."

"Unfortunately, Admiral," Morian said dryly, "I cannot do that. If I do, there will be no one left alive to arrest me."

"Arggg, ugggg," Hammond spluttered.

The *Avenger* rocked as a pair of plasma bolts tore into her topside, stripping away Missile Batteries six and seven and gouging a trench some fifteen meters long in the dutrinium armor cladding.

"Captain, we've lost power to section six, deck one," Lieutenant Fargo said. "Shields are forty-five percent."

Morian bit his lip. "Divert missile ordnance from six and seven and distribute among—"

"One, three and nine," Jadern finished for him quietly.

Morian nodded and said, "Mr. Sen, maintain heading five nine zero and rotate the ship as needed to keep our starboard hull facing the biggest threat."

"Aye, sir."

"Captain Morian, this is Fleet Admiral Hammond. I am officially relieving you of your command. You are now a criminal acting without the authority of the USF. Any fleet captain that renders aid to Morian will also be arrested."

Lowry looked up and said, "Captain, we're close enough to begin transmitting the codes to at least half the fleet."

"Send them," Morian said as *Avenger* rocked again.

"Hull breach on Deck Seven, section three port side," Volkov said. "Damage control dispatched."

"Codes sent, Captain," Lowry said. "They've been received by forty-seven percent of the vessels."

"To the captains and commanders of the USF Fleet, this is Captain Morian. We have begun to upload the codes that will enable you to disarm all of your conventional and nuclear warheads. Upload the codes to your weapons systems and your missiles will be disarmed automatically upon firing... You have to trust me; upload the codes and let's win this battle."

He knew Admiral Hammond must be having a fit at not being able to stop him from transmitting, but the thought flitted in and out of his mind as he paid it no attention.

"This is Avenger," he transmitted. "We are moving to a central position that will allow us to transmit the codes to the rest of the fleet, but we need help. We are almost out of ammunition, we have no fighter escort, and we're losing our shields. I need a Box and One formation around the *Avenger*. Acknowledge."

Nothing.

"I say acknowledge," Morian transmitted. Again, nothing. No USF ships were responding.

Another blast rocked the *Avenger*.

"Hull breach on deck four, section eight," Volkov said. "We're venting atmosphere. Life support in section eight is at zero percent. Damage Control deployed."

"Two minutes to target location," Jadern said.

"Missile ordnance at four percent," Fargo said.

"Why won't they listen, Captain?" Elio asked.

Morian shook his head. "It's called the fog of war, my prince."

"What's that?" Elio asked.

"The fog of war," Morian said, smiling grimly as he stared down at the hologram. "It means everyone is over-loaded with information and they are unable to unravel it, including Admiral Hammond. No one has the experience to figure it out and make the right decisions proactively. They simply react to what's being thrown at them. They don't know who to believe, me or Hammond. No wonder they're losing."

Again, the ship rocked, almost throwing them off

their feet. Morian, Elio and Jadern grasped the rail and hung on as the ship began to roll.

"Captain," Volkov said, "we have lost our topside thrusters. I am reconfiguring the port and starboard thrusters to compensate. Navigation is at seventy-five percent."

"We just fired our last missile, Captain," Fargo said and turned to look at him. "Fifty-cal rail ammunition is at twenty-two percent, but we have only three operational turrets."

"Keep sending those codes, Lieutenant Lowry," Morian said. *Stars, protect us,* he thought. *Just give us a little more time.*

He tapped the comm again. "Mayday, mayday, mayday. This is Avenger to all USF vessels. We are almost defenseless and need cover. Please form a Box and One around the *Avenger*. We need to stay afloat until we can finish transmitting the disarm codes."

There was still no response.

Hammond's threats must have been more persuasive than my offer to help, Morian thought bitterly.

Elio slapped the rail in frustration, pointed at the forward screen and said, "There are two cruisers right there. They could help us, and that carrier, there." Again, he pointed. "It's almost in position; they just need to speed up. If only that carrier could move into position, one is all we need."

"What do you mean?" Morian asked.

"It's just politics," Elio replied. "I've seen it so many times. Everyone is waiting for someone else to make the first move, but no one wants to be first. If only we could control it remotely, like a drone."

Morian turned to face the prince, his head tilted slightly and his eyes narrowed, a slight smile on his lips. "Maybe we can," he said.

Elio looked down at him, frowning, puzzled. "What do you mean, Captain?"

"I mean," Morian said, "maybe you can?"

The look on Elio's face changed from one of puzzlement to incredulity as he caught on. "An entire carrier?" he said. "I don't know if—"

"Give it a try," Morian said. "What have we got to lose, except our lives, which we've lost anyway if we don't get some help, and quickly."

Morian turned to Jadern and said, "Get Andra Graynir up here ASAP." Then to Elio, he said, "Maybe between the two of you, you can do it."

Elio closed his eyes and began to breathe deeply, slowly, trying to concentrate.

Another explosion rocked the ship and Morian and Elio both staggered several steps backward, then forward again and grabbed the rail.

Proximity alarms began to sound. Morian looked at the screens. Three enemy ships were hurtling toward them. Streams of kinetic slugs arched from one of the three remaining turrets. Two of the enemy ships exploded in eye-searing flashes of blue light. The third Swarm ship fired a long burst that swept past on the port side. The *Avenger*'s shields held, but barely. *Another hit like that and we're done for*, Morian thought.

"Rear thrusters are out," Jadern said. "We're maneuvering only on two forward thrusters. We're not going to make it, Captain."

"Just hang in there, Michael," Morian said. "We're not done yet. Not quite."

Why are they not trying to use the missile disarm codes? Morian thought. *If only they would give it a try, they would see it would work... Well, I can't control what another captain does. All I can do is... Wait. That's it. Maybe I can. If I could just talk to one of them... Or maybe just a gunner... or an engineer... What are the chances I can unlock the Psy in someone else? I'm able to talk to Danis.*

He closed his eyes, leaned with both hands on the rail and concentrated, sending his thoughts out to the surrounding ships. Nothing.

Metal screeched, the *Avenger* jolted and an alarm sounded. Someone fell into Morian. They both fell to the floor. Morian lost his concentration. He opened his eyes to find Jadern had fallen against him and was lying on top of him. Jadern jumped up and apologized. Morian just shook his head and scrambled to his feet.

"Power cells five and six have just combusted in their compartments," Jadern yelled. "It is time to abandon ship, Captain."

"Not yet," Morian said as he grabbed the rail to steady himself. "Hold on. We're still not done. Not yet."

It was then that Morian looked at the forward screens and saw something he couldn't believe. The A-class carrier was increasing speed and turning toward them.

Elio's eyes were shut tight, and his fists were pressing into his temples.

"Captain Lir," Admiral Hammond shouted. "What are you doing? Reverse course immediately."

"This is Captain Lir, Admiral. I am reversing course, but the ship is not responding. We're locked out. Something has taken over our systems. She's out of our control."

Morian was stunned when he saw one of the two cruisers turn toward them.

"Cruiser *Rock Fire*, reverse course," Hammond shouted. "I say again, reverse course."

"Sorry, Admiral, this is Captain Shuster of the *Rock Fire*. I'm moving to aid Captain Lir."

"It's not me," Lir shouted. "The ship is moving by itself."

"That's impossible," Shuster said. "Besides, Fleet Regulations state that we must go to the aid of a ship in distress. Captain Morian has broadcast a mayday call for help. We are duty bound to provide help if we can. I can, and I am. Rock Fire out."

The fog of war was lifting.

Danis, Andra and Gian entered the bridge.

"Andra, can you help Elio?" Danis said.

Andra stepped up beside Elio, took his hand and closed her eyes.

"I have one! I have someone," Elio said. "I'm linked with him. He's uploading the code to his destroyer."

"Who is it?"

"Someone on the Destroyer *Fearless*, a gunnery technician."

Richard glanced at the hologram. Two more ships

had moved into the Box and One formation off *Avenger*'s stern.

"One minute to code transmission range, Captain," Jadern said. "But we lost one of our forward thrusters."

"This is Captain Faraday of the Cruiser *Fearless*. We have disarmed our warheads as Avenger has advised. And... Stars. It's working. Our missiles are destroying their ships. I advise all fleet captains to do the same. Faraday out."

Morian checked the hologram. It showed a total of four vessels occupying the corners around *Avenger*, and two more were moving into position below.

One of the cruisers just off *Avenger*'s bow took a direct hit and exploded as the plasma tore into one of its fusion reactors.

He swallowed, then looked up at the forward screens. Another battleship off the port side was firing pattern after pattern of missiles. Enemy ships were exploding all across the battlefield as the smart kinetic weapons homed in on them.

Another explosion rumbled somewhere in the lower decks. The deck beneath Morian's feet shook.

"That's it, Captain," Jadern said, grabbing the rail to steady himself.

"What?" Morian asked.

"That was our last thruster. We have no maneuvering capability. We can't turn and we're off course. We can't reach our target."

Morian shook his head and then said, "If we don't have thrusters, how are we turning?"

"I don't... know," Jadern said.

Morian looked at Elio and his eyes widened. Elio's face was a mask of pain, drawn, white, his eyes tightly closed. Beads of sweat rolled down to his chin.

"Course please, Mr. DeLong?" Morian said.

"Five eight three... Five eight seven..."

Everyone looked at Elio. His entire body was rigid, his hand clamped on the rail.

"Course five nine zero," DeLong said, and Elio relaxed and almost fell.

Morian again glanced at the hologram. The *Avenger* was inside a cube formation comprised of an assortment of eight ships that formed the standard Box and One formation, and more ships moving to fill in the sides.

"In range, Captain, we're in range," Jadern said.

The ship shook again. Morian looked at Lowry, who was hanging onto her console, fighting to stay in her chair. He nodded and said, "Send it, Sandra."

She tapped the screen, looked up at him and said, "It's done, Captain."

Blue plasma blasts streaked by in front of the forward view screen. An enemy ship, spinning, its port wing shot away, hurtled across the screen, smashed into one of the A-class cruisers on *Avenger*'s port bow and exploded in a flash of blue. The cruiser's shields held. But an F32A fighter circling in from the port side flew directly into the blast. The fighter exploded, the blast rocking *Avenger*.

"More ships have uploaded and executed the codes, Captain," Jadern said. "The results are positive. The tide is turning. The word is spreading."

Morian glanced at Elio. He was holding onto the rail, a stream of blood running from his nose to his chin and to the floor. Andra stood next to him, grimacing in concentration, her hand on his.

"Fires on deck three in sections four, nine and twelve. Damage control deployed," Volkov said, seemingly unconcerned.

Danis stepped to Elio's side.

Danis put her hand on his arm but got no response. "I don't know how much longer he can keep this up," she said, looking at Morian.

Elio stood at the rail, his back straight, head back, eyes closed, his hands an iron grip on the rail. He was sweating, blood trickling from both nostrils.

Morian looked again at the hologram, realizing they hadn't taken a hit for several minutes. *Avenger* was surrounded by fifteen ships, one of them the carrier, two battleships, four cruisers and an assortment of destroyers and frigates. He watched as the battle continued to rage around them, but the box formation was holding, and the enemy ships were dying under the withering fire from the fleet.

Morian knew there were still many ships and fighters that were outside of the range of his comms net, but for now at least, they were winning.

"This is Admiral Hammond to all ships." His booming voice echoed around the bridge. "The enemy is breaking. They're in retreat. Repeat, the enemy is in retreat."

Morian smiled. It had worked.

"The fires are out," Jadern said, "but we've had to shut down all but one of the reactors. We have grav and life support, but our thrusters are gone and our engines are shut down. We're dead in space."

Morian nodded at Jadern, looked at Elio, stepped closer to him, put a hand on his shoulder and said, "It's all right, son. It's all over. You did well. You can relax now."

Slowly, Elio opened his eyes, blinked several times, looked around, his arms shaking, and his knees buckled. He let go of the rail and fell back into Gian's arms, who lowered him gently to the floor, unconscious.

"I wonder if someone will give us a tow?" Jadern said to nobody in particular.

Chapter Forty-Six

Welcome Home

The Orso Royal Palace
Planet Caerus
Orso System
Two weeks later

In the two weeks since the Battle of Luna, no Swarm activity had been detected anywhere in any of the known or occupied systems. It took *Avenger*'s engineers two full days to repair her main thrusters. That done, Morian was able to limp the ship home to the Orso System and deliver Prince Elio to his father.

Although he wanted what he thought would be a well-deserved rest, the two weeks passed in a flurry of meetings, debriefings, intelligence reports, audits, inventories, after-action reviews and, worst of all, funerals and memorials. Morian attended enough USF funerals to last a lifetime. But now, he had one more meeting to attend, and he was dreading it. He had no use for pomp and ceremony.

When Captain Richard Morian stepped out of the shuttle onto the landing pad of the Summer Palace, King Orson Lorne and Prince Elio were waiting to receive him; they were alone.

Elio looked well, and Morian was glad to see it, because Elio had spent the two days during the repairs in *Avenger*'s sick bay in a semi-conscious state. But now, there he was, standing tall, dressed in a black uniform trimmed in gold but devoid of rank.

The three greeted one another formally, then, setting formality aside, the king stepped forward and hugged him. Morian was stunned. Elio grinned at him. Morian glared back at him, then smiled, and they moved inside the palace to one of the king's receiving rooms.

Inside were several more high-ranking officers, including Prince Felder, Marshal Ugo Tan and Fleet Admiral Hammond.

Morian snapped to attention and saluted.

The Admiral waved a lazy salute. "At ease, Captain. This is an informal gathering. Please, Your Grace," he said and looked at the king, "shall we sit?"

"By all means, Admiral," the king replied.

Before Morian could find a seat, however, Prince Felder stepped forward and offered him his hand.

"Captain Morian," he said as they shook hands, "the hero of the Battle of Luna. It was an honor to be aboard your ship at such a trying time, though there were times when I wondered if we would survive. You are a true leader, Captain, and I would be honored to call you my friend."

"Of course, my prince," Morian replied. "And thank you, but I am no hero."

"Au contraire, Captain," Felder said, smiling. "Do you know they are calling you Captain Tenacious Morian?"

"Who is they?" Morian asked skeptically.

"Just about everyone," Hammond said and raised his glass. "The news media is having a field day with it, but we believe the sobriquet is rooted on the *Avenger*. You, so the media declares, possess a battle-hardened resolve to make the tough call, to fly into a battle, directly to the heart of the action where you were most vulnerable. And most of all, you had the will, or should I say the unmitigated gall, to stand up to myself, a commander who wasn't in full possession of the facts. You did the right thing, Morian. Just don't do it again," he said smiling.

"The real heroes are those members of my crew who gave their lives," Morian said.

King Orson took a drink off the center tray. "Everyone, please. Sit down."

The receiving room was decked out with extravagant luxury. Morian had seen it all before. It was a grand show designed to impress. And, knowing what he knew about royal events, he'd expected nothing less. He took a drink from a uniformed footman and sat down.

"Captain Morian," the king began, "I would like to personally thank you for saving my son's life. He's here now because of you, and I thank you."

Morian nodded. "It was... Thank you, Your Majesty."

"We all know you and your crew had a tough time out there," the king continued, "and that the last two weeks of debriefings have been hectic. That being so, we wanted to... Let's just say we wanted to give you a heads-up of what will be happening over the next few days. Admiral Hammond?"

Hammond sat up straight on the edge of his seat. "For your undoubted bravery, your leadership, and your ability to serve with distinction under fire, you are to be promoted to Commodore. The ceremony will take place tomorrow on base."

"Thank you, sir," Morian said and bowed his head.

King Orson finished his drink, looked at him and said, "Also, at the ceremony you will be awarded the Concentric Star, Orso's highest honor."

Morian, not knowing what to say, simply bowed his head.

"Not only were you responsible for saving the fleet and, by definition, the Beta Cephei system," Hammond said, "you are the only fleet officer to have taken part in battles in three systems. This, along with the four others who have exhibited telekinesis and telepathic abilities, puts you in a very special group, one we intend to utilize."

"A special group?" Morian raised an eyebrow.

"Indeed," Hammond said, nodding enthusiastically. "We must discover why and how this ability has suddenly manifested itself. We also want to find out if there are others."

"You said four others," Morian said. "As far as I know, there's only myself, my sister Danis Morian, Andra

Graynir and... Prince Elio." He looked at the prince, his eyebrows raised.

"Yes, that's correct," Elio said, looking at his data pad. "If you recall, Captain, I was also able to make contact with a gunnery technician whose name we have yet to determine. However, I was also able to make contact with another individual, a fighter pilot, Commander Handry Markkum. You will be meeting him tomorrow morning."

"What about Andra and Gian?" Morian asked. "Have they returned to Tor?"

"Not yet," Hammond said. "Pricus City was virtually destroyed but is under reconstruction. The natural resources on the planet are just too valuable and necessary to leave unmined. A great many of the people on the planet survived in tunnels beneath the city and in the hills. They are helping to rebuild. Emergency management teams are already there and at work, but it will take time."

Hammond leaned back in his seat, crossed his legs, took a sip of his drink and said, "With her father's permission, Andra Graynir will enter the Fleet Academy, along with Gian Vastum. People are volunteering for service with the Fleet and local defense forces in the thousands."

Morian nodded, and Hammond continued, "And that brings us to your colleague, Captain Paris. Her court-martial is scheduled eleven days from today. You will, of course, be called to testify, as will members of your crew and Prince Felder."

"Understood," Morian said.

"Yes, I'll be there," Prince Felder said smiling.

"Thank you, my prince." Morian returned his smile.

"As of today." The Admiral leaned forward and set his glass on the side table. "There have been no Swarm sightings in any system. But we know from what Prince Elio and— well, more about that later—from what Prince Elio has told us of his contact with the alien in Pricus City, that they will be back and we need to be ready. We need to rebuild and restructure the Fleet.

"We must accept that they will learn from their previous encounters with us, as have we. This new enemy requires we develop new weapons, new shielding, new armor. Your devotion to the antiquated *Avenger* provided us with a wealth of intelligence, Captain. If these Blues are going to fight on the streets as they have, we are going to have to meet them on the streets. That being so, we must also beef up our marines."

No one else spoke, but Morian was uncomfortable. "May I, Admiral?"

"Of course."

"With my new rank and being a member of this new 'special group,' will I retain command of the *Avenger?*"

The Admiral exchanged a look with King Orson and Prince Elio, then said, "Yes, of course. You will keep your ship and your crew with several additions," Hammond said.

"Thank you, sir," Morian said, then continued.

"If I am going to be part of this special team," Morian said and turned to Prince Felder, "I assume, by your presence here, I'll be working closely with you and the Alastor System, as well as Orso?"

"You will indeed, Captain," Felder said.

"Then, with your permission," Morian said, "I would

like to request that Mister Tenilo join my crew. The man is a genius. I'd like to have him work with my science team."

Felder nodded and said, "I see no problem with that, so long as that's what he wishes. I'll talk to him. You'll have an answer no later than tomorrow."

"Thank you, my prince," Morian said and turned to face Admiral Hammond. "Again, if I may, when you said the Swarm will return, you mentioned something about telling me more later?"

The two princes looked at Hammond. Hammond nodded, slapped his knees and stood up. "We have something to show you, Captain. If you will come with us."

Morian was smart enough not to ask questions during the gravcar ride to the sprawling USF base or when it arrived at an unmarked building. Morian had been a member of the fleet long enough to know that unmarked fleet buildings were unmarked for a reason. They exited the gravcar and entered the building. Security was tight; even Hammond had to show his credentials. That done, they passed through body scanners, eye scanners and voice recognition.

After passing through the final scanner, they were met by a security officer who motioned for Morian to hold out his arm. He did so, and the officer pointed a hand-held device terminal at Morian's data pad. The screen lit up and the terminal beeped. "There you are, Commodore. You now have level five security, the highest."

Richard checked his data screen and sure enough, it was true. He looked up at Hammond.

"Consider this your first briefing as part of your new intelligence role."

They took an elevator down three levels and stepped out into a heavily guarded laboratory.

"Commodore Morian," Dr. Jyra Dowd said as she walked toward them with her hand held out for him to shake.

"Doctor Dowd." He shook her hand and then said, "Why are you here?"

"We have a surprise for you," she replied. "If you'll all follow me?" And she turned and walked almost the length of the laboratory and entered a small room with white walls and a stainless-steel table at the center with a body strapped to it, not a human body, a Blue.

It was Morian's first sight of one of the aliens, but he'd seen enough images and footage to know what he thought they looked like. This one didn't look impressive, but it *was* alive, and it was right there in front of him.

He could see it had a badly injured left leg. It looked as if it had been both burned and crushed, but there was no blood.

Admiral Hammond stepped up. "This is the only enemy captive we have."

Dr. Dowd joined him on his other side. "It's harmless enough," she said. "Prince Elio has been interrogating it for days. It doesn't appear capable of contacting its own kind. We feel we're at the point where there is not much else we can learn from it, but everyone agreed that it would be a good idea if you came and took a look, see if maybe you can get anything out of it. Its biology is... bizarre, to say the least. We still don't know its basic chemistry, but we're working on that. I do think, however, that it doesn't have much time left. The leg injury is too much for its body to recover from and I don't know enough of its physiology to be able to help it."

Morian took another step closer and looked into its eyes. They were like nothing he'd ever seen before, totally black, glass-like. He not so much saw the alien stare back at him as felt it. As far as he could tell, it had no facial muscles; it was expressionless, nor did its small mouth move. But suddenly, Morian could feel something he'd never felt before, even when he was connected to Danis. He was linked to it. It was as if their minds had become one. Words, thoughts, and images entered his mind.

Who are you? it asked.

Morian was so surprised he was speechless.

I know who you are. You are the being called Morian. What do you want with me? Be quick, Morian, for I am about to become one with my reality.

Who are you? Morian asked. *Why are you here? Where have you come from? Why are you trying to exterminate us?*

None of that matters, it replied. *All that matters is that you and your kind have caused a rift in our reality, a rift by your indiscriminate use of the flux. Your kind has caused much suffering among the kindred. You may have me, but we are legion. There are more of us than your puny minds can imagine. We are replicating, waiting, and studying. We are learning. We will exterminate all sentient life in this universe. There is nothing you can do to stop us. Peace must be restored to the reality.*

Richard felt an overwhelming sense of contempt

emanating from the alien. The being hated Morian. It hated humanity. Its words were not threats. They were what it believed.

Morian broke the connection and stepped back.

Prince Elio touched his shoulder. "I heard it too, Commodore. Do you have any more questions for it?" he asked.

Richard shook his head, still in shock at what the alien had just shared.

"Then it is time." Elio said.

Then, still connected to it, Elio stared at the alien, closed his eyes and concentrated. After several seconds, they all heard a mushy crunch. The alien arched its back, held it for several seconds, then fell back, lifeless.

"You killed it," Morian said.

Elio opened his eyes, stared at the body, then nodded and said, "It was in pain. I put it out of its misery... These new abilities, Richard... don't you find they're getting easier to control?" He turned to Morian and continued, "I've been thinking: there must be more people out there who are experiencing an awakening of the abilities of the Heroes of long ago. We have to find them. You and I, we know the aliens will return. We must be ready for them."

The End